Mexico City, 1968. The year of the Olympics, the first sponsored by a developing country. There's a lot at stake, especially when activist students and their hundreds of thousands of supporters launch a summer-long protest aimed at reforming a ruthless authoritarian government. Ten days before the Olympic games are to begin, the government plans an armed assault. The result: hundreds of innocent victims — men, women and children — are murdered, imprisoned and disappeared…and the games go on. Known as the **Tlatelolco Massacre**, it was the first and the worst act of repression in the nation's 20th century.

PRAISE FOR
JAMES A. JACOBS
Days of the Dead
(A Daniel Mendoza novel)

"In this high-minded historical thriller, Jacobs portrays the murderous repression unleashed in 1968 by the Mexican government and an American journalist's efforts to ameliorate a deepening crisis. A compelling, harrowing, realistic and moving story. The journalist's subsequent mission to rescue his wife and daughter from the compound of the country's most-wanted guerrilla leader is sensationally-plotted."

USMC Captain (ret.) and FBI Special Agent (ret.) John E. Denton
(International Espionage and Hostage Rescue), Knoxville, TN.

"In this sequel to the coming-of-age novel, *Transgressions*, Daniel Mendoza, 28, an ex-Marine boxing champion-turned journalist, is burned-out from covering the murder and mayhem of the Civil Rights crises in the U.S and seeks escape to cover the Olympics in Mexico City. Instead, he's plunged into an even-worse nightmare: The Tlatelolco massacre and the disappearance of his wife and daughter. Daniel undergoes a spiritual breakthrough which allows him to fully understand his personal and communal responsibilities. Set amidst personal and political turmoil, Jacobs has also crafted a beautiful and touching love story that is tragic but immensely uplifting."

Rabbi Eric B. Wisnia, Congregation Beth Chaim,
Princeton Junction, N.J.

"Within contained, beautiful prose, we follow Daniel Mendoza's brooding introspection in search of the right moral choices. Set among the dreadful events of the 1968 Tlatelolco massacre of hundreds of students and their supporters in Mexico City, this novel could not be any more relevant in light of the 2014 disappearance and murder of activist students in the state of Guerrero."

Isabel Izquierdo, Foreign Languages chairperson,
Diablo Valley College, Pleasant Hill, CA.

"Exotic settings, exciting action, and well-executed dialogue all keep the reader moving along as the narrative pace quickens to unfold its story. Climactic, earth-quaking events make for an explosive ending."

Russ Tarby, entertainment editor, Eagle Newspapers,
Syracuse, N.Y.

"Jacobs' sequel novel is set during the cultural clashes and civic unrest within the context of the 1968 Olympics and student protests in the U.S and worldwide. It features complex characters with devious motives as well as a detailed knowledge of Mexican political, religious, social and military cultures. The writing is crisp, and each chapter reads like a short story."

Ron Cochran, PhD anthropologist and U.S. Army veteran,
Billings, MT.

"Jacobs' second novel, featuring Daniel Mendoza, takes us on a storied journey through the festivals and furies of a complex world that should be shockingly familiar to readers concerned with the glories and agonies of Mexico today. Mendoza works hard to keep the lid on extreme violence exercised by the Mexican government, including enforced disappearances of hundreds of the nation's children. But that's just the first act of Mendoza's complicated mission to seek justice, retribution…and just possibly salvation. A searing but very satisfying story."

Timothy Kennedy, PhD, University of Tampa, author of
Where the Rivers Meet the Sky: A Collaborative
Approach to Participatory Development.

DAYS OF THE DEAD

(A Daniel Mendoza novel)

James A. Jacobs

DAYS OF THE DEAD
(A Daniel Mendoza novel)

**PALO VERDE BOOKS, 16 E. CRESCENT DRIVE,
SAN RAFAEL, CA 94901. ALL RIGHTS RESERVED**

Editorial Assistant: Susan Springer

Cover: David R. Johnson
*Photo of soldiers with rifles during the protests in Tlatelolco was previously published
in the book "Massacre in Mexico" by Elena Poniatowska (The Viking Press, 1975).
National Strike poster created by the Mexican students' National Strike Council
(CNH) in summer 1968.*

Typesetter: Carol Yacorzynski

Typestyle: Times New Roman

Cataloguing-in Publication Data is on file with the Library
of Congress

ISBN 978-1-4951-5480-5

For my wife, Susan

DAYS OF THE DEAD
(A Daniel Mendoza novel)

PROLOGUE

Mexico City, November 1, 1968
Día de los Muertos (Day 1)

It's night, the only safe time for him to venture out. Being careful, he crouches 15 meters inside an unlit alley, waiting for Prado to pick him up. It's time to say goodbye.

A taxi pulls up. Two short flashes from a penlight, and a rear door opens. Daniel Mendoza jogs from the alley, gets in, slams and locks the door.

Robbie Prado, U.S. State Department security specialist working out of the U.S. Embassy, passes him an envelope containing $500 in Mexican pesos. He pulls out a pack of cigarettes — *Delicados sin filtro*. Shakes one out. Daniel declines. He's got another wicked headache.

"Remind me where I'll be meeting the operative."

"You didn't write it down?"

"No."

"Good, but don't forget. You'll be taking a first-class bus to Acapulco. When you exit the terminal, ask anyone where you can catch a city bus to *Pie de la Cuesta.*"

"Pie de la Cuesta?"

"The Sunset Beach. When you get to that bus stop, it's a short walk to the beach and to the guest house, *Casa Elvira*. Ask the bus driver for directions. It's easy. Book a room. Relax. The operative will show up within 24 hours."

"How will I know it's him?"

"Don't worry about it. He'll know who you are."

"He can be trusted?"

"Most definitely. He's on my payroll, he's established himself in the Sierra peasant communities, and he's very good. Perfect guy to help you locate Yvonne and Sonia."

Daniel stared out the window as the taxi cruised around Chapultepec Park. Pitch dark. Nothing to see but headlights and tail lights of other vehicles.

"Don't get lost in your thoughts," Prado said.

"It's Inez. Leaving Mexico City without finding her. Her parents are freaked."

"Let that slide. I'm working on it. Something will turn up. Focus on the rescue mission."

"It's not just that; I'm fucked up and out of shape."

Prado didn't reply.

"I can't believe all this grew out of a fight between rival prep and *voca* gangs," Daniel said.

"It's the national universities' and colleges' and their feeder schools' autonomy issues. Been a thorn in the side of the government for decades. Radical left-wing students run the show. Any challenge to their autonomy when riot police show up, they whip into action mode. And they're fearless."

"Fearless, persistent, but incredibly bull-headed and naïve. It's one thing to protest, force the government to confront issues. That's standard operating procedure. But they made it bigger than it should've been. Police states do whatever they want. They don't respond to threats. They don't negotiate. And you can't threaten to shut down the Olympics."

"If you're the government of Mexico, what do you do with misbehaving children?"

Daniel didn't answer the rhetorical question, seeing no point. Instead, he continued to stare out the window, sickened by the nation's damaged soul, worried about his own.

That familiar thousand-yard stare, Prado thought. *Which hurts him more, his migraines or integrating all that he's experienced here? I'll do what I can, but he needs all the help he can get.*

Mexico City, November 2
Día de los Muertos (Day 2)

CHAPTER 1

He'd spent all day in Inez' room laying on her bed, in and out of sleep, shades pulled, trying to figure a way to counter-punch his wicked headache. Sleep didn't help because he woke right up to it again. Emptying his mind, deep breathing, even punching himself in the head to dislodge whatever it was that was killing him...nothing worked. He felt ashamed that pain was keeping him from the mission, so at 4 p.m. he forced himself out of bed and drank the coffee brought to him that morning. It was cold, of course, but brewed with chocolate, still delicious. He forced himself to re-examine the plan he'd finalized the night before with Prado, his most reliable contact in Mexico City. He also brooded about his brief love affair with Inez who he'd met at the end of July at a student rally on the campus of the National Autonomous University, at the end of a week when activist students were repeatedly ambushed and beaten by riot police, a night when she agreed to be intimately involved in his reporting, a night when Prado predicted even more dire consequences.

As twilight approached, he left Inez' room and walked into the parlor, confronting once again the family's Day of the Dead altar. Long, green sugar-cane stalks strung to the back legs of a table and tied at the top into an arch, representing the passage between life and death. On top of the table: brilliant orange marigolds, white floral crosses, elegant candlesticks, incense-burners filled with *copal*, brightly-decorated sugar skulls, miniature chocolate coffins, bowls of nuts and apples. The anise-scented loaf of bread — *pan de muerto* — that reminded him of *challah* except the dough on top was shaped into a skull and crossbones, and the entire loaf was glazed and sprinkled with sugar. A glass of water to quench the thirst of the spirits. The votive candles placed around framed family portraits none of which were Inez because this was the day when the souls of the departed were welcomed back, not those who were merely...absent.

Now Inez' mother thanked him, held him, wouldn't let go. A prolonged and perhaps final embrace in the cramped kitchen of a four-room working class apartment.

Inez' father knelt on the floor, choking back his own grief, wrapping twine tightly around a large cardboard box. Scotch tape covered a paper label with a fictitious name and address in case of theft or confiscation in transit. He'd been the wiser parent who, from the beginning, had misgivings about the 28-year-old married American involved with his daughter ("...*podría estar loco*...maybe he is crazy").

Daniel pulled himself together, wiped his eyes. He gripped the father's shoulder, pulled him to his feet. "Thank you for hiding me, Señor García, and for helping me."

It was a remarkable turnaround. The parents' generosity replacing deep resentment and anger. But he'd quit his International Press Association job, abandoning coverage of the upcoming Olympic games and subduing his natural instinct to fade into the background, to become such a ferocious gadfly on their behalf that now he was labeled a 'principal agitator.' Under Article 145 of the Mexican Federal Penal Code, a law which metes out punishment to persons guilty of 'social dissolution,' he could be sentenced to five years in prison, fined 50,000 pesos and deported. So Inez' parents harbored him.

"Just because I'm leaving Mexico City doesn't mean I'm going to stop looking for her. After I finish.... Once things settle down....

I'm certain she'll be...."

The man of words, the journalist, couldn't finish. Throughout the past weeks, he'd also held back from Inez' parents the deeper conspiracy — what they were really up against. At the very least, he owed them a shred of hope, of progress. If they knew the truth of it all, they might not have anything more to do with him.

Inez' father averted his eyes, talked out. His daughter's disappearance the night of Oct. 2 turned out to be much more sinister than anyone had imagined. What had happened to his little schoolgirl, like so many others at Tlatelolco, labeled *subversiva*? College students! What is this *matanza estudiantil*? Can't the government distinguish among its opponents: armed *guerrillas* on the one hand and union organizers, peasant leaders, student activists on the other? Who is responsible for such cowardice and depravity! More than one month after the bloody massacre, after visiting hospitals, jails and morgues, he'd heard nothing positive from her friends lucky enough to survive the final protest. It was clear that she hadn't just run away. His only hope was that she and others were being detained...somewhere. But, like hundreds of anguished parents, some represented by high-powered attorneys, he'd failed to pry open even the slightest seam in the judicial bureaucracy. Daniel had failed, too, despite his good connections. He couldn't even access his wife and child in that God-forsaken prison. *¡Dios mío!* Where is she?

From the street below, Daniel's partner pumped the horn more urgently. Calle Milán was crowded with evening traffic, especially on this second day of *Día de los Muertos*. Berto said he'd wait only for as long as it took the street vendor to mix up two *licuados*. "What's the matter with your friend? Doesn't he understand our risk?"

Inez' mother wiped her tears with the bottom of her apron. In the end, she'd conceded that Inez' disappearance had nothing to do with Daniel. Her daughter had been fully committed to the protest movement even before meeting him and falling in love. And if Inez were here today, she would claim it was the fault of the state; it was desperate tyranny that had taken so many lives and crushed a utopian agenda. All in the name of patriotism and the Olympics, the first to be hosted by a developing country. The president had been adamant: *"Watch out! The country comes first! Defend the Republic!"* Which meant that it had finally been decided that protests against the government, championed by hundreds of thousands and articulated through massive marches right up to the presidential palace, had to be stopped. The games had been scheduled to begin Oct. 12.

"Bueno pues, Dan-yel. Cuidado.... Ándale," Señor Garcia said. Meaning all right, then; in the end, you couldn't help us, but you tried your best. Be careful now. *"Buena suerte con tu vida."* And good luck with your life.

"Que Dios te bendiga," the mother added. God bless you.

Distraught and nauseous, Daniel could barely lift the cardboard box which contained his old USMC seabag packed with utility uniforms, a pair of combat boots, face paints, a .38 Colt Commander, and some of his pack, web and combat gear. Prado had the box shipped to the U.S. Embassy from Daniel's Uncle Jesse. Which burden was worse, he wondered, losing Inez and witnessing her parents' despair or beginning this daunting quest to discover where the *guerrillas* were keeping Yvonne and Sonia?

If he couldn't even arrange to visit his wife and daughter after their arrest and imprisonment at Casa Montenegro, if Yvonne had refused to even see him, what were the chances he could locate them since the prison breakout engineered by the *guerrilla* leader Blanco, who scooped up Yvonne and Sonia in the process and absconded to his Sierra Madre mountain stronghold? And the fact that Daniel had weighed his search for Inez against the rescue of his own wife and child indicated once again an ongoing and severe moral imbalance.

He closed the door and eased the box down the three flights of tiled stairs, close to blacking out from the headache that flared, a lingering, evil malady that jacked up the already-lopsided odds, that sapped his energy and threatened to instantly disable his split-second judgement and athletic grace. *All bets off on this fight.*

In the van, he rested his head against the passenger window, wishing it were a slab of ice.

"Those little devils striking again with pickaxes?"

Daniel sighed. "Just take me to the bus station, Berto. Slowly. And obey the traffic laws for once."

Berto chuckled. He worshipped inappropriate levity but, despite that, he also believed in retribution. A big part of him enjoyed Daniel's suffering. He passed him one of the OJ, banana and raw-egg drinks.

Daniel took a sip, then another, felt the icy sludge slide into his belly, closed his eyes and pondered his next move. For the first time since his childhood when his parents and grandfather had been murdered, disaster had ganged up on him again, followed by futility and disgrace. Then lethargy. But a plan had been set into motion, and Prado expected him to see it through. There *was* going to be a successful outcome. At the very least, he would be able to live with himself.

"Which bus station?"

"TAPO at San Lázaro," Berto said, grinning inappropriately. He flipped the butt of a *Delicado* out the window and checked himself in the rear-view mirror, his perfect white teeth and perfectly-combed black hair. The man with the practiced, happy-go-lucky noncha-lance that endeared him to most women. "You can get a first-class seat on Estrella de Oro, on one of their real nice four-axle Sultana Imperials. Just a few stops until Acapulco. There's probably 2,000 people milling about the terminal, so sit on the floor and pretend to nap while I buy your ticket. There's a good chance you won't be spotted."

Daniel propped his head against the window, sipping from his drink, too tired to argue. True, TAPO was always massively crowded, but it was located just south of Casa Montenengro peni-tentiary and just north of the Federal Justice complex. Risky. Tax-quena, the terminal further south in Coyoacán, sent buses directly to Acapulco, too.

He was about to suggest this alternative when the Econoline van lurched to a stop. Waves of licuado spilled onto the rubber floor mats. "Fucker cut me off!" Then the van screeched forward at an alarming rate of speed until Berto passed the offending dark sedan and swerved back into the lane just as a traffic signal turned red. He reached below his seat and pulled out his .22 snub-nose.

"What...!" Daniel shouted. "What the hell are you doing?"

The Mexican driver got out of his car, door wide open, and walked casually up to Berto's window as other drivers, stalled now in the evening rush, blared their horns.

Berto handed Daniel what was left of his *licuado*, calmly rolled down his window, cocked the hammer of his .22, and hid it beside his right leg. "I'm just gonna scare the shit outta this guy, like, 'what can I do for you, *pendejo*'?" Berto's grin wide and smug.

Fuming, Daniel shook his head, shoved his box further into the back of the van. Yet another bad decision by his unpredictable partner, but Daniel would make certain it would be Berto's last. If they got out of this.

The Mexican approached. He was dressed in tailored slacks and open-necked shirt, dress shoes and sport coat. A good-looking guy, *indio*, maybe 40, precise haircut, clean-shaven, fit, calm.

Berto reduced his grin to a smirk. *"¿Qué pasa, amigo?"*

The man pulled an ID wallet out of his jacket pocket and flashed his credentials: Investigator, Judicial Police. "Nothing much, just trying to get home. What's happening with you, *amigo*?"

Daniel's stomach flipped. *I'm finished before I even get started. Fucking Berto.*

"I assume you have a license to drive this piece of shit in such a dangerous fashion?" he said, his countenance emptied of affect.

Berto surreptitiously de-cocked his revolver and placed it beneath a small pile of empty food wrappers and yellowed newspapers. He showed the man his license. They chatted for a while, the cop maintaining a steady demeanor, impassive; nevertheless, a look to instill caution and, for once, Berto got it.

"For a *gringo*, your Spanish is very good. And you have a D.F. license."

"I am *chilango*. I was born here."

"Where are you going?"

"I'm on my way to the airport to pick up my mother."

"What does she do?"

"Teaches English to *hombres de negocios.*"

If the cop was flustered, he didn't show it. This was Mexico City. Cop tempers well-contained. A certain amount of macho was tolerated, even admired, if it was handled with some flair. If not, a nightmare.

"What is your occupation?"

"I'm a college student."

The cop smiled sardonically. "Politécnico or the National Autonomous University?"

"University of the Americas."

The cop compared Berto's license and his student ID. "You have too many years to be a college student, and you don't look or smell like the *gringo* hippies who go there."

Berto pointed to the Camp Pendleton parking sticker on his windshield. "I'm a military veteran, dual citizen. The U.S. gives me a free education after discharge, plus living expenses."

The cop studied the parking sticker, the eagle, globe and anchor superimposed.

"What was your military occupation? I presume not a truck driver."

"Heavy weapons. Mortars. M-60 machine gun."

"Vietnam?"

"Sí, señor."

The cop glanced at Berto's hands. Fingers without scars, smooth knuckles. Not what you'd expect of a heavy weapons gunsmith. He nodded, then peered at Daniel. "And what about him?"

"Mi profesor."

"Does he speak Spanish?"

"Sí, señor," Daniel replied, reaching into his back pocket.

The cop waved him off, much to Daniel's relief. "What subject do you teach?"

In a moment of sarcasm, he thought to say hotel management. But, no. "Philosophy."

"A very timely subject." Rolling his eyes.

"Some people think so."

"What are your special interests in philosophy?"

"In the historical past, Thomas Hobbes."

The cop nodded. "And what about the modern era?"

"Ortega y Gassett."

"¿Cómo?"

"Yo soy yo y mi circunstancia." Meaning life is a drama that exists between oppressive circumstances and freedom.

Horns blared as the signal changed to green. The cop glanced back at the line of cars and with his free hand, palm flat, pleaded for restraint. Then he turned his attention to the man who claimed to be a *profesor:* swollen brows, thin variegated scars, slightly-dented nose — a face like that of a boxer, but not a losing one. Somewhat battered but intelligent, *guapo.*

"Así es como es," the cop said, surprising Daniel with the succinct acknowledgment: Yes, that's how it is.

The cop tapped Berto's license against the door. "You should drive more carefully, *amigo.* You cause an accident, you lose your license." With his thumb, he rubbed the tips of his fingers. "Expensive to get it back."

"I'll be more careful, *señor,* it won't happen again."

The cop laughed. "You're not going to offer me a scholarship?"

Berto subdued his grin. "I believe you already graduated."

"Correct, *amigo.* National University, *Filosofía."* He returned the student ID and driver's license and walked back to his car.

"Drive away slowly," Daniel ordered, "turn here, go ahead a few blocks, turn again and park the van."

Berto raised his eyebrows.

"Just do it, *cabrón."* A dangerous anger surfaced out of a sense of betrayal. The same reckless anger that afflicted his father and that Daniel, as a child, thought he could never possess. Until the night he discovered the conspiracy and just how shockingly venal were the ones responsible for killing his mother, grandfather and, inevitably, his father Davey.

Berto pulled the van over beside a small park.

"Get out, lock up and follow me."

Daniel walked behind a low hedge. Berto followed, palming the .22 and gripping it like a hammer, bearing a scowl bordering on hatred. "It was you who brought all this down. You who ruined the lives of two beautiful...."

Daniel pivoted, leapt and delivered a quick and devastating three-punch combination — actually, palm strikes — holding back a fourth blow, the middle-knuckle punch to the throat because Berto had landed flat on his back, blood streaming from his nose and a split lower lip. Reaching down, Daniel grabbed Berto's wrist and applied a pressure point, unlocking Berto's grip. He thumbed a latch on the side of the revolver and, with a flick of his wrist, the cylinder snapped open, exposing all five cartridge chambers. All of them empty. Somewhat relieved, he handed it back to Berto.

Berto snatched back his .22 and fingered his bloody lips, making certain his front teeth were intact. "I know you think I'm a fuck-up. And I've caused you some grief. But you fucked up way worse than me this time, and you're not getting off the hook. I just wish I could cause you some significant pain, just…one…time."

Daniel shrugged. "Forget about that, unless you use the gun. And don't forget to load it."

"Why won't you let me come with you?"

"I know you're in love with Yvonne, but you can't help her. Correction: I won't let you help her. I don't want you anywhere near her or my kid."

Berto charged, bellowing, "You know I'm better for her than you!" He was lean and quick on his feet, but Berto was no match for his partner. Daniel took a few steps back, slipped a few harmless haymakers, then grabbed a fistful of Berto's shirt, planted one foot in his midsection and rolled back over his shoulder, sending Berto airborne into the hedge.

Gasping, Berto struggled to get to his feet. Daniel reached out a hand. Berto waved it off.

"Are…you…shitting me?" Daniel exclaimed, exasperated. "You can't be trusted! The guy who Prado hired to help me is a professional. His only stake is succeeding at his job. I can't have you jeopardizing the mission."

Daniel cradled his right hand, the one that had been broken twice and still bothered him. "I'll concede you're a good liar. Marine Corps? Heavy weapons? Very funny. But we've gone over this a hundred times: Your Navy record shows you scored straight 5.0 marks over five years for proficiency. But you consistently failed in personal conduct. At heart, you're ungovernable, disobedient; you've always lacked restraint. Office hours 22 times, busted once, a stint in the brig. Even a rubber room one time. As a photojournalist, OK, you've won awards, been brave enough. The only reason you didn't ride out into VC country like those stupid swashbucklers Sal Fazio and Dickie Stone is because a jealous grunt cold-cocked you with a two-by-four when you roared away from his girlfriend's hooch.

"But you've disappeared on some big assignments since I've known you. Drunk. Then busted here two months ago by civilian police for shooting film in a whorehouse after they chased you out! Then resisting when they tried to confiscate your camera? And this last stunt? Typical."

"I lack restraint?" Berto pointed to his eye with an index finger and glared, an Old-World Italian gesture. *I know you, bud.* "And if you're so smart, why did you claim to be a philosophy professor? They were the biggest fomenters of that commie-infested student protest movement."

"Idiot. You've already compromised the mission."

"Back there? C'mon, man. I adjusted, I handled it."

The investigator Guzmán parked his car under a shade tree, a few blocks behind the van, and checked his notes against the illustrated bulletin. White Econoline van and license-plate number. The photograph of the *subversivo* International Press Service journalist Daniel Mendoza, likely in the company of Alberto DiVincenzo, his sidekick photographer. Both of the Americans former *Marinas.*

Then he stared at the dashboard shrine his wife insisted on making two days ago: a photo of her 20-year-old brother, Emilio, student at Poli, probably a communist, given his proclivity for celebrating everything Castro, Che and Mao. One of the *acelerados* pushing the student strikers.

"What about Zapata?" Guzmán had asked him. His own hero.

Emilio had just laughed in his face. "He's been expropriated by the *Partido Revolucionario Institucional.*"

Guzmán looked at the photo, showing Emilio kicking a soccer ball with abandon, taped to a newspaper headline: *Justicia y verdad para los desaparecidos.* Justice and truth for the disappeared. Well, as far as the *PRI* is concerned, that meant Emilio's soccer days were over.

He decided to wait out the dispute between the two *gringos*, then follow them. The journalist's hand speed was impressive. A champion's kid. Correction: Almost-champion, murdered before his first title fight. Still, for Guzmán, a boxing fan, it gave him great satisfaction to see a father's fighting skill survive to the next generation. But he was surprised to see the judo throw, so practiced, so smooth, and he wondered where that came from.

"You're just trying to cover for your incredibly-poor, impetuous judgment. Only a fool like you would assume that cop is stupid. Judicial Police, fer Chrissakes. I've had it with you, Berto. Stay in Mexico City, if you know what's good for you."

Berto wiped his face with the bandana, struggling to breathe as he regained his feet. *Cold.* "That sounds ominous."

"Let it sink in. I'm not going to let you be an impediment."

"What about my fervor...?"

"...you mean maniacal lunacy under the influence?"

"God, I still can't...I still can't believe Yvonne left the prison willingly when Blanco's people broke him out. She must really hate you...to not want to be...hate you a hell of a lot more than I do."

Berto wheeled the van next to the curb at the sprawling bus terminal. Daniel wet a paper napkin with the remaining ice water from his *licuado*, leaned across the seat to wipe the blood from his partner's lips. Berto snatched it away, turned the rear-view mirror, dabbed and licked his split and swollen lip. He missed the investigator's car pulling into the terminal parking lot.

He handed Daniel a sheaf of yellowing *Excelsior* pages. "I'll meet you in the terminal, Estrella de Oro. But stay away from the ticket counter. Pick out a spot near a wall where I can find you, near the W.C. Sit on the damn floor."

He held the ice against his lip, watched Daniel walk away from the van: the ex-Marine, the fighter/athlete, body beginning to break down, the best American story-teller of his time. Part-Iroquois, Irish, Sephardic Jew. Jet-black hair, unruly. Weathered tan corduroy trousers that covered ankle-high, lace-up USMC work shoes — boondockers, faded blue work shirt, beat-up brown herringbone sport coat, woven-cotton shoulder bag. Daniel tried to persuade Berto that he could at least visually pass as a Mexican: working man's hands, somewhat-battered face, a convincing aura of *triste*.

Except he was extraordinarily handsome, lacked sufficient humility and he still moved like a panther most of the time, like a movie star strolling onto a set. A more-obvious demerit: Daniel spoke Spanish like a five-year-old *gringo*, a handicapped five-year-old *gringo*. *And he thinks he's a fly on the wall? Forget about it.*

Berto waded through the crowd, enveloped by a myriad of conversations in sing-song Mexican dialect, punctuated by amplified announcements about bus departures and arrivals. It didn't take him long to find Daniel, sitting on the *Excelsior* pages talking to a cluster of children, all clutching *liquados* with straws sticking out. Berto shooed them away.

"Here's your ticket. But you have to wait a few hours. Mechanical problems. When it's ready, the bus will board at gate 7. Got you a window seat in the middle. You don't wanna be too close to the aisle in case of a security checkpoint. Sit close to the bus' W.C. in case you have to duck out of sight. If your luck holds out, you'll meet a fragrant babe to sit next to. Piece of cake."

He handed Daniel a paper bag with grease stains. "A couple *tortas*, ham and cheese, no peppers. First stop is Cuernavaca. Twenty-minute break. Then Iguala and Chilpancingo. Then Acapulco. Takes about five, six hours during the middle of the week. You should be pulling in about daybreak. Ask where you can catch a local bus to *Pie de la Cuesta*."

Daniel started to get up.

"Cálmate. Stay here until they call your bus. You already said your goodbye. I don't need your *pinche abrazo*. I'll keep in touch with Prado, see how things are going. If you change your mind about me...." Daniel shook his head. "If you change your mind, phone him, or me. I can always fly down to the coast...."

Daniel shook his head, pinched his nose, looked away.

"Oh yeah, no phones where you're going. Well, I'd leave you with a *Semper Fi*, but you don't deserve it." Red-eyed, Daniel met his glare. Berto turned and walked away.

At 10 p.m., Daniel took his seat on the bus. He'd eaten his *tortas* earlier, drank just enough of a Corona to swallow three tranquilizers and four aspirins which he tapped out of a film canister. He looked forward to a smooth trip and several hours of uninterrupted sleep...until a young boy sat next to him, briefly as it turned out.

"Ssssst." The boy turned in his seat and looked behind. Daniel turned, too. *"Niño, ven,"* a young woman said to him. Meaning change seats with me.

The boy squeezed past Daniel. The woman took his place. She wore a belted dress. Narrow waist but top buttons undone as if her breasts couldn't be contained. A sweater over her shoulders, mid-20s, long, lush hair pulled back and held in place with a silver barrette which revealed the strong neck of an athlete with corded muscles that moved into different patterns each time she changed the position of her head. Smooth mocha complexion. Full, sensual lips. And when she smiled, even, white teeth. "I'm his nanny. Are you going all the way to Acapulco?" She gave him a look of appraisal and contemplation.

Daniel nodded. Some nanny. She looked more like a *telenovela* heartbreaker. The bus driver turned out the overhead lights as he pulled slowly out of the terminal.

At daybreak, Daniel awakened. How he'd craved deep sleep, the best way to forget, the best way to deal with those little devils with pickaxes. When the woman first sat next to him and so earnestly tried to strike up a conversation, he thought about what Berto had said in jest, but complied with just the barest of introductory details. Then as the tranquilizers began to take effect, he pretended to fall asleep, then actually fell asleep.

Now he had to take stock of an unexpected situation. Near panic. The woman's hands were in his lap, clutching Daniel's bandana, crumpled. His right arm was around her and she nestled there, as close as she could get. The boy slept next to her, in her seat, head in her lap. They looked like any intimate traveling family. But the bandana startled him. What had happened during the night?

Awakening from tranquilizer sleep always left him groggy, a side effect that he hated, always swimming against a current of memory. After a few minutes, he recalled that when the bus had left Mexico City and headed downhill to Cuernavaca, she'd volunteered how happy she was to be free, to leave Mexico City, to spend a week with the boy's family in a big house overlooking Acapulco Bay. She mentioned a death in her family, something about *"no puede seguir así."* It can't go on like this. He'd listened politely while she talked. And when words no longer came and she wept, he opened his arm, let her slide into an embrace, handed her his bandana. He was relieved. That had been it, nothing more, no seduction.

The big bus rocked as it changed gears and turned into the Acapulco station. Overhead lights came on. The woman jerked awake and stared at Daniel. "Your eyes. I couldn't see them last night," she said.

Piercing sea-green eyes with tiny fissures of amber. "My mother. She was half-Irish."

When she tried to return his bandana, he gestured no, keep it. *"Gracias, señor.* I hope I didn't offend you or prevent you from sleep." He smiled and bowed his head.

After they exited the bus and retrieved their belongings, she lagged near him, expectant.

"It was nice meeting you," Daniel said, intending to slip away as soon as possible.

She handed him an address and telephone number, written on a piece of a torn paper bag.

"You're welcome to phone me any time during this week. I will have a little free time. Perhaps...." But she read his face. *Triste....*

"Gracias, but I have an obligation. Acapulco is just one stop of many."

She looked into her hands, disappointed, twisting the bandana, then looked into his eyes, searching. "Where are you going?" Daniel smiled again, shook his head.

"Very well, then. *Buen viaje."* She hailed a taxi. While the driver loaded luggage, she watched Daniel — now wearing very dark sunglasses — disappear into a crowd outside the terminal, accompanied by a man with a pushcart. She paid her driver and told him to wait, *un momento,* pinching her thumb and first finger nearly together. Daniel walked a few blocks to a corner bus stop and shifted his box to the pavement. When the man with the pushcart returned, she intercepted him.

"Do you know where that man is going?" she asked, smiling,

as if she had a proprietary interest.

"*Sí, señorita. Pie de la Cuesta.*" The famous Sunset Beach.

"*Un minuto más,*" she told her driver. She ran into the terminal and found a pay phone, dialed. "He's taking a bus to *Pie de la Cuesta.*"

"OK, we'll send someone," Guzmán replied.

"What about me? Why can't I follow him?"

Because you've probably already fallen in love with him. Guzmán laughed. "Because, Marisol, we don't want him destroyed, just followed. Now back off; there might be someone tailing you."

"So what do I do now? I've got a taxi waiting."

"Get a room at the El Faro, watch the cliff divers for a few days."

November 3
Pie de la Cuesta
Acapulco, Guerrero State

CHAPTER 2

Daniel breathed in the warm sea air and fragrant tropical flora, admired the cloudless blue sky. Although black diesel fumes spewed from buses and trucks crawling along the main thoroughfare, there wasn't the overwhelming blanket of smog that plagued the mile-high capital city, a smog that seeped into hair and clothing and occasionally dropped particulates of ash that stained faces or freshly-laundered shirts and dresses, nearly suffocating at times, even in the depths of Chapultepec Park. It could be outrun, as when he rode Prado's Harley out Paseo de la Reforma from Lomas, the wealthy suburb where Prado and his wife, Phaedra, lived, and higher onto the Toluca highway to the bucolic 20-acre campus of the University of the Americas where Berto had an apartment. It took the rainy season, the spring-through-summer downpours, to temporarily wash the sky and cleanse the streets.

Rain-washed sky and streets.... He wrestled his cardboard box onto the roof of the much smaller bus, took a seat in front where there was the most leg room. His thoughts drifted back a month ago to the Plaza of the Three Cultures, water cannons gushing full blast, pushing blood and gore into gutters that torrential rains had previously only lifted into puddles. But neither rain nor hoses could entirely dissipate the sickly-sweet smell of blood or the acrid gas of thousands of high-caliber rounds, fired continuously over a period of several hours. And the tear gas. And torn and mangled bodies, some with eyes wide open and mouths agape in disbelief, reminding Daniel of Edvard Munch's masterpiece painting, *The Scream*, epitomizing the agonizing distortion of human integrity.

He took off his sport coat and placed it carefully in the overhead rack. Sweating, he rolled up his shirt sleeves. He now knew Yvonne and Sonia had survived. Inez, as much as it pained him to admit, probably not.

He'd arrived at the Plaza on Prado's motorcycle after the clatter of heavy machine guns and rifle fire had appeared to stop, along with the arrests. Berto had probably seen it all, captured it all on film: thousands of *granaderos* and army troops with fixed bayonets, truncheons, grenades, bazookas, helicopters flying overhead, hundreds of light tanks and armored cars equipped with two .30 caliber machine guns and a 37 mm canon, bystanders zig-zagging one way then another, desperately sprinting to get away from the deadly crossfire that lasted from 5:30 to 6:30 p.m. and then began to diminish when it started raining, which was when Daniel arrived.

He parked the Harley under a stand of trees that formed a broad canopy until the worst of the rain passed, then continued slowly along Paseo de la Reforma. At the south border of the Plaza, streams of people still in fear for their lives poured out of narrow streets and ran across Reforma to the Cuitláhuac monument, which honored the younger brother who succeeded *Moctezuma II* and who drove *Cortés* and the *conquistadores* out of the Aztec capital. One woman fell. When two students tried to help her to her feet, *granaderos* — riot police, most of them former felons, according to Prado, and nasty-looking motherfuckers — ran up from behind and clubbed them to the ground with their meter-long truncheons.

Tanks, armored cars, jeeps and troop transports lined the

surrounding streets. Army troops, police and *granaderos* wearing rain ponchos encircled the area. Daniel reached into his pocket and slipped on the white glove he'd been given. A few hundred meters ahead, at the Ministry of Foreign Affairs building, a small corridor left open by the soldiers suddenly filled with screaming people trying to flee the Plaza, horrified and soaking wet. But as they attempted to run the gauntlet, soldiers closed ranks and slugged them with clubs and rifle butts.

One of the officers directing the *granaderos* hailed Daniel, and several soldiers — helmeted and flashing fixed bayonets at the barrel end of their M-1 rifles — aimed at him. He waved his gloved hand. The officer shouted an order and the soldiers lowered their rifles and resumed beating their cowering victims to a prone position and cuffing their hands behind their backs.

Daniel fishtailed and sped back to Reforma. He found a place to park on the sidewalk next to a group of workmen who'd earlier erected a neon sign of the Olympic dove beside a series of similar neon displays of athletes and Olympic symbols.

He ran back toward the Ministry building, looking for an opening, a way through the perimeter. But there were no corridors this time, just more troops blocking egress from the Plaza. The tumult inside and the glaring lights reminded him of arriving late to a football stadium at the peak of action. On a hunch, he crossed the street and rounded the block, steadying his shoulder bag to run faster. Every soldier or cop he passed either hailed or ignored him when he waved his gloved hand. He found an unpatrolled alley that led into the Plaza.

Strewn about on the pavement were placards: "We Don't Want the Olympics," "Sell-Out Press," "Riot Police Assassins." A blood-smeared poster depicted a helmeted *granadero* wearing a plastic face mask and bandoliers of tear-gas canisters, carrying a truncheon in one hand and a shield in the other, standing on skulls labeled students. The poster read, *"¡Hoy los salvajes estudiantes golpearon a un heroico granadero!"* Today the savage students beat up a heroic riot policeman!

He followed a line of tanks rumbling toward a phalanx of armored vehicles, parked to seal off the entrance to the Chihuahua apartment building, one of many named after Mexico's states. A large, black, burned-out section left a gaping wound in the building's yellow facade; most of the building's windows had been smashed and all were darkened. On the elevated esplanade, a remnant of the sacrificial Aztec pyramid, he saw hundreds of discarded shoes, clothing and posters, some covered with blood. Prisoners passed by him with hands behind their heads, drenched, trembling, hair plastered to their heads, shoved along by cursing soldiers who hammered them with rifle butts and pummeled them with fists, ripping the shirts right off their backs.

They're taking revenge.

All around him, people stumbled along the pavement slippery with blood trying to get away from their tormentors, crying and screaming as they trampled over bodies of the dead and wounded. An officer shouted orders: "Get them out of their clothes! Search them for weapons!"

The officer spotted Daniel. "We have to get the snipers, the ones who started this bullshit! They hit the *comandante* right at the outset! They targeted him!"

A fusillade began again. A line of soldiers wearing rain parkas aimed their rifles from kneeling positions behind a troop-transport truck and fired magazine after magazine of .30 caliber rounds, yellow tracers lighting up the sky. They fired upward, aiming toward what seemed like sniper fire streaming back at them from one of the buildings. The tanks opened up, and the shooting continued sporadically until 11 p.m. Some sought shelter in the Nonoalco apartments bordering one side of the Plaza, part of the massive government-built Tlatelolco district — fourteen apartment buildings, from four to twenty stories tall, that housed nearly 70,000 people, some middle class, others low-income government employees. But many were hit as they observed from tiny balconies, foolishly poking their heads out to see who was trying to kill them. Another long fusillade — directed by men in civilian clothes wearing white gloves on their left hands — was so intense, parts of the Chihuahua building had caught fire and water pipes burst.

Another reason for Berto to despise him and why Daniel would never forgive himself: He'd been too debilitated by a searing headache to cover what he'd been told would be a rally to celebrate the withdrawal of army troops from the National Autonomous University. The students' National Strike Council had also planned a short march from Tlatelolco to the adjacent Santo Tomás campus of Politécnico which was still under martial rule. Except the small size of the rally — a crowd consisting mainly of students, men, women, children, and oldsters sitting on the ground, street vendors, housewives with babies in their arms, tenants of the housing unit, the usual idlers and curious, bystanders numbering around 10,000 — was irrelevant. The government's tolerance had run out. And as much as Daniel thought he knew about the government's plan to create another generation of martyred leftists, Prado didn't really know the extent of it and couldn't warn him how far they would go to end the protests. Although, to his credit, he did warn Daniel to prevent Yvonne and Inez from attending the Tlatelolco rally. In addition, Prado also met privately with Yvonne and tried to discourage her. However, with Yvonne's estrangement from Daniel and her distrust of Prado — "You're CIA, why should I believe anything you say?" — that warning fell on deaf ears. And since Inez was a prominent member of the National Strike Council, nothing, not even Daniel's pleas, would keep her from missing a protest.

Another line of prisoners, many of them stripped to their underwear, dripping wet from either rain or hoses, marched past, their hands behind their heads, shoved along by soldiers beating them with truncheons.

Berto was among them — camera bag ripped, cradling the smashed body of his Nikon *sans* lens, wearing a haunted expression. They were being herded behind the 16th-century Spanish church, Templo de Santiago. Before the beatings began, Daniel waded through the police, grabbed Berto by the arm, pulled him away.

Berto was stunned, trembling. "It was like Chu Lai, man; like war. I've never seen a fucking deadlier ambush." Daniel grabbed him firmly by the arm and led him away from the tumult, shoving him roughly ahead, trying to look purposeful and resentful rather than like a benefactor.

Berto stopped suddenly, unable to go any further, bent over and vomited the effect of tear gas, struggling to breathe.

"You...you're getting me out of here? How the fuck did you manage that?"

Daniel held up his left hand. He was wearing a white glove.

"Did they get all your film?"

"All of it."

"Who took it?"

Berto looked disgusted. "A guy wearing a white glove, like you. Maybe you can get it back. Who *are* those guys?"

"I don't know." *But Prado knows.*

It's sweltering. The only air comes from an open window and a small fan on the bus driver's dashboard which, in Mexico, always contains a religious shrine replete with little figurines, *la virgen*, a cross.

A copy of *Supermachos* sticks out of the driver's pocket, Inez' favorite, a comic book of political satire and black humor skewering the dominant political party, the *PRI*, with characters created by Eduardo del Río, aka Rius: Juan Calzonzín, a serape-clad *pelado* or lovable bumpkin who survives in the big city by his quick wits and whose three dogs are named Winston, Nixon and Lenin; his drunken sidekick Chon; Don Perpetuo Del Rosal, *cacique* of the town for 30 years and party member; the bureaucrat Gideón Prieto, whose name is a parody of President Gustavo Díaz Ordaz (GDO) and who is Don Perpetuo's brother; El Lechuzo and Arsenio, the repressive police under Don Perpetuo; and Pomposa and Enedina, wife and daughter of Don Perpetuo. *Supermachos* doesn't exactly help to fill the information void left by the city's numerous, castrated daily newspapers, but it certainly does a lot to raise morale among those who feel victimized by a government/media conspiracy.

Editorial control of Mexican newspapers and journals is strict. Coverage is slanted to the government's side or missing or, like *Siempre* and *Política*, slanted to the left. Even when 180 journalists tried to insert paid advertisements into their newspapers in support of the student movement, they were repudiated. Account executives refused to take the reporters' money.

After Tlatelolco, the Mexican press played it like it was started by armed radical students or foreign-agent sharpshooters. *El Día* had as their front-page headline: "Criminal Provocation at Tlatelolco Meeting Causes Terrible Bloodshed." *El Sol:* "Foreign Interlopers Attempt to Damage Mexico's National Image. The Objective: Preventing the Nineteenth Olympic Games From Being Held." *Novedades:* "Shots Exchanged by Sharpshooters and the Army." *El Universal*: "Fighting for Hours Between Terrorists and Soldiers." *La Prensa:* "Army and Students Exchange Gunfire." *Ovaciones:* "Dozens of Sharpshooters Fire on Troops."

Mario Rodríguez Menéndez, crusading left-wing editor of *Por qué?* had trouble with his printer when he came out with stories of police brutality against demonstrators, and the magazine vendors' union was warned by the government not to touch the magazine. He finally prevailed upon an old printer who had worked for Rodríguez' father, also a crusading journalist, using an old rotogravure printing press. Students managed to distribute 500,000 copies before Mexico City police found out. And just two days ago, the first issue of a satirical magazine *La Garrapata* was quickly censored by the government.

But Rius, whose prolific output was as great as his talent, was subject to the government's most severe wrath. A week ago, he agreed to meet Daniel for lunch at the International Press Club, in a dining room dimly-lit and quiet because the itinerant international press corps had left the country to chase other stories.

He wanted to sit in an obscure booth partially hidden by potted palms.

"If you have a tape recorder, please turn it off. And no notes."

"This isn't an interview for publication. I've quit my job; I'm no longer a journalist."

"You quit? Why?" he asked, incredulous. It was something he probably couldn't fathom, having stuck to his literary guns after all he'd been through.

"It's almost impossible to develop post-Tlatelolco stories. No one in government will talk to me. All the strike leaders are in prison. Officially, I'm a pest, a shit-disturber, *persona non grata.*

Some are accusing me of being an activist or, worse, an agitator, a foreign subversive. Even my benefactor at the U.S. Embassy has been warning me to cool down. The momentum now is all about the Olympics and, frankly, I'm not interested in covering that. So, I'm a full-time private investigator, but I feel like an impotent one. And now I've been warned to leave the country. I could be arrested any day now."

"I'm sympathetic to this predicament you find yourself in," Rius began. "Your search for the Poli student Inez, the mission to rescue your wife and child. You might want to consider what I'm about to tell you as a cautionary tale."

About a minute into Rius' narrative, Daniel pushed his plate aside and signaled for another Bloody Mary. Two, actually.

"After Tlatelolco, I received a phone call with a warning: 'If you insist on showing a lack of respect to the president and the army, we will disappear you and your entire family.' I told them my mission was to make the government see the mistakes they were making, the grip on the nation held by the rich and powerful who don't do justice, just make laws to prevent doing justice.

"Then, a few days later as I was walking to my office after lunch, three men from the Federal Security Directorate, the police force of the president, grabbed me and tried to force me into their car, but I resisted."

Daniel visualized the wide-bodied Rius digging in his heels.

"They beat me and shouted that I was an instigator of the protest movement. I lost my shoes in the struggle. Because the car was just a two-door sedan and people gathered to watch, they drove off, and I was able to avoid the kidnap attempt.

"A few days later, three cars with more agents stopped me again; this time there was no escape. I told them not to mess with me because my grandfather is Gen. Lázaro Cárdenas del Río. They took me to Military Camp # 1 where they interrogated me and accused me of having a special relationship with the *guerrilla,* Blanco. I denied it and said I was only a journalist. After about 20 hours, I was shoved into a car and transported to the Toluca military zone at the base of Nevado de Toluca, the huge stratovolcano. I was handed off to other agents wearing civilian clothing and holding walkie talkies, standing at the side of the road smoking *mota*. I saw them reach into a military truck and take out machine guns. Then they tied my hands and marched me 100 meters up one of the volcano foothills to where there were open graves and trees marked with white crosses. They said this was a place where many disappeared were taken to be assassinated. First, they told me, the disappeared were beaten and interrogated, then killed. They told me this one foothill contained many corpses. They forced me into one of the graves and told me they were going to kill me, too.

"*Empecé a despedirme de la vida.*"

"*¿Cómo?*"

"I started to say goodbye to life. After a few minutes, the chief of the soldiers pulled me out. 'You're lucky this time. Someone intervened on your behalf.'

"My wife Rosita and I had an agreement after the first kidnapping attempt: If I didn't report to her by a certain hour in the evening, she was to phone Gen. Lázaro Cárdenas del Río. She did, and he contacted the president.

"When the army guys walked me back to the highway, the agents who brought me up were waiting, pistols in their hands, standing in a defensive position. They told me if I had been killed, they would be, too, so no one would be around to testify. They drove me back down from Toluca to Reforma and the *Cine Chapultepec*. When I got ready to get out of the car, without a penny in my pocket, one of them grabbed me by the arm. He said he'd read all of my work and asked me for my autograph."

Rius chuckled at the gallows irony, but not Daniel. Instead, he was consumed by the notion that Inez was the daughter of working-class parents, and that if she'd had to face the same outcome as Rius, there was no one important enough to intervene on her behalf. The Bloody Marys churned in his stomach and rose in an acid column against the back of his throat, and his heart ached with the worst kind of dread. He'd gone about as far as he could to find her, and now his hopeful 50-50 outcome was greatly reduced, especially when he recalled what Prado had told him days after the massacre: That a source in the Olympic Battalion — formed to safeguard the Olympic sites but who were the most aggressive shooters at

Tlatelolco — reported seeing Inez pushed into an army truck with a score of other National Strike Council leaders and taken to the Toluca army base.

"And you want to hear the best irony? Gen. García Barragán, who was selected by Echeverría, the minister of government, to run this entire Tlatelolco operation including my kidnapping and attempted murder, is my mother's uncle. So one of my relatives wanted me killed; the other one saved me."

The bus slowed now, letting out passengers at various stops along what looked like a thin strip of beach. His would be the last stop.

"How do I get to *Casa Elvira*?" he asked the driver.

The driver gestured west, a sandy path that led to the sea, mist rising where rolling breakers pounded the beach. He adjusted his sunglasses, worrying about the bright light and how it might affect his balance.

"Allá...y a la derecha." Beyond and to the right.

As soon as he retrieved his cardboard box, he moved it behind the semi-enclosed bus stop where there were metal barrels used for burning trash. He looked around to check that he wasn't being observed, popped open a razor-sharp Italian switchblade he'd bought at the Thieves Market and cut the twine. Pulled out the seabag. Cut the box into pieces and pushed them deep into one of the still-smoldering barrels. Hoisting the seabag onto his shoulder, he took the road to the beach.

Prado didn't tell him exactly who he was to meet. Somebody trustworthy, Prado assured him. Get a room at *Casa Elvira* and hang out. He'll find you soon enough.

Waves at least five-feet high were pounding the beach. Close sets. Churning wash. Tide rushing back out. No place for swimming, Daniel thought, disappointed. He was dripping sweat after just a two-kilometer walk and longed to strip down and run into the sea.

Casa Elvira — a simple, white-washed guest house or *casa de huéspedas* — sat at the edge of a coconut plantation, shaded from the morning sun. A handful of tables with wood chairs lined the veranda and one young couple, hippie *vagabundos*, lingered over the remains of breakfast, sipping coffee and smoking what looked to be hand-rolled cigarettes, given the rolling papers and package of Drum loose tobacco. Europeans. The man was shirtless, slim and barefoot. His sun-bleached blond hair was pulled back into a ponytail. He wore loose, white cotton pants with a drawstring belt, like pajama bottoms. The woman, also blond, was deeply-tanned and wore white shorts and a short-sleeved peasant blouse, color-fully-embroidered across the yoke.

"You need a room?" the young man asked. "Best place on the beach. Nice family."

Daniel nodded, guessing from his accent he was either Dutch or German, and placed his seabag against the porch rail.

The young man pinched his thumb and first finger nearly together. "*Momentito*. I'll get the *señora*." He placed his cigarette in an abalone shell ashtray and disappeared through a darkened, open doorway. The girl said nothing while appraising him and his seabag stenciled USMC, her look measuring slight disgust.

The young man returned, followed by a stout *mestizo* woman with gray hair in a bun and a mocha complexion, wearing an apron over her dress, stockings rolled down to just below her knees, flats. Full face beaming a guileless, disarming smile.

Daniel removed his sunglasses and, after the usual exchange of polite greeting, he asked her if there was a room available. She turned her head to the doorway and yelled. "Lidia! Lidia! Come!"

A girl Daniel guessed to be about 11, a Dutch-Girl haircut framing her face like parentheses, wearing a simple, loose-fitting one-piece dress, ran barefoot onto the veranda. She stopped abruptly, startled, like most people when they first saw Daniel. "Show him the rooms; let him choose."

Past the darkened hallway, which included entrances to two family rooms and a private dining alcove, the house opened onto a two-story square courtyard consisting of a dozen guest rooms with screened doors and windows. A bathroom with a sink and shower was located on the ground floor. Daniel selected a room on the second level, small, containing a folding cot with mosquito netting, one small mirror and a bureau, a room he'd hoped would provide ventilation. Except the door and windows faced north/south. When asked about ventilation, Lidia dug into a bureau drawer and produced a small rotating fan.

After a shower and changing into shorts, a t-shirt and flip-flops, he paid Elvira for two days.

"Are you hungry, sir? I can make you breakfast."

Daniel took the table vacated by the young couple. Lidia served him orange juice and a pot of coffee and, after a brief conversation about the menu, shouted his order into the kitchen: French toast, two eggs scrambled, bacon. He took coffee first, saving the juice for later, and stared at the sea sparkling in sunlight. Beautiful to watch, but for only a few seconds, fearing it would make him dizzy. A half-dozen pelicans flew in low formation over the water. About 20 meters to the right of the guest house, an open-sided *palapa* shelter had been erected. Two empty honeymoon hammocks hung limply from posts. He hoped at least one of them would be available after breakfast.

"Is there maple syrup for the French toast?" Daniel asked when Lidia brought his plate. The expression 'maple syrup' puzzled her. She pointed to the small white pitcher in the middle of the table. Daniel picked it up, looked inside, poured a little into a spoon. "This is *miel*." Honey. A rich amber color.

"Yes, it's what we have." Daniel poured some into his coffee, which provoked an astonished giggle, then poured the rest onto the French toast. Lidia lingered, watching, pretending to sweep the veranda, wishing he would remove his sunglasses so she could study his eyes, until Elvira called her to the kitchen. Good honey, he thought. Not store-bought. He wondered where it came from, out here on the secluded beach.

After breakfast and despite the pot of coffee, Daniel felt exhausted, and both hammocks remained unoccupied. He took the one deepest in shade. Reaching down, he pushed against the sand and, as the hammock swung gently, he worried about his need for sleep, worried about the headaches that plagued him. *Maybe I should've taken Berto after all, that speed freak who hardly ever sleeps.* The rhythm of waves breaking on the shore was hypnotic. Daniel's breathing slowed. His collaboration and friendship with Berto replayed like a movie, prompted by the guilt of desertion.

Meeting Berto at Brant University's journalism school during Daniel's freshman year, just a few months after Daniel had been discharged. Brant's program to train U.S. Navy photographers and Berto, photographer's mate 2nd class, working as a dark-room assistant, helping Daniel process his negatives. Becoming as close as a brother. It was wrenching when Berto left Brant to sign up for another tour. During his final year, 1965, he distinguished himself as a combat photographer with the Marines during Operation Starlite, the first big battle against the Viet Cong 1st Regiment, and Dagger Thrust raids 1-5 during monsoon season, the beginning of the search-and-destroy strategy.

Reuniting when IPS recruited Berto after his discharge, and he and Daniel began working as a roving features team covering anti-war demonstrations, race riots and the civil rights movement, until Daniel began to confess his desire to extract himself from the rut of what they were doing, pursue something completely different, uneventful, possibly even uplifting: The 1968 Olympics in Mexico, a country Berto knew well since he'd been born and raised there. Berto had never complained about their assignments. He thrived on the relentless travel and preparation, the 24-hour-a-day grind, the drama, but he wanted to keep the team together, so he agreed on the scheme to transfer.

They left the country after the King and RFK assassinations, Daniel's last bitter sip from the well of hatred, mayhem and murder. "I need a break, man. It's one thing to photograph; it's another to write about it, write around it, insinuate myself deeply into other people's pain."

He still felt guilty about convincing two young Jewish civil rights workers to go south to help blacks register to vote. "A righteous cause," Daniel had said, preaching advocacy to the boys who'd approached him after Daniel's summer internship in Mississippi and Alabama with IPS the summer following his junior year at Brant University.

The boys seeking advice, admitting their fears.

"Defeat fear," Daniel urged. "Remember what our people went through."

The boys volunteered the following summer and wound up being chased, tortured and murdered within 24 hours of arriving and buried in a shallow grave by Mississippi Klan goons.

Little did I suspect that I would be in for more of the same in Mexico City. That it would affect me more deeply and personally than if I'd remained working in the U.S. For Berto, the man who loved irony, it was the perfect assignment: Even though our relationship was fraying, I would need to rely on him more than ever.

November 3
Sierra Madre del Sur
Blanco's Stronghold
Yvonne's Story

CHAPTER 3

S onia's nightmares have diminished. She sleeps in a cot right next
to me. The horrors of Tlatelolco and prison were the worst things
that ever happened to me. But it pains me so much that they were also
the worst things that ever happened to Sonia, and she's only eight
years old. They made her mute. Ironically, it's the same condition
her father experienced when he was an extremely frightened boy
after his family was murdered, when he was tormented and filled
with remorse because he blamed himself for their deaths. Just as the
Indian School on the rez gave Daniel a notebook so he could communicate his thoughts and participate in classes, I've given Sonia
a notebook. Her first comment was a question: "Where is daddy?"
It was heart-breaking.

I decided to lie: "He's coming. He's coming to get us. It's taking
time because we're a long way from Mexico City, and he has to be
very careful."

I'm all cried out. I can't get over the contrast of the dark Mexico
City war zone and the beauty of these forested mountains of Guerrero, so close to Acapulco. The beginning of the dry season, they
tell me. Mainly blue sky but with puffy white clouds drifting in

from the Pacific which some days I imagine I can actually see, but it's really just a distant haze. We still need mosquito netting at night because nearby streams are running strong, and a lake just above the 15-square hectare compound is filled to the brim. I'd like to say that it feels good to be free from those murderous thugs who killed, tortured and imprisoned so many of my comrades. But I'm still in mourning. I believe I always will be.

Since my days growing up on the rez, through the Iroquois struggles with the state and feds, the civil rights and anti-Vietnam War demonstrations, I've always wanted to be part of those moments that change everything. Here, I got in too deep. After all my American radical friends were deported, I stayed involved. Working-class students, some of them Indian, were being murdered, imprisoned and disappeared. Also, I was adopted by mostly working-class women from *Unión Nacional de Mujeres Mexicana* — National Union of Mexican Mothers — who supported the student protest movement. They were mostly young mothers who noticed I was showing up at marches alone...or with Sonia.

At first they thought I was Mexican. When I told them I was a full-blood Iroquois from New York State, they were impressed, which was different from most middle-class Mexican women who disdain any trace of Indian heritage, who try to prove their European blood by walking about with unshaved legs under nylon stockings. They admired me, coming from a tribe that ruled a vast empire, as did their Aztecs. They told me I was beautiful and that I carried myself with strength and dignity, but they also said they could see a wounded look in my eyes and posture, as if I'd suffered a serious defeat. Don't worry, they told me, if we stay together, there's always hope. They were my comrades, especially during the most troubling crisis in my marriage. But at Tlatelolco, everything blew apart.

Before we left New York, I heard about the forming of a new organization, AIM, the American Indian Movement. It sounds like something I'd like to be part of, something more directly involving me, my people, my future.

The *cívicos* broke Blanco out of Casa Montenegro two weeks ago, as corrupt guards stood by, sweeping me and Sonia out in the process, probably saving our lives. The way I understand it, he couldn't be contained in Guerrero. He'd already been broken out of the state prison at Iguala, and he and the *cívico* leadership decided to go beyond the narrow framework of the state of Guerrero, and they established the *Asociación Cívica Nacional Revolucionaria*. So the next time he was arrested, after a bank robbery in Petatlán he'd been blamed for, he was taken to Casa Montenegro. But the *cívicos* broke him out of there, too. He asked if I wanted to accompany him.

"I know it sounds crazy to you," he said, cradling Sonia in his arms and leading us past a smoke-filled cell block N, a section where student leaders of the Strike Council had been subjected to brutal interrogations by Mexican and U.S. agents. "But to them you are a communist, an outside agitator manipulating the student protestors. It fits their narrative perfectly: Mexican students wouldn't be relentlessly protesting if it weren't for provocateurs like you. As you know, there's a history of detaining people without charges…indefinitely. You'll either be imprisoned under Article 145, or maybe they'll put on a show trial for their benefit. North American communist Indian woman. What greater threat to established order is there than you? Or you'll be disappeared soon like some others in custody. Your daughter, too, because you're still a threat to the stability of the country. And your prolonged imprisonment without legal representation is too difficult to account for."

I was really scared, but what he said had a high degree of likelihood. I'd been held incommunicado in Casa Montenegro's prison for women for three weeks since the night of Tlatelolco. It was frightening inside. Bad food — corn gruel, watery stews, beans — screaming chaos, little sleep. They took Sonia away from me for a few days in order to force a confession that I was a principal foreign agitator, an American communist. I was beside myself, but I didn't confess, even though I was on the verge of a breakdown.

I'd heard rumors that Daniel was working hard as hell to get us out. But he never got to us, and no lawyer came to visit. No one from the U.S. Embassy came, despite my demands. Day after day of interrogations, some of them brutal. The prison authorities told Daniel I refused to see him, refused help. When an especially sadistic guard told me that, I didn't want to take any chances staying there, and Sonia was catatonic and dehydrated by diarrhea. It was fortunate that we had been brought back to cell block N in the men's prison that day to be re-interrogated when the *cívicos* crashed in.

Now we're in the country, far away from any village, Blanco's stronghold on flat terrain overlooking steep *barrancas* terraced for growing corn, tomatoes and other vegetables. Most of the buildings are constructed of concrete blocks, wood plank walls and tin roofs. A few others are called *jacales*, mud and stick construction, some larger than others. The roof and walls are made of *otate*, a wild tall grass like bamboo or cane, then made solid when covered with mud. For an Indian who grew up on a squalid reservation, along with Daniel by the way, and all the terrible places we've lived in the urban U.S., this mountain retreat, the light, new clean buildings, a communal social structure — albeit patriarchal — and sumptuous communal gardens is definitely a respite. But if something bad happens again, if I find out the State Police or army is coming after Blanco, I won't be able to bear it. I'll just have to find a way out of the country.

Peasants with mule teams from all over bring in sacks of rice and beans and other supplies and occasionally by truck so the core group of founding *cívicos* — only about 15, not including family members — are pretty much self-sufficient here.

Sonia received good medical care from a visiting doctor, and she's now well enough to play with the other kids here, even attend makeshift classes under a large *palapa* roof. When I say "well enough," I mean physically. She no longer slouches or acts depressed or complains of stomach aches. Her little-girl pudginess has disappeared; instead, sinews of muscle have begun to form in her arms and legs. Her calf muscles flex when she runs and climbs. The sun has restored the honeyed bronze of her skin. With daily brushing, her hair gleams again. It's cut short, just below her ears, parted on one side. Her prize possession is a thin, flat silver barrette shaped in the likeness of a pre-Columbian lizard that keeps the long side away from her eyes. The barrette is a gift from one of the women here who noted Sonia's fascination with the geckos that climb across the walls and occasionally pose before her, as if treasuring her silent and meditative presence.

Psychologically, it's another story. Her usually-delighted expression — so much like her father's — has faded, replaced by a mask of steady solemnity. Occasionally, I notice a sly spreading of a Buddha-like smile, as if she harbors some ineffable wisdom. But when I ask her what she's thinking, she just shakes her head, puts down her pad and pencil and looks away. It took Daniel a couple of years to regain his voice and some semblance of personality, but that was due to intense intervention by his uncles and our Iroquois community to reverse the corrosive loss of faith that plagued him. There's nothing like that here. Just me. But the parental influence I was once so capable of exercising over all aspects of her development now is only partial and fleeting.

I'm not just a guest here. My duties are to help look after children of the *cívicos*, help with house chores like cooking, washing dishes and clothes, feeding and butchering chickens — the only kind of meat here, except for the occasional goat — and collecting eggs. And cleaning weapons. This has required some training as the only weapon they have here that I'm familiar with is the 1911 .45 Colt semi, similar to Daniel's .38 Colt Commander. Shotguns are easy enough, but I had to be trained to break down the M-1 carbine and M-16. I'd like to keep the Colt .45 within reach, especially at night, but I'm afraid Sonia might find it.

It's clear Blanco likes me. He's never met a North American Indian before, and he's really impressed I'm full-blood Iroquois, "the biggest and most influential Indian nation in North America, from the Ohio River Valley to New England, and from Canada to Oklahoma. They had great warriors and, just as important, great negotiators." Blanco knows his history, being a former school teacher. His perspective makes me chuckle because — as I said earlier — Mexicans usually disdain their Indian heritage and blood. I'll never forget seeing an old series of Lone Ranger shorts in a movie house in Mexico City and kids laughing so hard some of them fell out of their seats when Tonto got the crap beat out of him, which regularly occurred whenever *kemo sabe* suggested he go into town to scout things out.

Yesterday I saw a small single-engine plane flying in low over the tree tops and heard it land. The airstrip is nearby, although the mountain terrain is so broken and so dense with forest it must take a really skilled pilot to get in and out. I was told the plane had come for a load of *mota*. Where it's taken to I have no idea, but it must be bound for *El Norte*. I've tried to talk to the pilot about the possibility of taking Sonia and me back to the states, just the *possibility* of it, but he keeps putting me off.

Blanco, grandson of an army general, was radicalized at the Rural Teachers College of Ayotzinapa in Guerrero state. He said he and his fellow students were expected to go out on risky 'fundraising activities' that ranged from passing the hat in towns to taking over a highway tollbooth and letting motorists drive through in return for a donation. It sometimes entailed highjacking buses or food delivery trucks or blocking highways, which led to clashes with the police. Now he leads an organization numbering about 70 men which he hopes will become international in scope. Needless to say, his 'fundraising activities' are much more ambitious, including bank robberies. He's also organized some groups of peasants to grow weed. He's got considerable leverage.

When he got started, he said, he tried to defend peasants confined to the furthest reaches of the Sierras, who came down only to work at slave wages for rich landowners. He decided to participate politically in state government, running the *cívicos'* candidate for governor and candidates for township offices controlled by landowners. Rather than face electoral defeat, State Police supporting the landowners attacked Blanco's *guerrillas* and murdered his supporters at an electoral meeting in the state capital. Army troops from Mexico City were sent in to arrest and imprison those who survived and to occupy the townships. Even though he was convicted and sentenced to life for allegedly murdering a state cop, it didn't deter him. In fact, while he was in Casa Montenengro, he leaked out a manifesto to striking National University law students: "We seek unity on the international level with the forces fighting our common enemy, United States imperialism."

He doesn't look anything like Che, however. He's dark-skinned from living in the mountains, with black hair swept back from a prominent widow's peak, wide-set eyes and a thin mustache. On most days, he wears western shirts with pearlized snap buttons, faded blue jeans that sit low on his hips secured with a hand-tooled leather belt and unpretentious silver buckle, and scuffed flat-heel pull-on work boots. His physique is slender, and he looks more like a scholar than a fighter. He wears wire-rimmed glasses while pouring over documents for hours at a time. He's a man of words but also a man of action who the peasants revere, not least because he protects them from police and *bandidos*, pays them for growing *mota* and bribes government clerks to confiscate and destroy their debt records. He's a man most people here would risk their lives for.

He was more than curious about Daniel, that I was married to a journalist who was one-quarter Iroquois, one-quarter Irish and a Sephardic Jew, the son of the great Davey Mendoza. I told him that he was considered to be one of the best young American journalists. He said he must be very brave. I agreed, but I didn't say anything about our deteriorated relationship, and I didn't say anything about him not being a subversive, not wanting to have anything to do with what I do. I told him about the principle that guided Daniel, being a fly on the wall, being a skilled feature writer. Blanco laughed. "You know what draws flies?"

I didn't have to answer that one. Daniel would probably agree with him about a certain kind of journalism, but that wasn't the kind he practiced. True, I gave him a hard time when he insisted on maintaining his emotional distance. I always argued that the story wasn't enough, and I used to quote Martin Luther King Jr. about the hottest place in hell being reserved for those who maintained neutrality during a time of moral crisis. We argued constantly about that and about my active involvement in Iroquois protests, and local civil rights and anti-war demonstrations.

"You have a child to take care of!" was his constant refrain.

"You have a job!" I always replied. "I don't have anything to do. I don't like being saddled with motherhood."

"What do you mean?" he'd say. "You have an important job at the Indian School."

Sure, while he travels around the country with that maniac Berto, having big adventures and God knows what else. The only time he took me with him was when he covered the march on Washington, and I got to participate. The closest I came to him was through reading his stories.

But everyone lauded his work, saying his stories were the best. It's true, and he worked really hard to make them that way. But I was left pretty much alone to do the parenting and every other domestic chore. I also really resented that he wasn't there to comfort me, and that he withheld affection. He was hooked on deliverance, on proving himself, his journalism.

Blanco and I share coffee each morning on the terrace attached to one of the bigger *jacales*. He wants to know Daniel's history, going all the way back to 1700 and his family's patriarch, Daniel Mendoza, the first prominent Jewish boxer and champion of England. The guy who Daniel is named after. Then, 250 years later, a new champion was about to be crowned, Daniel's father, Davey.

Blanco wanted to know, so I got deep into his family tragedy. The two vengeful murders of Daniel's mother and grandfather by mobsters who'd been humiliated and rebuffed when they tried to take command of Davey's career. Davey's escape to Brooklyn where he worked with a crew of Iroquois high-steel workers until he was finally discovered and also murdered. Daniel's three years being harbored on the Iroquois reservation in fear for his life and in deep mourning, living with his mother's brother, Jesse, the tribe's faithkeeper. Showing up at the Indian School at age 12, mute and in shock, and I was assigned to be his secretary, his recorder — just as I'm doing now with Sonia — so that he could participate in class.

Our wonderful friendship began with such shared intimacy. He would speak through his notebook and through me to his teachers and classmates. And we could speak to each other this way, especially and most poignantly during that first, hard winter, drinking hot chocolate while sitting in front of Jesse's fireplace.

I fell in love with him so easily, and he with me, but we were both Wolf clan and, coming from an orthodox family, I resisted his urges. Several years later, his Jewish and Iroquois uncles, Abe and Jesse, who believed that their faiths shared so much in common, reminded us that, in practice, kinship rules weren't that rigidly enforced in either tribe, Jewish or Iroquois, especially if both families consented. It was only then that we dared consummate our relationship. This was actually a good outcome because we both needed to be certain of our commitment.

When Daniel began to recover his voice, albeit with a stutter, he became a belligerent drunk. He told me that when he drank he became less anxious and more fluent and, in the process, he developed profound, over-arching truths about life.

"The two most important things you can do in this dog-eat-dog world are: don't be a sucker for others, and look out for yourself," he declared, so pleased to be going off on his own.

I was so hurt because this signaled that he would turn away from me, and I panicked that our friendship would dissolve. His new-found philosophy was also the exact opposite of what Jesse and Abe had been trying to instill in him. Jesse was furious: *"Oneka* causes the mind to split. The mind-changer brings great misery and hardship, even as you enjoy it." But by age 16, with the persistent help of the three of us, he had evolved from nihilism and rebellion as a way of dealing with unspeakable and crushing loss to a strong sense of community and self-confidence, to the point of actually solving the murders of his mother, grandfather and father. But when Daniel discovered the leading role played in the tragedy by his father's brother, an uncle who schemed to reap the family's resources and who'd masqueraded as Daniel's mentor, he made a decision that nearly tore us apart.

I told Blanco about Daniel wanting to drop out of high school, leave Brant and join the Marine Corps. The Marines are really big on sports, so when Daniel finished boot camp at Parris Island and advanced infantry training at Camp LeJeune, he was assigned to Special Services at Quantico where he became the starting end on the football team. That was fairly significant because in 1956 he had just turned 17, was somewhat undersized, and the team consisted primarily of recently-commissioned officers, guys who played four years in college. But he was good and really tough: All-City end as a junior on a championship high school football team and two-year veteran of Red League box lacrosse. They nicknamed him "Nails." Daniel had earned a number of nicknames over the years that testified to his fighting spirit, a far cry from the Iroquois name given to him when he was an orphan with a tortured soul, *He-Who-Sits-Quietly-and-Listens.*

When football season was over, he boxed. He wound up Marine

Corps light heavyweight champion. In spring and summer, he was a squad leader with the battalion that trained officer candidates. Then Recon went after him. That was a story Blanco avidly wanted to hear, the secret mission that almost got him killed. But I told him some other time. I really didn't want to talk about it.

When Daniel got out of the Marines, he won a scholarship to come home, play football and lacrosse and study journalism at Brant University. We'd finally gotten married. I'd already graduated with a useless degree in sociology, and Sonia was a year old. He was a very good college athlete, but often injured.

You know how men of an oppressed class practice that blank look — what we Americans call a poker face, what you might call stoic — don't let your face betray you. We Indians have practiced that look, so have you Mexicans. No expression in the eyes or the mouth. But the eyes take in everything. Silence before a storm. I've also seen this look in the eyes of Mexican police and soldiers. But for them, it's the look they adopt before they confiscate your soul.

Daniel was never like that. His face was expressive; it almost always registered joy, despite all the trials and tribulations he'd experienced as a boy. His eyes, an unusual shade of green, absolutely danced when he was delighted. Anger was an alien emotion. He just rolled with every difficult situation…. Except the past few years, especially with me. Sometimes his eyes seem not to register any affection, let alone recognition, seemingly shadowed again by torment. His smile emerged only when he was around Sonia. I believe his injuries had a lot to do with it, especially the concussions.

Daniel experienced his share of them in the Marines and playing football and lacrosse at Brant. But he'd also experienced his share of KOs, most of them of an unconventional nature. The first time was at age 12 when mobsters blew up his grandfather's store. It sent him to the hospital. His last lacrosse injury sophomore year finished him for the season. Wicked headaches, couldn't remember anything he'd studied or even what we'd eaten for dinner two hours earlier. And when we talked, he'd ramble onto unrelated subjects, unsure of how he got there. When I tried to get him back on track, he'd lash out at me, then afterward beg my forgiveness. It had us both really worried right up to his final exams two months later when, inexplicably, he recovered.

By his junior year, his professors in both creative writing and news reporting were raving about his writing and his ability to record what they called "sights and sounds." I believe he turned to writing out of a need to communicate when he was a child so traumatized he lost his ability to speak. Then it was about proving himself. Proving that he was good. It was a story he wrote for the student newspaper that spring that won him the IPS internship that took him to Mississippi and Birmingham. Brant University had hosted a community action training program led by Saul Alinsky. Part of it focused on learning how to protest and they chose to stage a demonstration in front of the city's power company, demanding it employ blacks. I was there, and I still remember Daniel's lead:

"Light from the hot afternoon sun reflected off the facade of the Brant Power building, causing onlookers to shield their eyes. The polished black granite wall mirrored the demonstrators protesting the company's alleged racist hiring practices. It was quiet except for the freedom chants emanating from the inner circle of parading demonstrators and one young man who yelled: 'We ain't invisible no more!'"

That was the beginning of a career as a roving features writer covering the civil rights movement, Vietnam War protests and everything in between. He and Berto.

We came to Mexico because Daniel demanded that he needed a career change due to a bad case of burnout. I tried to tell him how foolish that sounded coming from him, given the history of his people and my people — our people, actually — what we've both been steeped in. Oppression becomes institutionalized, if you let it. If you fight it, you may lose. But there's also a chance you might win, if only a partial victory. That's how life is, and it never ends. I've been terrorized, but I'm not quitting; I'd just rather fight for my own people some day soon. Plus there's less of a chance of getting murdered at home. Mexico is an unmerciful police state.

The worst part of his burnout is that he'd grown disheartened covering a never-ending, surreal string of stories even before he graduated from Brant's school of journalism, achieving fame during his internship with IPS, when they discovered just how good a reporter and writer he was. If you consider just the last three years: JFK's assassination, the Newark riots, anti-war protests that escalated after Tet, the Malcolm X murder, the Columbia University uprising, the deadly Detroit riots which didn't end until tanks rolled down the streets. Kent State. Jackson State. The King and RFK hits. That's what his editors wanted him to cover, with Berto, the perfect team, pictures harnessed to words of principal eyewitnesses and Daniel's narratives. But for Daniel, reporting became a burden. Toward the end, he began to experience sweat-soaked nightmares, and he finally confessed to me that his assignments were evoking the turmoil and depression from his childhood that he'd worked so hard to overcome.

"Good journalism isn't going to change the world," he said, rationalizing his decision. "And I'm tired of cataloguing evil."

While I acknowledged his reasons for wanting to quit political journalism, I told him that despite the personal agonies revisiting him, he ought to persist. Maybe I was callous when I told him to be more like Berto, who treated their assignments as exhilarating and purposeful adventures.

I also tried to explain to him my passion for activism. When Daniel was a boy, harbored on the rez with his mother's brother, Jesse, he couldn't understand how a decorated World War II hero, proud to be honored as an American icon, could on occasion be totally angry and bitter toward his country. Daniel lacked the context to understand that Jesse and other Indian leaders were also fighting for their Indian nations — against their country — fighting politically to protect their ancestral lands from being invaded and reduced, fighting to protect their treaty rights and their guaranteed sovereignty.

In my own lifetime, the Iroquois lost two legal battles which still generate bitterness among our people. The first was when the Power Authority of New York State, citing eminent domain, seized just over one-quarter of 4,000 acres of reservation land in northern New York to build a reservoir. Despite the efforts of Wallace "Mad Bear" Anderson, a U.S. Navy war vet — W.W. II and Korea — and an activist for Indian rights, the U.S. Supreme Court ruled in 1960 that the seizure was legal.

A few years later, also citing the power of eminent domain, the U.S. Army Corps of Engineers built the Kinzua Dam to provide flood control and power generation along the Allegheny River in northern Pennsylvania. The problem was that the ensuing lake created by the dam extended 25 miles to the north into New York State, which meant condemning 10,000 acres of another Iroquois reservation. It also forced the relocation of 600 displaced people. Another legal battle was fought and lost.

It took time for Daniel to realize that Jesse had divided loyalties: to his country, which nearly cost him his life, and to his Indian nation which chose him to be one of its principal leaders, to fight for our people's rights.

Years later, it was easier for him to sympathize during the civil rights movement what with the murders, lynchings, bombings, police dogs, his own arrests, beatings and jailing in the South because police thought he might be some shade of black.

What he never understood was my sympathy for and identification with the Mexican students who were confronted with deadly force. They want to change their government and educational system, like the Paris student protestors. They love their country, but they feel compelled to challenge something bigger, a corrupt one-party authoritarian state and also to advance their people's rights, as promised by revolutionary decrees 60 years ago. They want to challenge the "mummies", as they call the fossilized leaders of every institution in Mexico: do away with Article 145 of the Federal Penal Code which establishes penalties for the vague charge of 'social dissolution', free political prisoners held for years without trials, abolish the riot police, fire the police chief of Mexico City and his head of security, pay indemnities to the families of all those killed and injured since the beginning of the conflict, maintain autonomy of all schools from police and military invasions and determine which government officials are responsible for the bloodshed.

But deep down, the students' chief demand was nothing more radical than dialogue with the government.

Daniel was so looking forward to covering the Olympics, especially boxing. But he also wanted to experience a completely different culture, and he convinced me that Mexico seemed to offer the potential of an exotic and benign environment. He was told he would be the assistant to the IPS bureau chief, John Cogdill, who was just two years older than Daniel and who Daniel had met and briefly worked with five years before in Dallas when JFK was murdered. Cogdill said he wanted Daniel and Berto to get ready to cover the Olympics. He also wanted them to help set up the bureau's press center at the Olympic Village, and also welcome visiting journalists and get them situated. It was supposed to be a perfect confluence of a slow news period and preparing for the most modern and widespread Olympics coverage ever, perhaps one of the biggest news events of the year, considering the developing-world setting.

When we first arrived, it was June, the beginning of summer. Daniel was content to do errands for Cogdill: Driving out to the airport every day with Berto to collect incoming cargo intended for the press center and to prevent thefts, a persistent problem. It was also a good way for Daniel to get his bearings while Berto navigated his van throughout the huge metropolis. Sonia loved to accompany them because they catered to her and kept her entertained by joking...how they always interacted. They made her feel more like an equal rather than a dependent child, which she absolutely adored. Sonia with Daddy and her Uncle Berto.

This went on for several weeks as we adjusted to moving into our lovely cottage in Colonia Polanco, adjacent to Chapultepec Park, getting acquainted with living in a very cosmopolitan city and meeting a wide variety of people, all of whom doted on us. Because we were exotic to them. Most important, his working hours would be closer to normal. He would have more time for Sonia and me. Which turned out to be illusory once the shit hit the fan, and the writer in him.... He began living inside his head again.

It was disappointing that the only open window we might've enjoyed together here — a respite from study, work, travel and my solo parenting — closed almost overnight. Previously, our most passionate time together was just before I became pregnant, the summer we were married, between his Marine Corps discharge and his first college football season and the beginning of classes. That summer he played Red League lacrosse, representing our tribe, and worked as a lifeguard at a city pool. Life was easy. We lived in his Uncle Abe's apartment, bequeathed to us after Abe's death, rent paid for the next four years while Daniel finished his journalism degree.

It was a hot, humid summer. We wore as few clothes as possible, and we probably took five or six showers a day, some of them after making love. The first times, we experienced a slight physical strangeness because we had been apart for a very long time. But we soon got over the awkwardness of separation. We believed that we were meant for each other. Our people believed that our relationship was God-intended. For us, sex became a dialogue of sensuality based on a deeply-significant and abiding love. We kissed for hours just because it was so satisfying. And he stroked my body in deep admiration, as if he was a brilliant art collector and I was a priceless sculpture.

When I became seriously pregnant, it was the beginning of the change. Hard work, travel, and more hard work changed everything. Of course, there were still those rare moments, but nothing like at the beginning. I suppose that happens to every couple. But it seemed he just lost interest in me and preferred living in his own head, chasing stories.

One way to displace my disappointment was to enroll in a graduate anthropology course at the University of the Americas because we could afford a maid to look after Sonia a few days a week as well as clean and cook for us. What a relief! The course was a seminar taught by a visiting professor from Oxford University and it appealed to me because, as an activist, I was obsessed with the topic in real, contemporary life. It was devoted to revival movements – the belief by a religious, social, or political group or movement in a coming major transformation of society, after which all things will be changed for the better.

The professor told us to research and make a presentation of an example of a revival movement, which exist in many cultures and religions. It was an easy choice for me, and I was a big hit when I led off with my paper on a belief in a future ideal society brought about by a devout and dedicated spiritual leader. The movement was familiar to me, Handsome Lake's revival of Iroquois religion by preaching a code that combined traditional Iroquois beliefs and behavior with white Christian values. Recognizing the need to make adjustments in order to survive in their changing world, his code emphasized survival and creation of a new age in which human suffering would be dramatically reduced without the sacrifice of Iroquois identity.

Born in 1735, a time when the Iroquois Confederacy was at its peak of empire and prosperity through fur trading, Handsome Lake, a half-brother of an Iroquois war chief, witnessed the gradual erosion of wealth, influence, morale and spiritual welfare after the American Revolution resulted in our loss of land, displacement and disintegration of the traditional family unit. In addition, epidemics of infectious diseases and the introduction of alcohol furthered a downward spiral. The traditional Iroquois religious rituals were no longer applicable to the environment in which the Iroquois people found themselves.

In 1799, after a period of illness due to many years of excessive alcoholic indulgence, Handsome Lake experienced a series of visions. When he regained his health, he began bringing an inspiring message of Gaiwiio (the "Good Word") to his people who were suffering in despair. With the help of his relatives, his visions were written down and published in 1850, and the Code of Handsome Lake is credited with saving and reuniting the Six Nations Iroquois Confederacy. The Code is not only practiced in real life today, but also is passed on to future generations through an annual ceremony every September.

When I finished, the professor took me aside and said I should consider applying to graduate school. I did consider that...until it was no longer an option.

Things were made easier in Mexico City due to the intervention of Daniel's hometown friend, Robbie Prado, whose official job title was security specialist for the U.S. State Department working out of the U.S. Embassy. It didn't take long for me to suspect he was really CIA. They met for breakfast every morning at Sanborns, a short walk from the embassy along Reforma and nearly every evening for dinner at the International Press Club, right across the street.

Prado was frank with Daniel, admitting the unusually high number of revealed CIA operatives, meaning ones who the U.S.

openly identified, who worked out of the embassy, and his role advising the Mexican government on security issues. But Prado claimed he was shocked when student-organized protests evolved almost overnight into a massively-popular movement involving thousands of non-student sympathizers. Intelligence prior to July was that Mexico was one of the most stable and dependable Latin countries in the hemisphere, despite occasional student outbursts, and the Olympics were going to be a sensational success. Nothing comparable to the student riots in Paris, Berlin, New York, Rome, Rio or Warsaw could happen in Mexico.

When the *granaderos* and then the army started beating, shooting, arresting and disappearing students, all hell broke loose. Besides the CIA and State Department operatives doing their thing, Prado needed someone like Daniel to penetrate the students' National Strike Council via his intimate reporting style. And, frankly, Daniel needed Prado to tip him off about Mexican government strategy and tactics that provided him with the best intel and, subsequently, made him the most knowledgable, effective and admired foreign journalist in the city. And if he were to get into a jam, Prado would come to the rescue. And all of this really put him in good stead with his bureau chief.

Cogdill was already an experienced hand in Mexico and Central America, but he was most renowned for his work in Dallas: discovering Lee Harvey Oswald's sniper nest in the Texas School Depository and helping to break the story of Jack Ruby's murder of Oswald at the Dallas police station. His wife, Marta, was an elegant Mexican woman. She was kind and, along with John, possessed a bon vivant personality, going out of her way to make me feel welcome.

Cogdill had also served in the Army after he graduated college, and he loved it that Daniel and Berto were combat vets. He also got a kick out of their philosophical differences, their incongruous relationship: the liberal Daniel — taught when he was a boy by his Sephardic uncle that he had an obligation to heal the world and by his Iroquois uncle that he had to assume responsibility for preserving Mother Earth for the next seven generations — and Berto, the self-confessed *cabrón* womanizer who hated communism and worshipped Ayn Rand and psycho-cybernetics.

Daniel and Berto were equally good at their crafts. Neither one hitched his wagon to the other's star. Professionally, they were in lock-step, and they took each other to school. Personally? Well, you know what they say about opposites. It may actually be true in this case.

I think Daniel was drawn to Berto's reckless sense of adventure and, outside of work, his enveloping commitment to pleasure. And it gave Daniel a kick the way Berto justified his profane, outrageous misbehavior with cherry-picked intellectual reinforcement. To Daniel, Berto was amoral; he did what he wanted with no thought to consequences.

As for Berto, I believe deep down he admired Daniel's immersion into a principled life since his childhood. One forced on him, really, by his uncles Abe and Jesse, in order to help him deal with the pain and cynicism brought on by family tragedy. And even if Daniel seemed so often to lack faith or question it, faith and morality were decidedly the foundations of every significant progression that occurred in his life, both personal and professional.

At one of the big rallies at the National Autonomous University, Berto became furious and deeply offended when students began to burn an American flag. Daniel had to literally hold him back while explaining that seeming to be anti-American and carrying posters of Che, and chanting *"Ho-Ho-Ho Chi Minh"* was just symbolic theater, copy-cat antics, exactly what other students around the world were doing in their anti-government protests.

This is how it went down, according to what Daniel told me: "Berto, why do I have to tell you this history? It's the same story all over. Plus anti-Americanism has always occupied a prominent place in Mexican revolutionary nationalism, especially as it relates to Latin America. You do recall the Cuban revolution, the Bay of Pigs, the U.S. role in the capture and death of Che a year ago, right? It's all about a struggle against domination."

Eventually Berto calmed down and Daniel told him, "Go on over there and inflict yourself on them. They'll see your IPS tag and your camera bag, and I guarantee you'll be idolized for being a hip and groovy *gringo*."

So Berto pulled himself up to his full, indignant height,

smoothed back his hair and waded into the chanting, singing crowd where he engaged students in his typically aggressive/endearing manner, by turns exasperating and charming, but also making his presence indelible. Eventually, he was invited to a post-rally party by a stunningly beautiful girl, Inez, who said she had nothing personal against Americans and that Berto should bring his friend. That was the amazing thing about those kids: their ideology led them to despise America, but they always offered the warmest hospitality to young Americans who they just assumed were *simpatico*. That girl turned out to be one of the leaders of the students' National Strike Council. And that was the beginning of the end of my marriage.

November 4
Casa Elvira
Pie de la Cuesta

CHAPTER 4

S econd day, same breakfast, same exhaustion. Daniel stretched
out in the hammock, and the rhythm of the waves breaking on
the beach lulled him to sleep. Then a different sound, like knocking.
Who's that knocking on my door?

When he opened his eyes, he recognized the sound. Hoof beats.
He rolled onto his side and watched a big mule approach. It was
outfitted with a wooden saddle, leather stretched over it. The male
rider led a string of three small horses, sorrels with identical white
blazes on their foreheads. He wore a wide-brimmed straw hat, flat
on top with a small tassel in back, white peasant trousers and shirt,
red bandana around his neck, *huaraches*. The man dismounted,
tied the mule and horses to the veranda railing. Lidia ran out of the
kitchen. After they exchanged words, she pointed to Daniel. The
man nodded, took off his hat as he sat at a table and placed a bag of
bottles at his feet. He motioned to Daniel to join him.

Daniel was groggy from a tranquilized sleep, but his heart
began to pound in a chest compressed with alarm. There was something familiar about the man, but it couldn't be possible. A man he
knew a world away. A man who saved his life, then disappeared. A

shard of recovered memory disinterred.

He felt weak in the legs because all the blood in his body seemed summoned to his heart. But it was important to make it to the veranda and take a seat, to get a better look. Lidia brought a tray of coffee, two cups. The man pulled a bottle from the bag at his feet. An old tequila bottle, filled with amber liquid, a small corn cob for a cork. His very tanned, lined face, dark brown eyes with crow's feet etched with grime, a face lean from years of hard physical labor and endless training. His nose scarred at its bridge and beneath that sheath of scar a slightly-flat bend to the left. He possessed one of those unusual smiles that never altered his speculative gaze, his dark brown eyes signaling an ever-present and potent lethality.

"Lidia tells me you like honey in your coffee. I'm the delivery man."

It is *Frenchy. Pascal Archambeaux. Legionnaire.*

When Daniel reached the veranda, Frenchy stood and opened his arms. They embraced. All the pent-up despair of the last month began to leak with the shocking reappearance after 10 years of one of the most capable, confident soldiers he'd ever known. At 35, he hadn't changed much, his complexion slightly more weathered, his expression just as enigmatic. Daniel couldn't find words, and his eyes blurred. He pursed his lips but too late to dam the taste of salty tears.

"Your friend Prado told me you needed help. Sit with me."

Daniel took a paper napkin and wiped his eyes. He tried to speak but words wouldn't come. Just breathing was a challenge. He'd been so stalwart and persistent during the past month of searching for answers and trying to rescue the people who meant most to him, but now he was close to emotional collapse. The prerogative had to come from Frenchy.

"After Lebanon," he said in a slight French accent, earnest, confident yet relaxed, "I became an independent contractor. More recently…. Look, I'm not telling you something you don't already know. Since Cuba, Guatemala and the Dominican Republic, the CIA has stockpiled revealed operatives in Mexico City working out of the U.S. Embassy, safeguarding the hemisphere. Mexico City is a labyrinth of espionage, with spies angling for advantage: ours, the Soviet KGB, Cuba and Mexico. The president prefers meeting with the station chief rather than the U.S. ambassador, and Prado's an important cog in the operation. A political and security attache. He wanted me in Guerrero, making friends." *Code for the key to counter-insurgency 'sleeper': Make friends and those friends will help you gather intelligence. Pretty much how I used Inez to help me get stories. But our relationships differed in a significant way. Inez and I were lovers.*

"There's going to be a war here soon. The Mexican army is planning to move into the mountains again to take out Blanco, the most dangerous *guerrilla* commander in the country. I'm going to help you find your wife and kid, and while we're at it, we're also going to pinpoint Blanco's stronghold, map it out. But first things first. What kind of shape are you in? I hear you're not doing too well, and this mission is going to be a challenge. 'Mountains high, valleys deep,'" he sang in a wobbly falsetto. "You get to experience the passion proclaimed in your pop music," he said, grinning, his smile a crease of mirth while maintaining a steady, somewhat unsettling gaze, two aspects of his countenance perpetually out of sync. "Maybe one day they'll write a ballad about you."

Elvira came out from the kitchen and spoke to Frenchy. He got up and motioned for Daniel to follow him to the family table inside, out of view. Lidia trailed behind with the coffee and set it next to a bucket of ice containing a large bottle of *mescal*, a small plate of limes, a tiny saucer of salt and tall, thick translucent shot glasses with blue trim around the top. Frenchy filled one and set it in front of Daniel.

"On my count, ready...drink!"

Daniel laughed at the military cadence, at least a choking version of a laugh as if he'd forgotten how. He picked up the glass, sipped twice, threw the rest back. Frenchy re-filled Daniel's glass and went back to his coffee. Daniel threw that back, too.

"Shape?" Daniel said, mocking the concept. "I smoke an occasional cigarette, drink moderately. I've always liked *mota*. Tranquilizers for headaches, lots of coffee. Except for some occasional, friendly workouts at this gym in Tacubaya near Condesa...across from the *mercado*."

"La Lupita?"

"Yes. Except for those, I haven't really exercised for years. Too damned busy in the U.S. being airlifted from crisis to crisis, working 20-hour days. Then Mexico. The work has been unrelenting. Got a bum knee...my back.... Brain says 'do,' body says 'screw you.'"

"I know all about it. I've read your dossier."

Daniel looked over the brim of the shot glass before throwing back a third time, deliberating whether or not to be surprised.

"Santé!" Frenchy proclaimed, and he made a fist of calloused knuckles, thumb up. Meaning it's reunion time, drink up, tomorrow's another day, and everything is going to get better. "I'm going to put petrol in your tank, *mon frer.* You got it in you, we just have to bring it back to life!"

Berto pulled the negatives out of the final wash and hung them in the hotel bathroom while contemplating the guy riding toward Daniel and Daniel's shocked reaction. While peering through his loupe and studying the man's features, he remembered a photo of this guy taken at the end of the mission in Lebanon, the rescue of a reluctant hostage. The man still looked like the same Legionnaire scout he was years ago. Wiry, muscular, cagey, exuberant, ready to go to work. Which is good for Daniel, because he's gonna need all the help he can get.

Berto followed the bus to Acapulco, then followed the second one. He stayed far enough behind and parked the van on the road while Daniel got off, broke up the cardboard box and trudged to the beach. Once Berto discovered where Daniel was staying, he circled back to the van, drove back to Acapulco and checked into the El Faro Hotel where the cliff divers go off every afternoon. Despite the prime location, a room was cheap, and he could use the salt water pool belonging to the upscale hotel next door. Then he went back the next day with Marisol, a really hot Mexican chick he met in the hotel bar. They dressed like tourists in beach garb, hanging far enough back with his bag and towels, the bag containing a new, almost silent range-finder Leica — quieter than his old SLR Nikon viewfinder with a mirror that flapped up and down when he pressed the shutter, the camera that got confiscated back in Mexico City. He also had a compatible 400 mm telephoto lens. Marisol was a good sport. She did what he told her and got good pics.

Berto knew there was a helluva story about how Prado arranged this connection and arranged for Frenchy to be positioned here looking like some kind of local character. Not Mexican obviously, but a local character who could circulate. But whatever the particulars, right now he was just going to watch and make sure he didn't get left behind. *I'm the goat-fucker, El Cabrón, the Least-Valued but Top-Secret Spy.* That meant packing his necessities and going back up the beach in the morning. He asked the El Faro manager where he could leave his van, told him he was going on a fishing trip, maybe for a couple weeks. The manager said it'd be better if he parked at his cousin's auto repair shop three blocks away. It had a nice shaded spot in the back. Leave the key with him. Twenty pesos a day. Perfect.

He fired up a pipeful of *mota* and shaved a small slice from the ping pong ball-sized stash of crystal meth he kept in the small fridge in his room, then went down to the bar at 6 p.m. Empty. *Everyone's outside waiting for another interminable sunset. A constant unfolding and dispersing of intensely memorable moments, kaleidoscopic turnings of light above the sea, clouds banking.... The clouds a mute chorus of prophets who gather without being beckoned, who spread the width of their gowns as they slow-walk across the horizon. Whoa, whoa, whoa you goat-fucker!*

Daniel had told him about how the Hopi saw clouds as souls of the dead and how he saw his dead uncle and merged with his soul. Berto wasn't fond of religious interpretations. Insufferable. *When I get high like tonight, I might see things, but I know it's just the drugs. Makes life much more interesting.*

"Bartender. A Corona and a shot of *reposado, por favor.*"

"Can I have the same, *mi amigo*?"

Marisol wore a patterned silk fabric tied around the bottom half of her bikini. Tanned, her hair was now an untamed mane draping over her shoulders to the middle of her back. She kissed him on the cheek as she sat on the high-backed bar stool and scooted closer. Her perfume was dizzying. *Fun companion is one thing, but I desperately want to fuck her. Marisol, man; just talking to her is spiritually libidinous. I hope her blush contaminates her lower extremities. A hint of the garden of heaven.*

"I hear you're going on a fishing trip," she said, eyes gleaming with hope.

"Yes. I leave early in the morning. But first I'm moving, taking a taxi to the sunset beach, to a little guest house. I'm going out with a local fisherman."

"We need to talk, *mi amigo.*"

Frenchy nudged Daniel's shoulder. "D, You ready to evacuate the area?"

Daniel groaned and pulled himself to a sitting position at the edge of his cot. "What time is it?"

"0400. Are you in any condition to ride a horse?"

"How far?"

"Just a few kilometers."

"Why can't we wait until sun-up?"

"Might be too late by then, D. The moon has set; it's very dark. Nobody will see us leave so nobody will follow."

Against a backdrop of waves breaking on shore, the monotony of it, Daniel felt the pull of the mission and the dread it inspired, a foreboding that left him sick to his stomach. He had to force himself from the cot rather than sink back into the illusory comfort of lethargy, a self-defeating condition that still pulled hard on him but which he'd long ago learned to at least contain. He confessed to Frenchy the dread he felt.

"I'm afraid that when we get up there, when we find Yvonne and Sonia, she won't even agree to leave."

Frenchy gave him a look close to pity. "Then get her to change her mind, D, and do it quickly."

Lidia waited at the back entrance of *Casa Elvira*, holding the reins of two of Frenchy's little sorrels. Daniel and Frenchy swung up onto their saddles. She pushed Daniel's seabag over the pommel and waved goodbye.

They rode out of the alley, leading a string of the third sorrel and the mule, and then turned east up a dusty road of a now-defunct coconut plantation which would soon be bulldozed to make way for a tourist resort. The perfumed scent of tropical sea air gave way to the dank smell of jungle and swampy bog, chattering insects, the swoop of an occasional bat and crowing cocks. The road, barely visible under the thin crescent of a new moon, twisted and turned until they came up onto a rise. Below, a few dim shore lights outlined the surface of a lagoon with a 20-kilometer shoreline that Frenchy had told him about. It was spring-fed, but also had an opening to the sea. To the right of the lagoon was a cluster of buildings which sat in total darkness, except for the orange glow of a single kerosene lantern attached to the gate of a corral. They dismounted, removed saddles and bridles, and led the horses and mule to stalls. It was still two hours before sunrise.

Frenchy escorted him to a *jacal* that contained a cot covered by draped mosquito netting, fleetingly reminding Daniel of a *sukkah*.

"There is time for a short sleep, D. When you wake up, *empieza un día nuevo.*"

The taxi dropped Berto and Marisol by the sandy path that led to *Casa Elvira*. By the time they arrived at the beach, the sun had risen over the tops of towering palms, and the sea was sparkling and gay with the promise of a new beginning. Dew painted the few tufts of sea grass. But when they arrived at the veranda, it was empty. No tables were set for breakfast.

"I know this family," Marisol said.

"How...?"

"Never mind. Leave the bags and wait for me. I'll see if we can get a cup of coffee and something to eat."

Marisol tried the front door, then knocked. A tall dark man with a broad nose and thick lips and a thatch of white hair wearing faded work trousers and a sleeveless t-shirt opened the door. He was impressively muscled for an older man. His smile disappeared when he spotted Berto taking a seat at one of the tables, then he let her in. Berto decided he just had to wait this out.

"Don Julio." She gave him a hug and kiss. "Is the kitchen open? Do you not have guests?"

"We served the fishermen earlier," Don Julio said. "We do not have guests now, but Elvira will make breakfast for you. She decided to take a little nap. I'll wake her. Is it…just the two of you?"

"Yes. But please let me wake her. I need to talk to her before…."

He pointed to a room with a curtained doorway. *"Adelante, mi nieta."*

Marisol parted the curtain and walked into her grandmother's bedroom. She touched, then caressed Elvira's shoulder, reluctantly waking her from a sound sleep.

"Mmmmm. Who is it?" Elvira asked, eyes open but straining to make out the figure sitting next to her bed.

"It's Marisol, *abuela*," she said, turning on a table lamp.

It took a few minutes of whispered conversation to establish the situation.

"Good," Marisol said. "Frenchy needed to move Daniel from here as quickly as possible. The Judicial Police believe he's somewhere on the beach. I'm not certain if they know why he's here, but it's fairly obvious that he seems determined to go up into the mountains and find his wife and daughter. They know I followed him, although they warned me not to. I've been staying at the El Faro. The man's partner followed him here, too. He's out front, determined to find Daniel. That's why I broke my cover. Can you give us breakfast and one room?"

"Breakfast? Of course. But why only one room, my dear?"

"I have to go back to Acapulco. Someone from Mexico City will show up soon. I have to be there to say that I searched all the hotels and guest houses here, but that I never found him."

"What if they come here looking, and they find his partner?"

"That's the point. We have to make sure they don't."

The whinnying of horses woke Daniel. He slipped into his old Everlast shorts, dug into his flip-flops and opened the door of his *jacal*. Frenchy and an older woman were carrying buckets into the horse stable. A boy struggling with a bale of hay spread it in a corner of the corral where mules grouped in the shade of flowering jacaranda trees.

Daniel relieved himself in a privvy attached to his *jacal* then found a well where he doused himself with a bucket of water, then a second one. He put on a t-shirt and Frenchy waved for him to come over. The woman joined them, wiping her hands with a rag.

"*Dan-yel*, I would like you to meet Graciela, the owner of this little rancho, *Laguna del Ejido*."

They shook hands. Daniel guessed mid-40s, but she was still beautiful, like women he'd known on the rez. Smooth, unblemished skin, long black hair tied into a single braid streaked coppery by the sun, firm strong limbs. Thin, satin lips. Gleaming white teeth. Bright eyes framed by just a few grin lines. Only her fingers, calloused and misshaped, told of many years of manual labor.

"Did you sleep well, *señor*? Are you hungry?"

Frenchy laughed. "No breakfast yet, Graciela. But please bring us some herb tea, a big pot."

Frenchy led the way to a table and chairs set under a *palapa* shelter.

"Tea?" Daniel asked. "I don't mean to be rude, *mon amí*, but I'm dying for some coffee."

Frenchy gazed fondly across the table, reached across and patted Daniel's shoulder. "You're going to have some of Graciela's *té de bruja*, witch's tea. It's going to provide you with the immense energy that will take you through the first workout. Then lunch and, if you insist, some very good coffee. In the afternoon, we discuss a plan. Then dinner. At night, we go for a swim."

When Graciela joined them with the pot of tea and filled two large cups, he explained the setup.

"This is her place. Her husband was murdered two years ago. He was the leader of the communal farmers who worked that coconut plantation we passed last night. They were supposed to be the rural beneficiaries of the original revolution. Encouraged and trained by Blanco, they refused payment from the government which planned to appropriate their property for development. It was a big deal. He led hundreds of armed farmers into Acapulco to meet with the governor who'd agreed to a final, more generous offer. But the governor was afraid to leave the airport. Instead, the State Police showed up, and there was a gunfight. Twenty-three were murdered, including Graciela's husband.

"I approached Graciela as a volunteer. I call myself a Jehovah's Witness preacher, which isn't exactly true. But it's easier for people in authority to grasp. I'm really a member of a break-away group — Free Bible Students — who've discarded most JW beliefs. Instead, we rely on the Bible, the Old and New Testament, as God's inspired word, the only authoritative and infallible rule of faith and conduct for humanity. We believe that God, in time, will restore perfect harmony to all creation, and our mission is to save others. The spiritual kingdom of grace exists now, and it's our obligation to renew the earth into the paradise conditions that existed in the Garden of Eden. Christ will return to power and glory. His earthly reign of 1,000 years will be a universal kingdom in which all principalities, powers and enemies are overcome.

"I offered to help run the place, and together we made a plan. I go up into the mountains where I've made friends and converts of marginalized *campesinos* who've fled their properties confiscated by violent *marijuanos* or just to get away from violence. There's an incredible amount of feuding, banditry and murder going on up there. Even little kids carry guns. I return here with bottles of honey which I sell door-to-door. And in turn, I bring them store-bought goods they've requested and medicines they need. I've got quite a little network going."

"Just honey for that exchange? Sounds like a bad deal for you," Daniel said, raising an eyebrow.

"OK, I also bring back some *mota* which my friends grow, a special kind which I've taught them to cultivate. *Sinsemilla*, without seeds. I sell that to the hippie tourists who rent my horses with fine leather saddles. For guided rides on the beach."

"And the police don't give you any crap?"

"Ha! They're smart, D. Look at me: I'm a religious fanatic who's embraced a life of service and poverty. There's no money to be made from me. They go after some of the hippies, the ones who don't exercise caution."

"So, what's the connection with *Casa Elvira*?"

"Graciela is Elvira's daughter, her only child. And Elvira's husband is the founding leader of the coconut commune and a member of the town council. Nobody wanted to sell their livelihood, but they had no choice; they also had to survive. But they want justice, too. They know your story, your legend and your struggle. They'll do anything to help."

"But I have to keep a very low profile."

"But of course!" he intoned, imitating the voice of the French actor, Maurice Chevalier.

The tea didn't provide the wallop of a pot of fresh coffee; it's effects would only be felt as he worked out, Frenchy explained, sipping from a liter bottle of water. When Daniel finished the pot of tea, Frenchy stood up from the table, laughing, noting Daniel's apprehension.

"I was just teasing you, D. The tea is pure ginseng. A Jehovah's Witness friend from West Virginia sends it."

He pointed. "You see that large building? Meet me there in 10 minutes."

Outside the building, a chalk slate announced *Sala Frenchy*, with posted hours for training. Inside the building with its eerie light leaking in from breaks in the warped wood plank walls was a gym with a sand floor. Thin, canvas mats tied end to end lay in one corner. There was even a ring of sorts, with sagging ropes hanging from metal stanchions that could've used a strong application of naval jelly to clean them up. Frenchy came up behind him. Barefoot, wearing baggy shorts with garish Thai designs and lettering, looking lean, fit and deadly.

"Before he became a coconut farmer, Graciela's husband was a boxer. Evenings, he trained local kids. I've taken that over. Tell me, when you trained at La Lupita, what did you do?"

"I went four rounds on the heavy bag...."

Frenchy gestured toward a heavy bag hanging from four by four timbers. "Check."

"Then two rounds on a floor-to-ceiling bag...."

"We don't have one of those."

"Shadow boxing...."

"Which you can do in a jail cell."

"General conditioning...."

"I have a plan for you."

"And sparring...."

"Check," Frenchy said, grinning, revealing a dark empty space where he'd removed a bridge.

"D, don't you think it's ironic? In Lebanon, back in '58, we started from a beach like *Pie de la Cuesta*, rode our way on horseback into the mountain stronghold of Sheik Ahmed Arsalan with his goofball kid."

Until now, Daniel hadn't even considered it. And look how that mission turned out.

July 15, 1958
Damour, a Christian coastal town, 10 minutes south
of Beirut

CHAPTER 5

Daniel didn't witness the amphibious landing on the beach at Beirut by 1st Battalion, Eighth Marines, but he later learned it was as surreal as what Berto said he experienced when he came ashore at Da Nang in March 1965. Not only was there no resistance by, in this case Lebanese rebels, but the Marines were joyously welcomed by bikini-clad sunbathers and scores of beach workmen who dropped their tools and ran to the shore, and by villagers who'd galloped on horseback, waving and cheering.

Instead, he'd been put ashore the previous day an hour before sunrise by an Underwater Demolition Team in a small pontoon craft at the Christian coastal town of Damour, just south of the main landing near the international airport. It wasn't exactly smooth. Instead of walking ashore with Ismail, the sheik's only son, Daniel had to carry him cuffed, kicking and biting, until one of the UDTs broke open an ampule of morphine and jabbed him. No one expected the guy would resist repatriation.

Two and a half years after getting Uncle Jesse — his legal guardian — to sign a document allowing the Marines to enlist him, Daniel was a 19-year-old corporal with three months' recon training under his webbed belt. The original plan had been that Daniel would leave Brant, take his boot camp training at Parris Island and Advanced Infantry training at Camp Le Jeune, be stationed with a special services training battalion while he played football and boxed. Everything went according to plan, exactly, and for two years he reveled in all of his tasks. Then came that fateful day when he was abruptly transferred to the 3rd Recon Battalion. It began when five guys thought this late-comer should experience a hazing by tossing a blanket over his head and beating the crap out of him. Only it didn't turn out that way. Two of the unfortunates were hospitalized with serious enough injuries that they had to be transferred to less-strenuous duty, never to return. The other three, after washing off their bloodied faces, were ordered by the platoon sergeant to unpack and stow Daniel's gear. He was impressed with Daniel's outstanding desire to finish. The Marine known as "Nails" proved his mettle as soon as he walked into the squad bay.

Reason for the transfer? The planned invasion of Lebanon, and the repatriation of a sheik's son, a young, impetuous man who several years ago followed his American Jewish girlfriend who he'd met while vacationing in Israel back to Brant, a girlfriend who attended the same high school as Daniel. When Ismail found out about the repatriation, part of a *quid pro quo* deal with the sheik, chief of a Druze rebel clan, in exchange for intelligence regarding disparate rebel locations and weapons caches, he demanded that her friend Daniel —who'd always treated Ismail with respect — be the one to escort him home. Or he wouldn't go. And if he wouldn't go, no deal.

During intel briefings, Daniel had reminded the 1/8 op officer about Ismail's instability stemming from guilt over his relationship, his father's adamant opposition, Ismail's breakdown after the girlfriend's family demanded she break up with him, his subsequent flunking out of the university.

"He has no options left in Brant, which may be a motivating factor. But what if he changes his mind? He was crazy about that girl. How am I going to escort an unwilling party to a place where he doesn't want to go?"

The officer's response: "The guy admires you, trusts you. As a Druze warlord's son, his life is in jeopardy as soon as he reaches shore. He wants our protection, and he has a lot of confidence in you. In addition to the pull of filial piety, a factor leading to his breakdown, you're his link to his best past memories. He just needs a push. Convince him that he's doing the right thing, and that he has a bright future in his own country."

The Marines had been sent in — by invitation of the Lebanese president — to prevent a civil war breaking out between Christian and Moslem factions and to support the sitting president or, if that failed, to set up a new election. Conditions became critical when intelligence pointed to arms being supplied to the Moslem rebels by Syria and Nasser's Egypt and the toppling of a pro-Western government in Iraq's 14 July Revolution. Sheik Arsalan was a Druze rebel chieftain allied with the Moslems, one of six founders of the Progressive Socialist Party, headquartered in the Druze town of Baakline in the Chouf district, the southern part of Mt. Lebanon, about 3,500 meters in altitude.

The plan was to meet a French-speaking operative familiar with the region, ride horseback southeast along lightly-traveled paths — avoiding PSP checkpoints — to a small town, Mechret, then proceed to Baakline, one of many disparate Druze rebel strongholds. The operative would wait outside the town until the exchange of the sheik's son for promised intelligence, detailed maps of all the rebel strongholds, then accompany Daniel back to Damour where he'd be picked up by a UDT crew and delivered back to the USS Taconic, the command ship.

The French-speaking operative was Pascal Archambeaux, aka Frenchy, a former legionnaire sergeant who, at 21, had served in Vietnam until the fall of Dien Bien Phu in 1954 and later in Algiers and Lebanon. From a line of trees behind the beach, he signaled with a flashlight, then walked down to the shore, leading three horses. Like Daniel, he was dressed in mufti, including a *keffieh* worn like kerchiefs around their necks. They both sported short scruffy dark beards and long hair.

Each knew the other through briefings, including photos for ID purposes.

"*Bonsoir*, Devil Dog," Frenchy said.

Daniel sized him up. A tall middleweight with long arms, big wrists, hard-knuckled hands, the breadth of chest. He extended his right hand to Daniel, offering a slack grip, more like touching his palm. It was a classic fighter's handshake. He could almost be Daniel's twin with his dark lean frame, his wide empathic smile. Except his gaze seemed frozen into a disarming, ironic stoicism suffused with a kind of knowing superiority. The disconnect between his gaze and his smile could be disconcerting to a stranger.

Frenchy gestured at Ismail. Slender, pale, reluctant. "He looks seasick. Is he able to ride?"

"Homesick, or should I say USA sick. Misses his girlfriend, afraid he'll never see her again. He decided at the last minute he didn't want to come back. Doesn't want to face his father. Had to sedate him with a shot of morphine."

"Well, let's get him up on Trigger, loop the cuffs around the saddle horn. The trail is wide enough for you to ride beside him and prop him up. I'll lead. OK?"

"Will do."

"Good luck, Corporal," the UDT leader said, patting Daniel on the back. "Anything goes wrong, you have these hand-held radio transceivers. One for Frenchy, one for you."

Daniel nodded, already feeling snake-bit.

It was an easy, steady climb up the mountain path, through occasional canyons and past waterfalls and onto heavily-wooded plateaus, the famous cedar trees of Mt. Lebanon that provided ample cover. They skirted the town of Mechret. But on the outskirts of Baakline, a small PSP blocking party couldn't be avoided.

"No problem," said Frenchy. "They don't see us. You take him in. I'll remain here. Shouldn't be more than a couple hours to do the transfer. You'll call me when it's over."

Daniel rode directly up to the roadblock, one hand holding the reins of his horse, the other hand holding Ismail erect in his saddle. Suspicious looks as he pulled up.

One of the men squinted at Daniel. "What's wrong with Ismail? Is he sick?"

"Yes. He got seasick the other day, and the dramamine we gave him…. The sea voyage and the medicine had a terrible effect on him."

Another man spoke into his hand-held radio. After a brief conversation, he told Daniel to continue up the path into Baakline where they would be met by Ismail's father and his bodyguards. Daniel dug his heels into the flanks of his horse and, after several bends in the path, came upon a large cistern. Wearing a red and white *keffieh* fastened by a silver headband and looking stern rather than happy on this joyous occasion, Sheik Absalan waved to Daniel. "Bring him over here."

As Daniel approached, four of the sheik's men lunged forward and pulled Ismail none-too-gently off his mount and dragged him into a courtyard that contained several buildings including a small village mosque with white-washed walls and a round, tiled roof painted blue. When Daniel dismounted, he was grabbed and held, arms behind his back, by more of the sheik's men. The sheik was tall, with dark piercing eyes and a long scraggly beard. He walked over and swung a whip handle to the side of Daniel's head. When Daniel came to, he was dangling in the cistern, water up to his neck, his legs and arms entwined by heavy rope. What followed was a series of prolonged dunkings. Pull up, drop down. Leave him under water for a time, pull up, and on and on until Daniel was done coughing and sputtering and heaving. Half-drowned. Another blow to the head put him out.

When he came to, he sat chained to a stone wall in a cell, head pulsing with pain, ears ringing and lights exploding like fireworks disrupting his vision and with no sense of how long he'd been detained. He leaned over and vomited what little there was to bring up then segued into dry heaves. Rattled and disoriented, it took a while until he could breathe with a modicum of regularity. His eyes finally focused on Ismail sitting across from him, also chained, his shirt ripped open to reveal beneath sweat-matted hair what looked like tribal scarring. Except it was too fresh, too raw.

Ismail looked petrified. Daniel tried to question him, but couldn't form the words. The sheik pushed open the unlocked cell door. One man set a wood stool onto the stone-tiled floor, another brought a black pillow decorated with gold thread. The sheik took a seat, slamming the whip handle into the open palm of his free hand. His intent was so obvious, so earnest. Daniel flinched, anticipating another beating.

Instead, the sheik lashed out at his son, cracking him across the jaw. The two men assisting the sheik hauled Ismail to his feet, pushed him face-first against a wall and fastened his handcuffs to iron rings that were set apart just for this type of occasion. Ismail whined and howled and began jabbering in Arabic. The two assistants ripped off his shirt. The sheik handed the whip to one of them, and he began lashing Ismail until a dozen red welts began to leak blood. Then the sheik held up his hand for the man to stop, unfastened the cuffs from the wall rings. Ismail fell to the floor, weeping, ashamed, disconsolate. Then the sheik turned to Daniel, standing inches away. A disarming calm seemed to settle the sheik. But the calm was short-lived.

"A Jewess!" he exclaimed, spittle flecking his lips. "My only son, my heir, chased a Jewess halfway across the world! Why? Because the honey between her legs was sweeter than what was available to him here? And he could have anyone, the sweetest virgin in all of the Chouf. Thank Allah he didn't get that bitch pregnant...

"And now you, Mendoza, a Jew whose blood is contaminated, whose ancestor escaped the Inquisition, who persisted in remaining a blasphemer. But I've got you now, and I will see to it you will be the last of your line.

"But before I take away your manhood, Mendoza, I want you to tell me what you know about my son's ridiculous odyssey. I don't trust him to tell me the truth. The only thing I believe is that your people betrayed him. They welcomed him into their home and their school, only to abandon him and leave him penniless because he refused to convert, refused to denounce Allah. And now you're using him to get me to reveal secrets that will help your crusader armies to divide and conquer our country?"

He reached into his jacket and pulled out a packet of maps. With disdain, he threw them on the floor.

Ismail told him that?

Daniel shook his head, another plan gone bad, just like he learned in Marine Corps classrooms for two years. When it goes very wrong, it will bite you in the ass. Really hard. But he never expected this. This mission seemed so cut and dried. Now the only thing cut and dried would be him. *Take away my manhood? What does that mean? How?* The throbbing pain in his head intensified. He could speak, but only in a soft, choking voice, and only if he concentrated on every word.

"OK, but first, how long have I been here?"

"You arrived 36 hours ago. Answer my question."

"It's dark. Is it just me, or is it night?"

The sheik burst out laughing. "It's night, your last one as a potential daddy."

Daniel calculated. Frenchy said this operation would last just a few hours. A spark of hope remained. Just like in the song that now haunted him as he couldn't remember any part of it except for the refrain. His awareness was too impaired to make up a story, so he just told the truth. *What difference would it make?*

"From what Ninette told me three years ago, she and your son met on the beach in Tel Aviv. She was taken with him, and he was really smitten. He vowed he would follow her home and applied for admission to Brant University. He was accepted, obtained the necessary student visa. But when he arrived, he was broke, so she put him to work in her father's business."

The sheik scowled. *The Jewess.* "What kind of business?"

"Something that would let him take classes during the day and pay for his share of their apartment near campus. A night job."

The sheik slammed the whip handle across the back of Daniel's head, taking care not to lacerate his face. "She was still a high school student! How could her parents let her live with…this pig? What kind of night job?"

Daniel inhaled deeply and sighed, wondering to himself again about the sheik's imminent threat to his manhood. Mr. Sheik wasn't going to take to this sordid tale.

"Ninette's father owned a famous burlesque theater, downtown Brant. Ninette worked in the ticket office. Ismail tended bar…." Crack. Another blow to the back of his head. He nearly blacked out. Water was thrown in his face. Several buckets, one after another.

"What kind of 'burlesque'?"

Daniel couldn't shake the water out of his eyes. Any movement brought blinding pain. He hung his head and whispered. "It's a stage show where women take off their clothes, slowly, beginning usually with long-sleeve gloves, then a gown, then, undergarments. Seductive dancing done to music. Until there's nothing left to take off. Takes about 15 minutes. The women are called strippers."

The sheik's head dropped, too. He shook it slowly, side-to-side.

"Whiskey, strippers, fornication with a Jewess. He's ruined."

One of the sheik's men pushed open the door. "Pardon me, but there's a man outside requesting to speak with you."

The sheik grimaced. "Well, who is he?"

A shrug of shoulders, a look of chagrin registered on the man's face. "We don't know. He speaks fluent Arabic. His face is hard to read, like maybe there's some kind of partial paralysis. But he's very poised, confident. Claims he has important news about the invasion. He said something's gone terribly wrong."

The sheik stood. He ordered the two assistants to stand Daniel spread-eagled against the wall. Then he kicked Daniel, the toe of his boot aimed directly between Daniel's legs. Vaguely reactive, Daniel was still able to turn his torso just enough so that the kick landed on his inner thigh. But enough of the sheik's kick got through, and the impact felt crippling.

"Drop him."

Extreme pain followed by nausea and vomiting. He retained only a fraction of consciousness, couldn't move and desperately wanted to breathe. The room was spinning, and the voices were barely distinct. He felt as if his luck was running out, and there was nothing he could do about it.

"Bring this man to me," the sheik demanded. "We'll finish with this infidel next."

Right after the emissary left, Ismail sprang to his feet.

The suddenness of movement shocked Daniel into a greater percentage of awareness. *Ismail must've been playing possum.* Daniel was amazed at what he was seeing. Ismail quickly wrapped his cuffs around his father's neck. Bellowing with rage, he pulled the cuffs as tight as he could, making a garrote. As the two assistants tried to intervene, the sheik's man came flying back into the room, head-first against the stone wall, collapsing unconscious, followed by a sprinting Frenchy who grabbed the man's head with two hands — right hand under the jaw, left hand at the back of the man's skull — and twisted violently, snapping his neck.

Daniel had never seen a savate fighter in action. In Daniel's confused state, it looked like some kind of lethal can-can. A little hop and Frenchy throwing a high kick against one of the assistant's head. Another little hop and Frenchy kicking the inside of the other's knee, a grotesque crack, dropping him. Then a head kick for each downed man, the steel toe of his combat boot smashing in the sides of their faces. Gurgling sounds came from the sheik. Ismail sat astride his father, choking the life out of him. Frenchy let him finish, then went through the sheik's pockets. Finding a ring of keys, he unlocked the iron cuffs restraining Daniel. Spying the sheik's maps on the floor, he picked them up, looked them over, smiled.

"Can you ride?" he said to Daniel.

Grimacing in pain, Daniel seemed barely able to comprehend.

"Ismail betrayed me."

"I already came to that conclusion. Can you hear me, corporal?"

Daniel squinted, looked around: the sheik dead, cuffs still wrapped tightly around his neck, three of the sheik's men dead or unconscious. Frenchy took the key from Daniel's pocket and unlocked Ismail's cuffs, leaving him on his knees, obsessively running his hands through his hair, staring at his father's corpse. Daniel nodded assent, but Frenchy wasn't convinced.

"Can you stand?"

Daniel reached tentatively toward Frenchy who tugged him to his feet and held him erect until Daniel seemed able to bear his own weight.

"Can you walk?"

Daniel took a step, stumbled. Frenchy caught him.

"There's only the one horse I came in on. I'll put you in the saddle and sit behind. But we won't go back to the rendezvous point. I called a Marine motorized patrol near here. Told them about a possible FUBAR situation. They'll set up a blocking movement along our original exfiltration route. Instead, we'll head southwest to a place I know, Wadi Bnahle, about 3.5 kilometers as the crow flies. A Marine chopper flying reconnaissance will pick you up."

Frenchy slipped an arm around Daniel and began to help him out the door. "Did you get that?"

No response. Daniel was conscious but out of it.

Ismail limped a few steps. "Hey! What about me?"

"The deal was to bring you home. We honored our end of the bargain, the sheik didn't, and you bailed before we even got started. This mission is over."

Frenchy's assessment clearly startled Ismail, but it seemed beyond his ken, so Frenchy relented, laying Daniel carefully on the stone floor.

"Tell you what I'll do: I'll hogtie you with rope and gag you. There's only a few bodyguards left and they're all asleep 50 meters from here in the sheik's house. The rest must be out patrolling or engaging our forces. No one knows what's happened here, so when your people return you can blame it all on us and claim a hero's survival. That's the best I can do. The rest of your life is up to you."

Looking downcast, Ismail nodded and lay down on his belly. Frenchy tied him with a length of rope from his saddlebag. Gagged him with Daniel's t-shirt.

"Doesn't hurt too bad, does it?"

Ismail shook his head, a muffled reply. Frenchy stroked the back of his head as if he were petting a dog then reached in his boot and withdrew a double-edged, fixed-blade stiletto, parted the back of Ismail's lank hair and thrust the 7.25-inch blade into his medulla, then pushed Ismail's hair back into place, cleaned off his knife and inserted it back into the sheath hidden in his boot. He untied Ismail and removed the t-shirt gag, stretched him out next to the sheik, positioned his hands to grasp the sheik's neck. He looked once more around the mosque's dungeon and thought to himself: *Vous avez perdue*. Meaning you lost; you and your father's perfidy didn't work. Then he picked up Daniel and carried him outside and lifted him onto the saddle.

From behind, Frenchy held him in the saddle all the way to Wadi Bnahle, thinking it was better Daniel was out so he didn't have to endure the steady jostling and pain of the trek down the narrow mountain path with all its twists and turns. As they rounded the final bend and entered the courtyard of a Christian monastery, monks, children and old men ran out to greet him like a long-lost relative, which he almost was, having preached there many times during a Jehovah's Witness mission. Some brought gifts of fruit, cold drinks and wine.

Within an hour, the chopper arrived and, after a short flight, Frenchy helped Daniel walk along the white sand beach at Damour to the UDT pickup, the sheik's maps and a bottle of wine tucked in his knapsack.

November 5
Laguna del Ejido

CHAPTER 6

A white quarter moon, seven days old, lay on the horizon, bright enough to light a path across the lagoon. Handing Daniel snorkeling gear, Frenchy led the way into the water.

"This will be a relaxed-pace training swim, about 1500 meters through the lagoon to the sea, then another 500 meters, then south a bit, then back towards shore, body surf in. Lidia will meet us. We'll ride back to Graciela's. Call it a night."

"Why can't we just get rooms and spend the night at Elvira's?"

Frenchy adjusted his goggles. "Not safe."

It'd been a long day, and Daniel was already exhausted. At least the water was refreshing and being buoyant and able to breathe easily was a huge relief from having to bear his own weight. It didn't take long to find a rhythm.

The morning workout had begun with a lot of stretching, including stretch kicks. Then low horse-riding stance and a series of hand strikes, deep knee-bends, followed by push-ups and dips between two chairs, situps, leg raises. Then all of the kicks: front, side, roundhouse, hook, spin. Then all the jump versions of those kicks. Then bag work. Then more pushups — fingertips only — and situps and leg raises…again.

The sparring was done at half-speed with 12-ounce gloves, involving kick and punch combinations, elbows, knee-lifts, grabbing and tripping, finishing. Daniel's training with black-belt Korean Marines during recon, especially his work with the top-ranked KM fighter, The Cobra, who personally selected Daniel for one-on-one instruction, mirrored Frenchy's savate and muy thai and it amplified Daniel's combat-fighting repertoire. The sparring was flirtatious, tentative and defensive, until each realized the other's abilities. And then ego was dropped, and it was just two boys trying to trick the other, finally busting out laughing, playful, until Daniel's arms felt as heavy as lead, and his legs turned to rubber, and he collapsed from exhaustion.

Frenchy was right about the ginseng tea. Daniel's stamina seemed to remain consistent throughout the two-hour session. But after it ended and, after a shower and breakfast, he fell fast asleep. When he woke up, he could hardly move, so Graciela gave him a massage, and Lidia walked on his back and shoulders. And Frenchy treated him to a series of chiropractic manipulations. And then more sleep. At day's end, a light dinner and over coffee, Frenchy briefed Daniel about practice forays into the mountains, riding mules along various paths to his nearest honey and *mota* vendors to create the illusion that he'd recruited another Jehovah's Witness to help him with his work. Then the swim without mask, fins and snorkel, which proved tricky once they reached the ocean where they had to fight the riptide until they could finally catch a wave and tumble onto the beach.

A daily pattern of training would ensue, including service-animal packing, bivouac considerations, weapons, topo map and compass review, developing a plan of action, silent killing.

"I know you packed your K-bar. You got anything else?"

Daniel showed him his Italian switchblade, purchased at the Thieves Market in Mexico City.

"Nice action. Sharp. Six-inch blade. Faux black pearl handle. It'll do, especially if you practice opening it quietly. The next few weeks you have to focus every minute of training on the mission, from wake-up to nighty-night. Time to get back that icy blood. I'll get you ready."

Berto was really disappointed when Marisol left him alone at *Casa Elvira* to go back to the hotel, saying she had to finish up some business related to resort development. *She made me feel hornier than a 10-peckered owl.* But he was shown to a room, served a wonderful breakfast, and allowed to remain on the veranda as long as he wanted, watching the waves and the parade of tourists on horseback and snack vendors. He chatted with Don Julio as the stoic, sun-tanned, white-haired old man sanded a door to be refinished, his shoulder and arm muscles rippling beneath a layer of aging, wrinkled skin.

What really got Berto's attention was a procession of women sauntering along the beach, followed by a group of boys carrying colorful baskets and blankets and umbrellas. Like something out of a Fellini movie. Especially one gorgeous woman who led the group. Black, with a delicate facial structure, carrying herself with haughty insouciance, reveling in her infamy by pulling up her skirt and squealing with delight as she splashed in the shallows. Legs strong and gleaming, narrow hips and waist but high and sculpted buttocks and remarkable breasts straining against the damp fabric of her blouse.

"Don Julio, what is *that*? And who is *she*?"

The older man chuckled. *"La parada de las zorras.* It's their day to relax and have a little fiesta on the beach. The woman in front is Ana, *La Negrita*. Very sexy, eh?"

Berto raised an eyebrow. *"Mamma mia!"*

"Yes. The Spaniards brought African slaves to Mexico in the 17th century, to Guerrero, to work the mines and coconut plantations. Her ancestors were runaways who lived in mountain communities," Don Julio said.

"There's a little *burdel* here, down the beach a few hundred meters to a dirt road and up against the hillside. It's not fancy, but they can provide what a man needs."

Berto sat up straighter in his chair without taking his eyes off the procession as it passed farther up the beach. He ran back to his room, grabbed his camera bag, towel and his straw hat, stopped by the kitchen fridge to retrieve his ping-pong ball double-wrapped in red cellophane, and jogged onto the beach.

Gracias Dios mío. Don Julio signed with relief, his arms aching from three hours of sanding, even if it was a light version. *This is a job for my handyman.*

The brothel was a shack, really, and Ana's bed a cot, which really didn't matter to Berto. He couldn't recollect when he'd met a whore so proud and beautiful. First stop was the cantina next door, a bottle of *reposado*, then quickly out the door, past a guard cradling an M-1 carbine and a .45 tucked into his waistband, his face a mask of nonchalance. In her room, already trembling with desire and the effects of a sliver off the ping-pong ball, he retrieved some rolled joints from his camera bag. Ana waved him off. "No no no, Berto! Not in here!" So he climbed out her window and stumbled a few yards away, smoked one down to a nub then buried it in the dirt.

Two hours later, sometime after midnight, Ana was glowing. "How did you do that?" she exclaimed, tying back her hair and holding it into place with a comb. "I never met a man who could last more than a few minutes. Unless he was really drunk and then one time, maybe 15 minutes. But you: up/down; up/down; up/down. Six o' clock/six thirty; six o' clock/six thirty. I could barely hold on." Cracked Berto up. She'd held on longer than most, with uncanny flexibility and determination, driven by what seemed like continuous climaxes. *She's talkin' about the source of my self-esteem! I regard myself as king of the jungle, who wants only to enhance women's spirituality world-wide.*

Ana wiped the sweat off his face and chest, then herself. Berto grinned and stared at her big breasts high on her chest, dark nipples still erect. He was spent but still revved. "Can I stay? *Un poco más?*"

Ana laughed weakly, then exclaimed in a marvelous sing-song voice, "*Dios mío!* I can't do it again! But you can stay and watch me play cards with the other girls. You're so funny. The way you speak *caló. Canicas* for genitals. *De aquellas.* The best. *Prendido.* High. *Simón.* Yes."

"Yeah. Growing up, my favorite film star was Tin-Tan."

"Tin-Tan is from Juarez, the border," she said, in the manner of a haughty lecturer, as if to prove she possessed something more than just a body built for play. "That's why he speaks *Spanglish* and wears a zoot suit. He's the crude buffoon. But Cantinflas, the Mexican people's favorite, grew up in *Tepito*, the Thieves Market in Mexico City. One of us. The penniless underdog mocking the upper class, the police and the government."

"May I take photos?"

"Sí, amigo, lo que quieras." Whatever you want. Holding out her hand for U.S. currency owed her for an evening's pleasure of her company. Plus gratuity.

With her door opened, there was still barely enough room on the floor for Ana and two other whores, so the game spilled out into the hallway. The women wore rayon robes, and the scent of sweat and cheap perfume mixed with the aroma of *Delicado* cigarette smoke. Ana's robe kept coming undone, allowing Berto an exquisite variety of poses. A game of poker ensued, accompanied by riotous laughter and joking, a tequila bottle passed around, and money won and lost. Unequal to any of his previous bordello experiences. He took photos from various angles. Her bed, the hallway, the farthest corner of her room. A bare ceiling fixture and another in the hallway and her table lamp with beaded red shade provided all the light he needed for his fastest film.

Suddenly, heavy footsteps tramped through the adjoining cantina, approaching quickly. It was the guard with the carbine and two other men, long-barreled revolvers in ancient holsters slapping against their legs. Berto gestured with the lens of his camera. *Who are they?*

"Tira," Ana announced, her face a mask of imperturbability. Police. She scraped her winnings off the floor and took a seat on her cot. The two other women sat back against a wall, legs folded demurely and robes tightened.

While the carbine guy waited in the hallway, the police entered the room and went straight for Berto, who was wearing only skivvie shorts. They snatched his camera and dumped the contents of his camera bag onto the floor. Rolls of film tumbled out along with the cellophane-wrapped meth and shiny metal cigarette case which contained six tightly-rolled joints, several boxes of matches, two packs of cigarettes, his wallet. One cop opened the cellophane, sniffed and shrugged.

"Get dressed and come with us," one cop ordered, the cop whose pistol looked so heavy and unrestrained it would fall out with any untoward movement.

"Where? Why? I paid all my fees. I've been a very well-behaved customer."

"Never mind, *drogadicto*, just get dressed and come with us."

Berto slapped his forehead. *"Por favor,"* he muttered under his breath, a mix of irony and disgust.

No cuffs at least. Berto knew enough to go along quietly. The guy with the carbine led the way, and the two with pistols followed.

They escorted him through dark back streets to a small jail with only one cell, obviously not wanting a spectacle. Inside, a slender man sat at a cluttered desk, pomaded hair combed straight back, flashing Berto a lupine grin that revealed an impressive ridge of teeth going all the way back to his molars. He introduced himself as the *jefe*, and when the camera bag was dumped in front of him, he opened Berto's cellophane-wrapped ball and the cigarette case.

"You have marijuana. We know you smoke it. And there is this other thing, which will be tested."

"So?"

"So you're going to a state prison in Acapulco. Here, we don't tolerate the use of narcotics."

"C'mon, can't we just settle this here?"

"What do you mean, 'settle'?"

"How about $200 in U.S. currency?"

"You're offering me a bribe? That charge will be added to the list."

He nodded to one of the deputies. "Cuff him now. Take him to the car along with the evidence, and make certain to go directly to the prison."

"May I at least have my camera bag, camera and film?"

"These are confiscated for further possible criminal charges. But you can have this," he said sardonically. A warm bottle of apple-flavored soda.

Outside, a pink horizon, the sun poised to rise. In the car heading south to Acapulco — a car without a barrier between driver and prisoner — Berto was still wound up and began chastising the deputy for this bogus arrest, calling him every name in the book. In English, of course.

How absurd, Berto thought. *I wasn't even searched. I still have my wallet, cash, credit card, press credential and room and van keys. That* jefe *is a real ma-roon. Must think I'm really stupid to fall for this play. Somebody set me up and wants me outta here. Lumpage. In-fucking-credible.*

At a stop sign just before entering the coast highway, Berto gulped down the rest of the soda, grabbed the neck of the bottle and swung it hard against the side of the deputy's head, knocking him unconscious. Then he leaned over the seat, retrieved the key, unlocked the cuffs and scooted out a back door. He also retrieved the so-called bag of evidence against him and took all the peso notes from the deputy's wallet. Then, sizing him up, he stripped the deputy of his hat, shirt and pants. Standing outside, he turned the steering wheel, pushed the car off the road and watched it roll down a small hill, unimpeded by a thin stand of cane-like grass which parted like a curtain and closed again. *Show over. Next show: Agent goat-fucker is back in action.*

November 6
Pie de la Cuesta

CHAPTER 7

M arisol finished her morning coffee and strolled from *Casa Elvira* to the jail. The *jefe* was waiting for her. He handed her the camera bag.

"Gracias."

"De nada. It's always a pleasure to cooperate with the Judicial Police." Thinking he was so tired staying up all night waiting to arrest that *cabrón*, but he still could get it up for this really hot woman.

"So the deputy is going to arrange a bribe, return his drugs and put him on a bus to Mexico City — tied to his seat?"

"That's the plan."

"Perfect. Let's hope he doesn't put up too much of a fuss."

The *jefe* yawned. "It's a short drive to the bus terminal. He's cuffed. Some of my friends in the Acapulco police are waiting for my deputy and Berto to arrive. What could go wrong?"

Over a leisurely pot of ginseng tea mixed with regular black tea to give Daniel the caffeine boost he'd need before beginning day 2 of training, Frenchy posed the question: "How do you know

Prado?"

Sweat trickled down thin lines from Daniel's armpits to the waist of his shorts, the first sign of anxiety that his body tended to register.

"He's the one who convinced me to come down to Mexico City. Told Yvonne and me we could live in a cottage he owned right across the street from Chapultepec Park, in the heart of Colonia Polanco. Said he'd put in a word for me with the IPS bureau chief. How much fun it'd be to live and work here. How he'd help me make contacts. How many great feature stories there were to be had. That's how he put it. His contacts matched up with my nose for news. And within four months, the Olympics."

"But before this year. I know you two have a history."

Daniel took a deep breath and sighed. "You know how lasting memories affect the way you see a person?"

"What do you mean, 'see'?" Frenchy asked, drinking from a bottle of water.

"To determine whether or not a person can be trusted."

"What particular memory can you share? I know him only as a dedicated security operative, an avowed anti-communist. And for me — his employee — a man of his word."

Daniel finished his first cup of tea and poured another, glad that the pot had begun to cool just as the sun began to penetrate through breaks in the bamboo that formed the eastern border of Graciela's property. It was going to be another scorching day.

"I met him during an important transition in my life, moving off the Iroquois reservation where I'd been harbored when my life was in danger and moving in with my father's brother who'd returned from Brooklyn after my father was murdered. When the family enterprise was finished."

"Family enterprise?"

"The family's quest to have another champion. December, 1952. My grandfather was the manager. Uncle Jack was the trainer. Another uncle — Abe — was the spiritual leader. My father, Davey Mendoza, was set to fight Joey Maxim for the light heavyweight title. Davey was probably the only contender at that time who wasn't owned by the mob. And the mob's representative, Frankie Carbo, controlled the only boxing organization, the International Boxing Commission. Which meant sanctioning matches in just about every arena in the U.S. and radio and television programming of all title fights."

"And that was the problem?"

"Big problem. One of Carbo's associates was a local guy who represented all criminal enterprise in our area, a guy by the name of Ray DiNardi, also known as 'Rotten Raymond.'"

Frenchy laughed. "A good nickname, eh? Probably appropriate."

"Entirely. He tried to take over the family enterprise, but Grandpa Jake and Davey wouldn't have it. The whole point was to make a new champion after our patriarch, the man I'm named after, boxing's first prominent Jewish boxer and 16th champion of England, 250 years ago."

Daniel's voice grew tense, and Frenchy could sense his inner turmoil.

"After a particularly nasty series of rebuffs, DiNardi tried to have one of his top fighters maim Davey during his final sparring match days before the Maxim fight. That worked to an extent, but Davey's injury wasn't going to deter him. So DiNardi decided to burn down my grandfather's store, a stupid kind of revenge. But it went further than he'd anticipated. Grandpa Jake and my mom were inside the store. They were killed."

"If he didn't mean to kill them, how were they in the store?"

Daniel wiped sweat that was beading on his brow and raised both hands to his face then pulled them away, trying to regain composure. "It was my fault. They'd locked up. But I forgot something, my collection of new *Ring* magazines. They went in after them. In a matter of seconds, there was a huge explosion. It was supposed to happen after we left."

"Mon Dieu!"

"When Uncle Jack took my father to Brooklyn and Abe put me on the Iroquois reservation to live with my mother's brother Jesse, it was to protect us. Except my father was murdered — shot to death — in a Brooklyn bar.

"I spent close to three years on that reservation, under the protection of Jesse, who is the tribe's faithkeeper. Between him and my Uncle Abe, they brought me back to life. But I believed that I deserved better. And that's when Uncle Jack returned, law degree in hand. He took me from the reservation and planted me in a new house in the suburbs."

"And that's where you met Prado?"

"Prado was my main man, a fellow-Sephardic Jew, a distant cousin actually. He stood by me and helped me track down the guy who sparred with Davey and who hurt him so badly it jeopardized the title fight. By then I was determined to discover the truth about all those deaths, and it traced back to my Uncle Jack. He sold out the family enterprise to Carbo, bypassing DiNardi, and that was really the provocation that put DiNardi over the edge."

"So, at 16, you solved the crime?"

"More or less. Even then, Prado was helping to guide me, encouraging me to discover the truth. And then there was a final showdown with DiNardi. He'd kidnapped me and Uncle Abe and we appeared doomed. But I broke loose and ran into the street. Prado knew where we were. Miraculously, he showed up with a carload of my boys, along with police, and he was right there with us, throwing *chingones*. He helped save our lives. DiNardi was arrested and convicted of multiple murders, and my Uncle Jack was disbarred. At that point, I dropped out of my junior year of high school and joined the Marine Corps."

"But you kept in touch?"

"Right. We corresponded on a regular basis. He went to college, studied criminology, graduated law school, was commissioned an Army officer and chose intelligence as his specialty. Served in Vietnam."

Frenchy nodded.

"Then he began working for the State Department. We'd also see each other occasionally when he came home for the High Holy Days. You could say he was one of my best friends."

"And he continued to help you here?"

"Yes, especially when the trouble started in Mexico City. The only thing he didn't anticipate was the final outcome: Tlatelolco. And even then, he didn't know how bad, how complete it was going to be."

"Tell me about it, D."

At our first dinner meeting in the International Press Club after student protests and the police response became so violent, he listed all the good things previously accomplished by Díaz Ordaz.

"He's done even more in the way of public works than President Lopez Mateos," Prado said. "Because Mexico is hosting the Olympic games. And to benefit working-class and lower-middle-class Mexicans, he built the Tlatelolco project, 14 apartment buildings housing 70,000 people. A city within a city with shopping centers, schools, churches, playgrounds and the Plaza of the Three Cultures."

Wearing a tan summer suit and pale blue shirt with dark blue club tie, black hair cut short to minimize a slightly-receding hairline, Prado glanced suspiciously at every person who passed our table. He unfolded his hands and braced them on his thighs.

"But the reality of Mexico is somewhat different. A year ago, our CIA's Directorate of Intelligence, restricted to intel and propaganda — not involved in secret op — warned that the country was failing in some basic ways that the political elite ignored. Of Mexico's 45 million people, 40 percent are landless peasants. Thirty-five percent live on *ejido* lands, communally-held properties established after the socialist revolution but which are inefficient at best. Hunger, malnutrition and misery are getting worse, like a rapidly-spreading malignancy, especially in the countryside. Desperation is breeding violent rebellion. Especially in Guerrero where there've been clashes between *campesinos*, their *guerrilla* enablers and security forces.

"The *PRI* wants to keep the lid on this. The army is brutally effective, but D.O.I. doesn't believe that what occurred in France, the toppling of a government, can happen here. The problem for me is that we have wildly-conflicting reports about what's really going on.

"Of the CIA's 15 different sources and observers, some believe that the student movement is led by locally-grown communists inspired by Cuba and Vietnam; others are reporting that student radicals are armed with weapons smuggled in from Eastern Europe; others are convinced that Cuban, Chinese and Soviet operatives are providing guns with serial numbers filed off. I need you to penetrate the student movement and report to me what you can learn. I trust your judgment more than anything"

A month later, at another dinner meeting, I reported my findings.

"It's just like back home, all these student groups and their conflicting ideologies: communists, Trotskyites, Maoists, moderate social democrats. Quarreling constantly. But, unlike at home, the more the government cracks down, the more rapidly the movement grows. Now they're supported by a committee of professors and brigades of people from all walks of life — workers, mothers, literary figures, artists and journalists. But weapons? I've never seen any, nor have I heard of any students possessing them."

"I can tell you one thing," Prado confided. "The government isn't going to concede anything if students won't back down. Díaz Ordaz believes that giving in to their demands will invite further ultimatums, and letting the protests continue will lead to further disruption."

"What if I can influence the National Strike Council to agree to negotiate?" I asked.

"Only if they're not too deluded," Prado said, quite rightly. "I'm afraid this impasse could result in a kind of 'final solution.'"

"I don't hold anything against Prado. I know he never had control over Díaz Ordaz and his cabinet. He was trying to convince them to negotiate a settlement with the strikers before the Olympics. His job — unlike the CIA's — was to just monitor and analyze events as they related to U.S. policies. And bottom line: He told me he couldn't affect decisions made by Yvonne, nor could he arrange to save Inez. He could only save me."

"But he did help you save Berto."

"Yes, but in a bizarre way."

"And his wife, Phaedra. I'm told she's a real piece of work."

Daniel gave him a look. Startled, yet secretive.

"OK, *mon ami*. You can tell me about that later." He drained his water bottle, grinned and pointed to the pot of tea. "Finish up. We must go to *Sala Frenchy*."

Berto hopped a bus and returned to the auto repair lot to retrieve his van.

"That didn't take long, Berto," the shop owner said. "How was the fishing?"

Berto opened the van door. "The fisherman didn't want to go out. Said the weather could be bad. Said the marine radio reported a storm stalled off the coast."

"Storm? *Amigo*, look at the blue sky. It's really hot and dry. The rainy season is over. It must be stalled way off the coast." He laughed. "Maybe there's another reason. Maybe he's a drug smuggler and something came up."

"Yeah, something must've come up, maybe something like that." Berto closed the van door, checked to see that his .22 revolver was still under his seat and cartridges in a separate box. He turned on the ignition. *I'm going back to the El Faro, get some rest, chow down. Phone Prado. Clarify the situation. Then this goat-fucker will return to the scene of the crime.*

CHAPTER 8

The white lace curtains in Prado's bedroom were stained by the last blush of sunset. Daniel woke from a deep sleep, acknowledging with a muffled moan the remarkable transformation he was witnessing. And the miracle of a dissipated headache. And something else.

"What's that noise?"

"Probably distant thunder, lightning."

"Distant thunder? Lightning? You do see that pink sky out there, right?"

Phaedra nodded. She sat in a wing chair across the room, wrapped in a long Oaxacan shawl, her long blond hair radiant with the last light of day, proud of what she'd accomplished so far but wondering what more she could do to keep him there. She'd spent the early part of the afternoon as her husband, Robbie, had ordered. Keep him occupied. Discuss the subject that is most compelling to Daniel, his quandary over Inez and Yvonne. Comfort him with potentially satisfying resolutions. Encourage him to pop a couple of tranquilizers, smoke a bit of *mota*, drink a glass of red wine. Play recordings of the most soothing classical string quartets from our collection. Top it off with Daniel's favorite recording, Miles Davis' *Kind of Blue*. Until he finally feels relieved enough to fall asleep.

I don't want to lose him if what I think is going to happen, happens, Robbie told her. What with his wife, kid and girlfriend at Tlatelolco, if the Mexicans decide to drop the hammer because... well, in less than two weeks the Olympics are scheduled to begin. Anyway, his bureau chief and Berto are on the story.

Daniel had shown up at her home at noon, anxious and exhausted, let off by Berto. He told Phaedra that Prado gave him permission to borrow his Harley for a run to the National Autonomous University, UNAM.

Berto's departure was as abrupt as his arrival, claiming he was late for a last-minute urgent photo-assignment meeting, Daniel excluded. But privately, Berto was meeting with Prado to gather intel about the next protest. He believed Prado was more CIA than political attaché and that Phaedra was his partner in crime, and Daniel — the veteran journalist — should've been more cautious about embracing them as vital sources. But Daniel's judgment was compromised, what with his marital difficulties and, especially, his taking up with Inez, and his...what...lapses in mental acuity? What was it Daniel's wise old Uncle Abe had told him? *"This is what happens when you collaborate with the Philistines...."*

It was nothing to Berto, who admired spooks, their proactive approach to fighting commies and protecting America and the free world. Prado's warning to him to show up solo at the Plaza of the Three Cultures was something he knew he shouldn't discuss with Daniel because, after all, he was Daniel's backup, feeding Prado information that Daniel might otherwise leave out. But before he drove away, Berto spoke these last words to Daniel. *"Promise to stay by the telephone."*

Prado had enlisted Phaedra to pass on false intelligence that the planned evening rally at the Plaza — just a few blocks from the presidential palace — was going to be small and insignificant, not worth covering. He wanted her to convince Daniel to take advantage of a lull in action, take a tactical break, stay away from what could even be an embarrassing confrontation between his wife and Inez. Both women intended to show up, although allied with different brigades. Yvonne with the National Union of Mexican Mothers, which had adopted her, and Inez with the nursing students' brigade from Politécnica. If something really bad were to happen, a worst-case scenario, he knew Daniel would risk his life to save them.

"Take care of him like you're trying to cure his headache," Prado told her. "But don't get too deep into his problems."

When the telephone rang and Phaedra appeared not interested in answering, even at Daniel's urging, he became suspicious. He made a move to get up. But she beat him to it.

"No, he isn't here," she said, in a voice so soft it was barely audible. "I don't know.... I'm sorry, I can't help you."

Daniel could feel his face flush. "Who is it? If it's Berto, give me the phone."

She turned and whipped the receiver behind her back.

"Phaedra, give me the phone; he knows I'm here."

"You don't have to go to this one," she protested, her blue eyes pleading.

"Give me the damn phone!"

At wit's end, she slammed the phone onto its cradle.

Daniel swung his legs off the bed, struggling to break through the fog of sedation.

"What's the point of hanging up? If it's important, he'll call back."

Sure enough, the phone rang again. She made no move to answer it, so Daniel pushed past her and picked up the receiver. "It's me. *Qué pasa?*"

Phaedra followed him and searched his face, wincing when his squint deepened.

"I can't hear you!" he shouted. "What's that racket going on. That racket...*alboroto!*"

Defeated, Phaedra flopped down in the wing chair. Anxiously, she devised several possible reasons for keeping him incommunicado, only to abandon each one as futile. She felt herself a failure, and she worried about losing him. But his words filled her with dread.

"OK, good. Keep her away from the balcony, no matter what she says. Even if you have to sit on her. Keep applying direct pressure to the wounds until the *médicos* arrive…. You're right. I know I don't have to tell you how to do that. Where's Cogdill? How did he get out?"

He held the phone away from his ear so Phaedra could hear weapons firing, explosive and close to where Berto was located.

He brought the phone back to his ear. "What building are you in? Chihuahua! What floor?"

He ran his hand through his hair and began looking for his boots.

"On fire? Then try your best to find an exit…. Get someone to help you carry her out…. I *will* be there. I'm leaving right now!"

Daniel slammed the receiver in its cradle and stared at her.

It was embarrassing to lamely fend off his unspoken accusation. But there was nothing else for her to do.

"What?" she said.

"You knew, didn't you?" His face smouldered with rage.

Phaedra shrank deeper into the chair, gripping her shawl. "Knew what?"

"That this insignificant demonstration would be the finale," he said, knotting his boondocker boots. "That the army would finally put an end to it."

"It's the second of October, Daniel. The games begin in less than two weeks. The government had to end it; you said so yourself."

"Yeah? Well, I was supposed to be there when it fucking happened!"

She recoiled from his anger, but tried to keep a calm, empathetic presence.

"Who's bleeding"? she asked. "What did Berto say? It's not…."

"Thousands of troops. Army. *Granaderos.* They've ambushed the strikers in the Plaza. Caught them in a crossfire, throwing everything at them. Some ran into the Chihuahua building at the Tlatelolco/Nonoalco apartments."

"Is he with Yvonne?"

He turned on a lamp. His disgrace and guilt sickened him. *My weakness pushed Yvonne into this.*

"No, he's with Oriana Fallaci, the Italian journalist who never misses a thing. They and Cogdill were on a fourth-floor balcony where the strike leaders were to address the crowd. Then all hell broke loose. Cogdill went to an upper floor. Berto and Oriana were let into an apartment and ran to a balcony to observe and shoot film. She got hit three times. Berto isn't certain whether Yvonne is safe. He said he saw her on the Plaza with her Mothers' Brigade but lost track after the shooting started. Maybe she was with a group of women being herded onto a police bus."

"What about Inez?"

"I don't know. The last he saw of her she left the balcony and headed to the Plaza. But the police, the army, whoever, arrested all the leaders of the National Strike Council in the building. Hauled them all away."

Daniel pulled on his sport coat. Phaedra ran to the bedroom door in a desperate attempt to keep him from leaving. He pushed her hard to the floor. By the time he reached Prado's motorcycle and began kicking it to life, she'd caught up, only to thrust a white glove at him.

"When you get down there, wear this on your left hand!" she yelled over the full-throated roar of the Harley's engine.

"What?"

She was in a frenzy now. "Don't argue with me! Just wear it! It'll protect you!"

Daniel looked at her with such disdain she was afraid he wasn't going to take it. "If you insisted on going to the Plaza, Robbie told me to give it to you!"

Phaedra jammed the white glove in his pocket. "On your left hand! Just wear it! Promise me!"

She tried to embrace him, but he let loose the clutch, and the Harley lurched down the driveway.

"Daniel!"

Banking low around corners, Daniel raced through the streets of Lomas de Chapultepec, Prado's privileged sanctuary, to Paseo de la Reforma, a long, winding downhill run that would eventually open onto a broad Parisian-style boulevard when he crossed into Mexico City's *Distrito Federal*. At one point, tears created by his speeding descent blurred his vision. He thought he saw a thin splinter of light streak above the skyline. It startled him and opened a memory: Uncle Abe, the scholar of Kabbalah, who preached about divine emanation.

"Lights, Daniel, created in a twinkling of an eye. Divine lights. Some that descend to make evil stronger, and some that ascend to their divine source through a tikkun, a fixing of the world."

Years before, when he was a boy, Uncle Abe charged him with the task of *tikkun*. And when he was 16, something like that had actually occurred. But whether to credit it to his own intention, or to God's, he could never ascertain. Now, he almost didn't care, and that's when he began to feel rain drops pelting him, and then the sky opened and it began to pour. *A hard rain's gonna fall....*

CHAPTER 9

In retrospect, it was the perfect setting for an ambush. Ironic, too, because you could argue that the Plaza of the Three Cultures is the spiritual and historical heart of the country. Four hundred years ago it was the site of the Conquistadors' massacre of the Aztecs. The Plaza has been a natural choice for large public meetings since the protest movement acquired legs after the first serious clash with the authorities in late July. It's a paved area of two acres, including the ruins of an Aztec pyramid, part of the ancient city of Tlatelolco. On the right is a Poli prep school. On the left is the colonial Church of Santiago, dwarfed by the tower of the Ministry of Foreign Affairs. The most important advantage of the site is that the vast block of apartment buildings forming another side has balconies that make convenient platforms for speakers. In addition, many tenants had already committed to students harassed by security forces.

Students and their supporters had met there to demonstrate several times previously. Each time they'd been confronted by the riot police and army, resulting in beatings, shootings, arrests and disappearances. So you could say those were dress rehearsals for the real thing.

This day, the atmosphere was quiet. Students, supporters — many with their children — vendors, and residents of the housing units gathered in the Plaza. Relaxed. Chatting. Soaking up the sunshine. Students distributing handbills, posters and newspapers, collecting donations. Everyone was waiting for the Strike Council leaders to speak from a podium set up on the fourth-floor balcony of the Chihuahua apartment building.

I was standing on the balcony along with Inez, Cogdill and the Italian journalist Oriana Fallaci, thinking how Prado had told me to expect trouble tonight, although not to the degree he suggested. It certainly didn't appear to be that way at the time. But the small turnout and lack of an urgent agenda, more of a social gathering than anything else, was the perfect setting for an overwhelming endgame. Some of the speakers began to warm-up the crowd by urging them to keep up the fight because army troops had finally evacuated the campus of the National Autonomous University/UNAM.

Then thousands of army troops with fixed bayonets and riot police began moving in from adjacent streets — running actually — accompanied by hundreds of light tanks and other armored vehicles. A helicopter circled lazily overhead.

That pulled my balls up.

I pointed it out to Inez. We chatted for a while. Out of the corner of my eye, I saw her leave the balcony, and then a minute later, I watched her exit the building and enter the Plaza, just as I expected she would after what I had just told her.

Strike Council leaders huddled and one of them grabbed a microphone. "The scheduled march to the Santo Tomás campus of Poli to push for a military evacuation has been canceled in light of the deployment of forces to suppress us."

Just at that moment, red and green flares dropped from the helicopter, and a barrage of rifle fire exploded from the balconies above us. Reflexively, I ducked and crab-walked back to the wall. Through the opening in our balcony railing I saw some people in the Plaza fall, including a couple of soldiers. What the fuck! Snipers? Then all hell broke loose. Not only were the demonstrators being fired upon from all directions, but also troops and riot police cut off all possible exits from the Plaza. People ran back and forth, frantic to escape. When they began to hit the ground, I thought it was due to exhaustion. Until the bodies began piling up. Then there was shooting on our floor, and men in civvies poured onto the balcony and smashed through apartment doors, clubbing and dragging out every student they could lay hands on, including a visibly-credentialed photo-journalist — me. Oriana, who was shot three times, was pulled away from me, dragged down the stairs and left for dead.

Students tore up their identification cards into little pieces and swallowed them. When we were captured, soldiers ordered us to take off our shoes and drop our pants around our ankles to prevent us from making a run for it. They made one student kneel and lopped off his long hair with a bayonet.

The last time I was at Tlatelolco was just a few weeks ago, days after 5,000 army troops invaded the National Autonomous University/UNAM and sealed off the campus, taking several thousand prisoners, including students, teachers, staff, and even parents of students. Thousands of students battled riot police outside Poli, too, with the same results. Students on the Strike Council went underground, but they were still able to organize a meeting that day in the Plaza of the Three Cultures. More and more riot police began showing up, followed by more and more students from Poli's technical prep school from the Santo Tomás campus. Hundreds were tear-gassed by the riot police who, at that time, weren't yet armed, just wielding truncheons, shields, and tear-gas launchers. Students from one of Poli's prep schools lived with their families at the Tlatelolco apartments. All night long, while students were torching police vehicles with Molotov cocktails, housewives poured boiling water out their windows along with gasoline and kerosene, stones, jars, cans, paving blocks, garbage. Even little kids stood on the rooftops throwing stones. Students nearly overwhelmed the police, fighting them in hand-to-hand combat.

Inez and her brigade from Poli's School of Nursing and a brigade of the UNAM's Med School showed up to care for the wounded.

In retrospect, it was probably the hundreds of families at the Tlatelolco apartments supporting the striking students that day that led the government to believe they were facing an organized urban *guerrilla* movement. At least, that's what Prado told me.

The night at UNAM, late July when I freaked out over the burning of the American flag was when Daniel first met Inez. She invited us to a house party where her parents made a big fuss, plying us with a warm wine punch and hot chocolate and cookies. I could tell Daniel was smitten and vice-versa. She never let him out of her sight, and he seemed intoxicated by her radiance.

Now it's one thing to be vivacious, but this girl was a knockout: 5-5, slender, with a great rack and tight round ass, full lips, jet-black hair swept back into a single French braid. A few loose wisps framed her face. She had big brown eyes with such long lashes that when she held you in her gaze, any man would be mesmerized. She possessed a smoldering mixed-race beauty with a trace of insolence when she inhabited her revolutionary character, reminding me of a Latina version of that commie dilettante Bernadine Dohrn when she rallied those punk SDSers to the Weatherman cause.

But the longer you were in Inez' presence, it was clear she was free of poses and artifices, committed to something more profound, a collective truth that was greater than her own life and personal happiness. And when I noticed a framed childhood photo of her on a mantle — a close-up — she exhibited the exact same sparkling smile and bright eyes and goodness as now. Exactly. Which led me to believe that, deep down inside, her truest soul had never changed. A remarkable, historical continuity from 4-year-old child to adult that I'd honestly never seen before. Because of that comparison, I vowed to make a photo portrait of her as soon as I had the chance.

Daniel really lost himself in her plump glossed lips and so refocused his usual "look me straight in the eyes" gaze that I was embarrassed for him. To top it off, she had a collection of LPs that would even make a jazz fan like Daniel envious. Toward the end of the evening, when she put on the 1961 Oliver Nelson septet's version of "Stolen Moments," I thought our boy was going to freakin' swoon. What a prescient vignette. We stayed so late, some of us wound up spending the night, sleeping on the floor.

Earlier, however, the little apartment was filled with post-rally, raucous conversation, which quickly turned into a dialogue between the Mexican students on the one hand and me and Daniel on the other. Seeing as how we were the center of attention, attention that was, in turn, gracious hospitality, curiosity and ideological antagonism.

I started off by telling them what Prado told me about the government believing it was facing an organized urban *guerrilla* movement, that this student protest movement was unique among all others we'd witnessed or read about in the last two years. Radicalized students at Columbia University, led by SDS chairman Mark Rudd and his "action faction," folded as soon as the police hustled onto campus swinging their night sticks, which were about half the length of the Mexican truncheon.

"The president overstates our menace," Inez declared. "This allows him to act with extreme brutality."

"Overstates your menace? You're attacking police and army! Nobody does that in the U.S. And most of you identify yourselves as communists."

"So what? All of our intellectuals and artists are communists. And why did it take five years for your American student activists to evolve from non-violence," a Poli member of the Strike Council said, heatedly. "Except for stupid, self-destructive riots, why isn't there a pattern of aggressive, revolutionary dissent?"

Daniel responded quickly. "Probably due to the powerful influence of Martin Luther King Jr."

"What works on your people's conscience doesn't necessarily work on ours," the Polí boy said.

"I understand," Daniel countered. "But with the advent of Malcolm X and the Black Panthers and their passionate intellectual literati, *all* that has changed."

Inez interrupted, "Excuse me, but we have a much longer history of activism because we've never been allowed to participate in political decisions. Those decisions are made for us by a political party, the *PRI*, that's been in power for 40 years. Going back over the last decade, dozens of revolutionary and student groups have made the same demands we're making today, especially to abolish political imprisonment, Article 145 and the *granaderos*. There was the national strike in 1956, the Teachers' Movement in '58, the Railway Workers' Movement '58–'59, student protests in Morelia '62–'63 and '66 and in Puebla '62 and '64 and at UNAM '66 and Sonora and Tabasco in '67. Even doctors have gone on strike."

"It's not as if our movement has no precedent," another student blurted.

Right. Prado told me there had been dozens of significant episodes of student unrest during the '60s, led by *agitadóres*. I couldn't resist taking a pot-shot. "From what I hear, those university protests have resulted in the authorities allowing student demagogues — commies — to take over the universities, appoint teachers and directors who will kiss your asses. Even let you make decisions over curriculum. You're presiding over the dismantling of your educational institutions. So now the inmates are running the asylum."

Well, I couldn't have provoked a more reactionary outburst than if I'd been President Díaz Ordaz himself, speaking from the balcony of his palace. Nobody could get in a word edgewise, but they were all flushed with anger.

One student yelled: "You de-institutionalize society by de-institutionalizing education!" Others bristled, wanting to kick my ass, just the outcome I liked best. These SDS/VC/commie pricks.

That's when Daniel got into it, first enlisting a humorous approach. Until then, he'd been living up to his Iroquois name and oogling Inez, whose mini-skirt kept rising with each declamation.

"Now keep in mind," he yelled several times before commanding their attention, "my partner here is a disciple of Ayn Rand." It worked, provoking loud moans, booing and hysterical laughter. One guy laughed so hard he spit up red wine all over the front of his white shirt.

I didn't miss a beat. "You've been shot, José!"

I glanced at Daniel. He winced. José? It always amazed him how I was so willing to push the envelope. But no one seemed offended. In fact, when the guy's compadres saw his stained shirt, they got hysterical all over again. Once things died down, Inez looked at me with a strange mixture of admiration and disbelief.

"You speak like a *chilango*; are you Mexican?"

"My name is Italian, but I was born in Mexico City and I have dual citizenship. My dad was born here and worked as a chef and a hotel manager. He died five years ago. My mom was born in Texas. Now that she's a widow, she teaches English to businessmen here."

"Where did you go to secondary school?" a student asked.

"Preparatory # 1, San Ildefonso."

"So what did you think when the army took a bazooka and blew off the 400-year-old hand-carved door?"

I looked down at the floor and shook my head.

"Daniel," one student said, "I understand you are *mestizo*, like most of us." The others laughed, but they found it fascinating that an American journalist could have European/Spanish and Indian blood.

"Yes," he replied. "My people were Sephardic Jews kicked out of Spain who wound up in England and then the U.S. My father married a woman who was half-Iroquois and half-Irish. My wife is full-blood Iroquois." He took a photo out of his wallet to show around: Yvonne leaning against a granite boulder, deeply-tanned, with shoulder-length straight black hair, wearing a faded denim jacket and Levi's, desert boots. Lips slightly parted, an expression both pensive and sultry.

"I don't know you," Inez said, "but I sense you and Berto are very different. What is the glue that holds you together?"

Daniel jerked his thumb at me. "He speaks better Spanish." More laughter, but Inez' brow remained knitted, while I'm thinking it was really me wanting to be around Yvonne, the woman in the photo. My photo. I was crazy about her.

And that's when Daniel defused the situation by giving them a little entertainment, a gift of theatrical dialogue between the two *gringos*, him and me, what they really wanted to hear, the main reason they invited us. At first, to clear the air, he confessed that we were both combat veterans. Me with the Marines in Vietnam. Him with Marine Recon in Lebanon. There were audible gasps.

"Berto, did you kill anyone?"

"No. I was a Navy photo-journalist attached to Marine combat units." Out of the corner of my eye, I glanced at Daniel. He looked straight ahead. But Inez caught me.

"What...?" I asked.

Daniel came to my assistance. "Sometimes even a journalist might have to pick up a gun. In Berto's case, he photographed a combat rescue mission from inside a Marine helicopter. In very bad weather and against orders from his commanding officer, a young aviator flew to a pick-up point and back to base camp seven times to rescue a platoon that had been ambushed and pinned down. Most everyone was badly wounded. At one point, Berto had to man a machine gun until the last wounded were loaded. If he hadn't, the helicopter might not have been able to take off. He was awarded a Bronze Star for valor. The pilot won the Navy Cross, highest award in the Marine Corps, second only to the Medal of Honor."

"We aren't impressed with medals," the Polí kid said. "You were there to put down a spontaneous people's revolution. Your country created a war that's killed a million innocent peasants. How can you live with yourself?"

I shook my head. "You got it all wrong kid. It was the commies who started it. We were there to protect freedom-loving people."

Boos all around.

Inez waved her arms, quieting them down.

"What about you, Daniel?"

"No, I didn't kill anybody. I was sent on a secret mission. We were trying to prevent a civil war. My mission was to restore a son to his father — a sheik — in exchange for maps of rebel locations."

"Was it a success?"

"I believe so, but I was badly injured, and I never learned about the final outcome."

Then the dialogue began. Daniel first.

"Do you remember a few weeks ago when a whole bunch of us drove down to Cuernavaca so that our bureau chief could interview the Red Bishop, the most prominent advocate in Mexico of Liberation Theology?" he asked. "You were disgusted."

"Yeah," I responded. "Because I'm a traditional Catholic, and

I hate the way the Church has been poisoned by trendy political activism, interpreting theology only from the perspective of the poor, saying that Christ's mission was to bring the sword of social unrest rather than peace and social order. It's nothing more than Christianized Marxism."

More gasps. And a clamor of students to intervene before we even get started, sort of like a Greek chorus, but in the radical student-speak of *pronunciamento.*

"What's your objection to liberating people from unjust economic, political or social conditions?" asked one.

"What's your objection to democratizing one of the most oppressive institutions in all of Latin America?" another student demanded.

"...whose sin has been to ally with oppressive regimes and actually create poverty!" another cried out.

"So," I asked, "what is the outcome when socialists take over your country and condemn the Church? How many of you have read Graham Greene's "The Power and the Glory," set in post-revolution Mexico? The socialists confiscated Church property, banned Mass and giving the sacrament. They banned confession and hunted down and murdered fugitive priests."

More Greek chorus.

"What's that got to do with Liberation Theology?"

"What's wrong with acting on behalf of social justice and human rights? That's what we've been clamoring for all summer!"

"What's wrong with a call to action against poverty and raising up needy, defenseless and despised people who, instead, should be privileged by God's grace?"

"What's wrong with a preferential option for the poor?"

Daniel burst into laughter. "Sounds familiar, doesn't it, Berto, like our Cuernavaca experience."

"OK, OK. We'll get to that. But I'm opposed to Liberation Theology for the same reason I oppose communism. Jesus is now a Marxist? Who embraces class struggle and advocates a more just and equal redistribution of wealth? Up to and including expropriation, and solidarity with revolutionary movements? Sorry, but the role of the Church is to advance personal salvation through divine truth and faith. I need the Church to help me become more perfect: overcome the world, the flesh and the devil."

Not bad, I thought, coming from a lifelong backslider and horny bastard. Daniel gave me a look that said as much.

More boos and hissing, but they were really into the Daniel-and-Berto show.

"OK, back to Cuernavaca," said Daniel. "Ostensibly we were accompanying our editor for his interview with the Red Bishop, and afterwards Berto took photos of Mendez Arcéo...."

"Don Sergio!" a student interrupted. "He preaches that 'a true Christian is obligated to condemn any form of injustice, particularly the sort of injustice which becomes the prevailing order of things.' "

"Why do you refer to him as Don Sergio?" I asked.

"His poor, working-class parishioners honor him with this title for his weekly homilies on behalf of them...exclusively."

A moment of silence passed as everyone acknowledged the student's sentiment. And then the student urged us to continue our story.

"Berto, after you took photos of Don Sergio...."

I stepped on Daniel's line. "We were also traveling with a friend of mine from the University of the Americas, John, a young Marist brother on sabbatical from his teaching gig in Brownsville, Texas..."

Then Daniel interrupted. "... whose school, St. Joseph Academy, a college prep school, emphasizes 'a preferential option for the poor,' meaning serving the poor Mexicans living in the lower Rio Grande Valley..."

"...where they inculcate students in that propaganda!" I asserted, maybe with a little too much heat. "Force them to do community service rather than encouraging them to develop their own individual skills and preferences."

"...and you picked on him for that and for his vow of celibacy."

"Celibacy is the stupidest concept ever invented by man!" I yelled.

Greek chorus.

"You contradict yourself!" one astute student shouted. "A few minutes ago, you said you prefer traditional Catholicism: 'overcoming the world, the flesh and the devil.'"

"That's all metaphor," I said, lamely defending myself.

Inez piped in. "I think I see your game. You just like to argue; find a person's scab and pick it."

Daniel grinned. His girl was not only beautiful, but smart.

"So how different am I from your student leaders?" I asked. "The ones who argue incessantly over ideology, over who is more rigorously authentic: the Maoists, the Trotskyites, the Spartacists, the communists, Fidelistas, social democrats."

Inez piped in. "It's true. At the beginning it was disheartening to see the social class division between UNAM and Poli students, and then the quarreling when we all ached for action. But that all changed after the *granaderos* attacked our separate rallies as we marched on the Presidential Palace. And then when we retreated to barricade and occupy our *voca* and *prep* schools and the *granaderos* tried to break a three-day siege. When four students were killed, hundreds injured and arrested. When infantry, paratroop riflemen and military police backed by tanks and armored cars occupied the schools. When they fired the bazooka at San Ildefonso Prep. When they killed and arrested and disappeared many more of us.

"What did we do? We came together and presented our demands. We formed a National Strike Council. Now we're organizing a massive protest, and we're expecting more than 100,000 will show up. Eventually, we hope it will grow much larger — citizens from all walks of life. When they see how the government represses us."

I figured I'd better try to score some points. "Well, I admire your courage *(crazy Latin temperament?)* to confront armed troops and even fight with them, which is greater than what students have displayed everywhere else in the world."

Greek chorus, a spontaneous cry: *"Mé-xi-co — Li-ber-tad! Mé-xi-co — Li-ber-tad!"*

When the cheer died down, due largely to Inez' parents who worried about attracting undue attention from neighbors (it was getting pretty late) and who gently hectored the students to be a more polite audience, Daniel resumed our Cuernavaca dialogue.

"Your friend, John, wanted to visit a friend of his from New York, Barbara, the Maryknoll nun..."

"...who was ostensibly preparing for missionary work in Latin America," I said. "By studying Spanish at the Institute of Latin American Culture. But who spent most of her time with other nuns *(a coven of witches)* at Ivan Illich's think tank, the Intercultural Documentation Center. Fancy title for the free university for intellectual hippies."

"And what was the focus of their devotion?" asked Daniel.

"Supposedly, creating self-reliance groups among poor *campesinos....*"

"Why?"

I began to squirm. "Because the *campesinos* live far away from parishes with active priests."

"And what did she say she would do with these people?"

My voice grew softer with each ensuing word, and the students leaned forward in their seats or where they were standing. "...join together to study the Bible. Remind them that there is always someone to love them somewhere, and that they still have a chance in life. Service rather than creed."

"So?"

"It's nuts. If Mexico doesn't allow a public role for the Catholic clergy — they're practically invisible here for Ch...for crying out loud — how's she going to accomplish her goal? Oh, right, she's heading off to El Salvador."

"...is that where she wants to go?"

"That's what John told me."

"So, for you, what was the point of our visit?"

"To be humiliated."

"Is that what you felt?"

"She only wanted to talk to you, even more than John."

"What do you remember from that conversation?"

"You told her you were from Brant, N.Y., and she got excited, wanted to know if you knew Billy O'Dell."

"...who had joined the Catholic Worker Movement. Moved to New York City, and had teamed with Philip Berrigan to break into draft board offices, to pour blood in their file cabinets."

"...and she wanted to know if you knew David Miller..."

"...who..."

"...who was the first draft-eligible American to burn his draft card..."

"...publicly..."

"...publicly, and who a lot of people would like to strangle, including me."

"And who was *his* mentor?"

"Daniel Berrigan, Philip's brother, a Jesuit priest who taught at that Catholic College in Brant you told me about."

"Seems to be a trend here, huh?"

I just shook my head. Hell, Brant might've been just a small college town, but it was famous for something sinister. I needed something stiffer than mulled wine, or whatever it was that was being served. The students burst into applause.

But Inez wanted to have the last word.

"Berto, the first thing you told us — that a U.S. State Department employee gives you intelligence?"

"Well...?"

Daniel came to the rescue. "Not exactly intelligence. He gives us context more than anything. But, yes, he does have an ear to what is being discussed among your government's top officials."

Inez leaned forward. "Would you be interested in having exclusive access to our brigade leaders and the Strike Council and covering our story on a daily basis? You say you're free until the Olympic games begin. We'll tell you about planned protests and tactics. And in return, you can provide us with intel regarding how the government plans to deal with us; for example, are they willing to negotiate our demands?" *Giving him a look like, every day we'll be together, for at least a little while.*

Uh-oh! A deal with the devil. But in our case it's not so much of a deal because Cogdill was already chafing at the bit for more of our daily exclusives about these radicals and their confrontations. But Daniel didn't disappoint; he tilted his head, pondering the *quid pro quo* deal. But the man knew a priceless opportunity when he saw it.

"This could be a good partnership. And I can tell you a couple of things already. The *granaderos* are now being armed with rifles and bayonets, besides the tear gas grenades and truncheons they already carry. So things could get even nastier. And the government is relying on a strategy of dividing the students."

"So," I said, "you hope to get the government to agree to your demands? This can only be done through negotiations, right?"

"Right," she asserted. "But they must be public, not behind closed doors."

"Your condition?"

"Yes."

Daniel followed up, although he was listing badly in his chair, and I could tell another headache was about to take him out. "And what if Díaz Ordaz doesn't agree?"

"Eventually, we hope the student movement will grow much larger. Other campuses. Nationwide."

"Right up to the Olympics?" I asked, disbelief at her naiveté.

"...we don't know. That's months away."

By that point, everyone was tired of talking politics. Inez' parents laid out another plate of cookies and slices of cake and more hot chocolate, then went to their bedroom. Some students began to argue over which music should be played, just like in the States where, among the radical set, your music preference helped maintain your status. I loved to claim that Dusty Springfield was my favorite, and those dilettante radicals all just about puked. One of my favorite and vengeful moments in a little village south of Mexico City was when I played a Bob Dylan tape on my eight-track, and little kids who gathered around the van began howling with laughter at his affected nasal twang. The Great Folk Hero reduced to an object of ridicule.

Meanwhile, Daniel was looking done in, and Inez noted it.

"What's wrong with him?" she asked me. I explained his problem with severe, debilitating headaches.

"Do you think he needs to lay down?"

"Perfect. With the lights out."

She took him into her bedroom then came out a few minutes later and turned down the record player and began cajoling her friends to think about leaving, then went back to her room.

All I could think about was a scene from one of my favorite movies, *Battle Cry*, when a World War II combat-weary jarhead played perfectly by Aldo Ray begins to re-experience symptoms of malaria while on liberty. His girlfriend, a New Zealand babe, puts him to bed in her cute little cottage. He's really suffering, trembling with chills even after she tucks him in. Extra blankets don't help. He's shaking like there's an internal volcano about to erupt, but it's summer in New Zealand. So, in desperation, she pulls open the covers and dives right in, holding onto him real tight. Freakin' brilliant tactic! I've been waiting for an opportunity like that ever since. Instead, my boy pulls it off. He's beaten me to the punch! Life is so unfair.

As I stretched out on the carpet to lay on my back for the next few hours, entertaining myriad erotic fantasies, I pulled a pillow from one of Inez' chairs. I picked out the guy wearing a Mao cap, one of the assholes giving me shit earlier. I threw the pillow at him. He threw it back and gave me a mean stare.

"*¿Qué pasa, cabrón?*" he said.

Cabrón? Prick. "I gather you're fond of Mao."

"What of it, *gringo*?"

"Then you know they have their own Article 145 over there. It's called 'Disrupting Social Order.' You shoot off your yap, and they lock you up. Indefinitely."

"Why should I care about what *you* have to say? You're just a dumb, prejudiced *gringo*."

"Right on. And the world needs dumb, prejudiced *gringos* like me to witness on your behalf. To prevent the authorities from disappearing your ass."

He snorted, pulled the cap over his eyes and rolled onto his side, revealing a small piece of cake leaking out of his butt pocket. *The revolutionary cadre confiscating scarce resources. Too much!*

October 2
Tlatelolco Massacre
Inez' Story

CHAPTER 10

He wouldn't let me touch him that night, the night my parents hosted a party for a few of my friends from Poli who'd attended the protest at UNAM. When I sat on my bed to ask if he felt better and swept his brow with my fingers — delicately, and with barely contained trembling — he responded with such a pained yelp and tensing of muscles that it felt as if he were momentarily levitating. Simultaneously, what I imagined to be a current of electricity from him to me made me jump to my feet.

Now keep in mind that I'm a fourth-year nursing student, and I've seen a lot already. I was just shocked at my response, which was quite emotional, not at all what I'd expected. You see, I thought he was fooling around with me, trying a ploy to get into my room and into my bed, like a scene from a melodramatic movie. Uh-uh, no-no. I wouldn't fall for that.

I tip-toed a few steps to my over-stuffed comfortable chair where I often studied. I dimmed the light and sat watch over him or, more accurately, watched him suffer. Fighting pain by laying absolutely still. In this meditative state, he was able to slow his breathing, but sweat still beaded on his forehead and rolled down his face onto my pillow.

Dios me perdone, but all I could think was that he was the most beautiful man I had ever met, and his suffering made him beatific. Immediately, without knowing much about him, my heart went out to him. Meaning, I lost my heart.

The first time I saw Daniel was a few weeks earlier, before all the trouble started. He came to Poli on the hunch of a story. For him, it was a really unusual story that sparked his enthusiasm because he was convinced it would be a great feature piece for IPS's international sports wire. A 'side-bar,' he called it, that would be attached to some pre-Olympics feature story he had yet to figure out, since he'd arrived so recently from *El Norte*.

He showed up with Cogdill, his bureau chief, and Berto, camera at the ready. They sat on a grassy hill overlooking the football field where the Poli White Donkeys were scrimmaging. Apparently, while touring our rival campus UNAM because it was adjacent to the Olympic Stadium, he discovered they had a football team, the Pumas, and he had to see our team, too. He had no idea our schools played American-style football. He was absolutely delighted about it, and I was there in my capacity as student nurse assisting the trainer.

At one point, a coach waved them down to the field. A fairly lengthy conversation ensued between the coach and Daniel as he soon recognized who Daniel was, son of the famous Davey Mendoza and an acclaimed university football player. Excited, he blew his whistle, and practice came to a halt. Then he yelled for all the coaches to come over and meet Daniel. There was a lot of hand-shaking and animated conversation.

The next thing, Daniel took off his sport coat and rolled up his shirtsleeves. The first coach summoned all the ends and wide receivers and introduced them to Daniel. More animated conversation and gesturing. Then the coach blew his whistle and lined up his offense and defense, told them to run a passing play. The quarterback threw the ball to the most-accomplished wide receiver on the team who was obviously trying his best, as if he was auditioning for a starring role in an important movie. But a defensive back, alert to being victimized, charged in to break up the pass, bobbled the ball and fell to the ground with it cradled in his arms.

The coach blew his whistle and called the offensive team back into a tight huddle around Daniel. More animated talk, but on the next play, Daniel lined up at wide receiver. This time, he ran the exact same route and the defensive back charged in exactly the same way, probably thinking how easy it would be against this older guy dressed in civvies and military boots. But, at the end of his pass pattern, instead of waiting passively for the ball to reach him like the White Donkey, Daniel raced back toward the quarterback, leapt into the air just as the defensive back arrived, bumped his hips, and plucked the ball out of the air. The defensive back fell to the ground, and Daniel pivoted toward the sideline and jogged downfield about 20 yards, a crooked smile on his face. Well, more of a grimace than a smile, which he tried to disguise, but I saw it.

Berto worked his camera like an automatic weapon. Whoops and hollers from the coaches and Cogdill. A teaching drill about fighting for possession of the ball was born, and the entire team was let in on it. Berto continued to snap pictures of the rest of the practice and he, Daniel and Cogdill were invited to stay for dinner at the cafeteria.

Daniel was so boyish that day, but a damaged boy; that was clear to me, and it was clear that this opportunity to teach the Poli players an important, advanced lesson was something bursting from within him. I could see he had a good heart, and everybody else could, too.

Later, when I got to know him, he told me that he really wanted to move away from impressionist, mostly-tragic political writing to something more uplifting, and that he couldn't wait for the Olympics to begin to practice this craft. From my perspective of revolutionary fervor, I couldn't understand why a journalist of his stature would desire this change. But all I could think to tell him at the time was, I *hope* your dreams come true.

After the night of the party, when the protests were in full bloom, we made a plan for daily contact. He would phone me at my parents' apartment after his morning breakfast with Prado and again early in the evening after dinner with Prado at the International Press Club. I would meet him there, if possible, or phone there if I couldn't make it, or phone Cogdill; then he would meet me wherever I was. Sometimes we'd confer in one of the press club's hotel rooms, but he never made an untoward move.

Our morning discussions usually dealt with what he'd learned about the government's back-and-forth plans to either negotiate with or confront the protesters. He told me which police and military units were being mobilized against us and the kinds of weapons, armaments and tactics they were being schooled in. What statements were being made by Mexico City's chief of police and the secretary of defense. He told us about the role of the Olympic Battalion, formed to preserve public order during the Olympic games. Young cavalry officers and soldiers, Federal District Police, Federal Judicial Police, Federal Security Directorate, and the Federal Treasury Agency. He wanted me to seriously understand what we were up against.

In turn, he wanted to know what steps the Strike Council was taking to unify the two main student factions — *acelerados* and moderates — which wasted several agonizing weeks running off at the mouth and vehemently disagreeing at every turn. It was an experience that was all too familiar to him, the splintering of American protest groups, the impetus to be the most authentic.

"You can't solve the real problems of your country and create a new future unless you construct a united front. Remember, the government wants to divide and conquer you."

Moreover, he warned that it was really important to make it clear that the Strike Council's agenda should be finite in negotiating its demands with the government. "Do you want to achieve your political objectives? Because resistance for its own sake is just narcissistic and unproductive.

"And you have to promise and then reiterate that promise on a daily basis that you will not interfere with the Olympics; I can't emphasize enough how important that is. And that's straight from Prado."

I argued with him. "We don't want the Olympics! What a waste of $180 million! The government should be investing in social overhead, developing basic services for the poor. Paved roads, sewers, clean water, better schools and medical clinics. And don't you see how ironic it is? Díaz Ordaz is reaching out to everyone in the world, but he won't even talk to us, the children of his own country!"

"OK," he replied. "But at least it's good that cancellation of the Olympics isn't on the Strike Council's list of demands. That's a huge non-starter. There's a lot of money invested, a lot of prestige. Just think of all the tourist dollars that will pour into the country."

I shot back an exasperated retort. "Really? And who gets that money? Only the people who already have it!"

But to keep our relationship going and for the sake of a good story, he covered every protest and demonstration and filed stories.

"If you have a good grasp of recent history, you might recall 1968 as a particularly tumultuous year. From Paris, Berlin, London, Madrid and Warsaw to New York and Chicago and beyond. Popular rebellions against military, economic and political elites who respond with escalating repression. But in Mexico City it is something more like war. And the term 'to disappear' — referring to what happens after hundreds of activists are arrested, beaten, and taken off to secret military camps — is sprinting to the top of the list of the modern political lexicon."

Unlike Berto, he never dismissed my arguments. We discussed the issues, sometimes heatedly. But he was very intelligent and thought carefully before he spoke. He also understood the particular Mexican historical precedents and the modern philosophical underpinnings most Mexican students were steeped in, especially the writings of Frantz Fanon and Paolo Freire. How critical education leads its participants to transform their world. How oppressors must be willing to re-think their way of life. But if they stubbornly cling to their authoritarian principles and back it with violent oppression, that oppression must be met with violence.

He listened patiently, but he also reminded me about the government's point of view that violent protesters were subversives who must be subject to law and order, meaning repression that would serve as a warning to other student groups in the country. There had been plenty of skirmishes, but the Olympics were getting close. When the government decided to really crack down, he said, it might be worse than anything we'd yet endured or imagined.

I also told him about how the works of Herman Hesse, especially "Steppenwolf," influenced me. Learning to be myself, giving me the courage to go my own way, believing in my future. I told him I wanted to be a nurse in a rural village clinic, like a secular nun, a legend.

He gave me a copy of Anne Frank's "The Diary of a Young Girl," for inspiration — the innermost thoughts of this girl living under Nazi occupation, the tragedy of betrayal, a life cut short. A quote that had me crying for days: *"I don't want to have lived in vain; I want to carry on after death."*

One day, after discussing with Daniel the unhappy and unfulfilled life of the Italian emigre-turned Mexican film star and photographer and dedicated communist, Tina Modotti, I blurted out: "Promise me that if I'm killed and there is a memorial service, I want it to begin with Anne Frank's quote." And then a crazy idea took hold of me: "I would also like you to record on tape and play the fanfare that precedes every 20th Century Fox movie." I hummed it for him, with the appropriate passion.

He laughed until tears squirted out of his eyes. "How Hollywood," he said, joking.

Although he persisted in criticizing the Strike Council, especially the *acelerados*, he never made it personal. He worried about me. He followed our Strike Council through all of its planned protests. The violent clashes in the Plaza of the Three Cultures. The arrests and casualties. Smashed windows and burned-out busses and jeeps. The invasions and occupations by police and military of the two university campuses and their prep schools which the government had promised autonomy since their founding days. Beatings and arrests of thousands of students and teachers. He and Berto were always there, writing and taking photos. But always looking out for me. And when it became too dangerous, he'd insist I run to the van to save me from being beaten or arrested.

But he almost took it personally when the Strike Council reneged on negotiations with the president on whose behalf Prado was a broker, a neutral and invisible go-between. Just when it appeared that everything could be resolved before the Olympics, the *acelerados* held sway. *It's stupid to negotiate with the government; everyone is an agent of repression!* They not only wanted to continue the struggle but also wanted to emphasize our organization's name, the National Strike Council, in order to recruit other schools in the country to our cause.

But what Daniel said about unifying our polarized factions and having a finite goal to negotiate an end to the cycle of protest and oppression finally made sense to me. Now was the perfect time to negotiate change, change that would become permanent. And I found myself moderating my position which, unfortunately, jeopardized my standing among the Poli *acelerados* on the Strike Council.

He became a fixture at my parents' apartment, especially when his marriage was strained to the breaking point and when his headaches worsened and he needed a quiet place to rest. On the good days, when he felt well enough to test his competence, he let me watch him train at La Lupita. He talked about boxing as if it was war. "One guy claims a territory, one guy wants it back."

He talked about the ways of a counter-puncher but also about not surrendering the advantage if he had to fight to the finish — like the warriors of old, like all the great Mexican champions — with all of his heart. I really favored that philosophy. If I were a man, I told him, that's the kind of fighter I would like to be. He worked hard on his footwork; he worried about his balance, which he thought was failing. "I don't want to be in a bad position to avoid taking shots."

And we often mingled with the old coots who so admired Daniel's boxing ability: the peek-a-boo stance pioneered by his family's patriarch, his own modified and ambidextrous martial art stance taught to him by his Korean Marine mentor which nobody at the gym could break through, the powerful straight jab and out-of-nowhere upper-cut — punches that Daniel lovingly referred to in Yiddish slang as a *knak* and a *shtaysl*, and the uncanny resemblance to his dad. They lovingly nicknamed Daniel *El León* because of the Lion of Judah that was embroidered on his father's white silk robe. The last time we were there together, and I believe it was the last time he trained because the pace of protests and confrontations was escalating, he gave me a velvet box containing a gold pendant on a slender chain. Boxing gloves folded one over the other. It was a memento from his last fight when he won the Marine Corps light heavyweight boxing championship. In a corner of the gym, he discreetly clasped it around my neck. When I examined it close-up in a mirror, I was so deeply moved; my eyes welled with tears. I realized he was acknowledging our deepening relationship.

That night it was cold and raining, and when we returned to the apartment, a note from my parents sat propped against a vase filled with calla lillies. It announced that they were visiting my mother's only aunt who was ill and lived alone in a country house way out on the Toluca highway, and that they would stay over as a precaution.

I was chilled to the bone and wanted to take a hot shower. When I finished, I wrapped myself in a thick, white towel. Normally, I would put on my robe, dry my hair and go to bed. Instead, hands unsteady, I found myself applying mascara, a few sprays of perfume, and a new red lipstick. In the living room, Daniel was rewriting notes taken earlier in the day, so I snuck into my bedroom where I called out to him. "Do you need to take a shower, too?"

"No," he replied. "I showered and washed my hair at La Lupita."

"Then maybe you should come in here." Something had happened to my voice, disembodied and strangled with emotion. It became very quiet in the living room. I sat on the edge of my bed.

"Daniel…?"

My ears were ringing with an overwhelming expectation, so that I didn't even hear him cross the floor to my door, and when he opened it, I held onto the towel so I wouldn't jump out of my skin.

"…Inez?"

How I got the courage to respond, I have no idea. "In Mexico, everyone has a nickname. Would you please call me *cariño*? It means 'honey.'"

I felt so stupid. Everybody knows what that endearment means.

He sighed deeply and looked down at the floor.

"Dicen que el león es el rey de la selva." They say the lion is the king of the jungle. "Would you like some honey?" I said coquettishly.

I was flustered by my own words, my audacity. He kept shaking his head, wouldn't even look at me. Had I misjudged him, his hungry glances from the first time we met, the way he stared at my mouth when we talked rather than looking me straight in the eye?

When he did look up, his answer startled me.

"You shouldn't do this to me, Inez. I have an obligated life."

My heart began to pound, and I began to sweat, despite my shower, as if a heat wave had settled in the space between us. I let my towel drop, its edge sliding past my erect nipples.

"Just be obligated to me from time to time, like now, this stolen moment. I need your love," I pleaded. "Come closer." I desperately wanted to seal the promise of permanence between us.

I touched him, felt his tremor and his hardness beneath his corduroys. I unzipped him and took him into my mouth, caressing him with my lips, now slick with saliva. When he moaned, it sounded as if the sexual intensity between us terrified him. But I was wrong. He pushed me back onto the bed, parted my legs, knelt and began to slowly kiss me. I felt like I was dissolving.

"Take...take off your clothes. I want to feel your body," I insisted.

We sat next to each other, touching, trembling, and then I boldly pushed him onto his back and quickly straddled him. He immediately slid into me, and I was so aroused I began to rock in a frenzied pace. But he put his hands on my hips, trying to constrain me.

"Slow down," he whispered.

" I can't help it!" I yelled, defiant and needy, but his unyielding resistance was too great for me to persist, and we settled into a graceful dance involving my offer and his response. I didn't want it to end, but my desire overwhelmed me with spasms swift and deep, and he matched my climax with a long, exultant shudder. I fell away from him and collapsed into his arms, breathless and dripping with sweat. I'd never experienced such a profound, symbolic dialogue of reciprocal friendship, respect and desire, when my mind, body and emotions met another's in such an intensity of pleasure.

Before I fell asleep, I knew my love for him would only grow stronger and that I'd never forget this night.

✧　✧　✧

The Strike Council plotted actions for the rest of the summer. Classes at both universities were abandoned and the rectors resigned, blaming the government. Instead of studying, hundreds of thousands of students formed brigades within their particular academic departments, and we printed and distributed handbills all over the city, even on buses. And as the repression against us grew, so did support for our cause.

At one point, we organized a silent protest march, drawing nearly 100,000 people from all walks of life, including some who formed their own brigades, like the Mexican Women's Union. We began at Chapultepec Park and walked down Reforma all the way to the Presidential Palace. It was so moving. No shouting of slogans, just people carrying signs, some with white handkerchiefs over their mouths and walking with great dignity. Thousands of people along the way shouted their support for us and raised their hands, fingers forming the *V* symbol. Not for peace, but for *Venceremos*, we shall win.

A subsequent march drew 250,000. At the Presidential Palace we shouted for Díaz Ordaz. *"Come out on the balcony, loudmouth!"* We removed the Mexican flag and replaced it with a red-and- black strike flag. We spray-painted a slogan on the wall of the National Palace, *Díaz Ordaz is a dumb ox.* We convinced the priests at the Metropolitan Cathedral to turn on the outside lights while they rang the bells. We intended to spend the night there, but at 1 a.m. the army made a show of force with paratroopers armed with rifles and fixed bayonets and armored cars with two mounted machine guns and a cannon. Police indulged in more beatings and arrests. But because we outnumbered them, we fought back hand-to-hand. Then the *granaderos* regrouped, overwhelming us with their truncheons and tear gas until we dispersed.

Prado revealed intel to Daniel a few days later that Díaz Ordaz told his cabinet and in a joint meeting with U.S. State Department representatives that that night's action was the final straw. Basic law of physics: For every action there is a reaction. But the student strike had developed a momentum of its own, and with the mass support we were receiving and the Olympics just a few weeks away, we were told to expect the worst. "The worst" was part of a Mexican strategy that Prado promised Daniel he knew very little about, didn't quite know the nature of, or when it was going to occur.

The night of Oct. 2, I stood with some of the other Strike Council leaders on the Chihuahua building's fourth-floor balcony overlooking the Plaza. Waiting. It wasn't such a big gathering of people, nor were they particularly worked up. Instead, people sat on steps or on the wall that separated the modern Plaza from the Aztec ruins of Tlatelolco. Or they stood in small groups chatting amiably. Some ate food brought from home or snacks purchased from vendors. One member of the Strike Council estimated the size of the crowd at about 10,000 and it seemed that half were non-students. Quite a few brought their children. There were a lot of soldiers around, as usual, some sitting on vehicles polishing their bayonets.

At one point, Berto sidled up to me and pointed to a smiling little girl, her mother paying a vendor for a balloon. "That's Yvonne, with her daughter, Sonia."

I don't know what came over me — curiosity, guilt — but I had a sudden urge to see them up close. I edged away from the 20 or so of my *compadres*, exited the balcony through an apartment and into a hallway and pressed the elevator's down arrow. Nothing happened. I pressed several times, but the up/down signals failed to light up. So I took the stairs. When I reached the ground floor, a large group of young men were pulling white gloves onto their left hands. What a strange sight.

One saw me and trotted over.

"Are you a student, a striker?"

Alert to trouble, I lied. "No, I'm an office worker. I live here. I'm going out to buy food for my family."

"Well, hurry on then. You don't want to linger on the Plaza. And don't come back here for a while."

The next thing I knew, the men scrambled up the stairs. I could see the bulge of pistols under their jackets, tucked into waistbands or in short holsters. I left the apartment lobby and walked quickly onto the Plaza and into the crowd to where I thought I'd seen Yvonne and Sonia. I figured a balloon would be my marker, but there were several balloons bobbing aloft, so I began pushing past people to get a better line of sight.

Then I heard the high-pitched squelch of a loudspeaker and someone beginning to make a speech, and then someone else took over, saying the rally and march to the San Tomás campus of Poli was cancelled because of all the police and soldiers gathering on the periphery. Most everyone was standing now, looking up at the balcony. I thought better of my attempt to locate Yvonne and Sonia. Instead, I turned around and began to make my way through the crowd toward the apartment building. Suddenly a series of flares fell from a helicopter circling overhead, two reds and a green.

Flashes of gunfire spit from the helicopter and from windows above the fourth-floor balcony. People around me began screaming, and a few fell to the pavement, including a woman near me who clutched at a gaping wound in her throat, gushing blood. Then gunfire erupted all around us as troops with fixed bayonets stormed the Plaza from all sides. The clatter of machine-gun fire raked the crowd and pounded the apartment building. Again, I looked up toward the fourth floor balcony. It had emptied. Confused and panicking, people raced one way across the Plaza then back again as they tried to escape the incoming rounds. Soldiers began to fall, too, wounded by what appeared to be sniper fire. For some reason, I didn't scream, even as bullets whizzed around me like angry bees.

A large man ran into me, knocking us both to the pavement. Several other people tripped and fell around us and on top of us. I could feel the thud of bullets striking them. I couldn't see anything, and I could barely breathe due to their weight. But the racket of sustained gunfire, screaming victims and pounding feet sprinting back and forth made it clear to me, even in my state of terror, that a massacre was going on all around me! My face felt wet and sticky. I couldn't raise my arm to wipe it away. I knew it was blood seeping onto me from the people sprawled beside me and on top of me. There was nothing to do but wait. Except the overpowering din of battle went on and on and on!

November 6
Hotel El Faro
Acapulco, Guerrero, Mexico
Berto's Story

CHAPTER 11

I turned on the overhead fan and opened the doors to my veranda, dumped a rucksack on the floor containing my necessities, including gun and ammo and the deputy's duds, then took a long shower. A plan had already formed in my head, but I wanted to run it by Prado. I filled a glass with ice and *reposado*, carved a slice off the ping-pong ball and fired up a joint.

Since I had his private number at the embassy, I didn't have to wade through several layers of bureaucracy. I filled him in. He also filled me in.

"That girl Marisol? She's Judicial Police."

"She set me up!"

"To simplify things. Judicial is working with the Guerrero State Police to track Daniel because they're also interested in locating Blanco's exact whereabouts to eventually take him out. But her loyalty is with Blanco because the State Police killed her father, Elvira's son-in-law, who was head of a communal coconut plantation. He led a resistance against a plan to take over and develop the land for a big tourist resort. Frenchy knows her well because he's living with her mother. He's using her place as his base of operations."

"Did I hear you say *'simplify'*?"

"Here it is. The most important thing is Daniel has met up with Frenchy, and Frenchy is getting him mentally and physically ready. Now we have to get you back in the game."

"What you mean *we, kemo sabe*? And what do you mean, *'game'*?"

"OK, Berto. You. But this *is* a collaboration with the embassy and CIA. Always has been. We aren't engineering anything, but we need to know what's going on with Judicial, the State Police and maybe even the Mexican army. And we need to know more about Blanco's intentions.

"You've been good about being persistent. Nutty, but persistent. I want you to re-join Daniel. I know Frenchy prefers a two-man op. More than two will raise suspicion. After all, we're talking about trekking into the mountains, eventually through the guarded perimeter of Blanco's stronghold. But we need your camera up there and someone who really knows how to use it. They're planning to use your camera, but who knows for what purpose and how proficient they can be under stress.

"I'm not certain about what's going to happen, but photo intel is essential. It shouldn't be too difficult for me to argue this point with Frenchy. His primary job for us is to locate and recon Blanco's territory, get inside, photograph and map out the layout. Pics of the captives, Yvonne and Sonia, are also very important. Marisol believes this is purely a rescue op. But we need to know where Blanco is located, exactly, and as the *numero uno guerrilla* leader in the country, what he's up to and how it could affect hemispheric security. It's not a Che/Bolivia mission... yet. So, how do you plan to get back in place?"

I plopped the slice of speed on my tongue, swallowed half the glass of tequila and took a giant hit off the joint. Then coughed for about a minute.

"Well," I finally said, "I can't just show up at *Casa Elvira*."

Prado agreed.

"So...."

I tell him about checking out of the El Faro and changing into the deputy's modest clothing. About working my way back to *Pie de la Cuesta's* bordello, very late at night. About making my pitch to Ana. Prado liked that.

"When should I approach Daniel? How?" I asked.

"Make certain Ana hides you, and stay put. No wandering around in broad daylight or at any other time. Give Frenchy some more time to get Daniel right. When that's accomplished, we'll send someone to take you to him, a trusted confidant."

"How will this someone find me?"

"Don't worry; it'll happen."

I parked the van where I'd left it before, changed clothes, substituted a woven-cotton shoulder bag for my rucksack and walked down to the bus stop. It was late, and I caught the last bus to *Pie de la Cuesta*. I made my way carefully up side alleys to the bordello and waited until closing time. My pulse was beating so fast I pressed my fist against my stomach and forced my breathing to slow down, which was not easy considering how high I was. Correction: High, yes, but also super alert. Through her window, I watched Ana count her earnings, then knocked quietly. Of course, I startled her, but when she came to the window, I took off the deputy's straw hat so she could recognize me. Her look of pure disbelief segued into annoyance, then something else, like intrigue. She opened the window. I reached in, dropped my bag on her floor and crawled through.

"Berto!" she whispered in her delightfully musical voice. "What are you doing here? I heard you were taken to prison!"

I explained my getaway, and that I needed a place to hide, maybe for a week, until I could join my friend who was planning to rescue his wife and child from Blanco's stronghold. A short, concise version of a long story.

"Aiieee! You can't stay here!"

"I know, *huisa*, but somewhere." I pulled a roll of U.S. dollars from my pack and put in in her hand. She counted it out, smiled, then lay back on her cot.

"OK, I know a place. Now take off your clothes and cuddle with me. We have only a little time. We have to leave while it's still dark."

I quickly complied with her order. But *"cuddle?"* Little Berto had another, much better idea.

Ana led me up a hill behind the bordello. Good thing she knew where she was going because in the dark of a quarter moon on the horizon I couldn't see a damn thing. Of course, I was hallucinating a little bit, speed mixed with enormously-satisfying afterglow. Eventually, we came to a narrow dirt road and a concrete-block shack with a molded-fiberglass roof. All the windows were open but barred for security. Wood shutters could be closed in case of rain.

"This is my cousin's house. No one will think to look for you here."

She fished a key out of her purse.

"He's working construction at the new tourist resort and usually stays at his girlfriend's house. There's no food here, no electricity, no refrigerator. There is coffee, a pot, and a small propane stove. Soon, someone will bring you water, condensed milk and some food. My little boy. He'll tell you the price, OK?"

"You have a son?"

"Yes. Rafael. He's only nine, but he's very smart and very discreet when I tell him to be."

She gave me a little kiss on the cheek, but when I tried to pull her closer she punched me in the chest. "Not now, Berto! *Más tarde.*"

Yeah. Well, I guess I'll lay in the cousin's rack and twiddle my thumbs 'cause there ain't nothin' else to do up here but wait. Sweat and wait. Solitary. *Más tarde* my ass.

I woke up way too late the next day to a knock on the door. A cute little boy, not as dark as Ana, but with the same fine-boned facial structure, wild black hair and perky nose. He was holding two plastic bags of groceries. A friend about the same age placed two plastic buckets of water just outside the door. I invited the boys in, but there was no place for them to sit, just one chair and a table and the bed. They knew I had nothing to offer them and that *they* were the ones hosting me, sheltering me. *De nada* was implicit in their body language.

"Eat and rest," Rafael said to me. "Soon you'll be ready to travel." Probably not a good idea to get too friendly, so I asked for the bill and paid it, plus tip. Rafael said he'd come by tomorrow after school, the same time, about noon.

I turned on a burner and heated water for coffee. One bag contained mostly canned goods and jars of refried beans, condensed milk, peaches, salsa, peanut butter and jelly but also a half dozen freshly baked *bolillos* and four bottles of pop. Something smelled good in the other bag. Tamales, wrapped tightly in tinfoil.

After eating, I washed out of the bucket, soaking a bandana with a little bit of soap, focusing on those parts of my body that smelled of sex and b.o., then a little more water to rinse the bandana and hang it to dry. I stripped down to my skivvies and took another nap, a long one.

When I woke up, it was to a cool breeze. It was dark and quiet, except for the buzz of an occasional mosquito and, from down below where the shacks were wired, music from the local radio station. Smoke from cooking fires. Cocktail hour. I pulled the bottle of *reposado* out of my bag, my K-bar, a couple green *limones*, my ping-pong ball, a joint and a pack of *Delicados*. My choice of after-shave cologne for this one-man party was a few dabs of mosquito repellent. I got high and sucked on lime slices, salt and the tequila bottle as if I were a greedy, nursing piglet. After everything clicked into synch, I lay back down on the rack to take advantage of my confinement and let my mind try to sort out ideas I'd been keeping in reserve for the past few weeks.

Like what the fuck I was doing here and why. Besides what Prado wanted.

I wish I hadn't been right about the hammer falling on those strikers. Tlatelolco was a game-changer for me. I usually keep a tight lid on the seething contempt I feel when I witness a terrible injustice. Instead, I project a clownish cover. I guess it's a major personality flaw, but it's who I am. Cutting through that husk and all my anti-commie bullshit, it's obvious to me — even to me, *el cabrón* — that the murder of those students, men, women and children was totally outrageous and unacceptable. Pinning the blame on student snipers is a ridiculous lie. Government snipers were firing on the crowd from right above us. Whether purposely or not, they even hit their own people. Right now, when I apply my guiding principles to that fucking massacre, the big picture hits me like a ton of bricks. The Plaza of the Three Cultures was visited many times by the student strikers and their allies, but also by the security team that helped plan the massacre. The individual lives of those victims were snuffed out by a totalitarian government and its brain-locked minions. Forget ideologies. Forget the Mexican-standoff shit due to the stubbornness of the two sides involved.

This is state-sponsored murder we're talking about. Washed away, over-and-done-with, and now the Olympics can begin. It was just abso-fucking-lutely wrong to deprive innocent, defenseless individuals of their lives. Lives that could've been fulfilled or not, but lives to be determined by free choices. And they almost got me, too. And some witness I am. No film, no record of the murder and mayhem, the conspiratorial ambush led by those men wearing the white gloves, the specially-formed Olympic Battalion. Even before being allowed to tour all the police precincts, hospitals and military-camp morgues with Daniel and Inez' parents, I was thoroughly searched. Couldn't even smuggle in a miniature camera.

The morgues overflowed with corpses. Men, boys, girls, women — some of them pregnant. All tables filled. Bodies ripped by high-caliber bullets and bayonets lay sprawled on metal morgue trays placed on the floors in every room and hallway. The stink of death overwhelming.

At one military-camp morgue I stood next to a girl, the sister of a 15-year-old boy, as a medical examiner told her she could claim his body only if she signed an affidavit testifying that he died from another cause, like a freakin' auto accident. The girl was there with her little brother, a kid about 10 years old. When he saw the brutalized body of his older brother — a beloved older brother — he leaped into the air as if shot, arms flailing, and collapsed onto the floor where he pounded the concrete and screamed non-stop. I saw scenes like that repeated too many times. Reminded me of Vietnam, commies vs. ARVN and their allies. But that was war.

I swear, if I ever get my camera back.... Forgetaboutit, *cabrón*. It's too late. The damage is done. The government won. Another "final solution."

I lit my joint and took a few more puffs. Who're you kidding, goat fucker? It's over. There's only one thing left to do, help find Yvonne and Sonia. There's gotta be a role in this for me.

I can understand Daniel's anger and why he doesn't want me to be a part of this op. He knows I fucked his wife. Or, I should say, Yvonne and I fucked each other. He left the door ajar when he took up with Inez, but I'm the one who kicked it wide open and filled the vacuum he left. It may be why he hasn't killed me. His guilt.

It happened the night he asked me to pick up his belongings after Yvonne kicked him out. I drove over to their house. It was late. Sonia was asleep. It was just Yvonne and me. His stuff was sitting just inside the door, but she was very upset.

She embraced me and held on a few moments, crying. This was the closest I'd ever been to her, smelling the scent of jasmine in her hair. I tried to diminish the excitement I felt, tried to just respond to her embrace with requisite tenderness. But it had the opposite effect on me. I just wanted to crush her, feel her hard breasts against my heart, grab her tight ass and press little Berto between her legs. But it was a brief embrace, like at someone's funeral. Which is what it nearly felt like, according to Yvonne.

"Come in, Berto. Come in and sit with me for a while," she pleaded. "I feel like there's a death in the family. I need someone to talk to. Would you like a drink?"

I'd guessed she already knew the story, but she wanted me to tell it anyway. How Daniel met Inez, what she looked like, was this girl really powerful enough to take Daniel away from her. I sipped shots of *mescal* along with a cup of fresh-brewed coffee as we navigated the modern-day trail of tears.

I went through the whole thing but in a way that would establish my empathy and give her some hope. How I couldn't really tell if he was crazy about Inez, which he seemed to be, or whether she was just a pawn in his game. How this strike story had mesmerized him, distracted him to the point of losing his mind.

"Yes," she said. "Losing his good mind. It's something that's happened to him before, looking out only for himself, going his own way. It had a hold on him when he was a kid, something maybe he never got over."

I played along, remembering that detail of his troubled childhood, crushed by the murders of his mom, dad and grandfather. The sheer evil of it which sank him into despair and which his uncles worked so hard to dispel. But, in reality, I just wanted to establish a level of intimacy which…might…lead to something.

I could tell she was exhausted. The school thing was over since the strike began. Now it was looking after Sonia, helping her leftie *gringo* friends who were being deported pack up their most important belongings and box up the stuff that could later be shipped to whatever leftie U.S. metropolis they came from. Berkeley, Madison, Boston, New York, even LBJ's bastion of illiberal education, Austin. Keeping abreast — *whoops, excuse me* — of events involving the National Union of Mexican Mothers with whom she'd developed particularly close friendships.

I yawned out of boredom. I was tired of trying to lift her spirits when all I really wanted to do was lift her mini-skirt, turn her to face the wall and take her from behind, beast that I am.

"I'm sorry, Berto. I must be tiring you out with all this talk. Plus you've probably had a long day chasing down stories."

I just nodded, trying to restrain myself.

"It's really late," I admitted, lying like hell because it's never too late for me. "I don't know if I can make it up the hill. Plus there's a big meeting tomorrow with Cogdill. An early meeting. Real early." How much more of a hint could I give?

"You can sleep on the couch. I'll get you some sheets, a blanket and a pillow."

I watched her climb the stairs, the mini-skirt rising rhythmically above her lithe, mocha legs each step of the way. I quickly combed my hair and pulled a bottle of mouthwash out of my camera bag, swished some around and spit out the window.

When she came down, we made up the couch together. I watched her every second: the tautness of her blouse against her breasts, the way her hair fell like a veil across her face, the natural satin sheen of her lips. She'd been sipping *mescal*, too, and she stumbled against me as we reached simultaneously to spread the sheets across the couch cushions. She regained her balance and stood straight, very close.

I didn't ask. I didn't hesitate. I just blurted it out. "I want to kiss you."

She put her hand against my chest. Closed her eyes. Her breath came fast and with the scent of *mescal*. I was determined to show my wanton desire for her, exploit the situation in the absence of the one whose desire for her was only a distant memory. I knew what I was doing.

We met like that several times, usually after long, agonizing and mutually-apologetic and regret-filled conversations over the phone. But I never took hesitancy for an answer, and I always showed up at the same late-night hour. My persistence won out along with my desire to reignite her sexuality which had been so repressed. And I ensured this with my secret weapon, the little ping-pong ball. Of course, I also adored her and hungered for her, more than any other woman I'd ever known. So my hope for this mission is that, somehow, I can at least see her one more time and see the look in her eyes when Daniel and I both show up at her door.

November 10 — 13
Laguna del Ejido y la Sierra Madre

CHAPTER 12

It was only after several treks into the mountains that Daniel felt more at ease sitting astride a hard saddle, riding a mule and with the mission. Before the first time, after he and Frenchy had saddled up and packed the mules, he returned to his *jacal* and began to dig out of the seabag his combat utility uniform, faded to a pale green after hundreds of washings.

Frenchy walked in. "D, what do you think you're doing?"

"Getting ready for bush country."

Frenchy laughed and tossed him a package. "No, no, no, *mon ami*. You have to look like me, broken in, *un hombre del campo* who has vowed poverty and service." He cut the twine and opened the package. "Graciela saved her husband's clothing, which is what you're going to wear. Yes, this is a military mission, but it can't look like one. Remember Lebanon? How we wore mufti? We're just taking goods up to a couple of families, making *palaver* about possible locations of Blanco's stronghold, staying overnight, making the return. Just like I always do."

"What about weapons?"

"I've already stashed almost everything we need with my people in the mountains. We don't take anything with us now. We could be stopped at any time by police, *rurales*, soldiers on patrol, maybe even a *cívicos* patrol because I'm establishing a new pattern with the two of us. In fact, I want us to be seen and stopped so they can see we're clean. Just a couple of religious zealots on a mission to serve the *campesinos*."

So Daniel dressed almost identically to Frenchy, including cheap *huaraches* and wide-brimmed straw hat with tassel in the back. Graciela beamed when they showed up at the corral, then suddenly burst into tears.

"Forgive me, Daniel, but at first glance you reminded me of Jaime, my husband."

In addition to the mules they were going to ride, they loaded two pack mules with store-bought goods, filled their flat, wool-covered Mexican canteens with water, then rode slowly up to the two-lane coast highway, crossed it, and followed a stream bed into a narrow canyon and a half-day's climb.

"Why not take the horses?" Daniel asked.

"For an obvious reason, D. *Campesinos* don't ride horses with leather saddles. Also, only mules can navigate the steep trails and rocky stream beds we'll be taking. Mules can see at night. They can carry heavier burdens farther. Horses are impractical. They're strictly for tourist beach rides."

About 100 meters below a plateau clearing, Frenchy stopped and dismounted.

"We'd better eat some cold C-rations here, D, because we won't get much to eat up there. And give the animals some oats, let them drink from the stream."

At the first settlement, they were welcomed by a young man and his wife, who was nursing an infant, the Molinas, Pablo and Estella, both short in stature, dark-complexioned, in their mid-20s. Frenchy received a hearty *abrazo* from Pablo, Daniel a tepid handshake. They were then directed to a small, shaded corral, populated by two scrawny burros.

"Just wrap the reins around the saddle horn, D. We won't be here long, and these animals aren't going anywhere."

They followed the Molinas into the shade of their *jacal*. Frenchy led them in a prayer, one of his favorites, which he repeated at every stop, Paul's Epistle to the Ephesians: "Put on the whole armament of God, that ye may be able to stand against the wiles of the devil. For we wrestle not against flesh and blood, but against principalities, against powers, against the rulers of the darkness of this world." Afterward, he and Daniel were treated to a snack of hot tortillas into which a pinch of rough salt was rolled.

Frenchy glanced at Daniel when they were presented with this modest meal, a look that conveyed that this was standard fare offered to visitors by these dirt-poor subsistence farmers whose day-to-day existence was precarious. They depended on Frenchy not only for spiritual affirmation because they were unschooled and couldn't read any of the Spanish-language JW publications or the Bible. But they also depended on him for necessities that augmented what they were able to scratch out of a small plot of *maíz* and a vegetable garden, irrigated, when necessary, by a muddy *acequia*, a simple open ditch with dirt banks that meandered from a nearby river which could be dammed with rocks. They also kept a few egg-laying hens that could be butchered when their egg-producing days had ended.

Before they began to parley, Frenchy went out to the mules, unpacked a couple of boxes, then distributed their share of goods including Spam, baby formula, new under-garments and clothing, rice, coffee, sugar, medical supplies — iodine tablets for purifying potable water, tetracycline and flagyl, bandaids in various sizes, hydrogen peroxide — and a special treat prepared by Graciela, a dozen strips of beef jerky.

The dispensing of gifts completed, Frenchy inquired about their well-being and whether Pablo had heard anything about the movements of Blanco's *cívicos*. Pablo glanced at Daniel then pulled Frenchy closer and whispered into his ear. Frenchy took it all in, nodded, gathered everyone close and led them through a final prayer, Psalm 21.

Afterward, Frenchy and Daniel walked out to the corral, remounted and resumed the steep climb through the canyon until just before sunset when they arrived at another plateau and a larger settlement. They removed the saddles and bridles from the mules and the remaining boxes from the pack mules, then tied the mules to iron stakes in the ground. They were greeted warmly by several peasant families, all short in stature but hardy and devout, who treated them to coffee, fresh tortillas plus one hard-boiled egg apiece. After a very promising intel conference and distribution of goods, Frenchy began to preach, beginning with the "fear not, little flock" passage from the Book of Luke and about how Satan pervaded the earth, causing pain and suffering. But not all suffering was Satan's doing, Frenchy reminded them.

"Some suffering is part of God's design to test, teach or strengthen belief in Him," he proclaimed. "The greater the suffering of innocent believers, the greater will be their reward after life."

With the larger gathering of peasants, who obviously hungered for his presence, he also read to them from a JW text, translated into Spanish; namely, the chapter on the origin of evil, about a dispute between God and Satan and how Satan was cast out of heaven and, acting through the serpent in the Garden of Eden, led Adam and Eve into sin.

"In Genesis 2 and 3," Frenchy preached, "Adam and Eve forsook God and rejected the knowledge He provided them. They believed Satan and his lies, literally following Satan as their God. As a result, God sentenced them and the rest of humanity born from them, to be cut off from Him. However, God determined to call and use a few men and women throughout human history to advance His plan to save all mankind.

"God has permitted Satan's rebellion to continue on earth," Frenchy continued, "in order to demonstrate to angels and beings on other worlds that his law is righteous and necessary, and that the breaking of the Ten Commandments leads to moral catastrophe." Then Frenchy read passages of the Bible. Revelations, Isaiah, Ezekial, Genesis, Romans and Peter. So that the people could better understand the nature of this evil.

It reminded Daniel of his Uncle Abe's Kabbalist, more-nuanced preaching years ago on the *sefiroth*, the Tree of Life. Daniel almost felt like preaching it himself, but decided it wasn't appropriate to his role as Frenchy's assistant.

"When God created the world and human beings, he withdrew

a part of himself in a shattering explosion of his divine light. Sparks of that divine light flew either back into its divine source or downward to the earth. God had to exile himself in order for creation to occur. But an accident of great cosmic proportion happened, and elements of the lower lights broke away from the divine and became the powers of evil. These powers are opposed to existence and cannot survive on their own. In order to be, the evil powers must derive spiritual force from the good, divine lights.

"In order to unify all existence, God created man to make righteousness victorious, to bring forth the downfall of Satan and all of his realm. When men do evil, more divine lights are brought down, evil becomes stronger, and the victory of good over evil becomes even more difficult. The world could be destroyed in this way.

"Our task is to fix the world, tikkun, through a constant effort of raising the holy scattered sparks to their divine source. It's a tough fight, but living a life of mitzvoth is the way to bring this about.

"God made evil in order that man can achieve a righteous state without any outside assistance, against maximum odds, requiring maximum efforts. What God wants is for us is to make the maximum possible effort to reach the heights we are capable of. Without evil, that would be impossible to achieve."

Uncle Abe preached that to Daniel just before his bar mitzvah, when Daniel was deeply depressed, unable to deal with the murders of his mother, father, and grandfather. At the time, those moral guidelines were held up to Daniel by his devout uncle as obligations, to charge him, even though he was a boy on the verge of symbolic manhood, with the responsibility that no Jew should avoid: To pursue the guilty ones until they were punished. But for a boy who believed he'd never possessed courage and who'd lost everyone dear to him and who'd lost what he'd most expected out of life, the entitled glory and treasures due a champion's family, the moral tenets and real-life obligations advocated by Uncle Abe became burdens he rejected. Over time, however, in spite of guilt still gnawing at his soul, by age 16, with constant counseling, Yvonne's devotion, and overcoming a series of difficult challenges compelled him to discover the truth about those crimes, risking his own life to bring it all to a just conclusion. But now here he was in the most profound fight of his life, and after Frenchy's preaching to his JW network — his sodality — Daniel vowed to emulate the courage that these peasants possessed.

It was clear that Frenchy relished the role of special operative, but it was becoming more and more obvious to Daniel that Frenchy was equally dedicated to his role as a Good Samaritan. It shook Daniel to the core to witness the enduring faith of Frenchy's people, despite their poverty and hardships. But it inspired him to hear Frenchy promise them that for their best efforts they would be saved. It so reminded him of Abe and Jesse's efforts on his behalf when he was so impoverished of faith. Later, alone in his straw bed, he tried to resolve his conflicted emotions, comparing them to those he had when he was a boy. But the onset of a debilitating headache short-circuited reflective thinking. Struggling to sleep, he felt close to a breaking point.

There were three major stream beds leading up into the mountains from Graciela's rancho. Branching from these were numerous lateral trails leading to water holes, lookout points and tiny settlements amidst a mountain range of lush, green jungle, sanctuaries of natural springs, clear streams and seasonal lakes. It was at these plateaued locales where *campesinos* had fled from harm and established their subsistence plots.

Paramount in everyone's mind was how grateful they were for the dry spell which had established itself in mid-September, because it had been an unusually-relentless rainy season with a near-cyclone thrown in for good measure. They confessed there'd been considerable concern about the persistent rain and subsequent fear that their meager plots of corn, beans, squash and melon would rot. But the rain stopped, and they proclaimed that God had blessed them with prolific harvests.

Daniel learned another aspect of *campesino* life in the mountains. Despite their new religion, they weren't passive people. They all spoke of their displeasure with the lack of basic services that only local governments could provide. Roads instead of paths, electricity, water wells, schools. They used Frenchy's network to talk to each other, and they came to an agreement that something had to be done to promote and encourage these civic improvements. They decided to form an organization, to petition the mayor and town council at nearby San Mateo, whom some regarded as sympathetic to their cause.

They didn't have faith that Blanco would ever help them get what they needed. He hadn't won their hearts and minds.

Luis Moreno, leader of the struggling subsistence farmers, summed it up for Frenchy. "When he robs small-town banks, working people lose their money because their deposits are uninsured. Whenever he commits a crime, it causes municipal governments to shy away from negotiating our pleas for assistance, lumping us all together. He talks a good game with his ideas and his revolutionary fervor, but he's never going to accomplish anything for us. He draws the authorities to us like flies to dung. He's a wanted fugitive. His days are numbered. We don't want to suffer the same fate."

However glorious the advent of the dry season was to the peasants, the aftermath of a wet spring and summer remained evident. Streams that Frenchy and Daniel rode alongside were running strong, and the ground was saturated in areas, even boggy. Fortunately, wherever they went, they always slept in the comfort of straw beds in raised-floor *jacales*. It would've been pretty much intolerable for Daniel to sleep outside, rolled up in a canvas shelter half, especially as his knee and back were already troubling him after all of the hours being jostled in the wood saddle. And severe headaches came and went. Fortunately, however, Frenchy's daily chiropractic work and foot massages allayed the most debilitating effects.

Once back at Graciela's rancho, Daniel received a much-needed massage by Lidia who'd also brought a meal prepared by Elvira of ceviche, red snapper, fried potatoes, melon and flan, and a good night's sleep, combat training resumed in the morning. Frenchy was enthusiastic, as always. Training charged his internal battery. But Daniel lingered on the mat, stretching, a far-away look in his eyes, a melancholy that rubbed Frenchy the wrong way. *He's worried about how Yvonne will receive him, and he's obsessed about finding that disappeared girlfriend instead of committing body and soul to the mission. He's also got that fucking thousand-yard stare that I've seen so many times before. Meaning that whatever confidence and determination about completing the mission he tried to own is about to drain out of him.*

"C'mon, D," he snapped, unable to tamp down the urgency in his voice. "Let's get into it."

Daniel appeared lost in his own thoughts. He wasn't worried about the adequacy of his physical fitness. Frenchy had seen to that. But beneath that hard, refined and tested knight's armor lay his real vulnerability: An undercurrent of brooding and emotional wreckage that could jeopardize the entire enterprise. "I'm not a Marine anymore," he mumbled.

Frenchy turned on his portable record player and put on a short stack of 45s to needle Daniel, which was a daily ritual: "Our Day Will Come" by Ruby and the Romantics, "Baby I'm Yours" by the Shirelles, "My Guy" by Mary Wells, and the ultimate killer, "Gonna Find Her" by The Coasters.

After stretch kicks, bag work and calisthenics, Frenchy dug the 12-ounce gloves out of his storage trunk and motioned Daniel into the ring. They circled cautiously, one way then another, each fighter trying to get outside the other's lead foot. Jabbing, kicking, grabbing, elbowing. A searching, feinting pattern. Half-speed, as usual, but from Daniel more like nonchalance.

Every time Daniel sparred, it took him back to his father's last tune-up before his title fight with Joey Maxim. During what was to be a friendly sparring match, a tall, top-ranked local welterweight, Joey DeYoung, suddenly and deliberately altered the pace in the third and final round when he battered Davey in a moment of furious betrayal. It happened because the Mendoza family was never going to let Raymond DiNardi take over the management of Davey's career. So DiNardi, out for revenge, plotted to derail Davey's first big opportunity for a title fight just a week away by convincing Joey DeYoung to join his stable of fighters and promising him a title shot of his own against Jake LaMotta. To prove his loyalty to DiNardi, Joey was ordered to deliver a disabling attack.

Not nearly satisfied, DiNardi then went on to commit greater mayhem against the family. Multiple murders. No title fight. The family's ambition thwarted forever. Lost in that reverie, Daniel stood flat-footed and too relaxed, and just at that moment, Frenchy pulled Daniel's head down and hammered him with knee lifts. He caught Daniel off-balance and bull-rushed him hard into the corner where the ropes seared his back.

...Joey raised both forearms and, like a blocking fullback, drove Davey against one of the ring stanchions. Davey's eyes widened in alarm....Joey, cursing furiously, rammed Davey repeatedly into the corner. Forced into an upright stance, trapped by Joey's leveraged thrusts, Davey could only raise his gloves and lean side to side to avoid blows and head butts. Then he crumpled to the canvas.

Remembering that turning point, that searing moment of betrayal, that bitter disappointment when his father's hope of winning his first title shot ended, Daniel dug deep. A hot rush of muscle memory, repressed anger and a powerful instinct for survival all kicked in at once. Daniel squatted, wrapped Frenchy's legs and dropped him to the canvas. Grappling wasn't his strong suit, but he had to get the savate fighter off his feet.

But just as quickly as he'd been pancaked on his back, Frenchy applied a leg choke around Daniel's midsection, ripped off his gloves and rained blows against Daniel's face, drawing blood from old scars and from his nose. *Please, God, don't let it be broken. I don't have time....*

A sense of urgency kicked in, along with an empowering rage. Daniel ripped off his own gloves, leveraged to a near-sitting position and hammered hard rights into Frenchy's head and neck until he felt the leg choke relent. Then he hooked Frenchy hard between the legs which freed him to finish.

Furious, mindless and oblivious to the consequences, Daniel stood far enough off the canvas to plunge all his weight, knee-first onto Frenchy's collarbone. Timed perfectly, it would shatter. Then he'd win.

But just when Daniel seemed to have full control and momentum, just before he dropped his weight, Graciela appeared out of nowhere, leaned over the ropes and raked a chair across the back of his head and shoulders. Down he went. Frenchy rolled over and, with Graciela kicking Daniel in the ribs with her bare feet and screaming,

Frenchy pinned him to the canvas, trying to avoid punches.

"It's over! Stay put! I was just trying to shock you back into reality! You are too a Marine! Just too damned temperamental for your own good!"

He slapped Daniel and blood sprayed in a fine mist across the canvas. "Wake up! You get too hung up on emotions you'll get us both killed!"

Frenchy grabbed Daniel by his shoulders and continued to slam him against the canvas until Daniel finally relented, moaning like a mortally-wounded animal, wrapped in Frenchy's arms. After a few minutes, Daniel angrily pushed himself to his feet, tense, fingers half-curled into fists.

Frenchy admonished him. "Look, I brought you to a boil for a reason! I want you to remember that level of commitment. This is where you need to be in order to be successful." Frenchy's tone shifted to one of encouragement. "You're the perfect commando: a tested fighter, a born champion."

Daniel relaxed his fists and staggered out of *Sala Frenchy.*

Graciela leaned against the ring ropes, her breathing labored. "He's too used to holding back."

Laughing. A high-pitched nervous laugh. "Maybe we should beat him up some more. Make him cry," Graciela said. "We've got to make him cry some more! Squeeze out the guilt, remorse and doubt!"

Frenchy glanced up at her, flashing a macabre grin through bloodied lips. "Good idea, but what do you mean, 'we,' mi amor?

"You know, Graciela, when you've been a winner all your life like he's been, but then you suffer big setbacks, it can be deflating. We have to help him regain his resilience. He's like his dad, Davey. After his wife and father were murdered, he retreated into himself. The family counselor told him 'every mourner wants to withdraw from the world; every mourner sees fatalism and despair. Get out of yourself and back on track.' "

"Frenchy, you've done your best, you've trained him well: *'aprende como si fueras a vivir siempre...vive como si fueras a morir mañana.'* "

Learn like you're going to live forever...live like you're going to die tomorrow.

"Although he's never killed anyone before," Frenchy acknowl-edged, "he's got a soldier's sense of duty. The kid's a true champion. I like him," he said, smiling through cracked and bleeding lips. "He could be me someday."

November 17
Pie de la Cuesta

CHAPTER 13

Another interminable sunset. So bored with being cooped up for a week and sleepless the past two days. Berto didn't even want to get high. Well, maybe a little, now that he thought about it. Enough cooking fires down below, he could fire up a joint and no one would notice the stench of *la yerba maldita*, the God-damned herb. Then again, he might as well also take a slice from the ping-pong ball and wash it down with a slug of *reposado*. Boredom won't last too much longer. Ana's son told him she'd be by early tonight, so he could get in a good one before she had to go to work.

In the order of things, he punched a *Delicado* out of the half-full pack and lit up. He should've at least done some calisthenics inside the house while waiting to join the mission. But, no. He didn't work that way. He only shot film, then got out of the way. *Nobody takes cover as well as me.* Anyway, a good long fuck with Ana was like a wrestling match. He already felt stronger...except in his legs which he could remedy with some squat thrusts. *Nah. Hold on. Save your strength for Ana.*

Feeling light-headed and at the outer edge of intoxication, Berto felt a sudden urge to look into a tin mirror tacked onto the wall. *Holy shit! The eyes staring back at me are those of a red-ringed horror-movie monster! Maybe I should lay off everything for a while...or at least scale back.*

He stretched out on the bed, trying to calm his blood pressure, his mind a jumble of thoughts about Yvonne, Tlatelolco and, unaccountably, one of the more gruesome search-and-destroy missions back in 'Nam.

Am I hallucinating?

He'd been so far away in his thoughts he didn't hear her footsteps in the alley, only the key turning in the lock. He glanced over as she entered. He could see by the light of the kerosene lamp her light blue work shirt with an embroidered floral pattern on the yoke and long, dark pants that revealed the lovely sway of her hips....

Wait a fucking minute! Ana only wears dresses, the easier to disrobe.

"Hello, Berto. Ana told me to tell you she apologizes for not meeting you tonight. But she said she's looking forward to seeing you again...when you return."

Marisol! I'm at a loss for words. Well, not quite.

It was a struggle, but Berto sat up in bed and swung his feet to the floor.

"You could at least apologize for having me arrested."

Putting it on her.

"It seemed like the best thing to do at the time."

Not gonna squeeze anything out of her, am I. "I know, you were only following orders."

"Like I said...."

"OK, OK, OK. But now the orders have changed, right?"

"Different people, different orders."

Looking around the little house, she had a confession to make. "I'm no longer Judicial Police; I just wired in my resignation. I'd been working two sides for a while, but now it's only one. I had a good boss, a decent enough guy, but my loyalty is with my family, my people, and a part of that means helping your partner locate his wife and child. It will be more clear to you once we get to where we're going."

Berto nodded, but seemed to have nothing to say. She thought that was strange.

"I said *'my family, my people.'* Don't you want to know what I'm talking about, or are you so drug-addled you haven't the wit to ask?"

"I know about your family," Berto admitted. "I know about Frenchy. I pretty much know about the rescue mission."

"How do you know these things?"

"Because Daniel's mentor in Mexico City has kept me informed. He wants me in on the deal. I was expecting someone to summon me. I just didn't know it was going to be you. Actually, I thought we had a thing going, you and me. But Prado, Daniel's mentor, set me straight."

Marisol shook her head, barely hiding her disgust. *He thought we had a thing going.*

"How quickly can you pack your belongings?" Marisol asked.

"Everything's right here. I can pack this shoulder bag in 10 minutes. But what's the rush? How about a drink? For old times' sake. At least the few times we spent together." *When I thought we were friends.*

"There'll be time for drinks later. But you need to know how serious this undertaking is, and you need to know more about me. Make a pot of coffee while I fill you in."

Reluctantly, Berto lit the propane stove, boiled water in a small pot for Nescafé. Marisol sat on the cot, hands on her knees, wearing an expression of strength and goodness, gesturing emphatically every now and then as she dredged up history, a painful history.

"You say you know about my family's involvement, right?" Marisol asked. "Prado told you about that?"

"A short version," Berto admitted, spooning the instant coffee into two clay cups. "The death of your father...."

"It wasn't a *death*, Berto," Marisol said, correcting him. "He was murdered. Murdered because he stood up to the state when they wanted to confiscate our *ejido*, our birthright, our communally-held coconut planation. Valuable property that our community had worked for 45 years. Our only major source of income.

"My father knew that at some point the government would take it from us, especially as tourism development began moving up the coast from Acapulco."

Berto poured boiling water into the two cups.

"Sugar? Cream?"

She shook her head and placed the steaming cup at her feet.

"I am the only child of Graciela and Jaime. But even though I was a girl, my father's plan for me was to go to university, graduate, join a state or federal police agency, maybe law school. He thought that I could help the *ejido* avoid disaster.

"I attended UNAM on scholarship where I became an honor student and a field hockey player of national renown. When it came close to graduation, I didn't want to wait to finish law school. I applied for enrollment in the Guerrero State Police. I passed a series of interviews and excelled in the physical test. The head recruiter was very interested in me, said I would be one of the few women cadets that year. My father was very pleased."

Marisol reached down for her cup, blew across the lip of it, took a sip. Berto could see her hand shaking.

"There was only one hitch. The recruiter was just like you: a womanizer, obscenely confident, very pushy. He let me know that acceptance depended on one thing: His seduction of me."

Berto stared into his cup, then looked up. Marisol sat erect, took another sip then patted her hair which was pulled and tied into a tight bun.

"When I refused, he tried to force me.... This occurred in my dormitory room. I broke away from his grasp and struck him repeatedly with my hockey stick. His wounds were severe. I phoned one of my professors, Guzman, a Judicial Police investigator...."

Berto nodded. "Yeah, I know him."

"Fortunately, he was in his faculty office. He told me to tie up the recruiter with my belts, wrists and feet, and he rushed to my room, cuffed him and arrested him. That was how I became recruited to the Judicial Police, and he became my mentor. Within a year, I became one of his assistants.

"When the government planned to expropriate the coconut plantation, I was able to alert my father and his people. They quickly formed a committee of resistance. Blanco became their champion and chief negotiator. But it was futile. My father was singled out as the principal agitator and was murdered. After that, the best that Blanco and the farmers could do was try to force the federal government to renegotiate a financial settlement. This was accomplished, but the payments to each farmer, while adequate compared to the first offer, meant nothing compared to the loss of livelihood."

Marisol reached down, drained the rest of her coffee, her fingers clenched around the cup so tight Berto imagined she could crush it. Instead, her posture deflated. She pulled her arms around her knees. Eyes red-rimmed, she glared at Berto.

"That's when I knew that my loyalty to Judicial Police — to Guzman, really — would always be secondary to my family, our people and to Blanco. At first, Frenchy didn't want you here. Now he's changed his mind, at the urging of Prado. And that's why I played you, and that's why I'm here tonight."

Chagrined for one of the few times in his life, Berto started to speak, but Marisol cut him off. She stood, grabbed his cup and walked to the sink, rinsed them both, turned them over and let them rest on the counter.

"We must hurry," Marisol said. "They're waiting for us."

Berto nodded. He got up from the bed, slid his feet into the deputy's sandals, donned the flat, wide-brimmed straw hat with the tassel in the back, and stuffed the rest of his essentials into his shoulder bag. He gestured at the deputy's appropriated apparel, which was no different from any peasant's because the local cops didn't wear uniforms, except for the guns they carried. "What do you think?"

Marisol appraised his look. *What I think is you need to lay off your drugs. More time in the sun would help.* "You look a little tired. But that was a smart move on your part, changing your appearance."

Berto grinned, his smile wide and fatuous. But there was no hint of acknowledgment or verdict in Marisol's deep brown eyes, just a steady glare.

"Because now you're a wanted fugitive."

His face flushed. He ripped off his hat. A look almost like

terror replaced the goofy grin.

"Wanted? It was a set-up! I wasn't even going to jail!"

"You're wanted for murder. When you slugged that deputy in the temple, it caused internal hemorrhaging."

Berto sat heavily on the cot.

"So now we have to gather you to safety…"

"…because I'll never get out of here alive?"

Marisol pursed her lips. "Exactly."

Wow! Ana took a bigger risk than I imagined.

"So, where are we going, and how do we get from here to there? Without being observed?"

She threw a shawl around her head and shoulders. "Fifty meters past here the dirt road ends. There's a set of stairs that leads to an unfinished lot and horses waiting behind an abandoned adobe house. We'll ride a few kilometers to where Daniel and Frenchy will be waiting for us. I hope you can deal with more boredom because you can't be seen by anyone. Until we set off on the mission."

Berto pushed off the bed to a standing position, then sat back down again before regaining his balance. "Man. I'm weak in the legs."

"*No es problema, ése.* Tonight we ride."

CHAPTER 14

After washing, attending to some cuts with hydrogen peroxide and butterfly taping, followed by a nap, Daniel stepped into clean shorts and limped to the dining area under the *palapa* shelter. It was mid-morning. Frenchy sat at the table, sipping tea, a mirror image of Daniel's cuts and bruises. Lidia sat beside him, wearing — incongruously — a white seaman's cap with shiny black visor.

"Pardonnez-moi, mon amí," he said, apologetically. "I'd greet you with a smile, but it hurts too much. I'm taking the rest of day off. So are you." He nodded at Lidia, who pulled a portable ice chest from beneath the table.

"Lidia will be your guide for the rest of the day. She's going to take you to a lovely, secluded spot at the lagoon where a hammock is fixed to a large shade tree. You can rest there, take a few swims, meditate."

"What about you?"

"I have some research to do. A man is coming to visit, one of my main sources in the network. He's pretty certain he knows the precise location of Blanco's stronghold. We'll try to pinpoint it on our topo map. It's close to the time when we go, so I'm also giving him the rest of your gear to take there, including the Colt Commander and knives."

A slight breeze riffled the dry palm branches overhead. Despite the heat, it sent a chill up Daniel's spine.

Frenchy again nodded at Lidia. She stood, her usual mirthful and flirtatious mien clouded by the task at hand, and Daniel felt embarrassed that she was in charge of minding him for the rest of the day. Still, he was grateful for the way Frenchy read him. A break in training was just what he needed, and he was also relieved that he didn't need to request it. His mind was a jumble of imprecise, conflicting emotions, and he needed quiet time to sort them out, to reach some kind of operational resolution.

He and Lidia grabbed handles of the cooler and, together, they carried it about a kilometer down a dusty footpath, their shower thongs slapping in care-free cadence. Lidia was a lovely young girl whose everyday demeanor was marked by an unusual combination of playfulness and duty. It's not that she reminded him exactly of Sonia, but this short trek to the beach harkened back to a time, a precious moment from the not-too-distant past.

Before leaving for Mexico, Yvonne wanted to visit her family at the Iroquois reservation. It was an unusually hot day in early June. With no one her age to play with, Sonia was restless and cranky. Daniel was exhausted after playing one-on-one with one of Yvonne's cousins, a very quick, aggressive midfielder who'd finished his first year on the Brant University lacrosse team and was getting ready to begin his fourth Red League season.

"Daniel, why don't you take Sonia for a walk to the dam?"

The dam was a small limestone pool formed after the time when glacial meltwater sought escape into the Iroquois valley. By late spring, when winter run-off had subsided, a stream meandered through deeply-fissured folds of the eastern hills. Under the shade of towering elms, volunteers made a pool by fitting layered, loose slabs of limestone across its lip. When an enervating heat crept into the valley, people showed up to bathe and shampoo their hair.

Hand-in-hand, Daniel and Sonia approached. Fortunately, by mid-day, they had the dam to themselves. They took off their worn and scuffed high-top sneakers and entered the water, their thin, cotton shorts billowing out until they were soaked through. Daniel reached out to Sonia and pulled her in circles until her sour mood dissolved into shrieks of laughter. Water beaded her deeply-tanned skin; her brown eyes sparkled with delight. Then she climbed into his arms and, together, they chanted the Iroquois prayer of Thanksgiving.

"Daddy, I wish we could stay here. I don't want to go to Mexico." She said this in earnest, her brow knitted and her lips tight in a flat crease. Water dripped from her long, dark lashes and ran down her cheeks like tears.

Daniel understood how, in spring, the rez seemed to Sonia like a magical place, a time when wildflowers erupted all around them, in the woods and blanketing the hills, varied in color and riotous in abundance: red trillum and blazing star, furry stalks of hepatica, bloodroot and buttercup, ferns, green dragon, brome and loose strife, columbine and clematis. As he held her, he reminded her about a special time with his Uncle Jesse, his mother's brother, the tribe's faithkeeper and most devout practitioner of the longhouse religion. About being harbored on the reservation when it was believed his life was in danger, about the Iroquois tradition of giving asylum to certain people who were in trouble.

Like Daniel when he was her age, Sonia loved to hear stories about her own father's fabled youth. She knew them in detail, but pretended she didn't, preferring, instead, to hear them repeated and repeated, especially from him. Today, she wanted to be walked through it again.

"Is this where Uncle Jesse took you when you had throat sickness?"

"You mean when I couldn't talk because I was so scared?"

"After Grandpa Davey was..."

"...when he was taken from me by those bad men, and after my mom and my Grandpa Jake died in the fire."

"Yes, Daddy; that time."

"No, dear one, this isn't the place. We only came here to soak in the cool water. Uncle Jesse took me to the stream above the dam...."

"...the day you walked with him and the False Faces to cure people with certain sicknesses? And Uncle Jesse taught you how to breathe?"

"Yes, love."

"I'm cool now, Daddy. Will you take me there and show me exactly how he did it?"

He toweled Sonia dry, tied her high-tops and they walked upstream to the site that overlooked the valley. He squatted on the bank of the stream. She squatted next to him. He cupped his hands and dipped into the stream and drank.

"Go ahead, Sonia, now you take some."

And just as he'd struggled to accomplish this basic skill nearly two decades before, Sonia cupped her little hands, dipped into the stream, then watched with dismay as the water escaped. So he cupped water for her and she drank out of his hands, and then he wet her brow and stroked her hair, a jet-black sheen.

"Try it again," Daniel urged. "Keep your fingers close together, one hand slightly overlapping the other." This time she succeeded. She took a drink, then another, then another.

"I didn't realize how thirsty I was," she said, her expression so earnest as she re-enacted the story from memory. Daniel smiled, his jaw muscles working, choking back tears.

"What next?"

"Uncle Jesse pulled a plump, tan root from his pocket, called heal-all. We'll just have to pretend we have it," and he mimicked taking it out of his pocket.

"What is it used for?"

"Mostly for sickness caused by being sad, like when a relative dies. But it also provides athletes with great strength. They chew it, spit on their hands and rub it on their muscles before they play lacrosse."

Sonia pretended to take the heal-all from her father's hand, chew it, spit in her hands and rub it on her arms and legs. "Like this?" she asked.

"Yes, dear."

"Then what?"

Daniel knelt and sat back on his haunches, looked out into the valley and the green hills beyond. His knee ached from being stretched so far, but he began to breathe in deeply, then exhale slowly, and with the repetition, the pain faded, and he relived the experience that Jesse wanted him to learn: to control his breathing and, by doing so, to reduce the fear that seemed to lodge like a knot in his throat, the knot that dammed his speech, the knot that — over time — disappeared and freed him to talk.

Sonia imitated his posture.

"Just sit still. Relax. Breathe in from the water and out to the clouds, like this."

He took a deep breath, held it, brought his right hand to his belly until he felt it fill, then gently pressed and slowly expelled it. Over the years, he'd become adept at slowing his pulse rate within just a few minutes, and he understood perfectly how Jesse wanted him to learn how to lessen his extreme anxiety through deep breathing. It was the first step toward learning how to concentrate, then meditate. It was something he did before every game, every bout, almost every key moment in his life, until he became so adept at this exercise that he no longer consciously thought about it.

"Like this, Daddy?"

Sonia took a deep breath, held it, but let it go too quickly, even before she could bring her hand to her belly.

"How far down did you bring your breath, Sonia?" he asked.

"Like to about here," she said, pointing to her throat. "I was afraid to hold it for too long."

"Let's try again," he said, changing his posture to focus exclusively on her, one hand at the small of her back, the other poised on the surface of her belly, the smooth, silky skin of a baby.

"Keep your mouth closed; breathe in through your nose, but slowly. Push out your belly so your breath can rest in there. Hold it...." Then he pushed gently against the little mound that she'd created.

"Now expel it, but slowly."

It took her a while to get the hang of the rhythm of breath in/ breath out and, after a while, she could put her own hand to her belly, breathe deeply, hold it, and slowly expel. But she grew restless.

"Can we go back to Grandma's house now, Daddy? Maybe there's some kids around I can play with."

"OK, love," he said, and slowly got to his feet, massaging the circulation back into his knee, rotating his hips one direction, then another.

"But, Daddy, will you get me some heal-all so I can take it to Mexico?"

Daniel smiled. "Yes, love, I'll get enough for all of us."

Heal-all. He did manage to obtain a supply of it, wrapped tightly in foil and stored in a metal tin. He'd stashed it in a bedroom bureau after they'd moved into their Mexico City cottage, but in the whirlwind that their lives soon became, he'd forgotten all about it. *I could certainly use it now.*

The trail through the woods led to a bright, open vista and the aqua lagoon. Water lapped gently across a white, sandy shore studded with sturdy mangrove trees. Where the water bathed the base of the trees it was stained pale brown. Lidia nodded toward a shaded, dry hillock, and that's where they deposited the cooler. Closer to the water, but still in shade, a honeymoon hammock beckoned.

"Do you have thirst?" Lidia asked, smiling, her even white teeth like pearls, sun-tanned feet glistening in the shallows.

Daniel nodded. "Yes! What do we have?"

Lidia unlocked the latch and opened the lid of the cooler. Tucked into ice was a gallon jar of Daniel's latest favorite beverage, made from hibiscus flowers called *jamaica* — ha-ma-eeka.

"Oooh, so much."

Lidia gazed at him. Not the look of an 11-year-old girl; rather, the look of an old soul. It seemed she was poised on the precipice of a transformative moment, the Indian in her totally present. Again, a chill ran up his spine.

"To replace the tears you are going to shed today," she

announced.

Daniel's brow furrowed, and he walked closer to the cooler. "What else do we have in there?"

Lidia reached in and pulled out a small sardine tin, sealed tent-like with foil.

"What's that?" Daniel asked.

She gently folded back the foil. Three, spindly, white mushrooms with small caps stood at attention in a layer of dirt. Lidia pulled them out and wiped them clean with the hem of her dress.

"Frenchy wants you to eat these," she said, solemnly.

Daniel smiled. "Not even one for you?"

She shook her head. "For you, only."

Daniel hesitated. This scenario wasn't what he'd anticipated. Frenchy knew he needed a day off. Not only to put their brutal confrontation into perspective, but also to just rest, stretch-out, swim in the lagoon, get another back massage from Lidia, lay in the hammock, observe the occasional squadron of white egrets skimming the water, searching for their mid-day snack.

But he continued to be troubled by opposed aspects of the mission. Frenchy's priority of reconnoitering Blanco's stronghold for the purpose of eventually taking out Blanco, and Daniel's priority of extracting Yvonne and Sonia. How, exactly, was this mission going to turn out? How much improvisation was going to be required as it proceeded? Because, as he'd learned so many times in the past, hardly anything ever goes according to plan.

Daniel had eaten psilocybin before, when Yvonne's anthro professor had taken them along with a group of students to Huautla, Oaxaca, and they tripped with the legendary *mujer del espíritu*, Maria Sabinas. It was exhilarating, but he really wasn't in the mood to once again confront his disunited self, saint and sinner. Not to mention his guilt over the unmerited grace that had been bestowed upon him since his childhood. How could he lack faith and be undeserving, yet continue to be blessed with good fortune? Especially now, when the disintegration of his marriage and Inez' disappearance weighed so heavily upon him. He had a lot of trouble imagining a positive outcome.

But he also understood that Frenchy had his best interests at heart, so Daniel put aside all trepidation and once again took a leap of faith. It was dangerous and intimidating, but in the end he was willing to accept the psychic challenge.

...protect yourself at all times.... God was once again the referee, but there was no protecting himself once he ate the mushrooms. He had to take what was coming.

He accepted the first mushroom and began to chew the bitter pulp while Lidia handed him a ladle filled with *jamaíca*. "It's best if you don't chew so much, just wash it down."

"What's that other bottle?"

"Berry-flavored *mescal*, for later. To soothe your good mind."

Daniel nodded as he swallowed the last of the little mushrooms. "Any other surprises for me?"

She reached into the pocket of her dress and withdrew a couple of tightly-rolled joints, filled, most likely, with Frenchy's special *mota.*

"What now?" he asked, smiling at the irony of this child/woman serving as his guide, feeling a little stupid.

"Maybe you should go for a swim, but don't go far and don't exert too much effort."

Sweat trickled down his brow and beneath his armpits and down the small of his back.

"What about you?"

She reached into her shoulder bag and pulled out a shawl, shook it open. "I'll wait there," she said, pointing to the deepest shadows provided by a lush mangrove tree, branches spread like a giant parasol.

The first unusual perception he noticed occurred when he dove into the lagoon and landed amidst a vast school of tiny silvery fish. They immediately darted away from him, then returned, seeming to contemplate him when he wasn't looking. As soon as he turned his head, a portion of the school sped away while from another direction, his blind side, another group approached him with captivating speed. This went on for about a minute, this game of tag, of hide-and-seek. Whenever he tried to capture their gaze, each silvery swarm would slam on their brakes just inches from his face, then speed away. He started to laugh, momentarily forgetting he was submerged. He arose from the water, sputtering.

He looked back to where Lidia was sitting on the outspread shawl. She waved. He sank back onto his haunches, eyes just above the water, turning in a slow circle. The surface was quiet for as far as he could see, and it felt a perfect, soothing temperature compared to the cold Pacific whose waves constantly roiled along the western shore and which he could see occasionally as they broke against a distant jetty. A breast stroke carried him out a little ways. The only waves he would experience this day were internal surges of ecstasy.

Perfect buoyancy, perfect balance and rhythm. In Oaxaca, they'd tripped in a *barranca*, and he leapt from rock to ledge to rock along an icy stream, as sure-footed and pain-free as a boy who'd never endured what he'd endured, who'd never lost what he'd lost. Everything flowed with the surge of pure, restorative energy, and he had no need for memory, just experience. That was the best part.

He lost track of time, of how long he'd been floating in the water, but when he realized he felt chilled, he knew it was time to let the sun warm him. And that began a pattern of returning to the sandy beach and re-immersing into the lagoon and back to the beach, the rhythm of perfection.

Finally, he gazed at the horizon, huge billowing clouds sliding slowly toward him. It was a moment he both cherished and dreaded. So he began to contemplate, unlocking the door to the place where he stored his innermost hopes, dreams...and fears.

What's wrong with me? Why did I stray? Why am I resisting the sense of urgency I should possess in order to rescue Yvonne and Sonia? I feel like my mind isn't working right...decisions regarding my family...Inez...blameless Berto. Wicked headaches, occasional blurred vision, loss of balance, writing down things before I forget them.

Daniel sat on the sand, legs crossed, staring at the most bulbous, towering cloud. It seemed to be stalled in place, not really going anywhere, and Daniel knew it was meant for him. It took the shape of the back of a human head. And when it began to turn, he knew it would be Uncle Abe. He waited for his exalted emissary with a mix of profound sensations, including trepidation and joyous gratitude, a transcendent moment that defied explanation. The face was in no hurry to seek him out. It just rolled in his direction, first recognizing Daniel out of the corner of his eye, then rolling to directly face him. Unlike the last time in Oaxaca when he berated Daniel, Uncle Abe was beaming, his eyes dancing with joy, blessing him, approving him, redeeming him.

"You've been damaged, Daniel, and you've suffered great losses. But trust me. Help is on the way. Nothing will deter you from fulfilling your legacy. The path will be clear to do what is necessary. Yvonne and Sonia are waiting. This is the moment Uncle Jesse and I have trained you for, the moment you've prepared for your entire life. You can do it. You will win, my boy. Then you can go back and find Inez."

Daniel cried, so profound was the relief he was experiencing. He wept like a man who'd finally and completely breached a wall of uncertainty. Uncle Abe's grinning face remained, loving Daniel, fixed, while the other clouds continued to roil and roll past. Then a shaft of light peeked through the clouds, and he realized Lidia was standing beside him, beckoning him toward the hammock where she poured fresh water over his head and body, wiped him dry, carefully daubed his scar wounds, quenched his thirst with ladles filled with the sweetest most refreshing *jamaica*, handed him his sunglasses. And when he lay back and gazed at the sky, the cloud formation had passed, and the sun began its slow descent to the horizon.

CHAPTER 15

Marisol and Berto rode in at 9 p.m., Marzisol loosely holding her reins, back straight, Berto gripping the saddle horn, pushing his feet against the stirrups to keep himself erect, a cigarette stuck between his teeth.

Frenchy and Daniel sat at a table under the *palapa* shelter. "Your partner looks tense, D, uncomfortable."

"So would you," Daniel said, "if you were high and hated horses."

"Ha! Wait until he gets on his first mule. That should keep us entertained. I guess we all can't look like Pathfinders. Better to have one newcomer who's more religious fanatic than *vaquero*, one who's willing to suffer in order to do good work."

"Now that's really a stretch, on both counts."

Frenchy laughed.

"What about Marisol?" Daniel asked.

"She's a real *vaquera*. Been riding since she was three years old. Shooting since she was six. Are you concerned that Berto's not fit enough for the mission?"

"He could've used more preparation, but he'll fit right in. Maniacal vigilance is his singular strength. Berto loves living in a state of constant stimulation. When it doesn't happen in real life, he simulates it with bennies or crystal meth. He's always primed and ready to roll. He's also had plenty of combat experience in 'Nam. He wasn't just a combat photographer. He was more than willing to pick up a gun if conditions demanded it."

Daniel told him about Berto's Bronze Star commendation, about how he could've bailed on the Marine helicopter pilot who went back to an LZ seven times to pick up wounded jarheads, how he manned the chopper's M-60 machine gun that enabled the pilot to evacuate an entire platoon. Even performing emergency first aid with ad hoc training he'd picked up from various corpsmen during his tour, including a tracheotomy using a ballpoint pen.

"Berto also liked to go out into the bush with one particular five-man scout/sniper team for days at a time. Just to scout, mind you. But accidental confrontations with VC and NVA did happen, and it was common knowledge he could be counted on to 'hit in the clutch.' "

"¿Cómo?"

"It's a baseball metaphor. Performing under pressure. Late in the game, at a very crucial time, a batter gets a base hit that pushes his team toward victory."

"You play baseball, too?" Frenchy asked.

"No."

"Then how do you know 'clutch?' "

"Most American males know many sports, even if they don't engage. They talk about them, read about them, watch them on TV, listen on the radio. But combine sports with politics, like the Olympics, the baseball word 'clutch' becomes a whole other story, an extended and dangerous metaphor."

"Tell me about it," Frenchy said. "I hardly know what happened in the Olympics, except for those black Americans who raised their fists. Wearing black gloves. One guy on the right hand, one guy on the left hand. Photo on every newspaper front page. Pissed off the Mexicans."

"Black American Olympians were trying to figure out ways

to symbolically demonstrate their commitment to civil rights in the U.S. Equality and justice, dignity and respect. What the civil rights movement is all about. That black-gloved gesture was misinterpreted as anger, rebellion.

"Their leader, a black university sociology professor in California, created the Olympic Project for Human Rights. At first, he proposed boycotting the Olympics. Bob Beamon, for one, said no; he wanted a gold medal in the long jump, which he won...by a foot, setting a new world record.

"The range of responses among athletes and civil rights activists in the U.S. to create some kind of protest in Mexico City reminded me of the National Strike Council. There were *acelerados* and moderates. Among the black Olympians, some, like Beamon, chose modest symbolism; he wore black socks.

"Lee Evans, the quarter-mile gold medalist, grew up picking cotton and grapes in fields near Fresno. He received a telegram from the Ku Klux Klan the day of his event. After much agonizing and fearing being shot dead, he and the second- and third-place finishers — all black Americans — decided to wear black berets on the medal podium. Yet he was chastised by *acelerados* in the U.S. for not going far enough.

"George Foreman, who won the heavyweight boxing gold medal by beating a Russian, celebrated his victory by waving a miniature American flag while walking around the ring. He was called a traitor to his race.

"The most demanding *acelerado* was their leader, the sociology professor. But the last time he saw the black Olympians was when they completed their training at Lake Tahoe, which is at a similar altitude as Mexico City. That was June. He chose to not even attend the games here, fearing for his life."

"*His* life," Frenchy said. "What about the black Olympians?"

"*Exactamente.* They were left on their own to decide how to protest. Most declined. A few, like Beamon, wore black socks. Subtle. The women were just plain ignored. Only the two 200-meter sprinters, John Carlos and Tommy Smith, decided to make the grand gesture, bowing their heads and raising their fists while standing on the medalists' podium. Smith's wife bought a single pair of gloves for them to divide. I wasn't even there, freaked out about Yvonne and Sonia. Trying to locate Inez. Berto took that photo. The Mexicans booed, furious about the violation of Olympics decorum. Those *ricos* care nothing about racial equality. Especially in Mexico."

"Then Carlos and Smith were heroes?" Frenchy asked.

"But at what personal cost? This may be one of those heroic decisions — 'damn the consequences, we're in the right' — that can come back and bite them in the ass. They were hustled right out of the country, kicked out by Avery Brundage, the head of the International Olympic Committee and banned from competing in the Olympics for life. Either 'those boys' go home for violating Olympic standards of due order and decorum, he demanded, or the entire U.S. team would be disqualified.

"Frenchy, your point of view pales in comparison to the big shots. It'll be interesting to see how things turn out for them.

"In the past — Jesse Owens, for example — just winning was proof of your worth. He achieved everlasting fame for winning four gold medals in the 1936 Berlin Olympics and for pissing off Hitler. But too many avenues for financial enrichment were closed to him due to racism. He actually ran against race horses after he returned to the U.S. Now, it's not so much the message, it's the way it's delivered. It's a new era. Smith and Carlos decided to push the envelope. Hopefully, the envelope won't seal up on them."

Frenchy looked pensive. "I'm a nigger, too, D," he said, startling Daniel.

"¿Cómo?"

"I'm a *mestizo* just like you. My mother is Algerian. My father is white, military, from Marseilles. He was stationed in the colony. As a little boy in France, I had a very rough time. Got the shit kicked out of me. Over and over. The French are very racist. Only the Foreign Legion loved me. I don't ever want to go back there. Actually, D, this is the best place for me."

Daniel reached over and grasped Frenchy's arm. *Mestizos... maybe so much more.*

When Marisol and Berto reached the corral, Marisol raised her right leg high in the air like a scissors kick and slid from her saddle, then gathered Berto's reins while he dismounted, holding onto his horse's saddle horn for dear life. They walked the horses into the corral, removed saddles and bridles, and headed towards the *palapa* shelter, Berto rubbing his buttocks with each step.

"What are you going to say to him?" Frenchy asked. "You caused him a bit of grief."

"What are *you* going to say to him? You got his ass thrown in jail."

"Yes, but look at the adventures he had…and Ana," Frenchy said.

"It *is* a consolation to know he can think on his feet."

Frenchy and Daniel slid their chairs back from the table and stood. Marisol skipped onto the veranda and embraced Frenchy. He kissed her on both cheeks. She extended a hand to Daniel and smiled coquettishly, somewhat embarrassed because of her previous subterfuge on the bus but also because she realized that the attraction she initially felt toward him remained strong. It was genuine. In return, Daniel held her hand a bit longer than he should've, a dear moment of mutually-recognized admiration that, just as soon as it happened, he felt ashamed and let go. *The imperative to resist has to be exercised; that's all there is to it.*

"Good to see you again, *amigo*," she said. "I…I understand you've been training."

Before Daniel could reply, Berto chimed in, facetiously mimicking a southern drawl, grinning. "Y'all look like you've been training for a title fight. What gives?"

Frenchy and Daniel traded knowing glances. "Just a family scuffle," they said in unison, their diverse dialects melding playfully. Then they laughed loudly.

"Seat yourselves," Frenchy said. "Are you hungry?"

"Is there coffee? Some cake?" Marisol asked.

Berto reached into his shoulder bag and pulled out his bottle of tequila.

"Put that back, *mon ami*." Frenchy said. "We have something special."

Just at that moment, Graciela and Lidia emerged from the shadows carrying trays of cake, coffee and *mescal*, plates, cups and utensils.

Frenchy smiled his lethal smile and extended his hand. "My name is Frenchy. I...."

Berto reached across the table, clasped his hand. "I know who you are, man. Heard about you and Daniel back in '58. I have to admit, it's no surprise to see you here since Prado briefed me on the mission, recently in Acapulco, during a phone conversation, but even before Daniel split from Mexico City. Told me just the other day I needed to be included." He nodded toward Marisol. "Said someone would pick me up."

Daniel kept his hands in his pockets, feeling awkward and also a lingering resentment. But he feigned nonchalance and fellowship. "Have a seat, Berto. We'll catch you up on the plan."

Berto waved him off. "No thanks, bro. If you don't mind, it was a short ride, but my ass is sore as hell. I think I'll stand for a while until the blood circulates where it's needed."

"Do you want a pillow, *señor*?" Lidia asked.

"It's not necessary," he responded, then changed his mind. "Well, OK, if it's no trouble."

Lidia smiled. *"Para servirle,"* she announced and dashed back into the shadows.

"So, what gives?" Berto asked. "You worked pretty hard to ditch me."

Daniel waited for Frenchy to respond, but when it wasn't forthcoming he realized it was better if he took the initiative. "We need your help."

Berto sighed. *I'll just have to wait and figure out this change of heart. Put up a stoic, cooperative front.*

Lidia returned with a plush cotton pillow. Once Berto was seated, they discussed the plan hashed out days before by Frenchy and Daniel. It was going to be the four of them riding into the mountains. Frenchy, Daniel, Berto and Marisol.

"The Four Horsemen of the Apocalypse!" Berto blurted out.

Frenchy and Daniel glanced at each other, then at Berto, astonished by his impertinence. Marisol shook her head. *He speaks and acts just like he was described to me. Ungovernable, a man with no restraint, no tact. How much time would be wasted keeping him under control? Would the job fall to me?*

A topo map was spread out on the table. Frenchy traced the route they would take to the edge of Blanco's stronghold. One of Frenchy's most astute men, a devout member of the JW network, would meet them there, about 3,000 meters up in the Sierra. The stronghold was located on a high plateau, 15 square hectares, with mountains and a lake bordering on the east, dense forest and hills to the south, a steep, forested descent to the west.

"We'll infiltrate the compound from the north, off this dirt road," Frenchy said. "This road sees quite a bit of traffic — men on foot or horseback, an occasional four-wheel drive vehicle. It's regularly patrolled and *cívico* pickets are positioned high up in tree platforms and behind log barricades hidden behind stands of bamboo. There are clear lines of fire to the north because the *cívicos* have cleared quite a bit of forest and tied down brush.

"Rescuers will escort Yvonne and Sonia to exit the compound the way you went in. We have a plan to stymie pursuers."

"But what if something goes wrong and they can't leave that way?" Berto asked.

"In that case, we do have another option. But it's our one and only option." He moved his finger across the map. "There's an emergency escape path here to the southwest, very narrow with steep hills on each side. It could be a formidable defile for any pursuers. This path leads to another path which, in turn, leads to a narrow dirt road which forks in two directions, west to the coast and south to the town of San Mateo."

Frenchy also pointed out a small airstrip just to complete the recon survey, although it seemed of no strategic importance. It had been carved along the eastern length of the plateau, just above the compound. It was built to accommodate a single-engine Cessna piloted by a *gringo* from California, a trusted smuggler who flew in an out several times after the harvest season, bringing in weapons and supplies Blanco needed and leaving with as much *mota* as the aircraft could safely carry.

"How are we going in?" Berto asked.

Frenchy was tempted to respond, what you mean, we.... But decided to keep levity out of the discussion.

"It's been decided that just you and D will go in. They'll be expecting the two of you because you're a known team, inseparable."

Berto's eyes grew large.

"You mean, just walk right in?"

"Yes," Frenchy said. "But not walk. Ride right in."

"Armed...?"

"No weapons, just your camera. You ride in, insist that you're there only to remove Yvonne and Sonia from Blanco's protection."

"Those words?"

"Exactly."

"But what if he doesn't agree to let them go? What if he has other plans? What if Yvonne doesn't want to leave?"

"We'll play it by ear; there's no rush," Daniel said.

"They'll know someone led us to them," Berto asserted. "We don't know this country. Or at least we're not supposed to know it."

"D will tell them he had help from the French missionary he met at *Pie de la Cuesta*. The missionary pointed them in the general direction and D just reconnoitered the way. Blanco probably knows he's had ample recon training, assuming Yvonne has told him."

"How will you know what's going on inside?"

"Don't worry, I have a man there who works regular sentry duty. Like all sentries, he carries a hand-held radio. We have two radios tuned to the same frequency. He'll know our every move once we're outside the compound and, hopefully, we'll know Blanco's every move. If we need to smuggle in weapons, more supplies, he can do that."

"What will you be doing all this time? It could be days."

"Me and Marisol and my boys from the network will be making defensive preparations, in case anything goes wrong and we need to facilitate our withdrawal."

"What kind of preparations?"

"You're not privy to this information," Daniel said, firmly. "It's better you not know."

"You mean they'll torture our asses?" Berto asked, his voice rising in alarm. "Sounds risky."

"Are you willing?" Frenchy asked. "You went through a lot of trouble to make this trip."

Berto threw back a shot of berry-flavored *mescal*, reflecting on the reason why he insisted on accompanying Daniel on the rescue mission. Yvonne. *I continue to test the thickness of the ice. This all has to do with the power of pussy, and it's written in railroad sign-sized letters: Get Off The Track, The Train Is Coming. But the challenge is there, ever-lurking.*

"OK, I'm game."

Frenchy nodded. "*Bueno.* This could turn out to be a very good opportunity for you," he said, mimicking the taking of photographs.

"When do we leave?"

"Tomorrow," Frenchy replied. "We're five days into the last quarter of the moon. You probably noticed on the way over here."

"Yeah, it was darker than shit."

"It's two days to the new moon," Daniel said. "So at night for the next week..."

"...it'll be darker than shit."

"Correct," Frenchy said. "Best time to hunt."

"Can I have my camera back?"

Marisol reached into her shoulder bag. "We've been keeping it safe for you, *amigo.*"

The next morning, after a substantial breakfast and Graciela's stoic farewell embraces, they left. Four mules to be ridden, three pack mules. Frenchy took point, followed by Berto and Marisol with Daniel last, leading the pack mules. It was more humid, the air was still, and when Daniel glanced back before they began their ascent, the horizon was a pink glow, charcoal-gray clouds banking.

The going was slow and deliberate, beginning along the stream bed Daniel and Frenchy had always used, branching off into a narrow canyon cimmerian with jungle canopies that remained lush, despite the end of the rainy season. After Berto fell off his mule a few times,

Frenchy suggested folding a rain poncho and placing it on top of the saddle. Grateful for the suggestion, he did, uncomplaining. After a few hours, the canyon stream bed began to level and they reached a dirt road. Frenchy raised his right arm and the troop halted.

Frenchy dismounted, looked both ways, then crossed the road on foot. He began to give the all-clear signal, when something caught his eye. He crouched low to the ground and crept further along a forest trail. Daniel thought he remembered a grassy plateau where some *campesinos* took their small herd of goats and a few mules to graze. Perhaps Frenchy would decide to take a break there, let the mules graze a bit before heading further up the mountain.

After a few minutes, Frenchy reappeared at the road, looked cautiously in both directions and, in a crouching jog, crossed the road. He signaled for the others to come parley.

"Qué pasa, mi capitán?" Marisol asked.

"You're not going to believe this," Frenchy whispered. "But there's a helicopter parked in the middle of a grassy meadow."

"You mean," Daniel said, "the spot where we've previously seen *campesinos* graze their...."

"Yes," Frenchy said, his brow furrowed. "That one."

"So what do we do?" Berto asked, *sotto voce*.

"If something weird is going to happen, we'd be better off on the other side of the road. Otherwise, we might have to turn back. We probably won't be detected if we take this little hunting path that begins over there and veers along the tree line to where there's a cluster of *amate*, umbrella plants. We'll stop there, hobble the animals."

He reached into his saddlebag and pulled out empty grain sacks used to transport *mota*. He quickly cut them into squares and distributed rolls of twine. "Wrap the hooves. When you're finished, we'll move out."

Ten minutes later, dismounted, the troop led the animals across the road and followed the hunting path for half a kilometer until they reached the stand of *amate*, then hobbled the mules and waited.

Within minutes, they heard the sound of truck engines approaching. Almost exactly where they'd previously crossed the road, three small trucks parked. State Police climbed out the back end. They wore their trademark blue military uniforms with bloused trousers over combat boots and soft blue caps and carried M-1 carbines and shotguns. Other men, officers who wore straight-legged blue trousers and long-sleeved white shirts without caps and who carried drawn pistols, waved them into position, barricading the road, looking north.

An explosive ignition of a large engine startled the animals, followed by the whine of the helicopter's blades revving up.

"Berto!" Frenchy hissed, pulling a rolled-up green rain poncho from behind his saddle and shaking it open. "Bring your Leica and the telephoto lens!"

Berto reached into his saddlebag and jogged over to Frenchy.

"Put this on, including the hood. I'm going to give you a lift into this tree. Climb until you get a view of the chopper and the road. Photograph whatever you see. I trust your judgment."

"*Madonna*," Berto whispered as he slipped into the parka. Frenchy tied a rope around his waist to keep the parka from billowing and snagging on branches. He gave him a leg up, and Berto quickly climbed to a height of about 20 meters where he found firm footing amid dense foliage. Pushing aside branches, yet remaining surreptitious, he tested his aim in two directions. Toward where he believed the chopper was parked and toward where the police had barricaded the road. He signaled to Frenchy that he was set.

All of a sudden, the chopper lifted off. Berto recognized it by its dominant fat bubble of forward compartments. A Sikorsky UH-34 Seahorse medium transport. He aimed his Leica with the telephoto lens and quiet shutter. The chopper rose to about 100 meters then steadied while some kind of struggle inside ensued, ending with a gunshot. Berto could see a man being tossed out. Then the chopper banked and flew off.

"*Merde*," Frenchy muttered as he witnessed it. "*Parti avec la vente*." Gone with the wind.

Then the sound of another engine came from the north. Berto could see a yellow cattle truck with red wood-fence siding making its way slowly along the narrow road. Several dozens of raggedy *campesinos* stood in its bed. The truck halted when it came to the police barricade. Berto began snapping photos. Everyone was ordered off and herded to the side of the road. Once there, an officer stood beside them and raised his arm. All the soldiers drew back the slides on their semiautomatic weapons and pumped shells into combat shotguns. All except one.

"¡Chale!" he exclaimed. *"¡Ni creer que voy a hacer eso!"* Forget about it! Don't even think I'm going to do that!

The officer unholstered a big revolver, thumbed back the hammer and, with sinister nonchalance, shot him. Then he raised his arm again. His men took aim. When he dropped his arm, the police let loose a barrage that lasted only a minute, although to the flabbergasted troop, it seemed to last a lot longer. Nearly every *campesino* went down, except a dazed few who wandered aimlessly. The officers went through the pretense of placing antique shotguns and revolvers in the hands of some of the victims so the police could say they were attacked and responded only to save themselves. Then the commander directed his men to board their small trucks and they drove off. Berto descended from the tree, losing his footing several times, clearly rattled.

"What did you see?" Frenchy asked.

Berto told them what they saw for themselves. A man being thrown from the chopper.

"Was he dead or alive when they tossed him?" Daniel asked.

"Well, the poor bastard might've been shot first, but he looked alive when he got tossed, wind-milling his arms. Don't know about now."

Marisol was in tears. She could barely speak, but she managed to ask the next question foremost in everyone's mind: "And what did you see on the road?" Fearing the worst.

"Matanza. Just like Tlatelolco. Seems to be the season for it."

"I'm going to take a look," Frenchy said, looking more grim than Daniel had ever seen him. "D, you and Marisol go find the hombre tossed from the chopper. If he's dead, leave him there. Nothing we can do about it. Berto, how many photos did you take?"

"A full roll, 24 exposures."

"Give the film to me. Stay with the animals."

Berto took out his pack of *Delicados* and began to punch out a cigarette.

"*Amigo*," Frenchy warned, waving his hand. "Put it away. No smoking now."

Frenchy pocketed the roll of film and jogged to the scene of the crime.

Daniel and Marisol walked back to the road and north toward the stream bed that would take them to the embankment just below the meadow.

When they reached the spot, he clambered up, grabbing tree vines and branches to help propel him to the top. Marisol followed, gasping because she was still severely shaken. When they reached that part of the meadow that had been flattened by the down-draft of the chopper's powerful rotor blades during landing and take-off, Daniel signaled her to venture one way while he would scout in another direction. The grass was waist high.

"Keep me in view," he said. "If you find the body, re-trace your steps and get me."

She wiped sweat out of her eyes with a handkerchief and started off.

In a matter of minutes, she discovered the body of the man thrown from the chopper. He waved a hand, weakly. She used her handkerchief to stifle a scream. The man was still alive, but barely. She turned and ran back to where Daniel was searching, ran right into his arms, sobbing.

"Sshhh, sweetheart. *Cálmate.* We have to be very quiet. What did you find?"

Marisol clung to him, trembling, her eyes glassy with tears. She could barely form words.

"We have to hurry back. He's still alive."

He followed her and saw a man who looked as if he was taking a nap after a picnic in the country, except his arms and legs were bent in unnatural positions, like a discarded marionette. Blood was frothing at his lips. He was choking. As Daniel knelt next to him, Marisol cradled the man's head in her arms, beside herself with grief.

"Don't!" the man rasped, "there's...no... time. What... are... you...." His voice trailed off.

"We were on our way to Blanco's stronghold," Daniel said, "on a mission to meet him."

The man blinked his eyes as tears leaked out. He looked like a hard-working *campesino*, cracked skin and callouses on his hands, deeply-lined face. Daniel took off his hat and held it over him to keep the sun out of the man's eyes.

"What's your name, *amigo*?" Marisol asked.

His face grimaced with pain. "Moreno...Luis Moreno.... I'm...."

Daniel exchanged glances with Marisol. "Who are you?" Daniel asked, holding the man's hand.

A look of confusion clouded the man's face.

"Moreno.... Luis Moreno."

Daniel shook his head, remembering a conversation Moreno had with Frenchy a week previously.

"How did you wind up in that helicopter?" Marisol asked.

"Gustavo Olema...head of the State Police...." A froth of blood bubbled over his lips. Marisol wiped his mouth hoping he could breathe, hoping to hear more.

"Very angry...wanted to kill my people." He coughed up a sheet of blood which she washed from his face with a splash of water from her canteen. He gasped for air, wheezing. He could only manage phrases.

"Why was he so angry?" Marisol asked.

"I don't know. They held me in custody...wasn't too bad.... But something happened."

Marisol buried her face in her hands. "*Dios mío*, it's just like what happened to my father."

"I'm so sorry, Luis," she said, feeling helpless and distraught, her face streaked with tears.

The man was choking now, drowning in his own blood. With immense effort, he raised his hand to her face. "*Mío una recompensa.*" Pay back.

Then his hand fell, his expression went slack, and he was gone. Marisol buried her face in his chest to stifle her sobs. She was devastated but also frustrated because she didn't understand the meaning of his last words. Was it a pitiful acknowledgment of martyrdom, or was he calling down a curse? After a few minutes,

Daniel touched her shoulder.

"We have to get back. Now."

She nodded. He helped her stand.

"Can you make it?"

"Yes, but let me shut his eyes and cover his face."

She gently pushed his eyelids closed, untied a bandana from around her neck and covered him, weighting the edges on the ground with stones.

"What about...?"

"We'll tell Frenchy," Daniel said. "He'll arrange for someone to remove the body. Notify his family."

Marisol nodded, crossed herself, whispered a prayer. Daniel took her by the hand and led her back to the embankment. When they began to walk down the creek bed, her expression of grief had faded, replaced with something more resolute: a set jaw, eyes ablaze with fury, a merciless look.

By the time they arrived at the staging area, Frenchy had also returned, his shirt wrapped around his waist, his arms and upper torso smeared with blood. He squatted next to the stream and washed himself.

"I counted 17 dead, 21 wounded, some severely." He paused to pinch his nose, struggling to keep his composure. "The *campesinos* had formed a cadre and were en route to San Mateo to demand drinking water, schools, medical clinics and roads. They also called for the release of their imprisoned leader, Luis Moreno, who hadn't been seen in nearly a week."

"*Desaparecido y matanza,*" Berto said. "Some new Mexican trend?"

Marisol stepped forward. "Frenchy, Luis Moreno is lying in a pasture, dead. The guy who got tossed."

"What! Luis! Was he dead when you found him?"

"No. But we had only a few moments with him. Besides being shot, his body was badly broken from the fall, limbs twisted in every direction."

"Were you able to talk to him?"

"Yes. Gustavo Olema, the head of the State Police, was in the helicopter. Luis told us Olema held him in custody, nothing untoward, but recently he became very angry. Wanted to kill Moreno and his people, but Moreno said he didn't know why."

Frenchy shook his head. "Luis and some of the *campesinos* were from my JW network. It was to be their third protest. They were convinced they were making headway. Maybe not with the mayor, but with some of the members of the town council."

He looked at Daniel. "Remember Pablo Molina?"

Daniel sighed deeply. "Of course. Is he...?"

"When I came upon him he was wandering in a daze, his entire shirt soaked with blood from his collar to his waist. Grazed on the forehead and neck. I recognized another guy. He was hit, but only superficially, in the thigh. He said he could function. We gathered those wounded who were able to walk and took them to the truck. I told them to drive to the medical clinic in San Mateo, and the doctor there could contact the municipal hospital in Acapulco...get back here...tend to the others who are still alive...care for the dead."

"What about my film?"

"I gave it to Molina. Told him what it was, told him to hide it in a safe place."

Glances all around.

"We're still good to go?" Daniel asked.

Frenchy swung into his saddle. Tense, attentive to the trail ahead, but deep in thought. "More than ever."

November 18 — 19
La Sierra Madre
The Trek to Blanco's Stronghold

CHAPTER 16

The troop stopped briefly at the nearest settlement where word had already been received about the massacre. Frenchy recruited several men to retrieve Moreno's body, then the troop proceeded to the little farm belonging to Frenchy's closest network confidant, the man who possessed all of the supplies necessary to carry out the mission, including weapons and ammo which had been covertly transported. He lived five kilometers from the entrance to Blanco's stronghold. It was cooler at this altitude, and everyone brought out long wool serapes and knit watch caps. Their host already had a fire lit when they arrived, aromatic from well-seasoned oak and pine which he'd stolen from a lumber camp several kilometers to the northeast.

Once saddles and bridles were removed and the mules unpacked and staked in the small corral, Frenchy introduced the troop to their host, Héctor Sánchez, a short, dark-complexioned man, heavily muscled in the shoulders and forearms, clean-shaven except for a thin mustache that curled at the sides of his mouth. He led them to chairs set in a circle around a fire pit. Frenchy distributed C-rations which they ate hot, rolled in fresh tortillas. For dessert, Héctor distributed slices of melon while Marisol brewed coffee.

Frenchy broke the news to Héctor about the massacre on the road out of San Mateo. Told him about the entire episode.

"Que barbáridad!" he exclaimed, pounding his fist into an open palm. Once, twice, three times.

After his outburst, it was silent around the fire pit, reverent. Finally, Frenchy poured himself another cup of coffee, poured all around, except for Héctor who was trying to make sense of it all.

"A helicopter!" he said in wonderment. "What kind of pig was behind the *matanza*?"

"Olema, head of the State Police," Marisol said, "and someone else. Some other state government big shot."

"I think I got them on film," Berto said. "There wasn't any glare on the windshield because the chopper was facing north when they dumped Moreno. We'll see. Could be another of my Cartier-Bresson moments."

The story must've put Héctor into a mood. He stood up, walked toward a shed at the far edge of the corral and returned, cradling a long, heavy bundle. He set it on the ground, untied it and opened it up. Héctor was an expert gunsmith, and he showed how he'd cleaned and oiled the troop's supply of pistols, M-16s, and combat shotguns. Then he re-wrapped them in oil cloth and then again in a canvas shelter half which he tied with twine.

"You want to see the other stuff?" Héctor asked.

Frenchy spit out his coffee. Everyone looked at him, startled.

"What other stuff?" Berto asked.

Frenchy put up his hand, but he was choking so badly he couldn't speak.

"The claymores," Héctor said, smiling.

"Claymores!" Berto exclaimed.

Frenchy coughed to clear his airway, regained his composure. "M18A1 claymores. Named after the long, large two-handed Scottish sword. Used in ambushes and as anti-infiltration devices against enemy infantry."

Héctor placed one of the bandoliers of claymores on the ground. Frenchy pulled one out. Instantly, he became a weapons instructor.

"Each claymore consists of a plastic case that is concave and rectangular in shape: 8.5 inches in length, 1.375 inches wide, 3.25 inches high and weighs just 3.5 pounds. Notice that along the 'active' side are the embossed words 'Front Toward Enemy' while the rear is embossed with 'Back.' This helps the operator from making a lethal mistake.

"The claymore's 4" X 6" spike legs attached at the bottom allow it to be easily secured into soft ground. The concave nature of the mine's design allows for a forward-blast area that produces a fan-shaped pattern of 700 steel balls across a 60-degree horizontal arc to a height of about 2 meters with a maximum-kill radius of 100 meters and an effective-kill range of 50 meters.

"Up to 20 percent of the steel projectiles can blow back upon detonation, so we plant them in front of natural mounds or hills to reduce friendly-fire incidents. The projectiles are set within epoxy resin. A 1.5 pound layer of C-4 explosive is used for detonation, and the detonator is remote-controlled by a 'clacker' or trigger.

"Héctor, Marisol and me are going to plant three of them across the northern entrance to the stronghold. Each of us will have a detonator."

"*Madonna*," Berto said. "To cover our escape?"

"*Más o menos*," Frenchy replied.

"Well, that's a hell of a lot of *más, carnal.*"

"Correct," Frenchy said, staring into the glowing embers, rubbing his hands. "However many *cívicos* try to chase after you when you leave the compound, these claymores will mow them down. That should definitely help us to evade them and get a good head start."

"How did you get them?" Berto asked.

"From our man in Mexico City, Prado. Marisol transported several bandoliers, each containing seven claymores, from Mexico City to Laguna del Ejido, then to Graciela's, and me and Héctor brought them up here.

"Well, on that note, I'm gonna *fumar* some *mota*," Berto said, eyebrows raised, shaking his head from side to side. "Anybody wanna join me?" He reached into his shoulder bag and removed a plastic soap dish where he stored his stash. The others gave him disapproving looks and waved off his invitation.

Berto was relieved to be able to smoke again. But he was told the evening's indulgence would be his last for a while.

"You think you can handle cutting out all your daily bad habits in order to make the final haul up to the stronghold?" Frenchy asked.

"For the good of the mission?"

"Yes!" the others answered in unison.

"Héctor, you wouldn't happen to have a little bit of tequila or something stored away? We weren't able to bring any with us. It was deemed unessential."

Frenchy conferred with Héctor.

"There is a bottle of *mescal.*"

Berto clapped his hands with glee.

"But it's for *after,*" Frenchy admonished, "when the mission is completed, and we can celebrate."

"So we're all coming back here?" For some sane reason, that outcome seemed unlikely.

"It's possible," Frenchy lied.

Berto thought about confronting Frenchy regarding the unlikely probability of that outcome and argue that he ought to be allowed to at least have a little taste. But he kept quiet about it and remembered the recent promise he made to himself to cut back his drug and alcohol use. Now he felt really self-conscious. He took a huge hit, then another, then pinched the burning end from the joint and returned it to its carrier. He punched out a *Delicado* and lit up, the only smoker in the group. *Oh, well; at least the cigarette helps to keep my high going. I might as well have my share of great Mexican tobacco. It's all the Indians had, back in the day. American Indians, that is. And anyway, I'm gonna be an Indian for at least the next few days...and nights.*

Héctor pointed upward.

"What?" Frenchy asked.

"What do you see?"

"Tiny sliver of moon. A very dark sky. Just like we planned."

And then it hit him. Just a few clusters of stars, disappearing, reappearing elsewhere as if they were being pushed around by some unseen hand. They should be plentiful, permanent and twinkling like crazy.

"Cloud cover moving in from the sea," Héctor said. "Did you see the sunrise this morning?"

"No," Frenchy countered. "Too busy."

"You, *señorita?*"

"No, Héctor. Also too busy, too distracted with preparations."

"I saw the sunrise," Daniel volunteered. "Red sky on the horizon. A bank of clouds moving in from the west. Milky, pastel-colored clouds, rising as high as I've ever seen."

"Holy shit!" Berto exclaimed, remembering his conversation with the auto mechanic in Acapulco. The lie he told him about his alleged fishing trip being cancelled because of a storm alert, a storm that was stalled somewhere off the coast. He shared that with the others.

"Something… the air, the weird multi-colored clouds of incredible height," Héctor said. "It's possible something is building. I don't like to bring it up, considering your mission. But it's not unheard of to experience a storm at the beginning of the dry season."

As a patina of gloom settled over the group, Frenchy acknowledged the reality. "Well, if it happens, it happens. We'll just have to deal with it."

"If it does rain…or storm, at least Daniel and me will be indoors. In the compound, I mean. But what about you guys? You'll be outside, waiting, setting up whatever defensive perimeter you referred to last night."

"I've worked outside in all kinds of weather," Frenchy reminded them. "Vietnam wasn't exactly a desert, as you recall. We'll prepare for that contingency. We'll figure out how to shelter once we're finished with our work. We can weather it out, so to speak."

Héctor nodded, gazing into the fire.

"We should all turn in," Frenchy advised. "We'll have our work cut out for us tomorrow. There's room in Héctor's main *jacal* for all of us to sleep on the floor. Ponchos for pillows, canvas shelter halves to wrap ourselves in. It *is* much cooler up here."

At daybreak, everyone awoke to the sound of a strong wind and steady rain falling.

"So much for the dry season," Daniel said.

After reprising last night's dinner, Frenchy made Daniel take another look at the topo map and a map of the compound, both wrapped in clear plastic sheets.

"In case you need to know, our man inside made a map of the compound."

He pointed: "Here is where Yvonne and Sonia sleep. It's one of several rooms in a building, but closest to this kitchen and eating area. Memorize it."

"What's your man's name, and what does he look like?" Daniel asked.

"His name is Miguel. He's short and skinny but very strong, the face of a formidable fighter. Has a genial smile with gold front teeth. A full head of hair and a soul patch under his lower lip. Looks like a hard-living rock musician. He'll be our go-between. He'll tell you what's going on outside the compound; you'll tell him what's going on inside."

Frenchy stood. *"¿Listos?"*

"Sí," everyone answered in unison.

"I can't *hear* you!"

"¡Si, mi capitán!"

One last chiropractic manipulation and foot massage for Daniel. Then Frenchy bowed his head and repeated his favorite prayer. "Put on the whole armament of God...."

Before they broke to leave, Héctor offered his own blessing: *"Os saludamos con mucho respeto."*

Outside, the wind was rising and a scrim-like sheet of rain made it difficult to saddle up and re-pack the mules. Once back into the canyon, though, the dense forest canopy protected them from the worst of the downpour, and the wool serapes, parkas and knit caps moderated the accompanying chill. The mules clopped through the rocky creek bed, which ran deeper as the morning wore on. The wind-driven rain made it rough going. It took four hours to reach the point just below the road to Blanco's stronghold. By then, it was raining so hard that it appeared the canyon might be in danger of a flash flood. They found the least-steep and least-wooded embankment, dismounted, and led their animals up to the road. Their feet slid and slipped in the mud.

"We've got to find shelter, Héctor," Frenchy said. "We just can't work outside in this storm, or everything will get soaked. Ourselves, our cargo, and the animals."

Héctor nodded and jogged north along the road. Within a half-hour, he returned.

"There's an abandoned settlement ahead, behind a tall hedge, including a barn. I looked inside. It's empty. Looks like it's been used to cure and warehouse *mota*. Even has cots for workers. We can fit everyone in there. The animals, too."

"*Louez le Seigneur!*" Frenchy exclaimed. Praise the Lord! "Let's head up there as quickly as possible."

Once inside the barn, they freed the mules of bridles, saddles and cargo. Héctor and Marisol rubbed them down with towels and cotton shirts they found hanging on hooks, examined their legs and iron-cleated hooves.

"How are we going to feed them?" Marisol asked. "The storm.... They can't forage."

"Don't worry. Graciela packed cubes of alfalfa hay, soybean meal and fortification pellets in case of emergencies. Feedbags, too. Look around and see if there are any pails so they can drink."

Berto spied a pot-bellied stove in the corner of the structure. "I'm going to look outside and see if anyone stacked firewood."

"Good. But we can't use the stove. Someone might see smoke."

"What if we just make a small fire on the dirt floor?" Daniel asked.

Frenchy looked up at the cathedral ceiling, thatched roof and the extensive loft which was probably used to dry kilos of *mota*. "That would work."

Just then Berto re-entered the barn. "There's a big stack of logs and kindling under the eave out back. There's a well, too, with water buckets."

"Cool," Daniel said. "I'll give you a hand."

After the mules ate, Héctor and Marisol covered them with

wool blankets which she found on the floor next to the cots.

Soon, Berto and Daniel had a small fire burning.

"Here's some additional blankets." Frenchy passed them around. "I've got rope. Let's string up our wet clothes. Sit by the fire; I'll brew some cowboy coffee."

"Wow," Berto said, grinning. "All the comforts of home, and there's a bale of mota under a canvas cover."

"Where?" Frenchy asked.

Berto pointed. "In that corner over there, bricks wrapped in plastic."

"Someone readied it for shipment," Frenchy suggested. "Don't get any ideas, Berto."

As they sipped coffee and gathered warmth from the fire, Héctor unrolled the bundles of weapons and bandoliers of claymores near the bales of *mota*. The layers of oil cloth and canvas had kept everything dry. Their ammo was contained in a surplus, air-tight Mexican army container, so no problems there.

Draped in blankets, they quietly sipped their coffee. Rain pelted the barn with such force it discouraged conversation.

Frenchy stood and edged closer to Hector. "Graciela also packed some carrots and apples. See if the animals are interested."

"I was thinking the same," Hector said. "But, look, they're all asleep."

As night fell, they discussed the final element. Entering the compound.

Daniel reiterated the basic plan. "So, we're going in unarmed. Dressed in mufti, plus serapes and rain parkas. We're alone."

Berto objected. "I don't wanna be in that compound without a weapon."

"Our 'weapon' is our lack of guile. I show up with my best friend, my partner, against all odds, for one purpose only, to be reunited with my wife and daughter. And we tell Blanco what we witnessed on the road to San Mateo. He'll be grateful for the intel that police and God-knows-who-all-else are in the vicinity. Hopefully, it'll make him paranoid. And everything else about the op remains the same."

"Daniel, he'll think we're crazy."

"No," Frenchy disagreed, "Daniel is right. Blanco will be less suspicious if you show up unarmed. And he'll admire your abilities and *huevos* coming all this distance disguised as *campesinos*."

"Besides," Marisol added, "we really don't know whether Yvonne would be willing to hide weapons if you brought them in. Her loyalty may lean more toward Blanco than Daniel and Berto. After all, he saved her life. In this situation, it's best to come in with humility."

"Humble journalists," Berto said. Nods all around.

"All right, then," Frenchy ordered. "Saddle up the mules. Two for you, two for Yvonne and Sonia. You and Berto enter the way we planned, directly into the compound using their main road. We want the sentries to capture you. In the meantime, Héctor, Marisol and I will remain inside the barn. As soon as the rain lets up, we'll set up our defensive perimeter."

Everyone dressed in clothing that wasn't quite dry but which possessed a poignant aroma of oak mingled with pine. It seemed strange to Daniel how two different kinds of firewood could remind him of the fragrant copal incense burned by Mayans in Oaxaca.

November 19
Blanco's Stronghold

CHAPTER 17

If anything, the rainfall had intensified since afternoon, and they were soaked again by the time they entered the compound. Between the downpour and the total lack of outdoor lighting, visibility was less than 10 meters.

"Maybe the sentries won't even see us," Berto said. "Then what?"

"We can only hope they hear us. The mules, I mean."

"Good, because I don't wanna be shouting any *holas*."

"No, that wouldn't work."

Not knowing where to go, they loosened their hold on the reins, hoping the mules could intuit the right direction. Sure enough, they stopped just outside a railed fence which turned out to be a corral.

"Let's dismount and walk them in," Daniel suggested. "If we're lucky, there's also a barn to shelter them."

"Do you think maybe now is the time to use our flashlight?" Berto asked, a slight whine creeping into his voice. "I'm freakin' soaked to the bone. Check that. Even my bones are soaked."

"Wouldn't hurt," Daniel replied, as he reached into his

saddlebag.

Berto grabbed his arm. "Wait a minute. I think I see a faint light coming through a window, like from a lantern."

"I see it. Let's hustle over there before we all drown."

Peering into the window, they saw the inside of a barn much like the one in which they'd previously found shelter. But this one had stalls. Daniel hoped they weren't all occupied.

"Thank God," Berto hissed. "Now if only we can find the entrance. Flashlight."

Daniel kept the beam low until he found a long, thin vertical line of light that he hoped indicated a barn door. Upon closer inspection, it was, but it was locked from the inside.

He shared that intel with Berto.

"Shit! Now what?"

"Let's try knocking."

"What!"

"You heard Frenchy; he wants us to be captured."

"OK, OK, OK!" Berto gave the door a few raps with his knuckles.

Daniel pushed him aside. "With all the racket this rain is making, they won't hear that at all. This isn't your first-date's house."

He made a fist and pounded as loud as he could. Six times.

"That should do it."

Sure enough, the light inside shifted and a man holding a lantern opened the door a crack. Daniel pushed it wider, and he and Berto trooped inside with the mules in tow.

Once Daniel and Berto and the mules were sheltered, the man holding the lantern shut the door. He was joined by three others. Astounded, one of them looked at the parkas, then looked into the faces of their uninvited guests.

"Who are you?"

"Tourists," Berto said. "We got lost. You got any *mota* for sale?"

The man pulled out a long-barreled revolver, a .357, and pushed back their poncho hoods.

"*¿Gringos?*" another man asked.

"You got that right. Cold, wet and tired *gringos.*"

"You can say that again," Daniel said.

"OK. Cold, wet and tired *gringos.*"

"Quiet, *cabrón,*" said the man holding the revolver.

"Jeez!" Berto exclaimed to Daniel. "He knows my name."

The man with the gun waved Berto and Daniel away from the mules. Another man searched their saddle and shoulder bags.

"Remove your parkas," the man with the gun ordered, and he flung them to the ground once Daniel and Berto had struggled out of them. "Remove your serapes." And he threw them to the ground, too.

Berto and Daniel were mirror images. Shivering in thin white peasant shirts and trousers that clung to their skin, wet hair flat and dripping water, pretty much naked in front of their captors. There was no point in patting them down.

"*¿Entonces...?*" the man holding the revolver asked.

"*Nada,*" replied the one who searched their saddle and shoulder bags.

The men conferred. "Better get Blanco."

Berto winked at Daniel. "Now we're making progress."

Progress.... "I'm sorry I've been so hard on you, bro," Daniel admitted, his gaze meeting Berto's, grabbing his shoulder.

Berto, feeling relieved, hoping that Daniel would be willing — somehow — to surrender Yvonne to him, decided to play it light.

"Well, you know me. I never make the same mistake twice. I make it, like, five or six times, you know, just to be sure."

"But it's different with Yvonne, right?"

Berto nodded. "*Sí, mon.*"

The man holding the revolver waved it in their faces.

"Hey! The two of you. Shut up!"

The other man walked over, rawhide thongs coiled in his hand.

"I don't think we should let this motherfucker tie us up," Berto said.

"I think we should," Daniel countered. "We're supposed to be captives, according to Frenchy, so what's the harm in being tied up?"

"I told you to shut up!" the man with the revolver yelled and swung the barrel at Daniel's head. Taking a step back, Daniel grabbed the man's wrist and cracked the back of his elbow with a sharp, concise hand strike, then drove him face-down to the hard-packed ground and knelt on his shoulder.

Berto bear-hugged the other man and flung him down, took hold of the rawhide thongs and slipped them around his neck.

Daniel glanced back at Berto. "Like I said, I don't think we should let this motherfucker tie us up."

Berto howled with glee. "The team is reunited! *¡Órale!* Right on!"

His reverie was short-lived, however, as a group of heavily-armed men charged into the barn.

"Get off my men!" the apparent leader shouted. "Stand up! Back away! Hands up!"

Daniel and Berto relinquished their holds and stood, hands high above their heads.

Daniel gave the leader the once-over: slender, straight black hair swept back from a widow's peak, wire-rimmed glasses, bookish-looking. Not at all what he expected.

"Are you Blanco?" Daniel asked.

Blanco nodded, a sarcastic smirk distorting the symmetry of his face.

"Who are you?"

Daniel spoke up first. "I'm Daniel Mendoza, a North American journalist. I'm looking for my wife and daughter who I believe are living here since you liberated them from Casa Montenegro."

"And I'm Alberto DiVincenzo, better known as Berto. I'm a photographer. We work together."

A look of disbelief replaced the smirk on Blanco's face, but it was fleeting.

He questioned the man who summoned him to the barn.

"When you searched them, did you find identification?"

"No. They possess only some meager provisions and those four mules over there." Pointing to Berto. "And this camera, wrapped in plastic."

"Speaking of mules," Berto said, "will you let us remove their bridles, saddles and saddle bags? They need to be rubbed down."

Blanco seemed to weigh Berto's question.

Four mules.... They plan on leaving here with Yvonne and Sonia. This is a rescue mission.

"Never mind. They'll be taken care of. Put your hands down. The most pertinent question to be asked is, how did you find me?"

Daniel answered. "My mentor in Mexico City said I should come down to Acapulco, take a bus to *Pie de la Cuesta*, go to a *casa de huéspedes*, *Casa Elvira*, ask for a man named Pascal Archambeaux, a Jehovah's Witness missionary who is familiar with this country."

"I know the family at *Casa Elvira*, and I've heard of this man you speak of, but everyone knows him by the name Frenchy. He serves many poor *campesino* families up here."

Blanco whispered something to one of his men who walked to the back of the barn — a darkened corner — and returned with towels and two wool blankets which he handed to Daniel and Berto.

To another man, he commanded: "Bring *La India* and her daughter here."

Then to Daniel: "Where is he? Did he lead you up here?"

"He led us part of the way. Do you know the road to San Mateo?"

"Yes, I know it. But that's quite a distance from here and so many trails criss-cross and meander. Why did he stop there? Surely you needed more help finding us."

Daniel and Berto exchanged glances. Their expressions turned immediately more somber.

"There was a massacre of *campesinos* by the State Police," Daniel said, his voice tinged with emotion. "Seventeen dead, 21 wounded, some severely. Frenchy stayed behind to help. Several were associated with his ministry."

Blanco's eyes widened with shock. He took off his glasses, wiped the lenses with a bandana and stepped closer to Daniel who was drying his head with a towel, a blanket draped over his shoulders.

"Tell me about it. Did you see it?"

Daniel told him the story, leaving out the part about Berto and his Leica.

"They were standing in the bed of the truck?" Blanco asked. "Where were they going?"

Daniel nodded to Berto to continue the story. "They were on their way to San Mateo. Their third protest, to ask for basic services, schools. To gain the release of their leader, Luis Moreno. They said they believed they were making progress with the town council but not with the mayor."

A muffled shout came from one of the stalls, and the body of a man, gagged and tied to a chair, tumbled out.

"Fuck! Fuck! Fuck!" Blanco shouted. "Fuck!!"

"What...?" Berto began, but he was ignored as Blanco and two of his associates rushed to the man in the chair, set him upright, slapped him a few times and dragged him back into the stall.

Berto put down his towel and glanced at Daniel. "What the...?"

"I'm guessing Señor Captivo overheard our conversation and freaked out," Daniel whispered. "Would be good to find out who he is."

At that moment, the barn door swung open again, pushed hard by the rain and wind. Sonia and Yvonne were escorted in.

Sonia yelled, in a strange, guttural voice, more like a croak than a pronounced word, and she ran over to where Berto and Daniel were standing. She ran face-first into Daniel's legs, as if to tackle him and bring him down, bellowing in some kind of other-worldly cry of relief, of exaltation. Daniel knelt and held her as she cried and shook uncontrollably, clinging to him as if he were her life preserver in a storm-tossed sea.

"Oh, my God!" Yvonne ran over, awkwardly trying to find a way to worm into Daniel's embrace. But when Sonia wouldn't relax her grip, she turned to Berto and burrowed into his arms, crying and moaning with raw emotion.

"This is just like the welcome-home reception I got when I returned from 'Nam. Over and over again, no matter where I went."

Yvonne pushed away from his embrace, stared at him, her face streaked with tears. Then burst into laughter and clung to him once again, convulsed with competing emotions until she could barely breathe, until she chose tears over laughter. Sobbing, pausing to take deep breaths, sobbing even more.

"C'mon, girl; I just stepped out of the worst rain storm I've ever seen. I'm gonna need another towel."

Yvonne pounded her fists against his chest, then buried herself inside again.

"Well," Blanco announced, walking over, "I guess you were telling the truth."

He turned to one of his men. "Take care of these mules. Make sure they get something to eat and drink."

Daniel scooped Sonia into his arms and stepped toward Yvonne. When their eyes met, they intuitively abandoned all traces of grief and sorrow. Yvonne rushed into his embrace. They struggled for balance, grasping each other, crying and trembling. When Daniel regained a semblance of composure, he turned to Blanco. "Is there a private place where my family and I can go?"

"Yvonne will escort you to the kitchen," Blanco said. "I'll have one of the men bring extra cots and mosquito netting into her sleeping quarters. There is food and beverages. Help yourself. You must have much hunger, yes?"

"Gracias, señor." A little respect to help win him over.

"De nada. In the morning, we'll talk more about your... situation."

Once in the kitchen, Yvonne lit two kerosene lanterns. They all took chairs and sat around one of the large communal tables. Sonia remained in Daniel's lap, her face against his neck, crying softly, seemingly afraid to let go.

"Are you hungry?" Yvonne asked.

Berto perked up. "Starving."

"Not me," Daniel answered, "but I'd love a cup of coffee. I'm starting to get a throbbing headache. Maybe the caffeine will help."

"What happened to your face?" Yvonne noticed the scars on his brows that had opened up during the fight with Frenchy and which were now pink and in the process of healing.

Self-consciously, Daniel touched one of them while Berto answered. He couldn't resist. "It was just a family scuffle."

Hearing that retort made her laugh and cry all over again. It plunged her right back into the exhilarating nights in Brant, N.Y., with Daniel at *Chez Jake*, the retort that was always uttered by Gene the bartender after a Friday night brawl that he'd forced out into the street.

Yvonne wiped her eyes, stood and walked to one of three wood-burning stoves where a fire was still smoldering. She tossed in a couple handfuls of kindling and two logs. Then she took water from a bucket, scooped ground coffee from a can, filled a big blue-and-white-speckled metal coffee pot and set it on the stove. An awkward silence permeated the kitchen. There was too much to talk about and an uncertainty about where to begin.

Yvonne started.

"How did you get up here? How on earth did you find us?"

Daniel felt dread balloon in his gut. "Before I answer that question, are you willing to leave here with Berto and me?"

Sonia wailed and began trembling again, sobbing uncontrollably, her little body so taut and her grip so tight around Daniel's neck that he began choking.

"Easy, baby, easy. Daddy's here, and he's never going to leave you again."

Tears rolled down Yvonne's cheeks. Wiping her eyes didn't stem the tide. "Excuse me, I've got to get a bandanna from my room."

Daniel smoothed Sonia's hair, stroked her back, kissed her. Eventually, she loosened her grip, pulled back and stared at him.

"You look good, sweetheart. Have they been taking good care of you?"

She shook her head.

Yvonne re-entered the room. "She doesn't mean to answer 'no.' She became so frightened by the prison experience that she's lost her ability to speak. Just like you when you were sent to the rez by Uncle Abe to live with Jesse, when you were so freaked out by... by what happened."

"What did happen...to her...and to you?"

"Tlatelolco happened!" She wiped tears with the bandanna. "You don't know because you weren't there! We looked for you and looked for you! I saw Berto and Cogdill up on the balcony of Chihuahua just before the shooting began. Where were *you?* With that girl?"

Daniel told her the story, how he was deceived by Prado and Phaedra, the phone call from Berto, the white glove worn by members of the Olympic Battalion, how he took Prado's Harley and raced down Reforma, arriving there after the first long fusillade, locating Berto, pulling him away from a beating, the smashed camera.

"I don't believe you!"

"Believe him. Daniel saved my ass, and Prado didn't want Daniel there. He knew it was going to be rough, and he knew you and Sonia would take priority over journalism. He didn't want him running to his death. "

Yvonne shook her head.

"Why didn't you come get us out of Casa Montenegro?"

"I tried. Believe me, I tried. I went to every district police station. Same response: 'there's no one detained here.' Then Prado took me to the Attorney General who claimed he didn't have a list of prisoners. Then when we discovered most of the activists were being held in Casa Montenegro, I insisted on visiting, but they wouldn't let me in. Later, the warden admitted you were there, but he told me that you didn't want to see me. I still tried. Every day for weeks."

"Why didn't Prado help you? That's his damned job, isn't it? To represent Americans in trouble?"

The coffee began to boil over. Berto rushed to rescue the coffee pot, move it off the stove.

"He said it was part of 'the final solution,' " Daniel said. "Díaz Ordaz turned his back on the embassy. Said he was going to handle things his way. Pissed off at the Mexican students, even more pissed off at the foreigners his intelligence people alerted him to, the communist interlopers who he saw as the real provocateurs. Wanted you kept incommunicado, wanted to make you suffer, wanted to make you confess."

"How hard did you try?"

"I quit IPS. Finding you and Sonia and getting you out once I found you was my full-time mission."

Berto interjected. "His biggest fear was that you both were disappeared."

"Jesus! We heard about that inside. How many were... disappeared?"

"Dozens...scores...maybe hundreds. Nobody really knows."

"Disappeared to where?"

Daniel told her Rius' story.

"Oh, my God! Killed and buried in mass graves? What kind of sick government does that to its own people!"

"In our era, Nazi Germany," Daniel said. "They might've invented disappearing to create terror. But from what Prado tells me, we may be on the verge of discovering atrocities committed in many closed societies, like the USSR. But Mexico is definitely at the cutting edge."

Then Berto told the story about the massacre they witnessed while making their way up the mountain, building the narrative as he set coffee cups around the table and filled them.

"Fuck me! You've got to get us out of this country!"

Daniel reassured her. "Don't worry, I will. The only question I have is, will Blanco let us go?"

"I never considered that he wouldn't. But he's never committed himself to either way. Why wouldn't he?"

"I don't know, but let me tell you this. When we told Blanco about the massacre on the road to San Mateo, he freaked out. Then a man tumbled out of one of the stalls in the barn. He was tied up to a chair and gagged, but he certainly overheard us, and he certainly was freaked out, too. Do you know... who is that guy?"

Yvonne pushed her cup of coffee to the side and lay her head on her arms. Mumbled something.

Daniel gently touched her arm. "What? I can't hear you."

Yvonne raised her head, her face pale. She took a couple of deep breaths.

"That man...he's the mayor of San Mateo. Blanco said he's one of the most corrupt mayors in all of Guerrero, filthy rich. With deep ties to the State Police, the former secretary-general of Guerrero,

Gov. Castillo. Blanco ordered the *cívicos* to kidnap him, hold him for a big ransom. Maybe that's one way he bankrolls his operation."

Berto and Daniel exchanged glances.

"Who told you about the mayor?" Daniel asked. "Blanco?"

"No. He wouldn't confide in me like that.... He discusses his goals, his grand strategy for a revolution, but he keeps specific tactics to himself."

"So, how did you find out?"

"The wife of one of his lieutenants. She was very proud of it...snatching the mayor right out of his bed."

"OK, we're going to have to play this very carefully. Especially not let on that we know anything about the kidnapping. But I can tell you, Blanco's got to be seriously paranoid now because we told him about the massacre."

"Why did you tell him about the massacre?"

Daniel glanced at Berto. "It's what we were told to do. We were told to make Blanco paranoid. That it would work in our favor...distracting Blanco, to get you out."

Yvonne reached for her coffee, took a sip, thought for a minute, took another sip. Berto couldn't take his eyes off her mouth, the natural satin sheen of her lips, so remarkable in the soft light of the kerosene lamp. But there was something that startled him, some strange re-composition of her face. He tried to shake it off, but it wouldn't go away. He needed time to make sense of it.

"Who is this someone who told you what to say? Not Prado?"

"Oh, brother, this is going to get interesting," Berto said. "Can I have a *Delicado*? Got any cigs about?"

Yvonne reached into her shirt pocket, tossed a pack on the table.

"Aahhhh." Berto punched one out and lit up. "A life-saver."

"Just sit far away from Sonia, near the door. Open it a crack. Ever since Tlatelolco and prison, smoke makes her sick."

"Do you remember the guy who saved my life in Lebanon, Pascal Archambeau, also known as Frenchy?" Daniel asked.

"The CIA operative... the former legionnaire from Vietnam? The guy who guided you to the sheik's? When you tried to return that loser-of-a-son to him?"

"The same, the one-and-only," Berto said.

"What the hell's he doing here?" Yvonne asked.

"Technically he's not CIA," Daniel clarified. "He works for the U.S. State Department. More specifically, he works for Prado who calls him 'an independent contractor.' Prado hired him to develop intel on Blanco, just how dangerous he is. Prado sent me to meet Frenchy, ostensibly to get me back in shape, to help me find you. But also to map the exact location of Blanco's stronghold."

"A double-freakin'-agent," added Berto.

Daniel explained Frenchy's method of operation. Using the cover of being a legit ordained Jehovah's Witness to preach to and help *campesinos* survive in the Sierras, *campesinos* who are marginalized squatters. Meeting the family from *Pie de la Cuesta* whose beloved son was murdered by State Police because he was an activist for a communal coconut plantation that was resisting appropriation of their property and livelihood to make way for a big tourist resort. Creating an intel network.

"Except he really loves his family in *Pie de la Cuesta*. He's in a complicated situation. People in his network really need him, for both spiritual comfort and material necessity. And I think he really needs them, too. When we came upon that massacre on the road to San Mateo, it was really a kick in the gut for him. Some of the *campesinos* put down were his people."

"So, where is he?"

"He's outside Blanco's compound, somewhere near the entrance, setting up a defensive perimeter."

"All by himself?"

"With two others who know their jobs."

"What good does it do us if he's out there?"

"He's got a man inside here, a go-between. We play it by ear...literally. When we're ready to go...we go...with or without Blanco's permission."

Yvonne sidled closer to Daniel, caressed him and rested her head on his shoulder. "Whew! This is hard to take in. I think I need to just sit quietly with you. It's been a hell of a night. And this storm is really rattling my nerves. This is supposed to be the dry season, but the *cívicos* are saying that this is the worst storm since about a year ago. A cyclone, maybe."

"Biblical, man," Berto interjected, stubbing out his cigarette, fishing the pack for another one.

"Daniel, I have one more question…what happened to Inez? She must've been at Tlatelolco, too, right?"

"Disappeared. Her parents and I spent quite a bit of time looking for her."

Berto reviewed briefly the scope of their search. "Even morgues, all over the city. The aftermath of that fucking massacre was just brutal. Bodies in morgue pans, parts of faces blown away, bayonet…."

Yvonne waved him off with both hands, pointing to Sonia, asleep now in her father's arms.

"So, you're thinking…."

"I'm not sure," Daniel said. "Rius didn't offer me much hope. He said his story was a cautionary tale."

"But you still…."

Daniel looked down at his coffee cup. Empty.

"I don't know. I just don't know."

November 20
Día de la Revolución
Blanco's Stronghold

CHAPTER 18

E xcept for the hours between 4 and 7 a.m., it poured. And poured. Blanco had arranged for two more cots to be brought to Yvonne's room. But Sonia insisted on sleeping with Daniel, so Berto took one of the others and folded and stored the fourth. When he wanted to smoke because he couldn't sleep, Yvonne made him go into the kitchen.

Berto threw a couple more logs on the fire, smoked and drank coffee. His hands were shaking, and he worried that he was on the verge of losing his grip. Overnight withdrawal from his multiple addictions was worse than he expected, especially because he'd never considered quitting and had no idea of the consequences. What startled and unnerved him a couple of hours earlier when he'd viewed Yvonne in the light of the kerosene lamp, was seeing her progressively age in a matter of seconds.

I understand that I'm hallucinating, but the image of Yvonne going from 28-year-old to a 50-year-old with white streaks in her hair was like watching advanced time-lapse photography. It scared the crap out of me. But despite the crow's feet, her eyes were even more luminous and her skin was remarkably smooth, her visage sedate, like a saint. She was more beautiful than ever. It encouraged me to spend the rest of my life with her. But it also made me realize I better clean up my freakin' act, even if I have to photograph freakin' bar mitzvahs. Or I might not make it to 50 myself!

Throughout the night and into the morning hours, Sonia barely moved, except to turn on her other side. But being reunited and sleeping close to her father did nothing to dispel the nightmare. She didn't scream when it struck; instead, she moaned and whimpered and ground her teeth so hard that it woke Daniel and Yvonne out of a sound sleep. Because they'd moved their two cots close together, as if they were sharing the same bed like when Sonia was an infant, they collaborated in comforting her until the nightmare ended. The mosquito netting was large enough, like a tent that attached to a hook in the ceiling and cascaded to the floor so that it covered them all. Only an occasional mosquito buzzed the net, and the steady sound of rain falling on the roof eventually lulled them back into deep sleep.

They didn't hear Berto when he returned to his cot, nor did they notice the storm relent during the quiet, uneventful early morning hours. Quiet and uneventful except for Berto trying to psychically beat back his cravings, and for those sentries whose security concerns were most heightened, inside and outside of the compound.

At daybreak, the clatter of pots woke them and, reluctantly, they rose from their cots, rolled up the mosquito netting and took turns visiting the outdoor commode and washing out of buckets by a well, reminding Daniel of the rituals of ablution he and his Uncle Jesse performed during the years on the rez when he lived in Jesse's one-room log cabin. Under those conditions, even a little sliver of soap and a cotton towel provided inestimable pleasure.

In the kitchen, two *cívico* wives stacked blue metal plates and cups on a table alongside a mound of utensils while they brewed coffee in one of two large metal coffee pots. When that task was completed, one of the women left and the other heated tortillas in a cast iron skillet and heaped them in a stack, covered, inside a red plastic basket, then tended to a pot of beans. A larger plastic basket filled with eggs sat on the table next to a jar of salsa.

From Yvonne's room, Daniel heard the woman ask, "How

would you like your eggs, *señor*?"

And a deep, raspy voice answered. *"Revueltos, señora, por favor."*

Daniel put on his still-damp shirt and trousers, slipped into sandals and made his way into the kitchen. The man whose voice he'd heard was seated at the end of the communal table closest to the wood stove. It was the guy with the revolver who'd wanted to tie up Daniel and Berto, the one who tried to slug Daniel with the long barrel but, instead, found himself face-down in the hard-packed dirt. No damage except a bruised cheek bone and, possibly, an elbow, because he maneuvered his cup and sipped his coffee with his other hand, awkwardly.

"Buenos días, señor," Daniel said, taking a cup and filling it halfway to let it cool before taking a sip, so it wouldn't scald his mouth.

The man looked up. Nodded. Then took his cup filled with coffee and went outside.

The woman heating tortillas smiled. She was short, her face and arms muscular and Indian brown. Breasts and belly pushed against her embroidered peasant blouse. "Don't mind him, he's just embarrassed. A strong man who met his match. Someone can take his food out to him."

Daniel smiled then glanced at the door as it closed. She studied him, startled. *Aiieee! Este hombre es muy guapo!*

"You are the husband of *La India*, the father of Sonia?"

Daniel nodded.

"You're going to take them away?"

Again, he nodded.

"What's your name?"

"Dan-yel."

"My name is Romuela."

"Mucho gusto, señora."

"You must be very smart to have discovered where we live."

He took his first sip of coffee. Not as hot, but strong, dark. Good.

"Is there *miel*?"

Romuela laughed and reached for a small painted ceramic pot

with matching cover.

"Just like Sonia when she learned to drink *café*. She doesn't like the taste of it *sin miel*. And if we have fresh cream, even better."

Three other men walked into the kitchen, wearing Levi's, flat-heel boots, straw hats covered with plastic and serapes that bulged at the hip. Looking exhausted, they stacked M-16s by the entrance and sat down. Daniel guessed they'd been on sentry duty all or part of the night.

"Aiiee! You're tracking mud onto this dry floor! Go outside and wipe them clean!"

One pleaded. "At least give us coffee."

They filled their cups and went out, muttering, then re-entered a short time later while Romuela swept up their clumps.

As they took their seats, one of them sniffed the air.

"What's that smell?"

"What do you mean?" Romuela asked.

"It smells like *copal*."

Daniel didn't say a word, just slipped down to the other end of the table.

"You're imagining it. We're burning pine in the stove instead of oak. The pine was covered with canvas. Someone forgot to cover the oak." Her tone half-accusing.

The man stared down the table at Daniel. "You *La India's* husband?"

Daniel nodded.

"How did you find us, all the way up here?"

"Leave him alone," Romuela scolded. "Can't you see he's tired...and beat up?"

"All right, all right, Romuela. Make my eggs *revueltos*."

"Me, too," the other men said, in unison.

"*¿Por favor?*"

"*Sí, por favor.*"

Daniel poured himself another half-cup of coffee, stirred in a dollop of honey. The men stared at him but said nothing.

"What about you, *Dan-yel*? Eggs?"

"*No ahorita, señora. Yo espero por mi familia y mi amigo.*"

Romuela smiled to herself. He could pass for Mexican, except for the way he speaks Spanish.

The men scooped scrambled eggs from the skillet which Romuela had placed on the table and spooned them into tortillas, added salsa and pinto beans and began to eat. Yvonne, Sonia and Berto walked into the kitchen. Yvonne and Sonia looked refreshed and happy; Berto not so much.

Berto poured a cup. "I think I'll take my coffee outside, as long as it isn't raining. Nothing like a cup of joe and a smoke first thing in the morning."

"Then please take this plate of food to the man sitting outside," Romuela said.

Someone on the veranda was kicking mud off his boots. When he finished, he walked in, passing Berto on the way out.

"*¡Buenos días, Romuela!*" By his Spanish, Daniel couldn't tell if he was a *gringo* or Mexican, especially because all the men he'd seen wore Levi's jeans and flat-heeled work boots. He was dark-skinned, maybe from working outside, with a stubble of a beard and a full handlebar mustache. Serious expression. He also wore the uniform of the day: serape, rain parka and a straw hat covered with plastic. About Daniel's size.

He hung his hat on a hook. "What's that funny smell?"

Romuela scowled, but poured him a cup of coffee.

"We are burning pine in the stove today," she said, exasperated. "Somebody left the oak uncovered. What would you like for breakfast?"

"Same as everyone."

He sat opposite Blanco's sentries. They nodded to him as they pushed rolled tortillas into their mouths. He caught the tail end of Berto leaving, wearing peasant trousers, shirt and sandals. He looked at the other end of the table.

"*Hola, amigo*, I heard you came in last night with the other guy."

"He's Berto, I'm Daniel."

"*Mucho gusto*. I'm Jerry. Known around here as *Jerónimo*." He stood and reached out a hand.

He is *a gringo*. Daniel took it, briefly, then let go.

"Where you from, bro?" Jerry asked.

"Lately, Mexico City. Before that, New York."

"The City?"

Daniel nodded. *Too difficult to explain upstate New York and Brant.*

"This is quite a change of pace, then, isn't it?" Still no smile.

"Where are you from?" Daniel asked.

"Originally, San Francisco. But now I live south of there…Big Sur. Ever been there?"

Daniel shook his head.

"God's country. I've got some acreage. Building a house. Not so different from here, except it's right next to the Pacific and cold."

Romuela handed him a plate with scrambled eggs and beans which he folded into a tortilla and added salsa. Took a big bite.

Daniel waited until Jerry consumed half his meal. "How'd you get here?"

"Flew. Out of Half Moon Bay. A few stops along the way to refuel." Jerry chuckled. "Sure beats riding a mule."

"What did you fly? Staying long?"

"Single-engine Cessna. I've been here a couple of weeks. As soon as the storm passes, I'm outta here."

"Business or pleasure?"

"A little of both." Aloof, he took another bite from his rolled tortilla.

"How far is Half Moon Bay from San Francisco?" Yvonne asked.

"By car, about two hours. Why do you want to know?"

"You ever hear of a pan-Indian organization there, United Council of American Indians?"

"Can't say that I have. I'm not into politics, just the cultural revolution."

Daniel stared at Yvonne. "What's your interest in this organization?"

Yvonne's face a mask of indifference. "Just something I heard on the rez before we came to Mexico. Do you remember Richard Oakes?"

"The Mohawk from St. Regis, the iron worker?"

"Yes. I hear he's living in San Francisco now, married and

studying in the new Native American Studies Program at the state university. He's become an activist leader, to be exact."

"What's the attraction there?" Daniel asked. "It's hippie country."

Yvonne smiled. Noncommittal.

Berto entered the kitchen. "Rain is picking up again."

Jerry looked alarmed.

"Just a drizzle now, but dark clouds are moving back in, wind is picking up."

Jerry finished the rest of his breakfast, gulped down his coffee. "You all have to pardon me, but I need to get back to work. If the weather gets bad again, I'm sure I'll see you at lunch...or dinner."

Everyone nodded in acknowledgment, except Romuela, who began to break more eggs in a bowl. Jerry started to say something, then put on his hat and strode out.

Romuela glanced at the Americans seated together at the far end of the table, then turned back to her work.

"What is that funny smell?"

Berto raised his arm and smelled his shirt sleeve. His face turned red with embarrassment.

"We found shelter the other day during the worst of the storm, not too far from here. We made a small fire to keep warm and to dry our clothes. It's the smoke you smell."

"What kind of fire?" Romuela asked.

Berto shrugged.

"Well-seasoned oak with pine."

Behind Romuela's back, Berto theatrically and silently mouthed the words, *and my stash of mota and meth.* Daniel blinked his eyes tight and held them shut for a few seconds.

"Where could you find shelter near here to make a fire?" Romuela asked, then covered her mouth, like shutting the barn door after the horse has bolted.

Just then, there was the sound of someone cleaning mud off boots, and another man entered the kitchen and removed his straw hat and rain parka and placed a hand-held radio on the table. Daniel gave him the once-over. *Short and wiry... burnished cheekbones... dented aquiline nose and one split eyebrow...genial smile with gold front teeth...full head of hair...soul patch.*

"Buenos días, cara mía," he said affectionately to Romuela, and he took a seat at the near end of the table. *"Un café, por favor."*

Romuela kept her eyes averted from the Americans as she set a cup in front of the man and filled it from the metal coffee pot.

"This is my husband, Miguel. Miguel, this is *La India's* husband, *Dan-yel* and his *amigo*, Berto."

"Mucho gusto, Miguel," Berto and Daniel said in unison.

"Mucho gusto a ustedes." Miguel sipped tentatively from his cup, the steam rising.

"How is the weather out there?"

He looked at Daniel. "It was clear for a few hours, enough to get a little work done. But it's beginning to rain again, and I believe there's going to be much more, *a la vuelta de la esquina."* Around the corner.

"I'm sorry," Daniel said. *"Una mala situacíon.* But we hope it will soon pass."

Romuela patted her husband on his shoulder. "Miguel, everyone ate scrambled eggs with beans, tortillas and salsa. What do you want?"

"Lo mismo, querida."

Sonia wrote in her notebook and walked it over to show Romuela. *May I have sugar and cream with my café?*

"Sí sí, mi caramelita. Sit down and I will bring it to you."

Miguel stood. "I'll be happy to bring it to Sonia. You've got a pan filled with eggs, and you don't want to scorch them."

"Gracias, Miguel."

Scraping his chair away from the table, Miguel brought coffee in Sonia's favorite cup, brown ceramic with a hand-painted green and yellow parrot, and also a covered jar with cream. "It's fresh this morning, just for you."

As he passed where the Americans were seated, he gave each of them a large, folded paper napkin enclosing metal utensils. Included inside Daniel's was his Italian switchblade and a brief written message, *This is a test/destroy.* No one else saw it. He hid it between his legs.

Miguel ate quickly, with no further conversation.

More footsteps outside. Cleaning of boots. Blanco entered, his hat dripping rain. He took it off along with his rain parka and hung them on a hook near the entrance.

"Miguel, are you finished?"

"*Sí, señor.*" Miguel drained his coffee cup.

"Then return to your post. I'll call you when it's time for a break."

Miguel nodded, picked up his radio and hat and left.

"Everyone is eating *huevos revueltos* this morning, *señor.* Would you like the same?"

"*Más tarde,* Romuela. Right now, *café* is all I need, *por favor.*"

"*Sí, señor.*" She poured him a cup and set it on the table.

"Sonia, may I have some of that *miel?*"

Sonia smiled and walked it over to Blanco.

"*Gracias, caramelita.* I usually don't take *miel* with my *café,* but today I believe I need a little sweet with the bitter."

He stirred a dollop of honey into his cup and glanced at the Americans while he let the steam from his coffee dissipate, watching them finish their breakfast.

"What bitter are you referring to, *señor?*" Romuela asked.

"Romuela, please go to one of the back rooms for a half-hour. I need to talk with our guests for a while. When you return, you can make my eggs."

"*Sí, señor.* Just let me add some more fuel and put the other pot on the stove so there will be more coffee for whoever wants it."

A minute later, she was out of the kitchen.

He put an unlit cigar between his teeth. "About last night...."

"Before you speak, Señor Blanco, allow me to express my thanks and undying gratitude to you for rescuing my wife and daughter from that terrible prison. You accomplished what I was unable to, and I'm so relieved to see them safe and in good health."

"You're very welcome. I was only too happy to deprive the state of two more innocent victims."

"What is the bitter you referred to a minute ago?" Yvonne asked.

"Did you know that today is an important Mexican holiday?"

Daniel and Yvonne glanced at each other, shrugged. Berto nodded, but said nothing.

"Today, November 20, is *Día de la Revolución*, the holiday to commemorate the start of the revolution to overthrow Porfirio Díaz' dictatorship in 1910, a revolution that lasted 10 bitter years."

"Why is that bitter?" Daniel asked.

"Because the revolution failed. Now we have the dictatorship of the winning political party, the *PRI*, headed by Díaz Ordaz and his political elite, enforced by police and military at every government level, from the capitol to every state and municipality. Díaz Ordaz handles dissent just like Díaz — *El Caudillo* — and the rich industrialists and landowners he protects rule over the poor just the way they did 50 years ago."

"In other words, nothing has really changed, although the *PRI* calls itself the revolutionary party?"

"Aha, but don't forget the last word, *Institucional*. They are fossils, with no memory, no ideals."

Yvonne raised her voice. "Fossils…that's the same word the National Strike Council used last summer."

Blanco nodded, sipped his coffee. Like the sentries, he, too, looked exhausted.

"And they continue to kill off the real revolutionaries, the ones still struggling for change."

Daniel decided to take a risk, engage him. "You mean, like what happened yesterday with Luis Moreno?"

Blanco took off his glasses and wiped them with a paper napkin. Put them back on. Took a sip of coffee, lay the cigar on the table.

"Yes, like that."

"Did you know him? Was he part of your civic organization?"

"I knew *of* him. He attended some of our meetings, but he wanted to remain independent. He believed that if he and his people openly associated with us, he'd never make any headway with the conservative mayor of San Mateo and the town council. His concerns were finite, limited, whereas ours are more…grand. He was afraid he'd never accomplish his people's limited goals if the mayor suspected he was tied in with us."

"But the mayor was suspicious? That's why they captured Moreno and put off settling with his people?"

"Let me tell you," Blanco said, evasively, raising his voice, "those *campesinos* will never get anything dealing with that corrupt, rich *latifundista*. He and his council are *PRI*. They know never to give in to peasants. There's no profit in that. Large-scale agriculture, cattle, resources like timber, tourism development; that's where the money is."

"But why would the state kill Moreno and murder his *campesinos*?"

"Because they're easy targets. On the other hand, the state is afraid of me."

Daniel glanced at Yvonne, then Berto, and Berto thinking: *When Blanco kidnapped the mayor, for the state it was the drop that made the glass overflow. La última gota que derrama el vaso.*

"But you don't have that many men here," Daniel said. "Why would the state fear you?"

"My influence is much greater than the few men you've seen. I'm calling them all in right now. At least 75 will show up by tomorrow. We have sophisticated weapons. We're trained *guerrillas*. The State Police, the army are like bullies. They fight only against defenseless people. We could decimate them. They're also worried we'll take out their leaders, which isn't that hard."

"Who trained you?"

"Some of us are former military."

Berto re-filled his cup. "Who's the guy tied and gagged in the barn?"

Blanco sat up straighter. "That's what I'm saying. He's a leader, one of the biggest landowners in this part of the state. Many cattle. Hardwood and pine forests. We're going to confiscate his liquid assets, and then we're going to eliminate him. Dump his body on his estate veranda. Strike fear into the rest of them."

"So you're calling in your 75 *guerrillas*...."

"Strictly as a precaution."

"Then we should be leaving soon," Yvonne said.

Blanco nodded. "As soon as the rain passes. You can take your mules and leave from the other end of the compound, a narrow defile that's safe for you. One of my men will get you started, show you the way. I can also draw you a map."

Yvonne brightened. "Thank you so much!"

"No problem. Your mules are being looked after. We'll pack some food for you. I ask only that you remain here for now."

He looked at Daniel and Yvonne. "I'm certain you need some time to...make a plan about your next move. Can your mentor in Mexico City arrange for you to leave the country? It would probably be wisest to leave by boat."

"From Acapulco?" Berto asked.

"No. Too many police and *Marinas*. A bit further north. From a sleepy little fishing village, Zihuatanejo, a deep, narrow harbor we call *una boca chica*. In contrast to Acapulco's *boca grande*. I know the captain of the port, Armando Padilla. It's very secure. Have your man contact him and arrange for a good-sized ocean-going boat. There really is no coast guard to speak of. It's partly why we're so successful smuggling contraband in and out of the country."

Berto thinking. *Yeah. Mota out, guns and ammo in. By sea and by air. This guy's a real operator. A pioneering junior mafioso.*

"Thank you for everything, Señor Blanco," Daniel said.

"Call me Andreas. And maybe Berto can do me a favor."

"Seguro que sí."

"When the weather clears, take a few photos of me with some of my cadre. So far there are none."

"I can do that." *No style points for these guys. Not like the old days with Villa, his bandoliers, leggings, spurs, big sombreros, repeating rifles.*

"All right, then. I have to go back to work. Enjoy your reunion and the rest of the day. Maybe Yvonne can wash your clothes. They smell pretty funky."

Blanco slid his chair back and left. His coffee cup still half-full.

Berto turned to Yvonne. "He doesn't eat breakfast?"

"He does. He has his own house and kitchen...and cook. Better set-up than what we have here."

"For a little while longer," Daniel said.

CHAPTER 19

After breakfast, Yvonne and Sonia went back to their room. Daniel waved Berto over, walked him to the door.

"Bro, see if you can locate that pilot, Jerry. He's a smuggler, but find out more about his operation. It might be important to us."

"Intel, huh?"

Daniel nodded.

"Right up my alley." *El Cabrón in action.* He walked out into a misting rain.

Feeling suddenly dizzy, Daniel gripped the edge of the table.

"What's wrong, *Dan-yel?*" Romuela asked with concern as she re-entered the kitchen. "Do you need help?"

Daniel could manage only a whisper. "Yes."

Romuela hurried out and, in seconds, Yvonne came running into the kitchen.

"What's wrong?"

"I feel dizzy, like I'm going to pass out."

"You need to get off your feet. Let me help you lay down."

She took his arm and put it around her shoulder and wrapped her left arm around his waist. Together they shuffled into the bedroom.

She helped him to the cot. "A headache? Earlier, you said you felt one coming on."

Daniel nodded. "Bad timing."

Romuela handed Yvonne a blanket. She covered him.

Sonia wrote furiously on her pad.

What's wrong with daddy?

"A bad headache, just like before."

Can I lay down next to him?

"Yes. But don't touch."

Yvonne pulled back the blanket and Sonia snuggled next to Daniel, wanting desperately to have him hold her. As if intuiting her need and violating what was best for him, Daniel raised his left arm over her head. She scooted right in.

"Lay quiet, sweetheart. Don't put your arm on my chest or stomach. I need to breathe, like we did back on the rez. Remember?"

Sonia nodded.

Watching Sonia restrain her snuggle while trying to duplicate the rhythm of Daniel's breathing brought Yvonne to tears. She backed out of the bedroom into the safety of the kitchen, empty now, where she could cry. But as quietly as possible. Feeling bereft and disconsolate. *My daughter is doing what I can't, and I'm afraid I've lost her, too. She'll never trust me again.*

After a few minutes, she dried her eyes and looked out the window. Berto was chatting it up with one of Blanco's men, animated, arms raised, pointing. Asking directions it looked like. She waited until Berto began to walk away, then quickly wrapped a *rebozo* around her neck, slipped into her serape and rain parka, grabbed an umbrella and walked out the door.

Berto followed a narrow, muddy footpath that wound more or less in an easterly direction about 100 meters through matted grass to the base of a bluff. Here the trail forked. He guessed left. After a while, he came upon a wide stone stairway with about an inch of water leaking down. Patchy fog and mist caressed the mountain and obscured the stairway's end point, but he climbed until he reached near the top and could peer over the final stair. Ahead lay a runway which looked as if it had been bulldozed out of the side of a mountain. Narrow and flat, but he couldn't tell how long the runway stretched to the north due to the lack of visibility.

A blue and white single-engine plane was parked at the south end. Jerry stood off to the side while a driver of a small tanker truck pumped fuel. When the fueling was completed, Jerry paid the truck driver who then edged past the plane and drove north through growing puddles, a wake trailing behind him, then out of sight. Berto imagined that a dirt road somehow led down to the coast highway and to a fuel depot.

He climbed to the top stair and hailed Jerry, signaling that he wanted to join him. Jerry looked around, then waved him over.

"You're Berto, right?" Berto nodded. "What's up?"

"Do you mind if we chat a bit? I didn't get a chance back in the kitchen."

"Sure. Let's get out of the weather. We can sit in the cockpit."

"Where's all this ground water coming from?"

"There's a lake above this outcropping of rock. It's probably overflowing its banks."

At first glance, the plane resembled an O-1 Bird Dog, the single-engine Cessna that the Army, Air Force and Marines used as a low-altitude observer plane over the jungles of Vietnam. It was perfect for scouting out enemy troop movements due to its quiet noise footprint and tight maneuverability. In short, it was very effective and highly feared. When they settled into their seats, Berto shared that information with Jerry, and he also noticed that all passenger seats in back had been removed and the plane was loaded with large burlap sacks of *mota*. Sacks, not bales or bricks. The aroma was powerful and heavenly. He tried to keep his hands from shaking.

"This baby is similar to the O-1," Jerry said. "Both are Cessnas. This is the turbo-charged 210D Centurian. Cantilever wing replaces the strut-braced wing. Engine is 285 hp. Stripped down, empty weight approximately 2,000 pounds. Maximum takeoff weight approximately 4,000 pounds."

"What's the weight of your load in back?"

"About 1700 pounds."

"If you don't mind me asking, how much is that worth wholesale?"

"About $250,000."

Berto did some quiet calculating. "Sounds about right. How much did it cost to buy?"

"I'm not at liberty to say. But sometimes we just exchange contraband for the weed, stuff Blanco needs."

Weapons and ammo, most likely.

"I expect the guy needs weapons if he's gonna defend himself. I've seen M-16s. What else does he ask for?"

"On this last trip, RPGs."

"No shit? Where do you get those?"

"We have a friend at Fort Ord, near Monterey."

Berto nodded. *I guess if you're going big-time guerrilla....* "How many trips a year?"

"Three. Maybe four if they grow a little during the off season."

Berto aimed his thumb at the cargo.

"Why isn't it bricked?"

"We only take the *colas de zorras*, the foxtails, the flowering tops. Pressing it into bricks using Coca-Cola as an adherent ruins the quality."

"Who takes the rest"?

"Once the very tops are harvested, the plant's secondary branches mature in the same way. We'll come back a second time for those."

"What about expenses?"

"Minimal. It's all in the family."

"Do you mind if I take some photos?"

Jerry let that slide. "You were in 'Nam?"

"Yeah, '64 to'65. Navy combat photographer with the Marines, mainly out of Da Nang. Operation Starlight, Dagger Thrusts 1 through 5. Discharged E-6. How about you?"

"Marines. Stationed stateside and in Hawaii. My last tour in 'Nam, '64, Da Nang. I was a cook. Discharged E-4."

"Small world," Berto said, smiling. "How did you learn to

fly?"

"When I came back to the world. California. San Francisco, to be exact."

"How'd that happen, if you don't mind me asking."

"My dad and his two brothers run a business. Signed me up for lessons."

"Look, man," Berto confessed. "I'm really jonesin'. Gave up weed for this expedition to find Yvonne and Sonia." He looked back at the sacks. "You wouldn't happen to have a spare joint? I'd be much obliged."

Jerry nodded and reached into an inside pocket and pulled out a chrome cigarette case, opened it, pulled out two joints.

"Can't smoke in here, but you can save 'em for later. Just make sure Blanco doesn't catch you. He don't tolerate it."

"You're a prince."

"And to balance the effect, keep you on your toes, you might want to pop some of these." He reached into another pocket and pulled out a bottle of capsules, dumped three into Berto's palm. "Benzedrine."

Berto swallowed a cap.

"Out-fucking-standing, corporal. Your generosity shall not go unrewarded."

Jerry wanted to know Berto's story, how they happened to locate Yvonne and Sonia. Berto told him an abbreviated and censored version, pretty much what Daniel had told Blanco, but none of the relationship stuff.

"So you're just gonna ride those girls on outa here? On mules?"

"That's the plan."

"Helluva story. Gonna document it?"

"I guess. Starting with Blanco. He wants me to take a few pics of him and his boys. What about you? When're you leaving?"

"Soon as the storm abates. Atmospheric pressure needs to build. I need a cloud ceiling of about 2500 feet and three miles of visibility."

"Unusual storm for this time of year, eh?"

"I'll say. A cyclonic disturbance, severe convective activity.

Westerly gusts up to 75 miles per hour. Had to tie 'er down. Fortunately, we're tucked right next to this mountain. Gusts just smack up against her and die."

Berto glanced out his window. Rain pelted the fuselage and wind gusts continued to toss treetops. Just like the last two days.

"Any guesses as to when this is going to subside?"

"Latest en route weather reports predict within the next 24 hours."

"Well, that's good news. But if your range is only about 1,000 miles, how're you gonna make it back to the states?"

"First stop is a little rancho near Cabo San Lucas, about 670 nautical miles northwest of here."

"Where's that at?"

"Southern tip of Baja California del Sur. You know, that little peninsula that extends down from southern California."

"Then where to?"

"Another private airstrip just east of San Diego, Borrego Springs. Approximately 800 miles. Second refuel."

"And then?"

"Borrego Springs to Half Moon Bay, approximately 500 miles."

"That's a lotta flyin'. How're you gonna stay awake?"

Jerry shook his bottle of capsules.

Berto nodded enthusiastically.

"Jerry, you look Mexican."

"Second generation Mexican-American."

"So that's how you can work both sides of the border?"

"Yeah. My dad and uncles operate a little syndicate: San Diego, Frisco...."

"And the little rancho near Cabo San Lucas?"

"A cousin."

"Borrego Springs?"

"Another cousin."

"Cool. So expenses...."

"We own the plane, the properties in Cabo and Borrego Springs. Expenses are minimal."

"How did you meet Blanco?"

"Connections. You know how that goes."

"Man! I appreciate you telling me your story."

Jerry thinking, *No problem; you're never gonna make it out of here.*

" But, uh, Jerry, just one more question: If an emergency arises, do you have room for passengers?"

Jerry looked at him. Still no smile. "I told you my max takeoff weight, didn't I?"

Berto nodded.

"I don't take passengers. But if I had to, maybe one, for a fee."

"How 'bout one-and-a-half?"

Jerry looked out his window, rain streaming down the glass.

"Lemme think about it. Let's head back. I need some lunch."

Daniel woke up. Checked his watch. He'd been out three hours. Sonia had been sleeping, too. A string of her drool lay puddled on his arm. It was that wet, uncomfortable feeling and wondering where it came from that woke him up. He moved his head side to side. Headache seemed to have dissipated. He sat up. Sonia, too. She picked up her pad.

Feeling better?

"Yes, love. You're good medicine."

Her smile beamed.

Are we going back home?

Home? "Yes, dear one, we're leaving here."

When?

"As soon as the storm is over."

Are you and mommy going to live together?

Jesus. "I'm not sure."

Sonia wrote furiously, her handwriting more unsteady. *Please let me stay with you. Mommy doesn't make good decisions.*

Daniel held her, recollecting, thinking.

"You know Miguel, Romuela's husband?"

Yes.

"I'm going to write him a note and fold it so it fits into your hand. When you see him, give it to him, but make sure nobody notices."

Not even Romuela?

"Not even her. Can you do that?"

Sonia nodded. He kissed her on the forehead and held her. Then he began to write: *San Mateo mayor kidnapped. For ransom. Thus, matanza. B calling in 75 cívicos. My guess: he expects shit to hit fan soon. Prepare.*

He heard footsteps on the porch, kicking and scraping mud off boots. Looked at his watch again. Noon. Time for lunch. He folded the note and gave it to Sonia. She smiled and walked into the kitchen while he eavesdropped.

"*Hola, mi caramelita.* Sit. Do you have hunger?"

Not now. I just want to watch.

A marvelous aroma leaked into the bedroom. If he was not mistaken, it smelled like *mole*. Just then, Yvonne entered the bedroom. Daniel noticed her wet hair and sandals.

"You been out in the rain?"

"Yes, gathering eggs for tomorrow."

"What is Romuela cooking?"

"Chicken in *mole*. Chicken is the only meat available here, except for the occasional goat. The *mole* is as good as any we had in Oaxaca. How are you feeling? You look a lot better than you did a few hours ago."

He stood up. "Balance seems okay. I'm not dizzy anymore."

"Maybe you should see a good doctor when we get out of here."

"You mean back in the States?"

"That's where we're going, isn't it?"

"Do you have your passport?"

"Confiscated. What about you?"

"I have mine, but I'm a fugitive from justice. They'd probably nail me at the airport."

Her voice rising. "Then how are we going to get out of the country?"

He reached out a hand. "Calm down, they'll hear us. Sonia…."

She slapped it away. Her glare was piercing. "Don't tell me to calm down! I'm the one who almost got killed! And I have to depend on you? A cripple? And dumb-ass Berto? And...who? Prado? That duplicitous bastard!"

Breathing deeply, trying not to lose his temper, he sat back down on the cot. "Yvonne, sit with me. Speak softly. Berto and I got in here, we'll get you out. We've got good help; Frenchy is a pro. Prado needs us, needs our intel. He'll make certain we're safe, and he'll see to it we're returned to the U.S."

"How? In a diplomatic pouch? Where will we live until he gets us out?"

"We'll return to Frenchy's place. It's quiet and out-of-the-way. Maybe we can leave by boat."

"I can't wait that long! I'm on the verge of a nervous breakdown! Can't you see! Tlatelolco was hell! Casa Montenegro was hell! This place could be a hell if we don't leave soon!"

Sonia entered the bedroom, looking stricken. She stared at Yvonne and took a circuitous route to sit on the cot next to Daniel.

"You all right, baby?" Daniel smoothed her hair.

She shrugged his hand away.

"Men eating lunch?"

She nodded.

"Miguel?"

She nodded again.

"Did you slip him the note?"

Another nod.

She wrote on her pad. *No one noticed. They were too busy eating.*

"Is Berto back?"

Nod.

"Maybe we should join him, for lunch."

He stood and took Sonia by the hand, and Yvonne, containing her anger, followed them into the kitchen.

Berto and Jerry were seated at the table, finishing their meal and sipping coffee. Blanco's men and Miguel were filing out the door.

"How are you feeling now, *Dan-yel*?"

"Better, Romuela, much better. Thank you."

"What happened?" Berto asked.

"Headache. Felt dizzy. Felt like I was going to pass out." *Berto's eyes.... They have that look.*

Berto glanced at Yvonne. *Uh, oh. She don't look too happy. Sonia neither.* "But you're..."

"...good to go," Daniel said, looking revived, but distressed in a different way. "No problem."

"Then you should have some of Romuela's *mole*," Jerry suggested. *"Lo mejor en todo de Mexico!"*

Romuela just gave him a dirty look.

"Please, come help me, Sonia."

Sonia stood and walked to where Romuela handed her a stack of blue metal plates and cups and eating utensils. *"Gracias, mi caramelita."* Romuela tried to hide her worry.

A single tear rolled down Sonia's cheek, but she brought the stack to the table and distributed settings to Yvonne and Daniel and one for herself.

Romuela lifted a huge iron cauldron from the stove and carried it to the table.

"There's a pot of rice on the stove, too. I have to go out for a little while so help yourself."

She retrieved her serape from the back of a chair, hoisted a rain parka over her head and grabbed the umbrella that Yvonne had previously used. It was soaked through.

As Romuela reached the door, Jerry shouted, *"Hasta luego!"*

No reply as she pushed through.

"You on Romuela's shit list?" Berto asked.

"I married her only daughter. Took her back to the States."

"You don't bring her back here from time to time? To visit?"

"She don't want to come back here. And Romuela can't leave."

"Oh." Berto felt tongue-tied and, at the same time, felt grateful for that condition. *I'm gonna keep my mouth shut for once.*

Yvonne smiled. "Jerry, after you finish lunch, can I talk to you? In private?"

Jerry glanced at Daniel and Berto.

"Sure."

Daniel ladled rice and chicken onto two plates, one for Sonia, one for himself. The dark mole sauce awakened his senses. He offered to fix a plate for Yvonne, but she refused.

"I'll have some later," she said, icily, pouring herself another cup of coffee.

CHAPTER 20

At daybreak, there was a gentle knock on the bedroom door. Berto was already awake, reviewing in his mind the previous day's happenings. *Ideas flowing from my nose like a nasty coke habit.* Brimming with false energy, he flipped open the blanket, pulled on his freshly-laundered trousers and hurried to the door. Romuela stood there, a USMC seabag at her feet. She edged it toward him with one foot.

"Good morning, Señor Berto," she whispered, timidly. "I'm sorry to wake you so early. My husband gave me this bag. He said you needed it. I'd pick it up and hand it to you, but it's very heavy."

Berto bent over and pulled it into the room. *Heavy? That's an under-fucking-statement.*

"Thank you, Romuela. How's the weather this morning?"

"I saw the stars last night! Miguel said it stopped raining about midnight, but it's still cold outside. I'll start a fire in the stove immediately. Come out when you're ready for coffee."

"Gracias, señora. Hasta luego."

The others were still asleep. He opened the seabag.

Daniel's ankle-high boondockers with wool socks.

Surplus black jungle boots, soft and well-broken in, with another pair of wool socks. *For me?*

Daniel's USMC utilities and soft boonie cover.

Faded French paratroop cammies and matching soft boonie cover. *For me?*

He tried them on. Boots and socks, too. Perfect fits. Cool.

Underneath were belt-suspender harnesses attached to web belts. Attached to the web belts were holstered weapons. Daniel's Colt Commander and Berto's .38 Colt Python with four-inch barrel. Loaded. Extra ammo — fully-loaded magazines for the pistol, speed-loaders for the revolver — were in pouches positioned on the left and right sides of the front of the belt along with large, lime-green phosphorous grenades and M-67 fragmentation grenades secured to the ammo pouches. On the left suspenders, K-bar knives were taped upside down for quick and easy removal. The leather straps that held the knives were relocated next to the hilt for safety purposes.

One combat pump shotgun — Ithaca 12-gauge Riot Type, 20-inch barrel — with web sling, double-ought buckshot loads, extra shells in two cloth slings. One M-16 rifle with web sling, loaded, extra magazines in pouches.

Face paint inside small green metal push tubes with a cap on each end. Light green grease paint at one end, a darker green at the other.

Two hand-held radios.

Emergency first-aid kits.

A folded note. "Only a few of Blanco's men made it to compound. Others detained (?) I suspect trouble from outside. Claymores reversed. Mules repatriated and hobbled at SW exit. We'll maintain defensive firing positions as planned. Meet you at exit when it's over."

Holy shit! I'm back in the DMZ! Changing into uni's just perfect. Outrageous, sarcastic, ironic in-your-face stuff. My mental picture of Marines: Two of them with parachutes climbing lower and lower on a cliff, seeing who will jump from the lowest point.

Berto folded the note and put it in his pocket, then closed the sea bag and pushed it under his cot, which was closest to the wall in the darkest corner of the room. He crept to Daniel's cot, pinched his arm. Daniel blinked his eyes, closed them, blinked again, trying hard to focus. Berto signaled for him to be quiet, then curled and waggled his index finger. *Follow me.*

Daniel, wearing skivvie shorts, carefully rolled over Sonia without touching her and followed Berto to the corner by the door. Berto had awakened him from a dream about Sonia's nightmares and his own childhood nightmares about vicious mobsters after his family was murdered and when Sheik Arsalan had beaten him to helplessness and so mercilessly he wondered if he would survive. In his dream, a familiar song played in the background, one that his Uncle Abe admired from the 1940s, seemingly contra-indicative. About bad dreams, but also about dreams never being as bad as they seem and the ironic advice to continue to dream. Sonia was lying in bed and, as if reading her a bedtime story, he was urging her not to be afraid to dream. Meaning that someday her nightmares would be replaced with dreams about a bright future, hope, happiness. And love. And the singers in the background repeating the refrain: *dream... dream... dream.*

Berto recognized that Daniel was having difficulty coming out of sleep. He grabbed him by the shoulder, shook him, whispered what had just occurred, exactly, from the knock on the door to hiding the seabag under his cot. Then Berto showed him the note. Daniel's eyes grew big, and he nervously grabbed his throat.

"Whaddya think, man?" Berto asked.

"Oy," Daniel muttered.

¿Cómo?"

"Oy, like cement in a washing machine."

"You can say that again."

"Oy."

"So whaddya think?"

"I don't know, bro. This is one of those situations we have to play by ear. Show the stuff to me later. Don't mention anything about it to Yvonne."

"Romuela said coffee would be ready soon. Maybe we should get dressed and go out and have some. Not that I need any."

"Agreed. But I need a cup to wake up. Be as quiet as possible."

They dressed in their clean *campesino* outfits and still-damp sandals. Before stepping into his trousers, Daniel taped his switchblade to his right hamstring.

"Ready?" Berto asked.

"Ready. But leave the note here."

Berto slipped it between one of the folds in his cot blanket. They left the room and closed the door. Yvonne, awakened by the tearing of electrician's tape, watched them leave.

When Daniel and Berto entered the kitchen, Romuela glanced at them while she labored at the stove. Blanco and two of his men were already sipping coffee. Blanco was wearing a shoulder holster over a long-sleeved denim shirt with pearlized snap buttons. Strapped inside was a new Browning .45. Three M-16s stood stacked by the door with double magazines, one taped over the other.

"Buenos días, Dan-yel, Berto," he said, unsmiling.

"Buenos días, Andreas," Berto and Daniel said, in unison.

"We believe the storm has finally expended itself." His two men nodded. "Perhaps today is the day you can leave."

Daniel and Berto exchanged glances as Romuela placed two more cups on the table.

"That's really good news," Daniel said. "Maybe after a good breakfast, we'll go to the barn and pack up."

Romuela carried the coffee pot to the table. Blanco placed his hand on her arm.

"Todavía no."

Daniel and Berto looked at each other again.

"We've already visited the barn," Blanco said.

Berto tried hard not to blush. Daniel cleared his throat.

"It seems your four mules, bridles, blankets and saddles are missing. Also some of ours."

His two men rose from their bench. The one with the revolver pulled it from his belt, held it cradled in the crook of his other arm. The other *cívico* held loops of rawhide thongs. Same two guys as two nights ago.

Blanco drained his cup and put it on the table. "I believe we are facing a crisis this morning."

"Crisis?" Daniel asked.

"Yes. Only a handful of my 75 *cívicos* from the countryside have showed up as I commanded. That might mean that some kind of impediment has got in their way."

He gestured to the man holding the rawhide thongs.

"We'll have to prepare for a possible invasion."

Romuela placed the heavy pot of coffee back onto the stove. Hard enough that the top rattled.

"Can you explain to me what happened to your mules and gear?"

"No, *señor*. I've been sick in bed and Berto...."

"...I've been asleep, too, *señor*. Until just a few minutes ago. When I smelled coffee brewing."

"Well, I don't have time to sort this out. So just to be cautious, I'm going to detain the two of you."

The man with the rawhide thongs grabbed two wood chairs from a stack in the corner of the kitchen. He gestured for Berto and Daniel to be seated, and he tied their wrists behind their backs and fastened them to the chairs. He also bound their ankles, one to each front leg of their chairs.

Blanco stood. "This may be just a drill. My men may yet show up by mid-day. If so, I will return to discuss your situation. If not...." He shrugged. *"Hasta luego."*

He and his men picked up their M-16s and walked out. As soon as they left, Yvonne came out of the bedroom holding Sonia's hand. She placed Frenchy's note on the table.

"Some savior you are, Daniel. Hog-tied and helpless."

"We're not hog-tied. Hog-tied is when...."

"Stop it! I don't care about fine distinctions. You're out of action."

Sonia swept up the note, looked at it, slipped it into a pocket of her dress. Then she walked around the chairs, examining where the rawhide thongs were positioned around Daniel's and Berto's wrists and feet.

"I'm leaving," Yvonne announced. Sonia's head swiveled, a look of astonishment on her face.

"What do you mean, 'leaving?'" Daniel asked.

Sonia moaned, trying to articulate her distress.

"The sun is out. Deep blue skies with just a few patchy clouds. Jerry is taking me with him to California."

Sonia ran to Yvonne, a pleading look in her eyes.

Yvonne wiped tears. Her own and Sonia's. Out of her mind with desperation, all she could think of was her own opportunity to escape.

"I'm so sorry for the harm I've caused you." She held Sonia by her slumped, trembling shoulders. "But you're in better hands with daddy and Berto. I love you very much." Then she looked at Romuela. A silent plea. Romuela covered her face with her hands. Then Yvonne turned and ran out the door.

"Mommy," Sonia whimpered and sat heavily on a bench next to the kitchen table.

Daniel thinking. *¿Como? Was that a word? An actual word? Am I that out of it?*

Shocked, Romuela dropped her tear-stained hands and embraced Sonia. "Oh! *Mi caramelita*! Your voice has returned!"

Stung by Yvonne's sudden abandonment, Daniel tried to remember when he had regained *his* voice. It was after learning that his father, Davey, had been shot to death in a Brooklyn bar by DiNardi's gunners. *"Like Ezekial," Uncle Abe had explained to astonished cousins, "when Jerusalem and the temple had been destroyed by the Babylonians, and he regained his voice."* The shock of losing mother and grandfather had taken his voice away; another shock had returned it.

"Sonia, speak to me."

"Wh…why is mommy leaving?" With the end of her apron, Romuela wiped away Sonia's tears.

Thank God!

"Come here, sweetheart. I need your help."

She approached Daniel.

"Lift up my right pant leg."

Sonia rolled it over his knee. "Like this?"

"Yes, dear. You see the black tape?"

"Y…yes, daddy."

"Find the end of the tape and unwrap it. There's a knife inside."

Sonia got down on her knees, found the tape, unwrapped it.

"Place the knife in my right hand."

She did as directed. The blade sprang open.

"Now take the knife and cut the rawhide thongs around my wrists. Carefully. One thong at a time. And be careful. The knife is very sharp."

"Daddy, how did you get such big hands?" she asked, sawing through one thong, then another.

She last asked me that question when we were laying on the floor together at our Mexico City cottage. I was recovering from another headache. She took my hand in hers, fingering the prominent thumb knuckle, the fingernails dense like plastic. Her anxiety, witnessing my debilitated state. "Daddy, are you still strong? Will you take care of me?"

"Hard work, dear one. Now give me the knife. I can finish."

Daniel sawed through the thongs that bound his ankles, then cut through Berto's.

"Romuela, would you please make breakfast for Sonia. And, after, pack up any of her belongings."

"Sí, señor."

"Daddy, I...I don't have any belongings. J...just my notebook and a pencil."

"Don't forget your barrette and coffee cup," Romuela said, with tenderness, marveling at Sonia's recovered voice.

"And my barrette and coffee cup."

Daniel reassured her. "Right now the best thing to do is eat breakfast and wait for me. I'll come back as soon as possible."

Sonia looked panicked. "Where are y...you going?"

"To get mommy, and then we'll leave...to go home."

"How are you g...going to get her?"

"I'll tell you later. It'll be a great story. You can write about it." Sonia's slow-spreading smile signified the beginning of relief and restored trust, deflating the tension in the kitchen. Even so, Daniel took her into his arms until her sniffles stopped, until the rigidity in her shoulders dissipated, until she melted into his embrace. He held her tight and murmured quiet confidences and kissed her tear-stained cheeks.

He and Berto disappeared back into the bedroom where they opened the seabag and dumped its contents on the cot. They changed into combat gear, painted their faces.

Berto grinned at Daniel and posed. *"Con safos, carnal." Caló,* meaning nobody can mess with this, brother.

"You take the shotgun," Daniel said. "I'll take the M-16."

Berto opened the cylinder of his .38 to make certain it was fully loaded and, similarly, checked the shotgun to determine that its eight-shell capacity was maximized and racked the action, putting a shotshell into the chamber. Daniel ejected the magazine from his Colt Commander, noted it was fully stacked with .38 caliber cartridges, slammed the mag back in, pulled the slide and released it, slamming the bolt home, chambering the first round. Then he carefully eased the hammer spur down and engaged the safety. Re-holstered it. He also chambered the first round in his M-16 and engaged its safety.

"You need me to come along?" Berto asked.

"No. I can handle it."

"What do you want me to do?"

"Blanco said he wanted you to take photos. Here's your perfect opportunity. Sling the shotgun until you absolutely have to use it."

Berto laughed. "I'd kiss you, but it might smear my paint."

Daniel smiled. "Semper fi, bro. Pay attention to the radio. I'll see you when it's all clear."

They crept out a side door. A helicopter sounded almost overhead. The same UH-34 Seahorse that dumped Moreno. Then a huge explosion, and they looked up to watch the chopper shudder, then disintegrate as a fireball exploded.

"RPG," Berto said.

"Really? Where did...? Never mind. You can tell me about it later."

Berto headed for the compound entrance, darting behind the cover of trees and shrubbery. *Yvonne was right. It's clearing up.... Good day for an airplane ride. Fuck, fuck, fuck.*

Daniel found the path that Berto had told him about, followed it until he came to the stone steps. He heard the Cessna's ignition, the engine beginning to warm up. He slung his M-16 and ran up the stairs and to the passenger-side door. *She is clearly rattled by the specter of me in war paint and battle dress. But in the split second before her head turns, I am shocked by her triumphant smile. Jerry's keeping his smugness to himself, not even noticing me, checking out his instrument panel.*

Daniel pulled his K-bar out of its sheath. The black, seven-inch blade gleamed only at its sharpened edge. He smashed her door handle with the steel butt end of the knife. The handle fell off and the door popped open a few inches. Then he ran to the right front tire and punctured it with a single stab. The plane titled sharply.

"Nothing will deter you.... Yvonne and Sonia are waiting.... You can do it."

A tremendous blast and a subsequent ripping noise, followed by screams of men being eviscerated by hundreds of ball bearings. *Claymore. This is not a drill.* The pop of small arms and bursts from M-16s, some on full auto. Then another claymore blast...and another.

With the radical tilt of the plane, the passenger door swung open. Daniel ran back. Yvonne dangled helplessly. He slashed her safety harness with the K-bar and she fell over his shoulder. Jerry turned off his engine and sat there, defeated and scared.

Daniel re-sheathed the K-bar and trotted back to the stairs.

"Wh...what's going on?" Yvonne screamed.

"It's all my fault. I'll make it up to you."

"Let me down! You're hurting me!"

He set her on the ground and grabbed her hand.

"We're being invaded! Stay close to me! Don't let go!"

"Where are we going?"

"To the stable. I want to get the mayor. We're going to need him later."

Berto was astounded at the force of the claymores. Dozens of State Police lay on the ground or, rather, some lay on the ground, parts of others were scattered about and dropping from trees where they'd initially landed. Leafy tree limbs and shrubs were shredded. Blanco and his men were howling with glee as they picked off police trying to skirt their flanks.

Berto snuck up behind Blanco, triggering his Leica.

I got all of it! Great action shots. Close-ups of The Man.

Blanco turned suddenly. Berto flashed him a V sign. Not for peace, for *Venceremos*. Blanco looked shocked and mystified, until he saw the camera.

"Jesus Christ!" he yelled, as his men continued to fire at blue uniforms. "What kind of apparition is this!?"

"It's me, Berto, Daniel's...."

"I know who the fuck you are! How did you get loose? Where did you get that uniform...face paint...those weapons? Your people took out about 60 police! How? And what the fuck are you wearing? Grenades?"

Berto pulled the fragmentation grenade from his web belt, pulled its pin to unlock a series of mechanisms, and flung it at a squad of police charging straight ahead past the bodies of their fallen comrades, screaming bloody murder. *Boom! All gone.*

"Yeah, I got one more left."

"How in God's name...?"

"I'll tell you later. It's a great story." He saw more blue uniforms gathering at the compound entrance for another charge. "But I think we oughta retreat to a defensive position. Got any ideas?"

"Yes!" He pulled a flare gun and fired. A flaming red missile arced above. He yelled into his radio: *"¡Síganme a la salida!"* His men came running over, just four in all, Miguel included, laughing when he saw Berto.

Daniel ran into the stable, found the stall where the mayor was still tied up, his eyes bulging with fear and confusion.

Daniel reached into his pocket, pulled out the stiletto. The blade slid open, six inches of lethal chrome-plated steel that Héctor had said he "made better" — meaning he sharpened the hell out of it. He handed it to Yvonne. The mayor lurched back.

"What?" she asked.

"I need your help. Cut his bonds."

She began to carefully saw away at the rawhide thongs that bound his hands and legs to the chair.

Daniel heard men running. He unslung his M-16 and ran to the barn door. Berto and two of Blanco's men were dashing across the yard, while Blanco paused to help one who was wounded. Several dozen State Police were closing in, bellowing with rage.

Berto stopped, turned and unslung the pump shotgun, taking out six. When the remaining police tried a shortcut climbing over the corral fence, Daniel picked off half. The others fell back, looking around, trying to figure out where the shots were coming from. Two sprinted to the barn door. Daniel drew his Colt Commander, disengaged the safety and thumbed back the hammer spur. When they turned inside, their mouths opened in surprise as they confronted a painted Pathfinder.

If my Korean mentor The Cobra were in my place, he'd probably take them both out with a combination of kicks and open hand strikes. But I'm not The Cobra. Instead, he put them down with two center-mass shots each.

Daniel holstered his pistol. "We're going to the kitchen to get Sonia and Romuela. The mayor hasn't been on his feet for a while. Grab him by the arm and make sure he can make it. I might have to lay down covering fire."

Yvonne nodded. She closed the switchblade and handed it to Daniel.

"Keep it," he said. "You might need it again."

She slid it into her jeans' back pocket. *Wow! This is really something!*

They made it back to the kitchen, although Daniel had to stop several times to shoot pursuers, slam another magazine into the M-16 and shoot more. When others began to bunch up and prepare to fire their weapons from about 20 yards away, he armed the phosphorous grenade and tossed it. A big explosion sent shock waves, followed by a blanket of smoke and a shower of burning particles which clung to their skin and uniforms. Screaming survivors clutched their throats, choking, reeling, collapsing.

Romuela was ready. "Meet us at the back door! It's safer! I have your *campesino* clothing, hats and sandals in your bag. And blankets!"

When Daniel rounded the corner of the building he saw Romuela giving water to the mayor and Yvonne kneeling to embrace Sonia.

Miguel raced around the other side. "This way!"

When they made it to the beginning of the exit trail, only two of Blanco's men were standing with Blanco, who was bleeding profusely from his nose. One lay on the ground with what looked like a severe shoulder wound from the spreading stain of blood. Héctor and Marisol were waiting there, too, waving frantically. Berto continued to shoot film, working on his third roll.

"Where's Frenchy?" Daniel shouted.

"Here, in the shade!" Marisol hissed.

Frenchy was laying on his back.

"Are you hit?" Daniel asked, fearing the worst.

"I can't walk, D. Héctor and Miguel carried me here in a blanket stretcher."

"What happened?"

"I was high up in a tree, blasting away at the police as they massed at the entrance. Then we detonated the claymores, three different times because they kept advancing. The blow back was greater than I expected. It shocked me, and I fell."

"What do you mean, greater than expected?"

"I never fired off so many claymores before today. Usually one at a time and at a small group of infiltrators. Twenty percent blowback is one thing; twenty percent times three...."

"Are you in pain?"

Frenchy smiled. "Yes. Something feels broken. But Héctor hit me with an ampule of morphine."

"It's good you can feel pain," Berto said. "Otherwise your spinal chord would be damaged, and you'd be paralyzed."

"We have only eight mules!" Marisol hissed. "Five with saddles. How are we going to transport everyone?"

"Two of my men will stay here with me," Blanco said, "but please take my brother out of here. Leave your grenades with us. We have four M-16s with extra ammo and six RPGs. And you have four claymores left over. We'll take out whoever follows you down this narrow defile."

" 'Nosotros' no 'ustedes,' " Daniel said.

"What do you mean?"

"We're all leaving together."

"But I am the enemy. I need to stand my ground and fight."

"The hell you do," Berto said.

"You saved my wife and child, Andreas," Daniel said. He waved at Héctor.

"Héctor, do you have another morphine ampule?"

Héctor nodded and tossed it. "Hit Andreas' brother."

"Berto, look into our first-aid kit for compresses and tape. See if you can stop the bleeding."

Berto went to work. "His pulse is weak, but his breathing is regular. Hollywood heroes would be up and mounted in 10 minutes. But this is not a movie. Andreas, what's your brother's name?"

Blanco stammered, stopped, took a deep breath. "Javier."

"What happened to your nose?"

"I w...as s...s...standing beside him when he got shot. His arm f...flew back and h...hit me in the face."

"You got a broken nose. I'll straighten it in a minute."

Berto dumped sulpha power over Javier's entry wound, and pressed a field dressing over it for about 10 minutes. At the same time, he asked Javier several questions: his name, age, where he was, what happened to him.

"You hold the dressing," he ordered Blanco. "Press firm. I'll roll him a bit."

Daniel could see there was no exit wound. "How bad is it?"

"It would've been better had it been his right shoulder. The left shoulder is closer to the heart. The round hit just below his clavicle but it might've been stopped by the scapula, which means the bullet might be in fragments. If it'd been a through-and-through, there'd be a fairly unremarkable exit wound and less blood loss. It probably missed his lung because his breathing isn't too labored.

"His color isn't too bad, either. His skin feels warm to the touch, he's not confused. So that's good.

"But his pulse is somewhat weak. In terms of internal bleeding, there are two arteries to worry about, the subclavian artery and the brachial artery — the main artery of the arm. There's also the brachial plexus, the large nerve bundle that controls arm function. His upper arm is swelling, so I'm going to apply a combat-application tourniquet. When it's secure, it'll provide true pressure all the way around.

"But if one of those arteries is hit, and we're at least 24 hours from a doctor, he could die. Or lose his arm."

Blanco's face pinched with despair. He choked back a sob. Everyone looked away.

"We can take him to San Mateo," the mayor said. "Him and Frenchy. There's a good clinic, two good doctors. It's not that far away. Maybe 16 hours on foot, unless we get a ride."

The others stared at the mayor.

Tears welled in his eyes. "This entire experience has chastened me.... The *matanza*.... I was not responsible for detaining Luis Moreno. I admired him. It was Gustavo Olema, head of the State Police, and behind it all, Gov. Castillo. My council and I were considering negotiating with Luis. They threatened to arrest us if we did that, put us in prison. Didn't want a precedent set. So, indirectly, Señor Blanco saved my life, and directly, you did. Whatever I can do...."

Looking back toward the compound, Daniel could see State Police re-grouping, re-loading. Maybe a dozen. Despite their escape, it was no time for jubilation. The mission had yet to be completed, reaching safe haven.

"Sonia can ride with Romuela," Daniel said. "Berto and I are wearing boots, so we'll carry Frenchy. But we have to make a better stretcher. Héctor, see if you can cut two straight limbs from a tree, at least seven feet long. Make them as smooth as possible, like poles.

"Berto, we've got 50 feet of coiled rope tied to one of the mules. When Héctor returns with the poles, we'll make a stretcher by loosely weaving the rope between them, then pad it with blankets. We can also bind him to the stretcher to keep him stable.

"Yvonne, Héctor, and the mayor can ride. Javier needs a mount. Miguel, Marisol and Andreas, you walk beside his mule. Take turns to keep him steady."

They nodded.

How many police were there originally? A battalion?

The few officers remaining were shouting, re-grouping their men. Troop trucks lumbered into the compound, loaded with more police.

More than a reinforced company now. If they figure out where we've exfiltrated....

Daniel knelt, closed his eyes. His mind raced. Yvonne put a hand on his shoulder. Sonia embraced him.

"Trust me...help is on the way...you will win, my boy."

"Are we f...free, Daddy? Are we going to be OK?"

Blanco and another *cívico* sidled into position with their RPGs, released depleted magazines from two of their M-16s and slammed in replacements. Berto clicked on his telephoto lens.

From higher ground, Daniel looked down at the compound, a panoramic view that included the airstrip, Jerry cowering behind the Cessna, the downed helicopter, the mountain lake above it and beyond to the north entrance.

Suddenly there was a loud crack then a low rumbling that felt like an earthquake. The police in the compound froze. The Cessna began to slide and underneath it the runway, and then the rumbling turned into a loud roar. An entire section of mountain above the runway had broken away, followed by a huge surge of lake water. In seconds, the earth and water formed a wall of mud about 30 meters high. Trees twisted in the force of the mud, which raced toward the compound's buildings and the police and their trucks. A few police seemed to be frantically swimming on top of the flow, then disappeared as if it were quicksand. Within seconds, the Cessna, Jerry, the helicopter wreckage, trucks, the police... the entire compound had disappeared.

December 6
Laguna del Ejido
Daniel's Story

CHAPTER 21

Frenchy is sitting in a plastic and metal lounge chair, the kind that can tilt back. Marisol and I wheeled him to the shadiest spot provided by the mangroves at the lagoon, the spot where he arranged for me to… receive Uncle Abe. It's practically the only place where he feels relief because the cervical-thoracic brace he has to wear for the broken vertebrae in his upper back is cumbersome and uncomfortable in this tropical climate. In the shade at the lagoon, however, there's a refreshing breeze, and he can soak his feet in the cool water. While sitting, of course. He also has plenty of cold *jamaica* to drink. And *mota*, to help him relax and sleep. Lidia and Sonia tend to his needs there.

The doc at the San Mateo clinic told us on Nov. 24, the morning we arrived, that — based on X-rays — Frenchy fractured the T3 through T5 vertebrae when he fell from the tree. But he assured us that the spinal cord did not appear to be harmed. He allowed us to keep the X-rays, so when Prado showed up in a CIA helicopter and we flew him to a hospital in Acapulco, the orthopedic specialist there confirmed the initial diagnosis. He said surgery would've been required only if the fractured vertebrae were unstable and couldn't support the rest of the spine.

After a week in the hospital where he could be monitored and medicated, we were allowed to transport him by ambulance to *Casa Elvira*. In 6-10 weeks he should be able to begin therapy, which Marisol and I will supervise.

But what Frenchy is most concerned about is his JW network.

Héctor relieved Jerry of two 60-pound burlap sacks of *colas de zorras* during our escape from Blanco's compound. We packed it on one of the mules. Some is being used for medicinal purposes, but the rest will go toward financing continued support for the network, as the *campesinos* most likely have nothing to trade and, except for *miel*, won't have anything for another year. Yesterday, Marisol took her first hippie clients on a horseback ride along the sunset beach. She raised a decent amount of money. Soon, she and Héctor and I will make our first trip into the mountains with more than the usual supplies and medicines. They must be in tough shape up there.

Tropical storm Isaias packed winds between 70 and 80 miles per hour and dumped between 18 to 24 inches of rain. The Interior Minister declared a state of disaster in 56 Guerrero municipalities, including Tres Marías, just west of Blanco's compound.

A local newspaper quoted a survivor of one of the mudslides. "It was like an explosion burst open the mountain, and in seconds the earth came down and the houses appeared to run, while others were buried. Then it hit us and we were rolling. The house was in sticks. We were buried under things, then we dug ourselves out. It was apocalyptic."

The Interior Minister said the cost of repairing damages to roads, bridges, and structures was "incalculable." He also said people were desperate for food, drinking water and other basics. In Tres Marías, which was no longer accessible by road, the majority of villagers were feared dead, buried by a huge mudslide. He also said authorities were searching for a police helicopter containing the State Police chief and the governor that disappeared near Tres Marías the day of the mudslides. It was thought to have been lost during a heroic rescue operation. But there was no mention in the local press or radio about a State Police raid on Blanco's stronghold.

Acapulco was hit hard, as you can imagine. Main roads were flooded, thousands of dwellings damaged. More than 12,000 refugees were cared for in 47 shelters. The two main highways in and out of the city were blocked by mudslides. The road closures and flooding of the airport terminal meant that 40,000 tourists, mostly Mexicans visiting during the national holiday, were stranded. Although 100 military flights were able to evacuate 10,000 people within a few days.

There was quite a bit of grumbling among citizens and local journalists that repairs would most likely be stalled for some time due to local, state and federal corruption and political shortsightedness. Officials had not learned from earlier tropical storms and had failed to prepare for disaster. Turns out the federal disaster fund allocates only 5 percent of its budget on prevention and the other 95 percent on reconstruction, most of which will be siphoned off by officials and their cronies. The government could've taken preventive measures, like relocating settlements from the most vulnerable areas or investing in infrastructure.

Casa Elvira managed to escape structural damage. Of course, the palm shelters in front were flattened, but the honeymoon hammocks were rescued. Electricity and gas were restored on Nov. 30. Until then, Graciela, Elvira, Don Julio, Lidia, Marisol, Yvonne and Sonia and, eventually, the rest of us survived quite nicely. With air-tight quart canning jars of rice, several pounds of potatoes and onions, and canned tomatoes, Elvira and Graciela prepared turtle stews cooked over an open fire. Then they prepared another series of stews featuring *armadillo*, which Héctor captured. It tasted like pork. Over ensuing days, a local fisherman sold us *huachinango*, red snapper.

Once we arrived, Héctor, Berto, Marisol, Yvonne and a half-dozen recruited workers and I helped rebuild Elvira's palm shelters and Graciela's corral and *jacales*. *Sala Frenchy* remained largely intact, but suffered water damage. The canvas ring will have to be replaced and so will the ropes, heavy punching bag and gloves, which we had to junk.

Blanco was treated for his broken nose, but his brother Javier died from internal bleeding and shock. The mayor insisted that Blanco stay at his hacienda while he planned his brother's funeral and burial. The only other *cívico* fighter to survive the police invasion was also invited to rest and recuperate. Miguel and Romuela, too.

To me, the mayor offered to hide our uniforms, combat gear, weapons and the remaining claymores. "Just in case they might be needed again."

The mayor and his town council have been very efficient in organizing local relief teams to deal with the damage left behind by the storm, the aid required to treat the sick and injured at the clinic, even contributing his own money to pay for supplies, relief workers and medicines. He has also vowed to surreptitiously work with Blanco and his remaining supporters and to fulfill to the best of his ability Blanco's long-standing demands for resource and infra-structure allocation — within reason and through secret negotiations. The mayor also vowed to meet many of the essential demands of Luis Moreno's *campesino* organization.

Along with the mayor, Blanco appears to have undergone a life-changing metamorphosis.

"I deeply believed in what I was doing," he said about his becoming a *guerrilla* leader. "But, ultimately, my ego led me in the wrong direction. I am responsible for the deaths of my brother and so many of my *cívicos*. I put people's lives in jeopardy, the people I championed and who depended on me. I have many years of produc-tive life ahead of me. I don't want to be a revolutionary martyr.

"Learning about Frenchy, his humility, his efforts to rescue me from the State Police invasion, your dedication.... Like you, I want to be a part of his network. It's a better way to serve my people and meet their needs."

The mayor told him that state authorities believed he and his *cívicos* died in the mudslide that destroyed his compound. What that means, said the mayor, is that Blanco is a free man, free to begin a new, if anonymous, life. The old Blanco remains a myth. *Corridos* will be written about him, the mayor said. He also said he would help Blanco assume a new identity.

I wanted to believe this conversion, but I was still enough of a skeptic to wait and see if they could actually pull it off. Time will tell.

"Will you help me, *Dan-yel?*" Blanco asked.

"Por supuesto, mi amigo," Of course, I promised.

The mayor insisted we use his private telephone to contact Prado, who flew to the hacienda within hours.

He wanted to know how it all went down. Over a Thanksgiving dinner and brandy, we told him the details.

"And how did you get here?"

"We trekked through the narrow defile for about 10 kilometers," I said, "then along dirt roads that hadn't been completely washed out. We ate on the run, finishing off all our C-rations. It was painstaking and exhausting carrying Frenchy, making certain to step in unison, like a slow march, to keep him stable. We all took turns carrying him and keeping Javier in his saddle."

"I thought a truck would come along at some point," the mayor told Prado. "But, of course, the storm eliminated that possibility."

"So we rode and we walked all day, all night, and all the next day until we entered San Mateo," Blanco said.

The mayor told them, "It was just like a ghost town."

"Until we arrived at the clinic," Marisol added, "and the mayor went into action, tirelessly organizing everyone and everything to bring the village back to life."

"Wow!" Prado exclaimed, "some kind of higher power must've been watching over you!"

Tears glistening in his eyes, Blanco crossed himself. His surviving fighter, Miguel, his wife Romuela, Marisol and Héctor followed suit.

Frenchy, laying on his side and being fed by Romuela, nodded and exchanged glances with me, meaning how much Prado's words rang true. "It *was* a deliverance."

Frenchy thanked us for carrying him to San Mateo, using the most sincere and profound expression: *"Je vous remercie."*

The next day, he was loaded into the helicopter. Yvonne, Sonia, Berto, Marisol and I accompanied him, along with Prado, who was the chief of this mission. Saying goodbye to Miguel and Romuela was very moving. I almost had to pry Sonia from Romuela's teary embrace.

"You must come back to visit us, *mi caramelita.* I will miss you so much."

"I will, Romuela. I promise."

Yvonne took me aside. "My anthropology professor at the University of the Americas wouldn't believe this revival experience. It's better than anything we studied. Especially the outcomes involving the mayor and Blanco...their stress conversions, their willingness to cooperate, the implied balanced reciprocity."

Yes. A much more profound miracle than divine intervention...unless it's all of one piece.

"It might seem improbable to some," I said, "this sudden conversion to gratitude and generosity. But it makes sense that when Blanco and the mayor's way of being in the world did not work anymore, they changed. We all do that sometimes...remake ourselves. It's just like your Handsome Lake essay. Handsome Lake turned his life around, from alcoholic to preacher, revived the traditional religion with a revised moral code and became a renowned leader so the Iroquois Confederacy would survive in a post-colonial era. Maybe you can make Blanco, Frenchy and his JW network your dissertation."

She looked at me. Pensive. "Maybe.... Some day."

By the first week of December, the post-storm emergency status had eased and things began to settle down and work the way they're supposed to. That is, except between Yvonne and me.

No matter what we had gone through, and though the appearance of a reconciliation seemed a done deal, that wasn't to be the case. Before the rescue, I believed I wanted everything between us to be as it was. But I had come to realize that it couldn't be. Not ever again. When she revealed that before Tlatelolco her research indicated that the United Council of American Indians in the Bay Area was discussing the possibility of invading and occupying the former federal prison at Alcatraz within a year, she couldn't contain her enthusiasm.

"I have to go there. I have to be part of it. It's momentous; it's huge. They're staking a claim under a 100-year-old treaty permitting non-reservation Indians to claim land the U.S. government had once taken for forts and other uses and later abandoned.

"The simple fact of the matter is that your love for me no longer makes me feel fulfilled," she told me one morning while we walked to the lagoon for a swim. "I hunger to possess my own life. I want to make decisions that give my life meaning. More than anything, I want to be a fighter for our people...my people. I can't just be a back-up to you, be a wife and mother, and I have no interest in pursuing an academic career that only benefits me and a bunch of upper-middle class high achievers. It's a false accomplishment.

"Don't get me wrong, I'm very proud of you, and I'm eternally grateful for what you've done for me and Sonia, risking your life to save us. It might be different if you were willing to return to the U.S. with me and build a new life along the lines of what I want. But I can see you're determined to go back to Mexico City to look for Inez. And I can see that you're committed to staying here and helping Frenchy recover from his injury, helping him and Blanco reconstitute his JW network."

"Frenchy saved my life...twice," I reminded her, "in Lebanon and here. When it came down to nailing Blanco or saving you and Sonia, he chose us. He made that decision out of the purest of motives. He built me up to become a leader of that mission when I doubted myself and lacked commitment. He's like a brother to me, Yvonne. I can't leave him.

"I also owe Blanco for saving you and Sonia...and me. He could've killed me when I showed up, killed me and Berto. He could've immediately suspected our motives as threatening to him, but he gave us the benefit of the doubt. Even when the mules were taken from his barn, he merely detained us.

"About Inez, I can't let go. I have to find out what happened to her. 'Disappearance' is too vague, for me and for her parents. There has to be a final resolution."

"I respect everything you say and everything you've done, Daniel. But it still doesn't resolve my yearning to do something important with *my* life."

"What about Sonia?"

I understood the difficulty she had with this issue. She didn't *ever* want to put Sonia's life in jeopardy again. She already said so. But when she'd told Sonia that she'd be better off with me, she really meant that by choosing a life of activism over everything else, she would cause Sonia to feel unjustly subordinate, unhappy and, eventually, a burden. I could see her struggling to answer. So I decided to pursue a different but related tack.

"What about Berto?"

She bristled. "What about him? You had Inez; I had Berto. She met your needs; he met mine."

Touché.

"And I can see that look in Marisol's eye whenever you're around, appraising you. I'm no fool. She's crazy about you, and she's beautiful. It's just a matter of time...."

When we finally took our swim, we shared the same sea, but we'd drifted apart.

Berto and I bade a different kind of farewell, also at the lagoon that evening during one of the most beautiful sunsets I'd ever seen. Replete with *jamaica, mota, mescal.* He was saving his only remaining tab of benzedrine for the final stretch of his journey. Tomorrow, Prado would drive Berto and Yvonne to Zihuatanejo where he had arranged for a State Department-leased 42-foot motor-sailer to transport them to San Diego. Complete with a security team. Berto had no choice; he's a fugitive wanted for murder. Prado also provided cover passports and visas, just in case the Mexican Coast Guard hailed them on the open sea, which he said wasn't likely.

"I'm saving your pics of the *matanza* at San Mateo," I said. "They're not intended for publication. I have a hunch they might come in handy in case the state ever gives the mayor a hard time for what he's doing to help his people. Which is not exactly going by the *PRI* book.

"You have the photos of the police invasion of Blanco's compound and the only photos of Blanco — famed *guerrilla* fighter — before his spectacular demise. What are you going to do with those?"

"I'll try *Life* first. If they don't bite, some European magazine or an alternative rag like *Ramparts*. They're headquartered in San Francisco."

"Not IPS?"

"Nah. Those pics are too good for newsprint resolution. Anyway, I resigned after the Olympics."

"How did Cogdill handle it?"

"You know him. Mr. Congeniality and Bon Vivant. But underneath the surface? He probably feels betrayed."

"After all he did for *us*?" I asked.

"No. After all *we* did for *him*."

I took a hit off Berto's joint, one of the biggest I'd ever seen, the size of an ice cream cone, filled to the brim with about an eighth-ounce of JW sinsemilla. He was taking final advantage of our bounty.

"You going to stay in San Francisco?"

"That Alcatraz story has the potential to be really something. Couldn't be better having *La India* vouch for me."

"Just be careful. It's colder 'n shit out on that bay. June or December, makes no difference."

I passed him the joint…er…cone. He took a gigantic hit, then coughed most of it right back out.

"Yeah," he said, his eyes tearing. "I'm sure we'll have to shop surplus, pick up warm clothes and sleeping bags. Imagine, me in a pea coat and knit cap again."

I was curious about what his intentions were with Yvonne, but I was reluctant to ask him. I knew what he wanted, but I also knew that Yvonne had a different agenda. Nonetheless, with his reputation as a photographer and as a warrior, I had no doubt he'd fit right in with her crew. And her.

"I'm really proud of you, bro," I said. "The way you handled yourself on the mission. Beyond my wildest expectations, especially considering that I trained for it, and you just rode right in. Marisol said she was worried about you. Thought you were a *payaso*, a clown."

"I *am* a clown, a fool; it's part of my charm." His smile was wide and smug and tenderly reminiscent. "Exasperate, then penetrate."

"No, really. You forget. War…. I've been through this before.

You've never been. You needed the training Frenchy provided. For me, the mission just kicked right in. You broke your cherry up there. But I'm proud of you, too, for your tenacity. The way you took charge."

He burst out laughing. That hard, raucous laugh I hadn't heard in a long time.

"On second thought, the hardest part was riding the damn mule. My ass may never recover; it might be broken."

"Asses don't break."

"Yeah, well, you know what I mean."

"If the invasion and occupation of Alcatraz actually happens... no way the feds are going to let that last."

"If things don't work out there, I'm thinking of heading south again, some place in Central America or South America. Some place warm where there are beautiful women.... Man, I'm gonna miss Ana. I'm gonna miss Marisol, too."

He waved his hand. "Do you think you might, you know.... I think she's got eyes for you."

"Marisol is very cool. Very cool. But I've got other things on my mind."

"¡Qué lástima!" What a pity! "What 'other things' could you possibly have on your mind that would take precedence over Marisol? Or Ana, man. You gotta check her out."

"Inez."

"Oh." His smile disappeared.

"Are you going to pass me that cone some day?"

"Oh."

I took a big hit and coughed. Didn't matter if I held it in. Went right to my head. Last hit for me. Well...maybe one more...in a little bit.

"So, about Inez...."

"Prado told me he's working on something. He said he'd let me know after he returns from Zihuatanejo."

"I can't believe you're really going back to Mexico City."

"I have to."

"Are you at least gonna make the drive with us? I hear tell Zihuatanejo is a real pretty port."

"Nah. I have to prep a trek into the mountains with Héctor and Marisol, see how Frenchy's network is making out. It'll take us all day to pack loads." *Which wasn't really true. We weren't going for another couple of days.*

"You have a very different life now, Daniel. Very different."

I nodded. "I want to be a part of Frenchy's family. I want to raise my daughter here."

I took the *mota* cone from him. Berto seemed near-catatonic. He watched it disappear from his grasp as if he were losing his best friend.

"Here," I said, passing him the berry-flavored *mescal*. "You must be thirsty."

He took a long sip and grimaced.

"Jesus H. Christ. I'm gonna miss this."

"You *are* heading to hippie country."

"Yeah. But, you know, there's nothing like *this*."

Meaning our intuitive and remarkable friendship and all that we'd been through. Our symbiotic working relationship over many difficult years, the abrupt separation, coming together again to accomplish what seemed like an impossible mission. I began to cry. So did Berto, surprising me with sobs that matched my own. Ashamed, we smothered our outbursts and covered our faces while our shoulders shook with spasms of sadness and mourning. We sat apart, crying quietly yet completely.

He was first to pull himself together. "Shit, man. Let's go for my last swim." His eyes were red and brimming, his face crimped with misery.

"OK, *cabrón*." I wiped my cheeks and we waded into the lagoon just as the last of the sun flared and fell into the sea.

December 8 — 16
Laguna del Ejido and Mexico City
Daniel's Story

CHAPTER 22

Prado had Berto take passport photos for all of us. Fortunately, I had begun to grow a beard after arriving at *Laguna del Ejido*. The photos were rushed to Mexico City and the passports and visas were returned by special courier who flew into Acapulco. Berto's and Yvonne's passports and tourist visas identified them as husband and wife, William and Dolores Logan of Santa Fe, New Mexico. Prado said he would send new passports in their real names once they relocated in San Francisco.

Sonia and I were issued new passports under the names Jesse Isaacs — my Iroquois uncle's name — and Mary Isaacs— my late mother's maiden name. Jesse was alive, but he relied on his Iroquois Nation passport when he traveled out of the U.S., which was rare. We were also given Permanent Resident Immigrant visas. Those are issued to people who are professionals, among other occupations, and my new profession is religious missionary, assistant to Frenchy, whose new passport and resident visa identifies him as Raymond Tessier, an American missionary of the Jehovah's Witness persuasion, from Baton Rouge, Louisiana. Sonia will be able to attend government-funded schools.

Witnessing Yvonne's farewell to Sonia was one of the hardest things I've ever done, considering that what had transpired among us was largely my fault. Sonia took it a lot better than Yvonne and me, and when Yvonne rushed to the horse that would take her to *Casa Elvira* where Prado was waiting, Sonia actually tried to comfort me.

"It's all right, daddy. I understand what mommy's doing. I know she loves me, and I know I'll see her again. I'm happy to be with you in *Laguna del Ejido*. It's very pretty and peaceful here and at *Casa Elvira* and the beach. And everybody likes me, especially Lidia, my best friend, and Marisol."

She showed me a long letter that Yvonne had written, which ended with the closing lines from *"Poem"* by John Cornford, Cambridge Marxist and poet who died at 21 while serving as a machine gunner with the International Brigade in Spain, 1936:

Remember all the good you can;
don't forget my love.

We spent the rest of the day at the beach, riding with Marisol and her merry band of *mota*-loving *gringos*, then enjoying a dinner of red snapper at *Casa Elvira*, followed by ice cream and cake, then a quiet ride at sunset back to *Laguna del Ejido*.

The next day, Marisol, Héctor and I rode up into the mountains while Prado waited at *Casa Elvira*. It was hot and sunny, and the canyon stream beds we climbed to the first settlement were running close to normal. After a half day, we arrived at the small plot of land on a plateau settled by Pablo and Estella Molina. They and some friends were repairing their corral and *acequia*. Their *jacal* had already been rebuilt.

Most of their chickens survived the storm, but the Molina crew were in desperate need of food and supplies. We unpacked several kilo bags of *masa harina* and pinto beans, and Estella immediately set to cooking. We also gave her ancho chile powder and garlic for the beans, as well as kilo bags of rice, sugar, and a box of salt, cans of spam, powdered eggs, baby formula and medicines. Their first meal was a feast for all who were visiting. They repeatedly expressed their gratitude and their regrets that they had no measurable amount of *mota* to trade. And as for *miel*, "who knows when the bees will return."

I explained to Pablo that Frenchy and I had a very large supply of *mota*, more than enough until next fall, to finance our visits. I asked him to help me make a list of things they needed.

They all were too hungry to pray before dinner so, over sweetened coffee, Marisol and I went through Frenchy's litany. Then we told the story of fighting off the State Police at Blanco's stronghold, our retreat to San Mateo and the mayor and Blanco's conversion. Our stories were met with repeated exclamations of astonishment and celebration.

"When will Frenchy be able to return to us?" Estella asked.

I explained his back injury, then tried to reassure them that his mission would continue, and that more help would soon be on the way. "Probably Frenchy won't be able to ride up the mountain for quite a while. But we'll return every two weeks to make certain everything is satisfactory here. If Blanco shows up, don't be afraid of him. He has pledged to carry on the same work as Frenchy. As a matter of fact, he wants to drill a water well for you."

I checked Pablo. The scars on his forehead and neck from the wounds he suffered during the *matanza* were long, red and raised, like welts. But the doctor at the San Mateo clinic had expertly stitched him up, and the scars showed no sign of infection.

We said another round of prayers before retiring. I remembered how shaken by their poverty I'd been the first time I'd visited, and how moved I was by their steadfast faith. We'd all been through quite a bit in the last month, but everyone was hopeful for a brighter future. I remembered the phrase that Miguel had taught me, *a la vuela de la esquina*. Just around the corner. When I shared that thought with Pablo and Estella the next morning over coffee, they corrected me:

"Oh, no, *Dan-yel*," Estella said. "Thanks to God, the good time is now! New life is now!"

I must've look confused, so Estella asked me to read Psalm 37, of David, and then I understood: *"The wicked draw the sword and bend the bow to bring down the poor and needy, to slay those whose ways are upright. But their swords will pierce their own hearts, and their bows will be broken."*

Over the next two days, our receptions at Frenchy's other JW settlements were identical. Everyone was rebuilding, everyone was hungry, everyone was grateful to receive so much food and medicine, and everyone was filled with hope, especially as Christmas and New Year's were just a few weeks away. They were already anticipating roads, wells, electricity and schools.

Our ride back down to Graciela's corral was lighter, and not just because we'd delivered every last ounce of aid.

After a day of rest, a massage by Lidia and a leisurely swim in the lagoon with Lidia, Marisol, Héctor and Sonia, I had a quiet dinner at *Casa Elvira* with Prado.

He smoked a cigar with his after-dinner coffee and *mescal.*

"I've become acquainted with Marisol's former boss at Judicial Police."

"You mean Guzmán?"

"Yes. He was really moved by her resignation letter. He said she was like a daughter to him. He and his wife don't have children."

"Does he know what happened up in the mountains?"

"Yes, up to a point. The rescue, the mudslide, the loss of life. He was very impressed."

"He was ready to bust all our asses."

"Because he was working on locating Blanco. But since he learned that Blanco died in the mudslide, that job is over."

"You didn't tell him…."

"I said I told him everything…up to a point."

"The rescue mission…?"

"Yes. In detail. Including your rescue of the mayor and your trek to San Mateo. Carrying Frenchy all the way."

"The freakin' massacre of the State Police? The shoot-down of the chopper?"

"No. No one is discussing that. The official story is that the chopper with Gov. Castillo and Gustavo Olema aboard was on a rescue mission, and they died heroically trying to warn people about the imminent danger of mudslides, trying to save lives."

"Does he know about the massacre at San Mateo?"

"Yes. Some idiot among the State Police actually filmed it, and it was confiscated and then stolen. And then sold and delivered to Judicial Police."

"How does he feel about that?"

"Terrible, but it's being held under lock and key in order to maintain the government's heroic mudslide narrative. He's had a change of heart about Tlatelolco, too."

"Why?"

"Because he knows it was a government set-up, from Díaz Ordaz and his secretary of government, to the army, the Olympic Battalion...everyone involved. His own people from Judicial Police and agents of the Federal Security Directorate were the snipers who were the opening act of the massacre."

"How did he find that out?"

"I told him. At a lunch meeting with one of our top CIA agents."

"Why did you do that?"

"To gain his loyalty. To help you."

"And he believed it?"

"We presented him with a detailed oral report and incontrovertible evidence in the form of communication intercepts."

"When will the rest of the world know about it?"

"I don't know. We're not in a position to reveal it."

"Then...."

"It's going to take some enterprising journalists."

Daniel shook his head, meaning don't count on me.

"Don't worry, I'm not suggesting you get involved. That's pretty much impossible, if you want to thrive in your new life. Oriana Fallaci will never return. She hates Mexico for what was done to her."

"I owe my life to others now. My daughter. Frenchy and his family."

"I know. There are some brave, enterprising Mexicans working to get the truth out. Did you ever meet the journalist and novelist Elena Poniatowska?"

"Yes. I met her once, at a reception at the International Press

Club. And I saw her at plenty of protests."

"She's already conducting jailhouse interviews with strike leaders, professors and witnesses who avoided arrest."

"Good for her. So what about Guzmán?"

"He discovered what happened to Inez, and he knows who can tell us everything. In person."

Daniel shoved his coffee aside, drained a short glass of *mescal.*

His heart raced with anxiety, and he could feel sweat begin to trickle down his back.

"Including where she is?"

"Yes."

"When do we leave?"

"*Mañana.* We'll fly the Huey back to Mexico City first thing in the morning."

Prado and I met Guzmán for breakfast at Sanborns.

"It's good to see you again, my friend, although I'm sorry about the circumstances," Guzmán said, his expression no longer impassive like the first time we met, now replaced with intense concern, which made me uneasy.

"Yes, sir. I'm very grateful for your help."

"No problem. How is Marisol?"

"She's fine. She speaks very well of you and misses you. But she's very happy with the way things turned out. She's part of a missionary outreach now, working hard to help poor people living in settlements in the mountains."

"You, too?"

"Yes, sir."

"It was obvious Marisol was attracted to you from the first time she met you...on the bus. Are you...is it mutual?"

"No, sir. We're just colleagues."

Guzmán smiled inwardly. *For now maybe, but she will make herself irresistible. You're doomed.* "You don't have to be so formal with me, Daniel. Call me by my first name, Manuel."

"So, Manuel, who is this guy we're meeting, and how are we going to proceed?"

"We're meeting a young officer, a lieutenant with the 18th Cavalry Regiment. He was assigned to the Olympic Battalion that captured and arrested the student strike leaders the night of Tlatelolco. We're going to meet him at the Toluca Military Zone and then proceed to Nevado de Toluca. We told him to keep it confidential. He'll be off-duty."

I pushed my plate away. Inside my chest I felt another erratic thud of my heart. *Nevado de Toluca.... Oh, no. He's going to show us where Inez is buried.*

I told Guzmán the story told to me by Ríus.

"Yes," he said, "I'm afraid it's the same situation, only worse."

We discussed a plan of how to proceed. Stay calm. Let the guy take us to the place. Dig up her remains and put them in a body bag. Take it to an undertaker. Prado was driving a white 1965 International Harvester TravelAll confiscated from a big-time opium smuggler now rotting in a Mexican prison. Plenty of room.

"Will I be able to phone Inez' father? I believe he'll want to witness this."

Guzmán and Prado agreed. After a short phone call, Señor García said he'd go with us. We picked him up in front of his apartment. He slid in next to me in the back seat. His hair was a little grayer than the last time I saw him, his face more drawn. I introduced him to Prado and Guzmán.

He took hold of my hand. "I never thought I'd see you again, *Dan-yel.*"

I told him about the rescue mission, that it was successful, and that I was going to remain in Mexico and live with Frenchy's family at *Laguna del Ejido*, with my daughter but without Yvonne.

He nodded, seeming to understand, but really just being polite. He was too concerned about the scenario which was about to unfold.

"Do you believe...*es muerta*?"

"We believe so, Señor García," Guzmán said.

"This man is going to show us where she is buried?"

"Yes, sir," Guzmán said.

"And then we'll dig up her body and take it to an undertaker?"

"Yes, sir," Prado said. "Someone will do that."

He burst into tears, without shame, and he cried as easily as a child for about 10 minutes as we drove out Reforma to the Toluca highway. Prado passed me a package of tissues to give him.

He removed a handful, wiped away his tears, blew his nose. "Her mother and I will be very grateful to have her returned to us. Not knowing was the hardest part."

When we reached the Toluca Military Zone, the lieutenant was waiting 200 yards from the entrance as instructed, seated at a covered bus stop. We pulled over, and he slid into the front seat. We proceeded through formal introductions. Guzmán didn't tell him that Señor García was Inez' father, and Señor García was instructed to not say a word, even if he was provoked by anything the guy might reveal. Guzmán told Prado and me to also not say a word, as our accents would give us away. Flashing his credentials, he introduced all of us as Judicial Police.

The lieutenant's name was Ernesto Lopez, a suave guy with a classic military haircut, high and tight on the sides. He wore civilian clothes. Levi's and dark brown cowboy boots with a design of simple contrasting stitching, tan crew neck sweater, blue corduroy sport coat. It was chilly at this altitude.

Inside the car, the scent of his cologne — Old Spice — combined with body odor made my stomach churn. He really needed to have that sport coat dry-cleaned, especially the arm pits.

We drove to Nevado de Toluca, more or less in silence, except for small talk...his. When we parked and walked about 100 meters into the forest along a well-worn dirt path, he became more forthcoming.

"This is where we brought many of the *subversivos*. Communists. We had them dig their own graves. Then we finished them off and buried them."

"Who ordered this outcome?" Guzmán asked.

"I wasn't privileged to receive that information. But it must've come from someone higher up. Our battalion commander was in on it, but I know he wasn't the boss."

"Which *subversivos* were dealt this ultimate punishment?"

"Not the ringleaders. They were sent to Casa Montenegro, and they remain there to this day. As examples."

"Then who?"

"Those who actively resisted arrest, those who were caught red-handed with weapons, those who assaulted us during previous riots at Tlatelolco and elsewhere. They were going to pay for that."

"What weapons?"

"A few Eastern-bloc pistols, mainly."

"Those weren't planted?"

Ernesto shrugged. "How can I know?"

"No sniper rifles?"

Ernesto snorted. "No, none of those."

"So how do you know where this girl is buried?" Guzmán asked, subduing his disgust.

Ernesto smiled. "Because I personally brought her up here, that bitch. You see my neck?"

He tugged at the top of his sweater, revealing new, raw scars.

"When we found her, she was hiding, covered with blood from the bodies she had slid underneath to avoid capture. When I dragged her out, she fought like the devil, screaming: 'I will fight you to the finish!' "

Just as she promised she would the last time we were at La Lupita.

"It took three of us to subdue her. She kept punching me and screaming two words I didn't understand. Some strange language. Curse words."

Daniel whispered into Guzman's ear.

"Were those words *knak* and *shtaysl*?" Guzman asked.

"Yes! How did you know?"

Daniel stared at Ernesto, burning with contempt. *Curse words...a curse on you, you bastard.*

"Never mind, it's not important. What happened next?"

"Then we searched her and found her Poli student ID card. She was later identified by an informer as one of the *acelerados* leading the National Strike Council."

So she was alive when he brought her up here.

When Ernesto tugged at the neck of his sweater, I could see something else. Below the scars, a gold chain, replete with a pendant. Crossed boxing gloves, also gold.

Guzmán and I exchanged glances. "Do you box?" Guzmán asked.

He shrugged. "Yes, of course."

"Can my detective see it? He also used to box."

"Sure."

I fingered the charm I had given Inez, turned it over. On the back was engraved USMC 1957.

I nodded at Guzmán and gave a thumbs-up to Ernesto.

"OK, lieutenant," Guzmán said. "Take us to where you believe the girl is buried."

He led us through the forest to a sun-dappled glade and an area that had been 'dozed clear.

Several dozen low mounds of earth marked the graves of *los desaparecidos*. A row of trees marked where they lay. Inez was buried in front of a tree with the number 21 etched into the bark. Ironically, her age.

I pulled Señor García aside.

"There's going to be a certain amount of violence inflicted on Ernesto before we retrieve her body," I whispered.

He nodded, drained of emotion.

Prado pulled out a miniature camera to photograph the site and every single grave. It took a while.

Ernesto looked at his watch. "Inspector Guzmán, are you almost finished? I have to return to the base by 1700 hours. Evening formation."

"No, you don't. You don't have to officially report back to duty because you didn't officially request leave from duty. That was our agreement."

Ernesto watched Prado work his camera.

"Sir," Ernesto said, his expression anxious, "I agreed to your condition only because you said it was a top secret operation, ordered by the highest authority."

Beads of sweat formed on his upper lip. "I'm wondering what the purpose is of this interview and tour. Perhaps you can explain?"

"It is a top secret tour and interview. And you are correct about the highest authority. Soon, you will meet Him."

Guzmán placed a leather gym bag on the ground, unzipped it, and withdrew an entrenching tool.

"What's that for?" Ernesto asked.

"Take off your sport coat. You're going to dig her up. And remember, when you lift out the dirt, don't be sloppy. Throw it out to the sides. When you get close to her remains, go gently. It'll be the closest you get to being intimate with her."

"What? What do you mean? We can't disturb this place."

Guzmán reached into the gym bag and withdrew the body bag.

"You're going to dig her up and put her in this body bag and give it to her father," he said sternly.

Ernesto's brow furrowed. He looked more carefully at the three of us standing in front of him.

"Where? Who is her father?"

Guzmán glanced at Inez' father, nodded.

"I am," Señor García said, his voice clear and determined.

"You can't make me do this!" Ernesto said, indignant.

I walked over to him, gripped the lapels of his sport coat and pulled it down over his shoulders, trapping his arms. I reached for his neck and yanked off Inez' chain and pendant and put it in my pocket. Then I grabbed his shoulders, lowered my head slightly and rammed his face, smashing his nose.

"I told you my colleague was a boxer," Guzmán said. "Let me clarify. He was United States Marine Corps light heavyweight champion, 1957."

Ernesto was dazed. He moaned. Tears leaked from his eyes. Blood covered the front of his tan crew neck sweater. I ripped open his sport coat, spun him around and pulled it off. Guzmán handed me the short-handled shovel. It's blade had been sharpened just for this purpose. I turned him back around so that he faced me. I clenched my right fist, middle finger knuckle exposed. A short punch to his throat dropped him to his knees at the edge of Inez' grave. I thrust the blade of the shovel into the soft earth that trapped her remains.

"Dig, motherfucker."

"*¿Cómo?*" he sputtered.

Guzmán answered while pulling his blued .45 Colt 1911 with pearl grips from his shoulder holster, working the slide back and chambering a round, pressing it against Ernesto's forehead.

"*El dice que tiene excavar su cuerpo. Hijo de la chingada.*"

Ernesto seemed paralyzed, maybe from shock.

"Why are you doing this to me? We're on the same side."

"That's not quite true. We may serve the government, but we don't kill innocent people, especially girls."

Ernesto protested. "But they weren't innocent, they were communists, enemies of the state, embarrassing the nation in front of the world."

"I must be misinformed," Guzmán said, matter of fact. "I didn't realize embarrassment was a capital crime." He grabbed Ernesto by the wrist and guided him to the shovel. "Dig."

He began to dig. I conferred with Guzmán, quietly, out of earshot, then stood aside.

Guzmán approached Ernesto. "How did you kill her?"

Ernesto stared at Guzmán, pulled himself erect with a mixture of duty and false dignity. "With a bayonet."

"The truth?"

"Yes."

"I believe him," Señor García said. "Curiously, in my nightmares, I have felt something like stabs of a knife. In various parts of my body, and saw daggers covered with blood."

Just as I feel and see them now.

"I believe the shovel has struck her," Ernesto said, pausing.

"Shallow grave," Daniel said.

"Dig around her, *pendejo*," Guzmán said, pulling from his pocket surgical masks for himself, Señor Garcia, and me.

Ernesto did as ordered, but he had to put one foot inside the grave in order to gain leverage. The sun was getting low on the horizon. The sky was still blue, but the density of the forest made it seem like night, an unlikely contrast so reminiscent of a painting by the French artist, Magritte. Prado reached into the leather bag and removed a powerful flashlight. When he shined it on Inez' body, it appeared to be moving.

"Agghhh!" Ernesto shouted, pulling his leg from the grave. "Things are crawling inside my boot!"

He pulled off his boot, turned it upside down and shook it. Fat, white maggots spilled out. It was the maggots crawling over her body, working in a feeding frenzy, that created the false impression that she was alive and struggling to be free. The stench, the putrid sweet smell of death and decay emanating from the shallow grave was overwhelming. The masks helped us somewhat, but Ernesto gagged and vomited and fell away. He clawed the earth, trying desperately to remove himself from the edge of the murderous trench he'd uncovered.

"Okay, Ernesto," Guzmán said. "Now lift her out."

"I can't! It's disgusting!"

"Do it anyway She's small. Reach underneath her and lift her out. We'll put her in the body bag."

"I can't! I can't! God have mercy on me."

"He will, but first He wants you to lift her out," Guzmán said. "Do it quickly; it won't be so bad."

Ernesto jumped into the grave, put his hands underneath her torso and legs.

"Gently, gently," Señor García pleaded.

Ernesto lifted her, straightened his legs, rotated his upper body and deposited Inez on solid ground, weeping hysterically, leaping from the grave, sweeping maggots from his arms and legs, and kicking his boots against the trunk of her number 21 tree.

Guzmán and Señor García crossed themselves three times and whispered a prayer. I fell into Prado's arms. The beautiful, charming, idealistic and passionate girl who loved and trusted me now lay on her back, completely defiled, barely recognizable. Prado held me for a few minutes.

If I'd been there, I could've saved her.

"Dan," he whispered. "We have to finish quickly and get out

of here. Help me put her in the bag."

Ernesto gathered his wits. Seeing us preoccupied, he began to run. I lunged after him and dove at the back of his legs. He tried to beat me off. Once again, I punched him in the throat, and he lay there kicking his feet and gasping for air, like some kind of beached mammal. I grabbed a fistful of his hair, greasy now with sweat. I stood and pulled until he regained his feet, crying out in pain.

"We've got to shut him up," Guzmán said.

I dragged him back to the grave, made him kneel and face the desecrated cavity.

"What are you going to do with me!" he screamed, trembling.

I pulled out my Italian stiletto and opened it quietly against my leg.

"Why don't you just let me shoot him!" Guzmán hissed, enraged.

"No! No!" Ernesto pleaded.

I waved Guzmán off and hushed him, pressing the slender blade against my lips.

I patted Ernesto's head the way Frenchy had taught me, patted and stroked him like a dog. I parted the back of his hair and thrust the blade into his medulla, thoroughly wiped it clean against his sweater and shoved him into the grave. I tossed his sport coat in after him.

"Manuel, please hand me the shovel," I said. Stepping around the edges of the grave, I shoveled dirt over his body until the earthen cavity was completely filled. Then I walked into the woods and dragged out recently-fallen branches to smooth over the surface and make it resemble, more or less, the other graves. While Prado and Guzmán carried Inez, followed by Señor García, I brushed the branches over our footprints until we reached the main trail. Then I threw them behind some bushes.

December 28
The Day of the Holy Innocents
Mexico City

EPILOGUE

In 1963, the Pope lifted the ban on cremation. Until then, because Christ's body was buried, and believing that resurrection of the body occurs after death, and believing that the body is a temple of the Holy Spirit, traditional burial was required by the Roman Catholic Church.

But, according to Church doctrine, any cremated remains should be entombed in a burial plot in a cemetery or mausoleum or in a columbarium. Options such as scattering of the ashes on the ground, floating them on the sea, or keeping cremation ashes at home are not considered respectful.

The 1917 Code of Canon Laws strictly forbade cremations, except in times of natural disasters, plague or other public necessities that required fast disposition of the body. Later, this was modified for hygiene, pathological and other justifiable reasons.

And so it was determined — by the Garcías and their priest — that since Inez had been murdered in a heinous manner, her body desecrated by burial in a shallow grave and the remains so horribly mortified, that she was, indeed, a candidate for cremation. Moreover, the priest allowed that her ashes, contained in a proper urn, plain black marble, could be kept at home. The reasoning being that besides Inez, the Garcías were childless and once reunited with her, they couldn't bear to be apart. The priest did set one condition, however. The Garcías had to purchase a family plot at the *Panteon Civil de Dolores*, the largest cemetery in Mexico — 590 acres — located in Chapultepec Park. Then, when the time came, they would all be interred together in a safe and sacred repository.

In 1966, Catholic priests were allowed to officiate at cremation ceremonies. A funeral service was held for Inez at the family church. It was brief, reverent and respectful and attended only by close friends and relatives.

"This is the body once washed in baptism, anointed in the oil of salvation, and fed with the bread of life," the priest intoned, as everyone wept.

December 28 is both a sacred and a profane holiday.

The Day of the Holy Innocents is the biblical narrative of infanticide by King Herod the Great, the Roman-appointed King of the Jews. According to the Gospel of Matthew, Magi from the east went to Judea in search of the newborn king of the Jews, "having seen his star in the east." Herod directed them to Bethlehem and asked them to let him know who this king was when they found him. They found Jesus and honored him, but an angel told the Magi not to alert Herod. Avoiding Herod, the Magi returned home. Then an angel of the Lord appeared to Joseph in a dream. "Get up," he said. "Take the child and his mother and escape to Egypt." They stayed until the death of Herod.

When Herod realized that he'd been outwitted by the Magi, he was furious. He gave orders to assassins to massacre all boys in Bethlehem and its vicinity who were two years old or under. Thus was fulfilled an Old Testament prophecy. *"A voice is heard in Ramah, mourning and great weeping. Rachel weeping for her children and refusing to be comforted, because her children are no more."* The Holy Innocents have been claimed by some as the first Christian martyrs. And in Mexico, December 28 is a day to commemorate the souls of departed children, in line with a pre-Hispanic tradition.

On the other hand, the Day of the Holy Innocents is also celebrated as a kind of April Fool's Day, when Mexicans play jokes and pranks and trick friends and family members.

So it was only fitting that at a memorial service for Inez, Daniel took the opportunity to speak about the dual nature of the holiday. Then he announced Inez' final request in the event she was killed and juxtaposed Anne Frank's quote from "The Diary of a Young Girl" ("I don't want to have lived in vain; I want to carry on after death") with a tape of the fanfare that precedes every 20th Century Fox film. Everyone was stunned, jolted by the contrast.

At first, people seemed shocked by the prescience of her final request.

Then they wept when Daniel read Anne Frank's statement on immortality. A few shouted out:

"We will never allow your death to be in vain!"

"We will always remember you!"

"You will be our guiding light!"

When they heard the fanfare, they laughed so hard that some spilled drinks and food on the saltillo-tiled patio adjoining the suite of an art deco hotel, rented for the occasion by Phaedra and Robbie Prado and Marta and John Cogdill. The suite's patio lay nestled under a canopy of lavender-blossoming jacaranda trees. The view on this clear, sunny day included the palm-filled Parque España across the street and, in the distance, on Reforma, the towering, majestic white Angel of Independence monument.

The attendees continued to cry and laugh, seeking solace in each other's arms. Emotionally spent, they then began to celebrate Inez' life with impromptu *in memorium* speeches and toasts of the best-tasting *mescal* and champagne the hotel had to offer. They toasted in front of two framed photos of Inez, one from her childhood and one taken by Berto just before the massacre. He had previously told Daniel he wanted to capture her everlasting incandescent expression, an exact match to the earlier one. A parting gift and a testament to Berto's unique aesthetic that Inez' parents told Daniel they would always treasure.

Daniel and her friends also played some of Inez' favorite jazz

LPs. She especially loved Oliver Nelson's *The Blues and the Abstract Truth*, featuring the track that she believed epitomized her love affair with Daniel, "Stolen Moments."

When the track ended, a friend from her Nurses' Brigade spoke up, through tears. "When Inez discussed the melody with me, she said she loved the haunting echo that gave Nelson's tenor sax solo a distant sound. Like it was not part of the present time and place." She played it over again. They all agreed.

Daniel also presented the Garcías with a glass vase, filled with thin-stemmed miniature white calla lilies, on which was etched: *May Her Memory Be a Blessing, 28 December 1968*. Before having it engraved, Daniel asked the Garcías if they would prefer it in Spanish. *Que su memoria sea una bendición.* They said they preferred English and Hebrew, Daniel's languages, because the vase was his gift, and they held him in high esteem, not least because Inez loved him so much. They also asked him to fasten the gold chain and pendant of boxing gloves around the vase because it was her most cherished possession.

The etching read *Zichronah L'vracha* with the English version beneath it and the date. An additional blessing, *May the family know no more sorrows*, seemed unnecessary. Because Daniel, the Garcías, and all of Inez' relatives and friends lived in a country that murdered its innocents, and they knew they would be mourning — for Inez and for all the victims of *La Matanza de Tlatelolco*, and perhaps the massacres to come — the remainder of their days.

HISTORICAL BACKGROUND
AND
ACKNOWLEDGMENTS

In 1968, Mexico became the first developing nation to host the Olympics. The games that began October 12 were successful, and many Americans won medals and achieved lasting fame. But 10 days before the games began, on October 2, Mexico achieved another milestone. Federal, state and local security forces conspired to launch a military assault on 10,000 activist students and their supporters – men, women and children. Between 80 and 100 people were murdered in one night, and hundreds more were imprisoned and forcibly "disappeared." That incident, which occurred at a public housing project adjacent to the Plaza of the Three Cultures — the spiritual heart of the city — became known as the Tlatelolco Massacre. It was the first and largest massacre and enforced disappearance of innocent citizens by Mexican authorities, and it is the subject of this novel.

According to Jefferson Morley, author of "Our Man in Mexico: Winston Scott and the Hidden History of the CIA," (University Press of Kansas 2008), Jorge Casteneda, the historian who later became Mexican foreign minister, interviewed many of the participants in the events that occurred during the summer of 1968 when radical students led a two-and-a-half months' series of demonstrations of popular opposition. Students and their supporters who demonstrated and resisted aggressive security forces demanded that the government (1) eliminate Article 145 of the Federal Penal Code which establishes penalties for the vague charge of "social dissolution," (2) free political prisoners held for years without trials, (3) abolish the riot police, (4) fire the police chief of Mexico City and his head of security, (5) pay indemnities to the families of all those killed and injured since the beginning of the conflict, (6) maintain autonomy of all schools from police and military invasions, and (7) determine which government officials are responsible for the bloodshed.

Casteneda concluded that President Díaz Ordaz and Minister of Government Luis Echeverria had tacitly worked together to strike a decisive blow (the Tlatelolco Massacre) without leaving a paper trail of who gave the order.

Thirty years later, according to a revelatory account published in 1999 in the newsweekly *Proceso*, by Julio Scherer and Carlos Mosivais, two of the country's best-known journalists, Luis Gutiérrez Oropeza, chief of staff of the Mexican military, had posted ten men with guns on the upper floor of one of the Tlatelolco housing project buildings and gave them orders to shoot into the crowd. This prompted army troops which had surrounded and trapped the crowd to fire from rifles, machine guns and cannons mounted on light tanks and armored transports.

Five thousand soldiers fired a total of 15,000 rounds. In addition to those murdered, imprisoned and disappeared, 2,000 people were arrested, many of them stripped, beaten and abused. Lights were extinguished, telephone service was cut off, photographers were forbidden from taking pictures, and even ambulances were turned away. Intelligence agents claimed the first shots were fired by activist students, and that's how the Mexican press reported it. It took 30 years for the truth to be told.

One could say that publication of *Days of the Dead* is timely because on Sept. 26, 2014, 43 male students from the Raúl Isidro Burgos Rural Teachers College of Ayotzinapa, children of poor farmers historically associated with activism, went missing in

Iguala, Guerrero. According to student survivors as reported by *The Guardian* in March 2015, the activist students commandeered several buses and traveled to Iguala to hold a protest at an annual conference for local dignitaries hosted by the mayor's wife. Local police intercepted them and a confrontation ensued. Six students were shot and killed, 25 were injured, and the 43 trainee teachers were forcibly disappeared and handed over to the local Guerreros Unidos (United Warriors) cartel (crime syndicate).

State and federal investigators later determined that 15 of the kidnapped students died from asphyxiation, and the remaining were interrogated and killed. Their bodies were dumped in a huge pit near a rubbish dump and burned, according to Austrian forensic scientists from the University of Innsbruck. Their smashed bones and ashes filled eight plastic bags and the remains thrown into the San Juan River in Cocula. The forensic scientists could confirm the identity of only one student, admitting they have been unable to recover sufficient DNA from 16 charred remains to make any positive matches, leading friends and relatives of the missing 42 students to remain hopeful that they are alive.

Hundreds of thousands of people took to the streets throughout many cities, including Mexico City, and social unrest led to attacks on government buildings in Guerrero and the resignation of the governor and three leaders of the Party of the Democratic Revolution (PDR) which governs Guerrero state and Iguala. Eventually, authorities arrested 22 police officers and many cartel members and charged them with aggravated murder.

The mayor of Iguala and his wife were charged with masterminding the abduction. They were subsequently arrested, imprisoned and convicted of homicide, organized crime and forced disappearance. Iguala's police chief remains a fugitive. In the process of locating the site where the cartel members dumped and burned bodies of the murdered students, dozens of other clandestine mass graves were discovered, and prosecutors have linked local police to at least 100 disappearances of community leaders and activists in the past two years.

The forced disappearance and murder of the students became

the biggest political and security scandal Mexican President Enrique Peña Nieto has faced during his administration. But the repression of social protest should come as no surprise since he has shown himself willing to viciously crack down on communities in resistance when he was governor of Mexico State.

In 2006, state and federal police inflicted cruel, inhumane or degrading treatment on hundreds of people in San Salvador Atenco who were protesting confiscation of land and subsequent inability to make an adequate livelihood. Police arbitrarily arrested 145 people, raped or sexually assaulted 26 women and men and killed two persons (see *Atenco: Breaking the Siege*, a documentary by Canal 6 de Julio and Promedios, June 6, 2006).

Moreover, in April 2015, Reuters reported that Mexico's delegation told a U.N. Committee on Enforced Disappearances that 11,300 people were unaccounted for in the past eight years. During that same time period, according to a statement by Amnesty International, more than 22,600 had gone missing amid "a huge problem of impunity." In their findings, the committee's 10 independent experts said they had received information that "illustrates a context of generalized disappearances in a great part of Mexico, many of which could be qualified as enforced disappearances."

"Enforced disappearances" are those linked to detention or abduction by state agents such as police or security forces, or their allies, who conceal the victim's fate, according to the committee. "Mexico has informed us that in contrast to the thousands of enforced disappearances that we assume...there are exactly six persons put to trial and sentenced for this crime." The committee urged Mexico to establish a special prosecutor's office to lead specialized investigations and prosecutions.

In the second half of *Days of the Dead*, I portray a second massacre, the Aguas Blancas massacre, one which actually occurred June 28, 1995, in rural Guerrero, in which 17 peasant farmers were killed and 21 wounded. Members of the South Mountain Range Farmer Organization were en route to Atoyac de Álvarez to attend a protest march demanding the release of a peasant activist more than a month before (who has never appeared since). They were also marching to demand drinking water, schools, hospitals and roads, among other things. According to survivors, they were ambushed by State Police who also filmed the event (see: *La matanza de Aguas Blancas (http://www.patria grande.net)*. Weapons were subsequently placed in the dead farmers' hands and the police said they acted in self-defense. Implicated but never charged were the ex-secretary general of Guerrero, head of the State Police, and the governor.

When I was 26, I decided to leave New York City in June 1968 because of a busted love affair, and because I was unhappy in my job as a publicist for Loew's Hotels. Previously, I'd worked as a reporter for the *Rochester Times-Union* (Gannett). A friend of mine who was studying at the University of the Americas in Mexico City invited me to leave the U.S. and live with him. It sounded like a great idea, even though I knew very little about Mexico except for occasional visits to Tijuana and Ensenada when I had weekend liberty as a U.S. Marine. And while I'd studied Spanish in high school and college, I was hardly fluent.

I lined up some promises from newspaper editors I knew in the New York area who promised to consider buying free-lance writing assignments, sold my meager possessions and flew out of J.F.K. International with $800 in savings, my Honeywell Pentax camera and portable Smith-Corona typewriter. However, when I landed in Mexico City and took a taxi to my friend's apartment, no one answered the bell or my loud knocks. Finally a light went on next door, and I was told my host no longer lived there. He and his wife had been deported that morning because they were considered foreign political agitators. Of course, my friend hadn't told me anything about their political activities.

Fortunately, however, he had given me a list of names I could contact and one of them, a U of A drop-out, let me stay at his place, a grungy studio apartment on Calle Milan. He strung a hammock over his bed for me to sleep in. It was the beginning of my immersion into the police-state culture of Mexico that ended with the

Tlatelolco massacre, when the government authorized the murder, imprisonment and disappearance of hundreds of student activists and their supporters.

I wrote my first free-lance story for the *Asbury Park Press* about U of A students from New Jersey. I also took a group photograph. When I wrote students' names for the photo caption, one of them, a smirking Alex Mason, confessed he really wasn't from New Jersey; he just wanted to needle me. When I got over that, we became friends. Recently discharged from the U.S Army, Alex lived with his mother, an English-language teacher, and worked part-time for United Press International as a van driver and telephone operator. He introduced me to the night editor, Terrance McGarry, and Alex and I ran errands for him, driving out to the airport and picking up equipment destined for use at UPI press quarters at the new Olympic Village adjacent to the National University campus (UNAM). In addition, McGarry let me occasionally work the re-write desk.

On July 22, a street fight broke out between students from Vocational School No. 5 and their traditional rivals from Preparatory School Isaac Ochoterra. When fighting continued a second day, 200 *granaderos* (riot police) armed with meter-long truncheons invaded Voca. No. 5, beating students and teachers indiscriminately. One student was killed. Three days later, activist students from UNAM and IPN (*Instituto Politécnico Nacional*) organized protest demonstrations. They were ambushed and beaten by riot police as they marched to the National Palace. Four days later when the riots ended, four students were dead; hundreds were injured and arrested.

Because we were young and Mason was fluent in Spanish, McGarry suggested we attend rallies at the two college campuses, make contact with students and professors, think about possible story ideas. But as far as UPI was concerned, this was not a prioritized story. Getting ready for the Olympics was *the* priority.

The underlying principal behind the student protests was violation of government-guaranteed school autonomy for all college and prep campuses, meaning police or army should never enter for any reason. That began a series of larger protests organized by a National Strike Council (*CNH*) formed by students from UNAM and IPN and from voca and prep schools. Students commandeered buses and blocked streets at the Zócalo, bringing traffic to a standstill. They also barricaded themselves on their various campuses and drew up a list of demands that eventually was presented to President Díaz Ordaz.

An attempted march on the U.S. Embassy was repulsed. Mexican infantry, paratroop riflemen and military police carrying bayoneted rifles and backed by armored cars and tanks invaded the barricaded campuses. Students retaliated with molotov cocktails. An estimated 40 students were killed. Hundreds were injured and arrested. Many were "disappeared," the first time I'd ever heard of that strategy but which later was repeated by authorities against citizens they considered subversives during the 1970s and 1980s in Argentina, Chile, El Salvador, Guatemala, Honduras and Nicaragua.

Demonstrations continued the rest of the summer, augmented by non-student brigades, including labor groups and others, such as the National Union of Mexican Mothers (*Unión Nacional de Mujeres*). The Teachers Coalition for Democratic Rights led a march of 200,000 people on August 13, denouncing authorities and pressing the students' demands. Battles between authorities and students and their supporters continued. On August 27, 400,000 people marched to the Presidential Palace. Students threatened to sabotage the Olympics.

Repeated violent clashes occurred at the Plaza of the Three Cultures near the Zócalo and at the nearby Tlatelolco housing project. Hundreds more demonstrators were injured, killed, imprisoned and "disappeared."

It was astounding and frightening to witness some of these confrontations and the invasions and occupations of UNAM and IPN. I'd covered anti-Vietnam War and civil rights demonstrations and riots in the U.S., but this was more like a civil war. By then, Alex and I had interviewed many protestors, including students on the Strike Council. We were also invited into students' homes, met their parents, and even stayed for dinner and, occasionally, overnight. As the opening day for the Olympics grew closer, tensions increased, especially as it became clear the president was not interested in negotiating students' demands.

On October 2, we were at UNAM attending a small rally. McGarry attended another small rally at the Plaza of the Three Cultures, which turned out to be the Tlatelolco Massacre, a planned military assault which was so complete and so deadly it ended all protests and demonstrations and which is represented in this novel, *Days of the Dead.*

It was not a big story in the U.S. or international press, except for possibly Italy because the famous journalist Ariana Fallaci was shot three times and left for dead. *Time* magazine gave it one column, including a small photo of the wounded Fallaci, but it was buried deep on an inside page. For the Mexican press, of course, it was a huge story, but it was played as if the students' started the gun battle, and that they were armed by Eastern bloc countries, the U.S.S.R, or Cuba. Typical headlines among dozens were: "Army and Students Exchange Gunfire" (*La Prensa*) and "Dozens of Sharpshooters Fire on Troops" (*Ovaciones*).

At the time, I was in the middle of something I didn't really understand. I would later learn about government suppression of anti-war students in the U.S. Kent State University, May 4, 1970, the shooting of unarmed students protesting the U.S. invasion of Cambodia, perpetrated by the Ohio National Guard, killing four students, wounding eleven. May 8, that same year, eleven protesting students were bayoneted at the University of New Mexico by the New Mexico National Guard. And on May 14, two students were killed and twelve wounded by police at Jackson State University. However, the differences between occasional lapses of human rights violations, however terrible and inexcusable, exercised by a democratic state and total, brutal, reprehensible repression by a police state which represents itself as a constitutional democracy such as Mexico are as obvious as they are stark.

It wasn't until I read, Elena Poniatowska's book *Massacre in Mexico (Noche de Tlatelolco)* Columbia: University of Missouri Press, 1994; *The Tlatelolco Massacre, U.S. Documents on Mexico and the Events of 1968*, by Kate Doyle, The National Security

Archives, Oct. 10, 2003, a complete set of the most important documents from the secret archives of the CIA, Pentagon, State Department, FBI and White House – many of them declassified in response to Freedom of Information Act requests filed by the Archive; the revelatory series published by Scherer and Mosivais in the Mexican newsweekly *Proceso* in 1999 mentioned above; and the Jefferson Morely book (2008) also mentioned above that I finally understood the totality of the Tlatelolco Massacre which, as I stated before, was only the culmination of two-and-a-half months of student-led protests.

I was so frightened and disgusted by the government's murderous response to those events, so worried about my personal safety, that I decided to leave Mexico City before the Olympic games began. I didn't know where to go, but I wanted the best place possible to heal psychically and emotionally. I was advised to travel to southern Guerrero state and to the then-sleepy little fishing village of Zihuatanejo. I followed that advice, and I found lodging in a small guest house (*casa de huespedes*), *Casa Elvira*, named for the owner. She, her husband Julio, the captain of the port, their daughters Vici and Olga and teenaged maid/food server Lidia treated me to hospitality and friendship that I will never forget.

I stayed for six months and was treated like a member of the family, and it was there I learned about Genaro Vázquez Rojas, former school teacher, civic association leader, militant and *guerrilla* fighter, champion of marginalized peasants living in the Sierra mountains that rose abruptly from behind the fishing village. These illiterate *campesinos* earned 50 *centavos* a day, exploited by big landowners *(latifundistas)*, Mexican and foreign big businesses and corrupt union organizations.

His parents were peasant leaders. With his father, Alfonzo Vázquez, he attended assemblies of rural workers and learned their plight. He attended primary and secondary schools in Mexico City and graduated from the National Teachers School and then attended law school at the National Autonomous University (UNAM). Throughout his studies and his work as a teacher, he never lost contact with the Guerrero peasants and eventually encouraged the four main agrarian organizations there to form the *Asociación Cívica Guerrense*. Led by Vázquez Rojas, the *cívicos* first protested the low prices set by the U.S.-owned companies for the region's farm produce. Then they campaigned against the Guerrero governor who was finally removed on charges of administrative corruption and bribery. As a result, repression against the *cívicos* increased, and its leaders went underground.

In November 1966, Vázquez Rojas was arrested and sent to prison in Iguala. Among the charges against him was killing a policeman. He was given a life sentence, but on April 22, 1968, guerrilla commandos broke him out of the prison. The *ACG* then prepared for a struggle on the national level and re-formed as the Guerreran National Civic Organization, inspired by Fidel Castro's National Liberation Movement (MLN) and created to sustain a prolonged *guerrilla* struggle. In response, they were pursued by army battalions, helicopters and paratroopers, trained in counter-insurgency warfare as practiced in Vietnam. Vázquez Rojas was captured after fleeing a car wreck. It is believed he died from his injuries, but this outcome is questioned by some who claim a more sinister ending.

One of the results of this incident was the creation of the Popular Revolutionary Army, a leftist *guerrilla* organization.

In my novel, the fearsome *guerrilla* leader Blanco is loosely based on Vázquez Rojas, but I must emphasize that Blanco is an imagined fictional character.

One day while I was eating breakfast on the patio of *Casa Elvira*, a man dressed like a peasant walked by and offered to sell me a large bottle of honey corked by a tiny corn cob. It was delicious. We became friends. He was a Jehovah's Witness from France who lived with and ministered to the spiritual needs of *campesinos* in their tiny and impoverished Sierra communities. He invited me to ride with him into the mountains, and those experiences are represented in imagined fictional chapters and characters in *Days of the Dead*.

In addition, the imagined and fictionalized accounts of marijuana (*mota*) growing and smuggling in *Days of the Dead* are based on personal observation but are also informed by the best-seller

Weed: Adventures of a Dope Smuggler by Jerry Kamstra, Harper & Row, 1974. The book grew out of a $25,000 fee *Life* magazine paid Kamstra, an experienced marijuana smuggler and gifted writer, which helped him buy an entire field of *mota* in the mountains of Guerrero and bring it back to the U.S.

One section of *Days of the Dead* refers to the 1968 Olympics and the Olympic Program for Human Rights organized to promote the civil rights of African-Americans. It represents the infamous black-gloved, clenched-fist salutes by the sprinters Tommy Smith (gold) and John Carlos (bronze) on the medal stand and their subsequent banishment from the games by International Olympic Committee Chairman Avery Brundage. It is based on the documentary film, *Fists of Freedom*, co-produced by George Roy and Steven Stern (Black Canyon Productions) for HBO Sports, 1999.

When I returned to the U.S in 1969, I was hired as a field representative for the Syracuse Human Rights Commission, specializing in ameliorating racial unrest in the city's public high schools. I also enrolled in graduate school at Syracuse University's Maxwell School of Citizenship and Public Affairs, where I earned a MSS degree (Interdisciplinary Social Science), focusing on Latin American Studies and Cultural Anthropology with a special interest in Revival (Millenarian) Movements. Previously, I earned a BA degree (English) and MA (Newspaper Journalism). I returned to journalism as editor of the *Glenville Democrat*, Glenville, W. Va. Then began teaching journalism (10 years) and English (24 years) at Diablo Valley College, Pleasant Hill, CA.

I published a coming-of-age novel, *Transgressions*, Palo Verde Books, in 2010, featuring the teen protagonist Daniel Mendoza. *Days of the Dead*, Palo Verde Books, 2015, is a sequel.

Besides the research mentioned above, I owe heartfelt thanks to many who read all or parts of *Days of the Dead* and offered support and wise counsel: David Pfeifer, Ron Cochran, Isabel Izquierdo and Yesenia Molina (principal and secondary translators), Gail Taback, Chris Junior, John E. Denton, Russ Tarby, Timothy Kennedy, Manuel Gonzales, Jay Schaefer, Douglas Century, Rabbi Eric Wisnia, and Lawrence I. Schwartz, MD.

Special thanks go to my typesetter Carol Yacorzynski and my graphic artist David Johnson.

Final editing kudos go to my dear wife Susan Springer, whose keen eye and sense of aesthetics greatly improved the final product. She wouldn't let me stop working until the novel met her highest standards, and my debt to her is immeasurable as is my love.

Finally, although I extensively researched and included parts of some scenes from historical, military combat and medical documents, this book is a work of fiction and should be construed as nothing but. I am solely responsible for everything portrayed.

James A. Jacobs
San Rafael, California
May 2015